Also from 1stBooks Library

*Four Corners Mysteries
by HP Hanson:*

The Dean's Murders

Classical Villainy

Excess Homicide

* * * * * * *

A Four Corners Mystery

**by
HP Hanson**

This book is a work of fiction.
People, events, and situations in this story
are purely fictional. Any resemblance
to actual persons, living or dead, is coincidental.

© 2003 by Howard P. Hanson. All rights reserved.

No part of this book may be reproduced, stored in a
retrieval system, or transmitted by any means, electronic,
mechanical, photocopying, recording, or otherwise, without
written permission from the author.

ISBN: 1-4107-2816-1 (e-book)
ISBN: 1-4107-2817-X (Paperback)

This book is printed on acid free paper.

1stBooks - rev. 05/20/03

Excess Homicide

Prologue

WHEN JOE LOUGHLIN arrived at work on the Friday morning before the long Fourth of July weekend, it was definitely not written in his day planner that, at 10:10, he'd take a bullet for the President of the United States.

Hell, Joe hadn't even voted for the guy, being a registered Democrat, and he had tried to plan his day to avoid all the hoopla and security weirdness that would accompany the Presidential visit. With the crowds of summertime tourists, the weekend of the Fourth in Boulder was going to be bad enough, but with the President there as well, Joe just wished he could be on vacation for the whole thing, somewhere up in the mountains.

Later, Joe would tell anyone who asked, including reporter after reporter after reporter, that it really wasn't that big a deal, he'd have done it for anyone. Well, just about anyone, maybe not that junior U.S. Senator of theirs, though, some politicians being better off out of their misery.

Joe was getting to that age when two mugs of coffee in the morning, followed by sitting for an hour in a meeting, caused far too much pressure in his bladder to be ignored. Crossing the lobby on his way to the Men's Room, he was surprised when the Secret Service detail swept in, pushing him gently to the side of the room, over by the couch, so that the President and his retinue could have the right of way.

Then Joe noticed something strange, something that shouldn't happen. A little door popped open on the solar telescope display, and he could see what looked like the business end of a rifle barrel peeking out. Just above the door was a lens of some sort, and that wasn't supposed to be there either. Later, the Secret Service people would explain that they were too unfamiliar with all the gadgetry in the displays to have been able to distinguish the lens from all the other stuff, and during their sweep they simply hadn't had the chance to disassemble any of the scientific equipment on the mezzanine to see what was inside.

But Joe's sharp eyes, honed by years of deer and elk hunting in the Rockies and quite familiar with the displays up there on the mezzanine, recognized the fore-sight of the rifle, probably a bolt-action .30-06, he thought. So he did what any red-blooded American citizen would do if they saw a gun pointed at the President. First, he froze in amazement as he felt his adrenalin level skyrocket, and, because he hadn't made it to the Men's Room, he tried hard not to wet his pants. Then he panicked, grabbing the Secret Service agent standing in front of him.

"Uh, hey! Look up there! That looks like a rifle pointed this way, hidden inside that box up there," he managed to stage whisper and point simultaneously.

Because the agent had grabbed Joe back, they had hold of each other, and when the agent screamed "GUN!!" and lunged for the President, Joe was just sort of dragged along. In the ensuing tangle of bodies, Joe was in the line of fire when the rifle went off. Or, more precisely, Joe's right buttock was in the line of fire.

"So, Mr. Loughlin, how does it feel to be shot in the butt for the President?" was the first question the first reporter asked him, and it was repeated, in various forms, until Joe became thoroughly sick of it. To tell the truth, it hurt like hell, but Joe managed to keep both his sense of humor and his dignity, mostly. After all, it was really only a flesh wound, passing through a considerable layer of fat and some muscle, and then out again. His friends would never let him forget that the gunman had quite logically hit what was the biggest target in the room.

But the more immediate result of the rifle shot was a fusillade of semi-automatic weapons fire from the several Secret Service agents, leading to the complete destruction of the solar telescope display. The lobby of the National Center for Atmospheric Research would require a substantial amount of spackle, to patch all the holes in the plaster walls and ceiling, and a complete new coat of paint.

After the hubbub subsided, it was discovered that the rifle had been mounted inside the display with a miniature video camera sighted along the barrel. This, in turn, was connected to a gray box with a small antenna on the top, and there was a curious, home-made-looking triggering device on the rifle also hooked to the box. At least that was the reconstruction. The barrage of lead had pretty much destroyed the original set-up, and it appeared that the contents of the box had been wired to self-destruct if disturbed. Except, that is, for the bottom of the box and the message laminated to its outside:

Dear Mr. President:
You've been SCREW'd!
Hope you enjoyed it as much as we did!

But none of this information would be released by the Secret Service for some months, long after Joe's wound had healed, leaving small, Presidential, entrance and exit scars.

Excess Homicide
A Four Corners Mystery

Part I: The Year Before

H. P. Hanson

Excess Homicide
A Four Corners Mystery

ONE

SEPTEMBER SUNRISE, southwestern Colorado – and New Mexico, Arizona, and Utah: the Four Corners.

A light dusting of early fall snow covered the chamisa and sage, still grayish-green from the warmth of summer, and it made the juniper bushes on the hillside across the way sparkle in the glow of the young sun. But the body that lay sprawled across the engraved brass monument marking the only spot in the U.S. where four states touch was still warm enough that the snow falling on it had melted.

It was the dark form against the white background that got Billie Sweetwater's attention. She had unlocked and opened the gate across the entrance road and was headed toward the visitor center's service entrance when she noticed it. As soon as she came close enough to recognize what it was—a young man, with long dark hair, lying face down in what looked like a pool of something dark—memories of the works of her favorite author, Tony Hillerman, put her on guard. Rather than track everything up, she headed for the phone.

She knew—once again, from Hillerman—that the FBI would eventually become involved in this, but she called 911 anyway, instead of looking up the number for the feds. The local call would bring in the Navajo Tribal Police first, and it would also spread the word throughout the close-knit, albeit scattered, Four Corners community that another tragedy had struck in *Dinétah*, the land of her people.

Considering the travel distances involved, as well as the bureaucratic communications needed, it was surprising how quickly the investigation proceeded. By 2:30 that afternoon, a telephone was ringing in the Durango police department.

"Durango investigations. This is Winders."

"This is Todd Sweeney, FBI. The CBI told me to talk with, um, an Annette Trieri. Is she in?"

"She's on medical leave, recovering from getting bunged up on a case. This is Sergeant Fred Winders, her second in charge."

"Well, I got called in to investigate a murder down on the Navajo Reservation this morning, and, according to a driver's license, the victim was a Durango resident, a Luke Begay. I thought I'd see if the name rings a bell with you folks."

"Hmm. Not immediately with me. But let me have a look on our database. Let's see." Fred was typing furiously at the keyboard of his new office computer. "Luke Begay. Right. Nothing big. Arrested for civil disturbance, once. Apparently had to do with a demonstration for Native American rights. It says here that he was the chairman of American Indian Restoration. I've heard of that for some reason. Oh, I know. It's a local advocacy group. Wants to ship all of us European types back to the coasts, or something like that, and let the tribes have all of their land back. Return nature to its true stewards. Stuff like that. Does this help?"

"Maybe it does. His body was found this morning, lying on top of the Four Corners Monument down here southwest

Excess Homicide
A Four Corners Mystery

of Cortez. Shot once in the back of the head, execution style. Looks like someone planned this carefully."

SITTING IN FRONT of a window in her suite in the Lodge looking out over the valley, Carla Fraser was wishing that she had already succeeded. The trouble with trying to become a travel writer, she thought, is having such lovely things to write about and no readers. She lowered her eyes to the screen of her laptop and reread her latest effort.

> It's early October, and through the window we're watching the morning sun creep down the northeast face of McIntyre Peak. A mere bump by Rocky Mountain standards, the peak is distinguished by cliffs that expose a dozen or so strata of different colored rock near its summit. The colors of the rock are muted, however, because aspen dressed in all shades of green, gold, and even orange command the view. They spread in sweeping stripes, random patches, and single, startling trees over the mountain and in both directions along the side of the valley. As the sunlight hits them, they explode into brilliance against the deep green of the spruce and fir, under the crystal-blue of the sky. A patch of red—kinnikinnick?—on a high scree slope and the white of yesterday's snow on the peak punctuate the scene.
>
> Because our room is up on the hillside, we're also looking out over the treetops in the valley. Perched nearby at eye level on the top of a ponderosa pine, a magpie watches to see if we

might offer breakfast. A few yellow leaves still cling to the elm, willow, and ash along the river, but most have fallen, leaving behind gray and tan skeletons brightly lit by the sun, in stark contrast to the shadowed valley wall. They provide a hint of the winter to come, a hint reinforced by smoke curling lazily down the valley from the wood stove in a cabin across the way, and by the frost on the corners of our windows.

As the morning matures, the little settlement that calls itself Horca begins to come to life. Guys in insulated overalls are standing around in the parking lot of the restaurant, little puffs of breath evidence of their discussion. The occasional semi whizzes by on the highway. Pickup trucks towing horse trailers appear, converging at the restaurant for morning coffee and conversation.

These are the San Juan Mountains of extreme south-central Colorado, a few miles from the New Mexico border, where State Highway 17 from Antonito crosses the Conejos River before its winding climb up La Manga Pass to the south. From our window, we can see the road curving gently up the grade into the distance, disappearing into an aspen grove. We're about halfway between Antonito, to the east, and Chama, south over the pass. There is history here, and, because our Spanish-English dictionary tells us that one definition of "horca" is "gallows," it may be dramatic history.

From here, the Conejos Valley continues upward to the northwest. After about 25 miles, the gravel road along the river passes the settlement of Plataro before ascending the aptly named Stunner Pass on its way over to the Alamosa River Valley…

As she read, trying to decide if this was too much or not, Carla kept checking the scene outside to gauge her accuracy. When she looked to see if there was anyone left in the parking lot of the restaurant, out from under a Volvo station wagon crawled one of those men dressed in overalls. How curious, she thought.

Just then, she heard a huge yawn behind her, and turned to see Kevin finally emerging from the bedroom, mouth wide open, scratching his hairy belly. How romantic, she thought. Now he'll probably want to Do It again. Maybe I can divert his attention.

"I made some coffee, sweetie. Good morning!" She turned back to her laptop and the scenery. A couple had emerged from the restaurant and were climbing into the Volvo. They headed off south, in the direction of Chama.

As she was working on her last paragraphs, trying to make them sound somewhat less clinically directional, she noticed a flash over the top of her reading glasses, out the window. She looked up just in time to see a large puff of smoke, with pieces of flying debris, where the Volvo should have been. Three seconds later, the noise of the explosion rattled the windows.

IN THE FOUR CORNERS STATES, hunting season, especially big-game hunting season, is a good time to stay out of the woods. And the mountains, and the desert—and anywhere else there might be, could even remotely possibly be, big-game in season. It's much better to stay indoors, behind eighteen inches of adobe, if possible.

It's not that the local citizens are irresponsible; quite the contrary. The danger is from the thousands of men—this is a guy thing, mostly—from neighboring states who have too much disposable income. With it, they purchase equipment by the ton, including large trucks and trailers to haul it, fancy firearms, and gallons and gallons of whiskey. Nothing like slugging down a pint or so of 86-proof spirits to improve one's ability to aim a high-powered rifle. Fortunately for the Four Corners states, many of these purchases are made locally, and the cash flow keeps many a small town in the back-country solvent. Locals who used to make a living from mining and logging are now able to survive as big-game guides. Some like it more than others.

Jake Colvin was one of the others, but he needed the money. His six weeks of guiding, run out of Cedaredge, Colorado, north of Delta on the road up the Grand Mesa, paid most of the bills for the year. He managed to defer the rest. But dealing with the people who hired him was almost not worth it.

Take that bunch from Oklahoma who came in for the second rifle season in November. Six guys in three extended-cab, doolie pickups, each crammed full and pulling a twenty-foot flatbed trailer loaded with two of those stupid little four-wheel-drive all-terrain travesties, a freezer, and several additional crates of junk. Including a Hell's Angels' convention worth of Wild Turkey, which they consumed while sitting around telling each other lies about their successes over the summer catching women and large-mouth bass. Jake wondered idly what activities coincided with which catch.

Excess Homicide
A Four Corners Mystery

And why they needed all that stuff was a complete mystery. Hell, Jake supplied tents and cooking equipment, and he would have supplied horses if they hadn't brought those ridiculous ATV pollution machines.

He'd much rather have been able to make a living by teaching silviculture down at Mesa College in Grand Junction, but the curriculum had changed, as had the requirements. You had to have one of those fancy doctorates to get on the faculty there now. The generations of experience he'd absorbed from his father and grandfather as a kid, on those trips up to the Grand Mesa with the six-mule team to take out bridge-truss-sized trees, that didn't count for squat. And logging, what there was left of it, was all done with machines now. None of the old-fashioned, gentler techniques were economically competitive.

But the rifle seasons were behind him, and they'd been good. His new, higher rates hadn't raised any eyebrows, all the sports had filled their licenses, and the tips had been astonishing. Must have been a good year in the oil and gas industry. At long last, all those giant pickups had left town, along with the usual contingent of Lexus SUVs with California plates, and it was back to the locals and their battered mini-pickups and ancient Subarus. He and his family would be having a good Thanksgiving later in the month.

He was on his way down the hill toward Delta for groceries and a trip to the hardware store, enjoying the view of the Gunnison River valley, as always. The snow line, he noticed, had come almost all the way down to Orchard City last night. So absorbed was he in the scene that he wasn't paying attention to the blue pickup truck with the oversized tires and reinforced front bumper that was following him, much too close for comfort, if he'd noticed.

When he finally did notice it in his rearview mirror, it was too late. Only the barest of nudges from the big vehicle behind him was enough to send his compact Nissan pickup out of control, and it spun twice before crashing sideways into a telephone pole, driver's door first. Unfortunately for Jake, he'd never gotten around to fixing the broken seat belt. Now he never would.

ARTHUR POWELL, who had felt more like a traffic cop than a National Park Service ranger in his previous assignment at Rocky Mountain National Park in Colorado, was still fascinated with his new world. It was smaller, and for sure drier, but it was his, or at least he was in charge. He made a point of arriving early every day, despite living some 35 miles away in Blanding, so he could have it all to himself for a little while.

Natural Bridges National Monument in southern Utah is to Rocky Mountain National Park as the little town of Blanding, Utah is to Denver, and Arthur was still adjusting. He'd even stopped wearing his sidearm, although the possibility of rattlesnakes, even this time of year, motivated his employees to wear theirs.

The drive over from Blanding was a pleasure every morning, and the return trip in the evening was just as lovely. With the sun behind him each way gently lighting the piñon and juniper scrub, making the solitary little trees cast long, long shadows across the desert and giving the red rocks a stark relief that vanished during mid-day, he felt as if he were driving through a travelogue. Ever since daylight savings time had ended, just over a month ago, the

Excess Homicide
A Four Corners Mystery

mornings were the better drive, with everything looking so fresh.

Another adjustment was in the political differences, and he was still getting used to this as well. The switch from touchy-feely, warm-and-fuzzy, north-central Colorado to stolidly down-to-earth Republican southeastern Utah was startling, to say the least. But these people had great respect for the land, too, and it was ingrained. He often felt that the Colorado Front-Range outdoors crowd had learned their environmentalism at summer camp or from reading about it in those slick advocacy magazines.

Also, since just about everyone hereabouts hunted for food and almost always carried a rifle in their pickup truck, there was a certain amount of self-policing that was not present up in Colorado. He was especially glad that he wouldn't have to deal with those groups of right-wing extremists who seemed to think that poaching elk in the Park was a God-given right.

For one thing, the elk around here stayed up in the mountains, in the Abajos, or over in the Henrys on the other side of Lake Powell. For another, everyone around here was pretty right-wing already, so the definition of "extremist" was quite different. And they all went to church and kept each other pretty honest. He was looking forward to a true community Christmas this year. Even though his coffee-colored skin set him apart from the others (man, these Mormons are *white*, he couldn't help but think), he had been welcomed into the Blanding community and had more dinner invitations than he could handle. He'd already gained ten pounds as a result. They all seemed to think that his foods of choice were deep-fried everything.

Arthur finally pulled in to the short section of pavement leading from State Road 95 to the Monument and stopped to open the gate to the day-use area. The air was cool, a pleasant wintertime cool, and it smelled of juniper. There was a hint of piñon smoke from a campfire somewhere. He took a deep breath, and stretched grandly. Looking around his little domain, he couldn't help but feel lucky.

Because the muzzle velocity of a Remington .30-06 is much faster than the speed of sound, he didn't hear the rifle's report, and the hollow-point slug caught him squarely in the side of the head, just above the tip of his left ear. He dropped like a rock.

EXCEPT FOR THE SKI AREA, Santa Fe in January would be nearly devoid of tourists, and that would have made Roger Colgate just about as happy as anything else in the whole world. Well, maybe not quite as happy as complete closure of the National Forests to all humans—assuming, of course, that he and his band of eco-preservationists could continue to have access. But close. The tourists just clogged up the narrow Santa Fe streets and made it necessary to make reservations for dinner. And even lunch.

This tourist problem was one of the reasons, not a public reason but a real motivating one, that he and his cohorts steadfastly opposed plans to expand the Santa Fe Ski Basin across its little valley to the next hillside. Roger and friends were all well-off enough, from trust funds and other annuities, that they could afford to take on the Forest Service in court, using the legal system to effectively strangle anybody's plans for anything. Rather than work at this themselves, Roger and friends hired lawyers, particularly young, hungry ones, from the huge contingent

Excess Homicide
A Four Corners Mystery

that needed such gratuitous work to pay off their mortgages in Santa Fe's up-scale foothills neighborhoods. They also donated large sums of tax-deductible dollars to various fringe organizations to do the actual protesting when it was needed. That way, Roger's group was able to spend its time on more relaxing activities.

The main vehicle for the legal action was the Endangered Species Act. It was pretty easy, especially in this undeveloped part of the country, to find some critter, or, if need be, some plant, that would be "threatened" by whatever the Forest Service, or anyone else, wanted to do. And even if they couldn't find a threatened species, there were possibilities. One time when they couldn't find a suitable candidate, they had been successful at stopping a forest-fuels thinning project over in the Jemez Mountains by inventing a new species of mouse, the "Jemez Springs while-tailed deer mouse." A picture of the cute little guy, created on a computer as a composite of three actual species, was one of Roger's favorites. He kept a copy, framed, on his desk. And it was a good thing that it was just a computer mouse, because any real ones would have been exterminated by the catastrophic wildfire they'd had over in the Jemez last summer.

Roger was thinking about tourists, especially the problem with their taking up valuable restaurant space, because he was waiting for a table for lunch at Santacafé, on Washington across from the old Federal Courthouse. Even though it was January, the mid-day sun was warm, and he was enjoying it while leaning against a massive elm tree on the courthouse lawn. The south light, crisp and clean, for which Santa Fe is famous, filtered brightly through the bare branches over his head. Twenty minutes, the maitre d' had told him, so he'd decided to wait outside in the sunshine and read the latest issue of the *High Country News*.

When, he thought, were they going to admit to being pawns of the logging and mining industries and quit pretending to be environmentalists?

He heard a polite tap on a car horn, and looked up to see who it was. Stella! Lovely Stella. She was waving to him from her Mercedes SUV as it rounded the curve from Washington to Federal Place. He waved back and smiled. Just seeing her drive by was enough to warm him up, especially in the vicinity of his lap. He went back to reading.

Lies! That "experiment" up in Oregon, where they fenced off the riparian area next to the stream bed, was just a sham. His friends on the west coast had told him all about it. Just getting the cattle away from the streams wasn't enough. Eliminating grazing altogether was the only solution. Let the land be the land, without all these four-legged bulldozers ranging around!

Thinking about cattle got him thinking about lunch again, and a vision of the Santacafé's green-chile smothered New York luncheon steak, medium rare, east-coast medium rare, lingered in his mind. His mouth watered.

A second polite tap on a car horn made him look up again. Could Stella be back? Despite the sunshine, his lap could use all the warming it could get. But, no, he thought, this horn didn't sound quite like the first one.

It wasn't.

This time, the car, actually a windowless black van with a sliding side door that had opened, stopped. Roger squinted, trying to see into the dark interior. There was

Excess Homicide
A Four Corners Mystery

someone kneeling inside, but he couldn't quite see what was happening.

Then there was a little twanging noise. He felt a horrible, blinding pain in his neck, and his knees buckled. But he couldn't fall. Nor could he scream. As he tried to reach up to investigate what had happened, everything went black. Unseen, the *High Country News* fluttered to the ground.

It didn't take long for the police to arrive, and they found him, quite dead, impaled through the neck onto the elm with a crossbow bolt, rather like a spindly-legged beetle pinned to an entomologist's collection case.

ON THE HIGH PLAINS of Northern New Mexico, west of Taos across the Rio Grande Gorge Bridge on U.S. Highway 64, it was easy to imagine that one had arrived on another planet. The houses there were built in quite a fanciful manner, supposedly self-contained and Earth-friendly, with curves, turrets, and angles that might be expected of a Star Wars movie set. Some were reminiscent of those sand dribble castles kids made at the beach; some looked like they were designed by Frank Lloyd Wright on LSD. And those were just the ones that could be seen from the highway. To come upon these dream-shapes rising out of the desert, especially after leaning over the railing of the Bridge watching the natural scenery of the Gorge, was quite disorienting.

Hidden in an arroyo out of view from the casual passerby was the house of Trenton Garcia, or SunMaster, as he insisted his acolytes call him. (He didn't have any real friends, so no one called him Trent.) SunMaster specialized in separating wealthy, insecure Taoseños and their friends from the coasts from their excess funds. He'd built his *ashram* in a location strategically chosen to enhance his ability to do this, due west of Wheeler Peak, the highest point—13,161 feet—in New Mexico. From SunMaster's place, sunrise on the equinoxes was just over the peak. And, on the solstices, it rose in almost equally impressive places, over another of the high Sangre de Cristo peaks to the north in June, signifying the "height" of summer, and over a dramatic saddle between two peaks to the south in December, signifying the "depth" of winter. As a result of these spiritual convergences, his clientele were *very* impressed with his powers.

Year 'round, his daily routine included rising before first light and running down to the very middle of the Rio Grande Gorge Bridge and back, some ten miles that he managed to do in about 50 minutes. Then, as the sun rose over the Sangres, he led a yoga class for whoever showed up with the requested "donation" of $75. Naturally, when the sun rose over some special landmark, there was a special ceremony and the checkbooks came out yet again. It was surprising how many of those special landmarks he'd identified up there in the Sangres.

The daily ten-mile run and the yoga kept him in fine condition, and he led the yoga class wearing only a bikini brief and his famous suntan. This combination was useful in maintaining his credibility in the private afternoon sessions he held for his female clients. The attractive, well-endowed ones, that is. Tantric yoga is a specialty that needs to be taught in private.

On Saturdays, the morning yoga class was generally over-booked, and his sun room was crowded. When he didn't show up on time one day in February, a completely

Excess Homicide
A Four Corners Mystery

unprecedented occurrence, confusion reigned. Finally, one of the more experienced women—experienced in both the morning yoga classes and the afternoon Tantric sessions—took charge and tried to conduct the class. But her attempts just didn't measure up.

Later that morning, Helma Lundegaard, visiting New Mexico with her husband as a respite from February in Minnesota, was standing on the Gorge Bridge, gazing down at the river some 650 feet below, when she spotted an unusual flash of color. Borrowing the binoculars from Herman, she was able to see that the color was a flame-orange pair of running shorts. Worn by a someone sprawled on the rocks.

It took the rescue team four hours to haul up Trent's badly mangled body.

SPRING SNOW! Jodie Pacheco knew the skiing lasted only briefly after each March storm this far south, but she also knew how to make the most of it. The trick was to catch it several times within a few days of its falling, before it had time to go through too many of the day-night melt-freeze cycles. The first day would be worth paying the lift ticket prices up at the Arizona Snow Bowl in the San Francisco Peaks. But after that, it was much better in the ponderosa forest south of town, where a first tracks descent of the Mogollón Rim always pushed her abilities to the limit.

Mostly, the ponderosa forest was too dense to ski, at least at the speeds she liked. In order to float on the new snow, speed was necessary, and to keep up speed, only the most gentle telemark turns were possible. It helped a lot not to have to dodge too many trees.

But she knew her way around the forest, in large part because she had been involved in thinning it. Her work with the faculty at Northern Arizona University had put her in a position to take a lead in the volunteer brigade that had been assembled for the task. Although it was an experimental program, they had managed to take out the undergrowth and small trees over quite a large area, and it now made for wonderful back-country skiing—towering ponderosas about 50 feet apart, with no lower limbs sticking out as obstacles. Like a park.

The thinning program was controversial, to be sure, because removing the slash, the downed trees and brush, had been denounced as "logging" by several noisy groups. Even Jodie had second thoughts. But leaving the slash in place wouldn't have reduced the fire danger significantly, and that was the whole point, after all. And it had also occurred to her that the piles of branches would probably not be covered with enough snow to be safe for skiing, either. So she pitched in with enthusiasm.

She and her three friends had arranged a complicated car shuttle to accomplish their run through the woods, leaving their cars in four places—at the top, at the bottom, and at two intermediate parking areas where they could ferry across flats. Why walk, even on touring skis, when you can ride? Besides, the chance to rest was worth taking advantage of.

They were on the last leg, a familiar chute that didn't take long to get skied out after new snowfalls. Because back-country skiing is a popular thing to do among the young and fit in Flagstaff, tracks appeared almost as fast as snow fell. Jodie felt lucky that hers were the first tracks this time. She was able to stay well ahead of her companions

Excess Homicide
A Four Corners Mystery

because of the workouts she forced on herself—running, wall-sitting, weights, the stair-master. It was paying off.

She made the last of the series of turns that had started higher up with long, sweeping telemarks, which tested the stamina of her quads, and ended in the chute with short, choppy jump turns. Then she checked to a stop above the final, straight shot at the bottom of the chute. Looking back, she was tickled to see her smooth, convergent S-shaped tracks proclaiming her expertise. Pleased with herself, she set her skis straight downhill and flew out of the bottom of the chute. But she didn't notice the piano wire stretched tightly across the opening, about shoulder-height off the snow surface, between two large ponderosa pines.

That's where her companions found her head. The rest of her was another thirty yards down the slope, but it was easy to find because of the bright red stripe on the snow leading to it.

NORTH OF GOLDEN, Colorado State Road 93 winds over grass-covered hills and valleys at the base of the Front Range Foothills, and Stuart Pendleton was enjoying the handling and power of his new Porsche Boxster. He'd waited six months to get the color and options he wanted, and now he realized how well worth the wait this car was. Even thoughts of his date in court, in which he was to defend a client against a defamation charge, couldn't distract him from the road.

Cruising over the crest of Davidson Mesa and down the two-mile grade to the South Boulder Creek crossing, he drank in the green of the springtime pastures. Ahead, the prominent Boulder landmarks were still limited to the National Center for Atmospheric Research, nestled on Table

Mesa under the Flatirons, the university dormitories at Williams Village, and the stacks of the power plant out east. The downtown area and the red tile roofs of the university campus were hidden by the pastels of April in the Boulder Valley.

Stuart was sufficiently mesmerized by the view that he almost didn't notice the traffic overtaking him—it was the erratic patterns in the mirror picked up by his peripheral vision that finally got his attention.

A gray, customized van of indiscriminate vintage was gaining on him rapidly, weaving across the yellow line into the oncoming passing lane and back onto the right shoulder. Farther behind, just beginning the descent, a blue pickup truck with those oversized, off-road tires was also closing quickly. A passenger was leaning out the side window with what looked to be a pipe on his shoulder, trying to point it at the weaving van.

Hemmed in by an embankment on his right and the guard rail protecting the drop-off across the road, Stuart's choices were limited. He shifted down two gears to fourth and stomped the accelerator, and with a roar from the engine compartment behind him, his new car leapt forward down the grade. He was glad there was no traffic in front of him.

As he rounded the curve at the grade's half-way point, he saw dueling 18-wheel gravel trucks occupying both of the southbound lanes coming up the hill, a pack of frustrated Boulderites in Swedish sedans and SUVs queued up behind them. At least the uphill traffic was staying politely on its assigned side of the double yellow lines. Stuart wondered vaguely about the weaving van and whether it would negotiate passage of the two trucks.

Excess Homicide
A Four Corners Mystery

He jumped the red light at the Eldorado Springs Drive intersection at just over 100. But despite the tension of the speed and whatever that thing was that was aimed generally in his direction from the blue pickup, he appreciated the irony of the "Welcome to Boulder – Please Drive Safely" sign as it zipped past.

It was not until the road straightened, metamorphosing into South Broadway, that he noticed the van was no longer in his mirror. It had not made it up the little curved hill from the bottom-land of the creek drainage. Stuart slowed to the speed limit, turned onto a side street at the first opportunity, parked, and tried, with deep breaths, to stop shaking. He picked up the car phone and punched 911.

"Hello? I'd like to report a very strange event on South Foothills Highway, south of Boulder, and there may well be some kind of medical emergency." He related matters as well as he could, given his adrenaline level, and got put on hold while the operator called in the troops.

The 911 operator finally got back to him with silly follow-up questions, which Stuart tried politely to deflect. No, at 100 miles per hour, he wasn't able to read a backwards license plate in his mirror, being preoccupied with other matters. He couldn't tell if there had been gunshots. All he knew was that the van didn't come over the rise up South Broadway by Chambers Road. Yes, he'd be happy to await arrival of a police officer to answer more questions. He provided his car description and location, and settled back for a wait. Time to call the office, he decided.

By the time several sirens zoomed past, southbound on Broadway, and a police cruiser finally pulled up behind him on the side street, he had rearranged his schedule to accommodate the delays. In his mirror he saw the officer approaching, so he lowered his window, and readied his license, registration, and proof-of-insurance. He took a breath and put on his lawyer face.

"Mr. Pendleton? I understand you called in this incident?"

"Indeed I did. What happened back there?"

"Would you mind stepping out and sitting in my car? I'll need to take notes." Stuart gathered himself and got out, listening for the chirp of the alarm as he locked his car behind him, and followed the officer back to the cruiser.

"I'd like to get a statement first, so your information isn't influenced by things you didn't see." Despite his mostly civil-court case load, Stuart knew enough about police procedure not to argue, and related the incident yet again.

"You said 'over 100,' did I hear that correctly?"

"Um, yes, well, I don't like to incriminate myself, but I expect that it's relevant for you to know my state of mind. Like running the light. Not my usual approach to driving, I assure you."

"It's fortunate that there wasn't very much traffic. And I won't be writing you up—you're right, though, everything's relevant. Now. What happened back there is that the gray van you described appears to have been hit with some kind of explosive device. It's completely destroyed, off the road, on fire, with two dead people inside, a man and a woman. There's no blue pickup truck anywhere around."

"So it sounds like that thing I saw on the guy's shoulder was some kind of rocket launcher, or bazooka, or something like that."

"That's my guess. It suggests that your decision to speed away was probably a good choice."

"Well, considering that it was the only thing I could figure out to do, it sure was. Is there anything else I can help with?"

"Where can we reach you if more questions come up?" Stuart gave him a business card, and they went their respective ways.

Neither was aware of the blue pickup truck off in the distance, at the pullout at the crest of Davidson Mesa, or of the two men dressed in camouflage fatigues using high-powered spotting scopes to inspect the scene far below.

Two

AS THE MID-MAY SUN settled down behind Sugarloaf Mountain, Hal Weathers unpacked and mentally organized his schedule for the next two weeks.

Because Annette would be joining him tomorrow and staying for the duration of his conference, he had decided to splurge on a top-floor suite in the old part of the Hotel Boulderado, downtown. Not the official conference hotel, and definitely not on the approved travel list for Frémont State business trips, it was still worth the extra cost. He could either walk or take the shuttle bus up to the campus, and Annette could have the car to drive up into the mountains to contemplate her navel while trying to figure out her future. She needed the time to think about whether to leave her position with the City of Durango Police Department and accept an offer to take over the satellite office that the Colorado Bureau of Investigation maintained in Durango.

As he was unpacking, he caught a glimpse of himself in the big mirror. How, he wondered, did I manage to get into this fancy hotel looking this scruffy? A week of fly-fishing solo with an empty tube of sunscreen and without shaving had given him the appearance of one of those guys who slept on the benches over in Central Park. Scratching the stubble, he examined it closely in the mirror to assess the

Excess Homicide
A Four Corners Mystery

gray and came up with a conservative estimate of 35% on his face. Fortunately, it was still only about 1% on top, a few flecks of salt amidst the full head of brown pepper, if you didn't count the temples. Those, he remembered, were supposed to make him look distinguished.

"I think," he said to the guy looking back at him through humorous brown eyes flecked with gold, "I'd better shave."

He got cleaned up and decided to call Annette. On his checking in, luck was smiling on him and he was given a west-side suite, so he was watching the evening sun over the foothills when her phone rang, twice.

"Trieri, investigations."

"Hey, darlin', I got here…"

"Hal! I want to talk, but I'm on the other line. Can you hold on for a couple of minutes?" He didn't have time to answer before she switched back. He used the wait to continue organizing his schedule and to review his reasons for being in Boulder.

As Dean of Natural Sciences at Frémont State University and a faculty member of the Earth Sciences Department, Hal was always getting all sorts of invitations to this meeting or that conference, and he had learned that he could not possibly attend even a small fraction of them. So he was very selective, not only about the topic of the invitation but also about the location. Living in Durango meant that most of the standard vacation spots held little attraction for him.

Not that all was sweetness and light in the little southwestern Colorado mountain college town. Frémont State continued to struggle with its perennial budget woes, and Durango's continued growth was becoming more and more depressing. At least, for long-time residents like Hal, the growth meant his home's value continued to appreciate, but the university's budget problems didn't seem to have any such silver lining. If only, he thought, the Board of Trustees hadn't been swayed by the pie-in-the-sky ambition of that long-gone university president back in the '80s. Then the school wouldn't have morphed itself into a second-rate research university, and it would still be able to take pride in its identity as the premier undergraduate college in the State of Colorado system. As things stood, Hal was forever working hard to increase Frémont State's visibility in the scientific community, with a frustratingly low success rate. And that was one of the reasons he was in Boulder, to try yet again.

The invitation to the two-week-long symposium and workshop on the increasing sensitivity of arid- and semi-arid-land ecosystems to climate variations, to be sponsored by the National Center for Atmospheric Research and held at the University of Colorado, had intrigued him for two reasons. For one thing, he had in mind a plan to bring the next such symposium in the series to Frémont State, so he needed to attend this one. Holding high-visibility meetings would be one way to increase the reputation of the foundering school, and, as a dean, that was one of Hal's responsibilities.

For another thing, between semesters at the university, Boulder was actually quite a pleasant little city, and it was only a short drive from world-class trout streams along the Rocky Mountain Front Range. The Cache la Poudre, the St. Vrain, and the South Platte were all calling out to him. Hal was sure that the conference, being two weeks long, could manage to stumble along without him for a day or two. If he

Excess Homicide
A Four Corners Mystery

got lucky, the freestone streams might not yet be flooded with runoff—spring seemed to be running a little late in these parts. But even if they were, the South Platte in Cheeseman Canyon and below would always be there, protected from runoff by the dam.

"Hal? Are you still there?"

"I'm here and you're there, and I wish you were here or I was there."

"Me too. How was the drive?"

"Nothing unusual. Pretty. Spectacular. You know. But on this end, yecch. The development down by Golden is way out of hand. Makes me glad we don't live here. I did have a great time yesterday and the day before, though. The caddis hatch on the upper Arkansas was in full swing, just on schedule. And there was still a little snow on the banks of the Blue River, but the blue-winged olives were awake, and so were the trout trying to eat them."

"And now you've got to go to work at that conference. Well, good luck getting your head into it. By the way, that phone call was the CBI again. They're really turning up the heat. They sent me a package this afternoon and wanted to know if I got it."

"A package? Candy? Flowers?"

"No such luck. A case file, or a set of case files. They have this idea that a bunch of homicides are somehow linked, and they think I'd be the perfect person to head up the investigation as my first CBI assignment."

"A *bunch*? To me, that implies, oh, more than five. Wouldn't you already know about something like that?"

"One of them, I do. And I recall hearing about a couple of the others. The Colorado ones. There are others in this package, too, a couple in New Mexico, one in Flagstaff, and one over in Utah. A bunch."

"What do those have to do with the CBI?"

"They don't, at least directly, but if they're linked to the four Colorado ones, they do."

"Four? When?"

"Over the past eight months. One down south of Cortez, at the Four Corners Monument. One up in Cedaredge. One west of Antonito, and one up in Boulder, last month, and both of those were doubles so it's really six homicides."

"So somebody's been busy. Or several somebodies."

"Quite. But there's no indication of who. None. Completely clean crime scenes. So they're appealing to my considerable ego and suggesting that I could solve the whole package, if only I signed up."

"But you didn't, at least yet, because you're coming up here to think about it."

"Yeah. That's what I told them and that's when they sent this package. Anyway, I'm on the early flight tomorrow, gets in about seven."

"And I'll be there to meet you. At the gate, if they'll let me out to it—they seem to keep changing the rules. Otherwise, at the top of the stairs after you get off the train, OK?"

"If I remember right, that place is bigger than all creation, so I hope you can get to the gate. Then you can buy me breakfast. I don't want to eat before getting on the plane, in case it's bumpy."

"I'll find an ATM before I meet you."

IN A GLASS OFFICE TOWER on the north end of Colorado Springs, in the midst of several other such glass towers that

Excess Homicide
A Four Corners Mystery

contained mostly religious non-profit groups, Charles Shure sat in a conference room with an unbelievable view. The Pikes Peak massif and the setting sun behind the Rampart Range dominated the scene, but the city of Colorado Springs, the U.S. Air Force Academy, and Cheyenne Mountain all provided variety, spread across the landscape in front of him. Lights were beginning to twinkle in the city.

UNELECO headquarters occupied the top three floors of the Christian Families Association, Inc. building—UNELECO owned it, truth be known—and the top floor consisted of the executive conference room and the offices of Shure and his senior staff.

Shure had the conference room, on the building's southwest corner with two walls of glass to look through, to himself. He had chosen to use it to open and examine a curious package that had been delivered earlier in the afternoon. Lying on the massive conference table was a leather-covered book, apparently hand bound, and, printed on 40-pound parchment paper, a letter.

7 May

Dearest Charles,

My colleagues and I have followed your extraordinary career with the greatest interest, and we all agree that it is now time for you to be made aware of your proud heritage.

When your grandparents immigrated to the U.S. at the end of the Second World War, they, like so many other people displaced by the War, had to begin a new life with only the clothes on their backs. Through hard work and the perseverance that one would expect from solid Aryan stock, they built a business from scratch, a business that your father would use as a springboard for his career and that you have brought into the 21st Century as one of the powerhouse organizations of the new economy.

UNELECO has matured from its origins supplying electrical equipment for the post-war housing boom in Colorado Springs to a multi-national conglomerate that stands at the center of the digital communications world. It is now poised, through its various subsidiaries, to surpass all expectations for profitability. We are aware of this because we have been stockholders since the IPO fifteen years ago. You, my good Charles, have made us rich.

It is now time that we return the favor.

Of course, given your personal fortune, it is unnecessary for us to return the favor in financial terms. But we believe we can return it in another way, one that fits with your Aryan heritage, and one that will make your professional life far easier than it is now. We can help UNELECO.

First, we should explain about your heritage. Enclosed with this letter is the final volume of your Great-Uncle Heinrich von Scheuer's laboratory notes. You may not know that your grandparents changed their name from von Scheuer to Shure upon emigrating from Germany. This was because the family name had become contaminated by the slanderous lies told by the Jew traitors in Germany and Europe at the end of the War. Your Grand-Uncle Heinrich was one of the premier Aryan scientists working on the problem of how to

Excess Homicide
A Four Corners Mystery

eliminate the inferior gene pool that had been spreading like a plague across Europe for centuries. As we all know, this is a problem that haunts us even today, and, with the continuing flood of inferiors sneaking illegally into our country, it will continue to be a problem, given their insistence on breeding like cockroaches.

You may be interested to know that the first twenty-four volumes of these lab notes are now a part of the propaganda on display at the so-called Holocaust Museum, where the Jew power structure continues to spread its malicious lies. How this volume came into our hands is a long, convoluted story, one that we hope to have the opportunity to relate to you personally some day soon.

Now, to return your favor. We believe that we are now in a position to assist UNELECO in two ways.

The first is related to your Grand-Uncle Heinrich's work. We have made arrangements to liberate a copy of the rest of his laboratory notes from the so-called Holocaust Museum, and we believe, with this final volume, UNELECO's biotechnology division will be in a far more competitive position to develop new pharmaceuticals than it is now. Of course, it will also be in a perfect position to work toward cleansing the gene pool.

Second, we have already begun to assist UNELECO's natural resources divisions by paving the way toward simpler approaches to new acquisitions in both the minerals and forest products groups. It is too soon to be specific about this, but, as you will soon see, many of the legal obstacles that UNELECO has been encountering will no longer be troublesome.

We regret that, for now, we must remain incognito, but we look forward to the day when we can meet with you, toast your successes, and discuss our common heritage in more detail. In the meantime, you have our

Sincere regards,
The Aryan Rights Foundation

Charles Shure was aware that his grandparents had changed the family name, but the rest of the letter's information, and the book itself, were news to him. By the time he finished reading the letter, his hands were shaking badly, and he walked to the sideboard to make himself a stiff drink, a good six ounces of Glenlivet over ice. Then he sat in one of the leather chairs facing Pikes Peak to try to calm down.

With friends like these... He took a large gulp of the Glenlivet.

Who, he thought, could these people be? The last thing UNELECO needed was a bunch of racist crazies doing things to "help." The timber and mining divisions were facing the same legal problems as the rest of the industry, and negotiations for new resource acquisitions were in a very delicate stage right now. UNELECO's public image simply couldn't stand any more tarnish. What in the world was the "Aryan Rights Foundation?"

He cleared his throat and raised his voice slightly above a normal conversational level.

Excess Homicide
A Four Corners Mystery

"Comm-access!"

"How can we help?" came a disembodied, metallic voice from the general direction of the ceiling.

"Susan Mackovich, voice, please." He enunciated carefully and almost immediately heard a ringing.

"UNELECO, Susan Mackovich." This voice also came from the ceiling, but it was natural, a real human.

"Susan, Chuck Shure. Glad you're here late. I need help. I'm in the conference room upstairs. Could you come up, please? And please bring your CryptoCard."

He was confident that Susan, computer wizard extraordinaire and head of UNELECO's executive research group, would be able to find the answers he needed. With her CryptoCard and the conference room's workstation, she would have access to just about any database she needed, anywhere, even from the Defense Department's secure servers.

THE EARLY FLIGHT from Durango was right on time, and, at 7:20 the next morning, Annette walked off the escalator from the underground train at the Denver International Airport and into Hal's arms. He had been standing back from the little crowd gathered around, and, watching her come off the moving stairway and look around for him, he marveled yet again at how fortunate he was to have attracted someone as spectacular as she. Even though he was some 15 years older and couldn't, even on his best day, honestly consider himself a "catch," she had found something appealing in him. She had come along at just the right time for him, when he had finally put behind him the pain and heartbreak of losing his first wife to cancer.

Whatever it was that Annette found in him, he sure wasn't going to argue.

After a long hug she handed him her briefcase and they headed up to the restaurant level, to Pour la France for breakfast.

"Well, Mrs. Weathers, what's your fancy for breakfast?"

"I don't know, Mr. Trieri, maybe Eggs Benedict?"

They had kept their separate last names after marrying in March, and there was no end to other people's confusion. So they enjoyed the private joke now and then.

"This briefcase must imply that you checked a bag."

"Um, two. I'm going to be here for a couple of weeks, you know."

"I thought I brought all the stuff you'll be needing up here when I packed the car."

"But I've had time to think about it some more."

"So just how big do you think my car is, anyway?"

"You didn't have the back seats folded down before, so there's plenty of room."

She was right. Hal had used the ski sack to store his fly-rod tubes, but everything else had fit into the trunk, nice and neat. With Annette's two new bags, he wasn't sure that this strategy would work, however.

After a relaxed breakfast, they headed over to baggage claim and found Annette's two bags patiently waiting to be picked up. Sometimes, Hal thought, things actually work the way they're supposed to.

They carted her luggage out to Hal's new car and put her two bags on the back seat, on either side of the fly-rod tubes sticking through the back seat on top of the arm rest.

Excess Homicide
A Four Corners Mystery

Hal headed out of the airport and turned north on the new bypass, toward Boulder.

"So, if I know you, you stayed up half the night reading those files they sent you yesterday."

"Guilty as charged. I even brought them with me. It's fascinating stuff. The CBI is doing exactly the right thing in trying to recruit me. Giving me these files, getting my curiosity piqued."

"At least you've got that figured out. I mean, if you know what they're trying to do, at least you won't get suckered in."

"Yep. I'm paying close attention to that, believe me. The strange thing is, most of the cases aren't CBI's. One of the Colorado murders is actually the FBI's. CBI is helping with the two double homicides and the one in Cedaredge, which may be only a traffic accident."

"And there's nothing that is logically in the Durango jurisdiction?"

"Not really. The victim in the FBI case, the body found on the Navajo Reservation at the Four Corners Monument last September, was a Durango resident, one Luke Begay. No obvious reason anyone would want to kill him, at least not execution style."

"Does that give you an excuse to get involved without changing jobs?"

"I thought of that already. Walter says no. But he and I talked about a temporary leave, to go work with the CBI on this case. To see if I liked it enough to make the change and all. He doesn't want to lose me, but he doesn't want to stand in the way of a career move."

"And, by treating it this way, dealing with you honestly, he's going to treat you well enough that you'll have second thoughts about another job. Bosses that considerate are hard to find, and I bet he knows that."

"Right again. And he and I've had this conversation, so at least there aren't any hidden agendas at work on his part. I think I'm going to see if I can get the CBI to let me talk with the locals here in Boulder about their double last month. That'll give me a little better taste of what working with them would be like."

"Do they have any theories about how these things fit together? I mean, they must think they fit together somehow, if they've got 'em all in the same package."

"The only thing remotely similar about them is that the victims all have one kind of connection or another to some relatively extreme faction of the environmental movement. Either they were active in some organization, or they provided funding, or they had some official position. Like, the guy over in Utah was a National Park Service employee, at Natural Bridges."

"And the two double homicides as well?"

"Both were married couples with both partners active. The Boulder couple, um…" she rummaged in her briefcase, "the Mayers, they were the people behind the Boulder chapter of SCARAB."

"SCARAB. Ahh, Students and Citizens for Animal Rights and Biodiversity, right? The same organization as the one at the U? The one run by that guy that got killed up in the Weminuche a couple of years ago, right?"

"Yeah, that guy Jennifer went camping with. One of Sal Kelly's dealers. The Mayers were killed in their van, on the way into Boulder last month, by someone who chased them and, apparently, got them with a rocket launcher, or something like that. The other couple was killed by a car bomb, near where the road west of Antonito crosses the river."

"West of Antonito... Oh, at Horca? I've been fishing there a couple of times. What a beautiful place. How could a car bomb get them there?"

"A witness said that she saw some guy crawl out from under their car when they were in a restaurant. It blew up about a mile down the road from there. This was the Levines, Holly and Jack, from Denver. They were on their way to Santa Fe for a vacation, from what the CBI's figured out."

"An environmental connection?"

"Funders of various small, radical fringe groups, big bucks funders. Like the Old Stand Guardians people in Boulder, the Forest Rescuers in Santa Fe, groups like that. In addition to the Sierra Club and so on."

"What about the Cedaredge guy?"

"Interesting. He was a big-game guide. Came from a logging family, people who did things the old way, before machines. Took big trees off Grand Mesa, not for lumber mills but for single beams. Mules, sledges, all that. Had a reputation as a tree-hugger. But he ran off the road in his truck. There were some indications that he may have had help, a push from behind. But nothing conclusive."

"So someone's going around knocking off Colorado environmentalists?"

"And their pals in New Mexico, Utah, and Arizona, or at least some of them."

"Well, at least it sounds like there isn't a Frémont State connection this time, like there usually seems to be. That's a relief."

H. P. Hanson

IF YOU PLOP a rectangle the size of Wyoming squarely on top of the Four Corners, you cover a landscape that is the property, for the most part, of various governmental entities. The largest landowner is Uncle Sam, through his agents in the Bureau of Land Management, the Forest Service, and the National Park Service. Second on the list is the Navajo Nation, which controls almost all of the Arizona part of this landscape plus a significant amount of it in Utah and New Mexico. Other Native American Nations—two Ute tribes in Colorado and the various New Mexico Pueblos—follow in turn.

Individual landownership, at least in terms of large parcels, is far down the list. Yet there are some ranches, assembled by hook and crook over the last century or so, that include significant acreage. The profitability of these ranches benefits significantly from additional grazing leases on nearby federal lands.

One such ranch, located in southern San Miguel County about 30 miles due west of Telluride, was the centerpiece of Jarvis Schoenfield's empire. His great-grandfather, Johann, had assembled the initial parcels during the late 1800s, using the Homestead Act and the less-than-perfect record keeping at the county seat, which at that time was way over in Silverton. When Grandfather Xavier linked the parcels into the X-S Ranch in the 1920s, the core of the Schoenfield empire took shape. Jarvis' father and uncles had expanded the X-S holdings and diversified into mining in the Paradox Valley after World War II, when uranium became the object of federal attention. Because Jarvis had stuck with the ranch, he was able to watch from a distance as his uncles and cousins died from cancer, and eventually he became the sole proprietor of some 50,000 acres of hay fields, pasture, and timber, too many mining claims on federal land to count, and grazing rights all over the region.

Because much of the pasture was scattered in parcels of various sizes throughout the Paradox Valley and the surrounding plateaus, the sight of cattle with the X-S brand seared onto their flanks was familiar to residents of the communities of Nucla, Naturita, and Norwood. This familiarity worked to Schoenfield's advantage at election time, and he was able to keep his seat in the Colorado State Senate as a result. His seniority there paid dividends for both his constituents and his fellow ranchers throughout the state, as well as for his variety of personal interests. His seniority also allowed him his choice of committee assignments, and he'd been Chairman of the Committee on Law Enforcement for years.

And the best thing of all was that everyone called him "Senator" all the time.

An operation the size of the X-S, which involved not only ranching but also timber and minerals extraction, required no small number of accountants and lawyers as well as ranch hands, lumberjacks, and miners. The corporate office, in a small building next to the First National Bank up in Norwood, was the employer of choice for the town. But the real seat of power for the X-S was at Raven's Roost, the ranch headquarters. Sprawled across the flattish top of North Mountain, about 15 miles south-southwest of Norwood, Raven's Roost consisted of a cluster of buildings—a small village, really—dominated by a huge, rambling log cabin, where Schoenfield lived with his domestic staff and personal assistants. But no wife.

For after trying three times without a hint of success to maintain a marital relationship, Schoenfield was finally and permanently single. His only regret was his failure to produce an heir. For a time, he blamed this on his wives, and he divorced the first two largely because of it. Wife number three, however, had the sort of personality that wouldn't put up with such badgering, and she had insisted on medical tests for both of them. She passed hers, and he failed his. He thought about adoption as an alternative, but he finally decided to work toward making the X-S a self-perpetuating, autonomous corporation, held closely by a select group of directors on behalf of a carefully crafted trust.

Wife number three, meanwhile, had died mysteriously on a hunting trip. It was only because of Schoenfield's considerable political clout, and financial resources, that the coroner had ruled the death an accident.

Sitting at his huge mahogany desk with his back to the bay window that looked out to the southeast toward Lone Cone Peak, Schoenfield contemplated the sheaf of paper with the laser-printed Colorado Bureau of Investigation logo lying on the leather writing pad in front of him.

He scanned the first page quickly, recognizing it to be a cover letter to the Governor signed with "best regards" by Roderick Andersen, the CBI Director. The remainder of the report took him two hours to read and digest. He was sufficiently engrossed that he paid no attention to the setting sun, which, due to the high cloud cover, lit Lone Cone with a deep red hue. When he was finished, he took a key from the ring on his belt, unlocked a drawer, and put the folder in, locking the drawer again afterwards. Then he picked up the telephone.

"Send Pickle and Mad Dog up here, willya?" Whoever answered knew his voice, because that was all he said

Excess Homicide
A Four Corners Mystery

before hanging up. Then he set to examining a thick account book.

Ten minutes later, there was a knock on the heavy door to the office.

"Yeah? Come in."

The door opened, and in walked a curious pair, who were waved to two leather chairs facing the desk. The right chair was taken by a small, wiry man with a puckered expression permanently fixed on his face. The left chair, appropriately larger, was taken by a very big man, someone who, before he put on middle-age weight, had the build and size to play power forward in professional basketball. His calm expression was marked only by a wandering left eye, which appeared to be trying to track the random flight of a housefly, or possibly a hummingbird. They waited patiently for a full five minutes before Schoenfield looked up.

"You asked us to come up, Senator?" The smaller man was the spokesman.

"I just finished reading about your handiwork. Quite an interesting compilation, actually, what there is in the report. It leaves out several of the early operations, and it misses a couple of the more recent ones that looked like natural causes. Last time I met with Andersen, he didn't refer to any of these, so I don't think they're onto them."

"Ah, I hope there's no suggestion of who was involved."

"Nope, only the victims. You guys are good. Real good."

Pickle beamed, and Mad Dog's wandering eye almost focused on Schoenfield.

"And there's no hints about the others?"

"Nope. They're probably being treated as routine homicides, or accidents, and so Denver isn't involved. And this seems to be confirmed by the work Timmy's doing on their computers." Although almost everyone on his staff knew that Schoenfield was considered to be the CBI's staunchest political patron, he always referred to them indirectly rather than by name, at least in this company. He continued.

"In fact, I've got a little bonus here for you both." He opened the top drawer and took out two envelopes. He pushed one toward each man across the desk.

"Make sure that this stays quiet, and there will be more of these envelopes. Now, then. Let's talk about that little affair we've planned for July up in Boulder. How are things progressing?"

"We've got the equipment all ready. We've been extra careful, Senator. All the stuff has been brought in from out of state. The electronics were bought as individual parts from about a dozen suppliers. The rifle was smuggled in from Canada last year, and it's only been used once, except for being sighted in. And we've figured out how to get access to the display. It's being taken out to be fixed up, polished and all that, later this month. We'll get at it then."

"You said that the controller box will be rigged to melt itself?"

"Yep, that's the way it will be set up. We figured it will get blasted, so it will have an internal flash heat source hooked to a motion-sensitive trigger. And even if it doesn't get blasted, the recoil from the rifle will probably trigger it." The smaller man fidgeted in his chair, and his forehead wrinkled, accentuating his puckered expression.

Excess Homicide
A Four Corners Mystery

"And we've been practicing with the video system. I have to tell you, Senator, I'm really doubtful that we're going to have any chance at accuracy. With the thing fixed, we can't really aim, so we just have to take a shot at whatever walks through the sights."

"That's OK, I keep telling you. The idea here is to make a big impression on this new administration we're stuck with. Taking advantage of the President's visit to that research center in Boulder will embarrass them as well, maybe put them out of business and stop wasting our tax money on all that stupid global heating research. And it will register our dismay with this fool President's choices for his cabinet. Diversity, hell. He's picked so many token blacks and browns and other inferior types, not to mention women, that we'd be better off without him. I mean, look at that Secretary of Interior. That's what she should be doing, being somebody's secretary. So we don't really have to hit him, just the event will have its effect. But if we do hit him, and especially if we get lucky and kill him, it'll play right into our hands, because this Vice-President is really a better choice."

"If you say so. Senator. We'll certainly do our best."

"And I know that really to be the best. Now. One more thing. How are you two at kidnapping?"

Three

THE PREVIOUS EVENING, while he was waiting for Susan Mackovich to come up to the conference room, Charles Shure had decided to examine the leather-bound volume that had arrived with the letter. He picked it up, turned it around, and felt a knot form in his stomach as a glimmer of recognition of the blue numbers on the book's spine settled into his consciousness. Carefully, he opened the book, to a page that seemed stiffer than the rest. It turned out this was because the page had four photographs glued to it. Although old and black-and-white, they had obviously been taken by a professional, because the lighting and detail were exquisite. The six heads, sitting on the stumps of their necks severed neatly at about the Adam's apple, were lined up carefully on a table, and the four photographs showed them from the front, the back, and the two sides.

When Susan had arrived, she found him retching into the bar sink, the sour smell of used scotch permeating the air. It was the frontal angle that got him, the one with the staring eyes.

Looking back on it later, he decided that his reaction was appropriate, and that it was perfectly acceptable for her to see him this way. He had eventually shown her the volume, but not the letter, and her reaction was similar even

Excess Homicide
A Four Corners Mystery

though she knew what to expect. So if any gossip about the meeting got started, he'd be something of a hero.

After the two of them had recuperated from the shock of the contents of the book, Susan became all business, motivated to find out who was behind the whole thing, and her research instincts kicked in. Before too long, a dossier on the Aryan Rights Foundation was sitting beside the workstation's printer.

He was now back in the conference room, reviewing the dossier in preparation for a meeting with Susan and Jerry Perkins, head of UNELECO security. Although there was more information than he could absorb in one sitting, he could tell that it was shallow stuff, and quite anonymous. The Aryan Rights Foundation wasn't revealing any secrets, or even any names, on its web site. And it wasn't listed on any of the hate-group watchdog sites, strangely enough.

He'd been trying to figure out an appropriate strategy all day. Fortunately, he'd not shown Susan the letter, just the book. She had been so disturbed by it that she hadn't thought to ask why he connected something called the "Aryan Rights Foundation" with it. Good enough. But Perkins wouldn't be so easily distracted.

Shure strode back into his office, on the northwest corner of the top floor, and sat down at his computer. After thinking for a minute, he opened WordPerfect and typed into a new document the words "Courtesy of the Aryan Rights Foundation." Then he thought for another minute, reached down, opened the lid of his laser printer, and removed the toner cartridge. He turned it over and over in his hands, and then replaced it. Then he printed the brief document, and repeated the trick with the toner cartridge. Back in the conference room, he folded the paper in half, unfolded it and made sure to get his fingerprints all over it, and refolded it several times and put it into the book. Now he was ready for Perkins, as well as for any after-the-fact questions that Susan might come up with.

The information that Susan had found on the Aryan Rights Foundation site, although shallow, painted a picture of a well-financed, clandestine hate group, one that was able to use clever arguments to make its points. Any way he looked at them, however, Shure found those arguments disturbing. The notion that some ethnicities were inherently superior to others grated on his sensibilities. As the CEO of a large, international conglomerate, he dealt with bright, motivated individuals from all over the world. To suggest, as did ARF, that northern Europeans were somehow inherently better than people from Asia was just silly. Yet he recognized the appeal of the arguments as well, particularly to those who felt threatened by people who look different or who maintain different cultural traditions.

And it was hard to disagree with the premise that humanity could only benefit from improvements in the gene pool. Of course, the definition of "improvements," he thought, was the rub. And especially who was going to be doing the defining.

There was a soft knock on the conference room door, then Susan Mackovich and Jerry Perkins slipped into the room.

"Susan. Jerry. Thanks for coming. Jerry, did Susan tell you what this is about?"

"Just briefly, Mr. Shure. It sounds pretty strange, something I'd think of as the work of a crank, except for the picture Susan described."

Excess Homicide
A Four Corners Mystery

"My thinking exactly. The book's over there on the table. If it's genuine, this thing is pretty scary to me. There's also the issue of its historical value. There's a notation on the first page that suggests it's part of a set. If the rest of the set's somewhere, this could be an important part of it." Shure had thought carefully about how to avoid any references to the ARF letter.

Perkins had begun looking at the book, and, on seeing the pictures that it fell open to, he reacted just as Shure and Susan Mackovich had the day before. Fortunately for the conference room's carpet, he made it to the same bar sink the other two had. Susan picked up the page of paper that had fallen to the table.

"I didn't see this yesterday. 'Courtesy of the Aryan Rights Foundation.' Why do you suppose these guys would send this to you, Mr. Shure?"

"I was so rattled I stuck it in my pocket yesterday. That question kept me awake most of the night. The only thing I can think of is that my grandparents immigrated here from Germany at the end of World War II. They never talked much about their life there, but maybe there's a connection to this von Scheuer guy. Somehow this Aryan rights bunch got hold of it and decided I should have it. It makes my skin crawl just to think about it."

Perkins re-entered the conversation, wiping his face on a towel.

"Mr. Shure, please accept my apology. I feel completely unprofessional. But that, that picture took me by complete surprise. Now I understand what Susan was telling me. And now I do have to take this more seriously than just a crank thing. If I may borrow this book, I'll dust it for prints and have it analyzed for its paper and so on. We need to authenticate it. Um, is this cover made of what I think it is?"

"Probably. Check out the little blue numbers on the spine. You can have that tested, too, I expect. Susan, why don't we have this whole thing scanned in and then, after it's analyzed, we can just put the original away in a vault, an environmentally controlled one. Eventually, we should get an expert in these things to look at it and advise us on what we should do with it. Meanwhile, let's keep this as quiet as we can. Jerry, do you think there's any special precautions I should take?"

"Can I persuade you not to drive yourself around? I'd like to ask you to use the armored car, with a driver and an extra person with him, if I could."

"And maybe you could set someone to watching my house for a while."

"Right. Do you have any overseas trips coming up? Or any others? Maybe it would be a good idea to stay close to home until we get a better handle on all this."

"Agreed." Shure grinned. "I was supposed to go to Moscow next week, but this is the perfect excuse to cancel. I'll set up teleconferences for whatever else I need to do."

NEVER, EVER, ever ever again will I complain about the traffic in Durango, Annette said to herself. She was sitting in Hal's new Audi S4, waiting, according to Hal's careful instructions, instructions she suspected were totally unnecessary, for the two turbines to wind down and cool before shutting it off. She had finally found the parking lot next to the CBI offices in downtown Denver and pulled in, despite the $8 per half hour sign at the entrance. Even

Excess Homicide
A Four Corners Mystery

Durango, she thought, is getting so you have to pay for parking, but this is absurd.

It had been easy for her to make an appointment to see the CBI Director, but his schedule required an 8:30 meeting, so she had spent the previous 90 minutes negotiating the 35 miles from Boulder. The average speed of just over 20 miles per hour was misleading: most of the time had been spent sitting still, with the remainder spent at about 70, bumper to bumper—with lots of people weaving between lanes, attempting to "win" the daily "race."

Annette kept current with her various training courses, including defensive driving, and she was well experienced with various modes of traffic, including big-city traffic. Growing up and learning to drive in Chicago had seen to that. But the morning commute into Denver from Boulder was something she hadn't expected, couldn't even have imagined. It didn't help that she was driving Hal's new pride and joy. Although comfortable and powerful and a dream to drive, it still had no scratches, and she was certainly not interested in contributing the first one.

At least she'd been warned about the drive and had left Boulder with plenty of time. Her watch told her that she had fifteen minutes to get an elevator up to the nineteenth floor, to the CBI Director's office. She felt a mixed sense of elation and nerves. They, after all, were recruiting her, so this wasn't a job interview. But she still wanted to make the best possible impression.

Ten minutes later, Annette entered the door to the CBI suite. A receptionist, whose desk label said "Sandy McStain," looked up at her with just the right mixture of professionalism and warmth.

"Good morning. I'm Annette Trieri. I have an appointment with Director Andersen at 8:30. Ahh," she looked at her watch, "I guess I'm a couple of minutes early."

"He's expecting you. Would you like a cup of coffee? Help yourself, there's a fresh pot just over there. Take one of the clean mugs." Sandy pointed to an alcove at Annette's left. "I'll let him know you're here." She pushed buttons on a telephone.

Annette found, to her relief, that there was a choice of regular or decaf—she picked the decaf, because she was still jangled by the traffic. As she was pouring, she heard footsteps behind her.

"Lieutenant Annette Trieri, I believe? I'm Roderick Andersen. I'm so glad you could come down." Annette managed not to spill anything while she turned to shake his hand.

"I'm glad to be here. And, given the traffic, lucky. You don't commute from Boulder, by any chance, do you?"

He tilted his head back and laughed.

"Don't tell me you came down from the Peoples' Republic at this time of day! My sympathies. No, I live just across town a ways, on South Ogden, by Washington Park. I take a bus, about 20 minutes including lots of stops."

"I thought I was ready for big city traffic, but that was just ridiculous. If you really want me to come to work at CBI, your best approach will be to let me stay down in Durango. I guess I'm spoiled."

"That you are. Summer music festivals right in town and winter skiing only 25 miles up the road. No, our intentions are strictly, shall I say, honorable. We want you for our office down there because of your relationships with

Excess Homicide
A Four Corners Mystery

the southwestern counties and with Durango. And, of course, because Bob Weldon is retiring. Let me get a cup of coffee here, and we can go into my office and talk about it."

Two minutes later they were seated on the casual furniture in his office, looking west over downtown Denver, the western suburbs, and toward Mount Evans on the Front Range.

"As I said, I'm glad you could come down. And thanks for braving the traffic. I hope you're here with good news for me."

"Depends on what constitutes 'good.'" She smiled. "I'm sure that you know how flattering it is to be sought after, and, to tell the truth, I'm at the point in my career where this would be a good move. I really don't want to move up in the Durango PD, because the next thing will be too desk-oriented. What I think I'm good at is investigating, leading investigations. Field work, coordinating the people, putting the puzzle together, and all that. It's certainly what I like to do."

"And that's exactly what we're after. Someone who's a leader. I'm sure you know that CBI isn't a huge operation. We mostly function as intra-state coordinators of difficult investigations, providing assistance in investigating and in forensics to small law enforcement units, and we try hard to keep our bureaucracy to a minimum. Um, I don't want to say anything bad about Bob, he's a good friend of mine. But he's run the satellite office in Durango in his own way for years now, and he's retiring. I think that office may be in something of a rut, and I think that your hands-on approach is just what's needed to get us out of that rut. If you decide to join us, what I'll suggest is that you appoint Bob's second-in-command as your chief-of-staff, to run the office side of things and to keep you available for investigations."

"This second-in-command, is he, or she, also a candidate for the division directorship?"

"Derek Petersen. Yes and no. In the normal course of things, we'd advertise the position, and I'm sure that he'd apply and be a strong candidate. But there are two mitigating factors. First, he's been the primary field investigator down there. Bob ran the office and Derek did the leg work. Derek needs administrative experience before he'll be ready for the top job. I figure, with you in the top job, he could get the administrative experience as your chief-of-staff and then move to another division directorship when one opens up. And they do, reasonably often.

"Second, well, I want to be candid with you but I don't want to offend you. So please don't take this the wrong way. But we, that is, the CBI, are under pressure from the Governor's office to diversify our staff. Especially at the top, we're dominated by older, Anglo guys. So what I'm trying to do in recruiting you is to get myself some points with the Governor while adding the best investigator in the Four Corners to our staff. I got permission to go after you without the usual open search. My excuse to do this is gender diversity, but I hope you believe me when I tell you that my real reason is your talents and capabilities and potential. Your work in Durango, and with the sheriffs of several of the counties down there, makes you perfect for our office. I've done a lot of homework on you, so I'm confident about this."

Annette was shaking her head.

"Well, I guess I'm not offended. It would be nice to be past all this stuff, but we're not, so I might as well take

Excess Homicide
A Four Corners Mystery

advantage of opportunities when they come along for whatever reason. I have to say, I'm suspicious that I got to be lieutenant for similar reasons, and I've been working hard to prove that I'm worthy of the position because of that." She shifted in her chair and took a sip of coffee.

"My captain is being straight with me on this. He doesn't want me to leave, but he's not going to stand in my way. He's offered me a leave of absence to try this out. I think he's got a hidden agenda of improving the PD's relationship with the CBI, so this is a sort of perfect opportunity for him."

She smiled. "I like the idea of an experienced chief-of-staff, even if he's not an administrative expert. But I'll need to meet him and check out the chemistry before I can commit. I'm sure you understand that."

"Absolutely. And, if you're going to be up here for a few days, we may be able to arrange something. He'll be up this way later this week for meetings. We're working on what may be a serial killer."

"I bet that's the folder I got. Those environmentalists?"

"The same. Derek's dead-ended. He'll be up here to talk to the Boulder Sheriff and PD about what happened, so he could meet with you in Boulder. Then you wouldn't have to drive down here again." He grinned.

"I'll be in Boulder through next week. My husband's at a climate conference up in Boulder, and we're going to drive back together when it's over."

"I'll make sure that Derek sees you when he's up there." He looked at his watch. "I'm sorry my schedule's so tight, but I have a meeting with the Chairman of the Senate Committee on Law Enforcement. He and the Chief of the

State Patrol are coming in for something or other about budgets."

"I'm glad to have had the chance to meet you. And, while I'm in town, I thought I'd go to the Denver Art Museum and do some shopping. Do you suppose that Ms. McStain would know how to direct me to the Cherry Creek Mall?"

"Would she! I think that's her second home. And I'll get you a pass to the museum. We do have various perks."

Just as Annette was about to leave, the main door to the office suite burst open and in walked a large, imposing figure with an air of authority; tall, immaculately dressed, gray hair coiffed like an anchor-man. Sandy McStain scrambled to her feet.

"Senator Schoenfield! How nice to see you again. Director Andersen is expecting you, sir."

"No doubt. Is Chief Wilkerson here yet?"

"No, sir, he called and said he's running a few minutes late. Something about traffic."

"Well, then we'll just have to start without him. Where's Rod?"

Andersen emerged from his office right about then, and Annette was startled by the change in him. With her, he had been confidently in charge, in a quiet sort of way. Now, he was the obsequious servant. Standing off to the side of all the commotion, she tried to be invisible, but she knew somehow that it wouldn't work.

"Senator! Thanks again so much for coming by. I'm certain that Chief Wilkerson will be here shortly."

"Hope so. I don't have all day. I need to get back this afternoon."

Excess Homicide
A Four Corners Mystery

"Since we have a minute, I'd like to introduce you to someone, someone from your part of the state, actually." Andersen steered Schoenfield in Annette's direction.

"Senator, this is Lieutenant Annette Trieri, of the Durango Police Department. I'm hoping I can persuade her to replace Bob Weldon. Annette, Senator Jarvis Schoenfield."

"Weldon? What's happening with him?" Schoenfield obviously did not like being uninformed.

"He's retiring. I'm sure it was in last month's report. Lieutenant Trieri has been in charge of the Durango investigations unit for several years, and she has a solid history of working with law enforcement in the counties down your way."

Schoenfield turned his gaze on Annette, giving her a leisurely once-over. At 5'9", she was used to being able to look most people in the eye, but Schoenfield was a good head taller. It made her uncomfortable to tilt her head back—she felt like a rabbit being watched by a mountain lion.

"Pleased to meet you, Lieutenant. Bob Weldon's an old friend on mine. You'll have big shoes to fill. Hmm. Trieri. Interesting name. Where's it from?"

At times like this, Annette was able to participate in the situation while simultaneously observing herself as if she were acting in a play. It happened all the time, and she had learned to be both actor and director. This time, her directorial instincts told her not to be intimidated.

"How nice to meet you as well, Senator. I've had various interactions with the southwest CBI office over the years, and I've developed great respect for Bob Weldon and his people. Ah, my family is back in Chicago, if that's what you're asking. Generations ago, it was in Europe, like yours, I imagine, maybe a little farther south."

She met Schoenfield's intense stare without flinching, her green eyes focused like lasers on his. He was obviously not used to such behavior, for he turned away from her and changed the subject.

"Rod, I need to move along, so perhaps we should start." She was dismissed, just like that. He, she thought, is someone I'll have to be careful of.

ANARCHISTS ARE NOT the sort of people that I should be trying to organize. Why the hell did I ever talk myself into this?

Sitting in his north Durango apartment, Steve Rutherford was bemoaning his situation, trying to find a graceful, or even clumsy, way out. He had gathered together a group—no, that sounded too formal and organized; it was a bunch, a pile, a heap—of acquaintances from the area to discuss the formation of a new organization. Naturally, he'd picked the people he knew to be disenchanted with other groups, even the underground fringe represented by the Mother Earth Defense League. And if they couldn't get along in the MEDL, they were definitely loners by nature. Talk about herding cats.

They had shown up largely because he had promised beer—and wine for Lolly. About the only thing they had accomplished in their three hours of wrangling and arguing and, finally, laughing was to come up with a name they could agree on. And even then, there was controversy. Steve thought that it had just the combination of whimsy and topical relevance that was needed, along with the potential for name recognition and a really cool logo, should they ever need one: Southwestern Colorado Radical Environmental Warriors. To be known, obviously, by the acronym.

David Wellington, who always took everything, including himself, far too seriously, thought the humor would distract people from the purpose of the organization. Aaron Felterson objected to the use of "warriors" in the title, arguing that it would give away their strategy. "Radical" was also a cause for concern, for similar reasons. Lolly Markham argued against "environmental," reasoning that it was too restrictive. She thought "social" would be more appropriate. Even the "Southwestern Colorado" regional twist raised questions, but Steve pointed out that they needed to keep this group small and focused.

In the end it was the killer weed that Flip Chester always seemed to have some of that forged an agreement, or, more precisely stated, a reluctant truce. That and the distraction of Lolly's not wearing anything under her tee shirt. When she got agitated and waved her arms around, it looked like she had a couple of puppies squirming around in there, little dark noses poking against the fabric. Man, Steve thought, I'd sure like to get my hands on those puppies.

Lolly's point about the limitations of restricting SCREW to an environmental mission was well taken, but they did need some kind of focus. And the catalyst for getting together in the first place had an environmental basis, for sure. Too many of their friends and colleagues in the environmental movement, especially in the MEDL, were dying off, getting killed in suspicious circumstances.

Steve had wondered about it idly for several months, but it was the thing up in Boulder last month, where Bill and Jane Mayer got blown up in their van, that finally got his attention. He'd started a list, and he was surprised to see how long it was when he was finished. And he knew that at least half of the people on the list had been MEDL supporters. So he'd called around to friends and acquaintances within a couple of hours' driving time who weren't dead (yet? he wondered) to talk things over, and then to get together and try to get organized. A couple of them had been thinking along similar lines, so it was easy to arrange the meeting. The timing was a hassle, but it finally got put together.

They met in Steve's apartment, because his office at Frémont State was too cramped, and because he kind of suspected they'd end up smoking a joint, or two or three. Lolly, since she lived in town, arrived first, and he was proud of himself for not coming on to her, at least not too strongly, puppies or no puppies. Wellington had stopped in Pagosa Springs on his way over from Alamosa to pick up Felterson, and they wound up late. Reid Tompkins, who came in from Cortez, was always late for everything, as was Flip Chester, who had the excuse of being perpetually stoned.

"So, I talked with each of you a little about this meeting on the phone," Steve started out when they had all assembled. "If I'm right, the cops aren't doing anything about these killings, and we're on our own. I think, with a little organization, we can accomplish a lot. Find out who's behind this and deal with them ourselves. In the process, we'll eliminate an enemy of Mother Earth. We need to wear a different hat to do this so that we don't bring any attention to MEDL."

"You mean, violence?" Lolly was either aghast or delighted, Steve couldn't tell.

Excess Homicide
A Four Corners Mystery

"Isn't it about time that someone stepped up and fought on the side of the Earth? She's been raped and ripped open for generations. I think we owe her. MEDL doesn't condone violence, but I think that may be what's called for, in this case at least."

"What's this have to do with your list of dead people?" Wellington was always practical.

"They were all, in one way or another, fighting within the system on Mother Earth's behalf. And they got killed. Even Jake, who was a logger, was really a tree-hugger. And he got killed."

"Didn't he just crash his truck?"

"The police report had some suspicious stuff in it. It looks like someone gave him a shove and then he crashed. Meaning he was killed. Now it's time someone avenged him and the others, too."

Thus was the concept of the Warriors born, and eventually SCREW.

"Far out," said Flip, through his personal fog.

THEY USED the tried-and-true road construction ploy, and it worked to perfection.

First, they invented an opportunity, irresistible to the target, to lure him onto a secondary road in a relatively remote area. In Shure's case, the opportunity was to obtain a combined timber and mineral lease on private property, allowing extraction without most of the usual federal paperwork. They set up a phony meeting in Norwood for this purpose. Because the obvious itinerary for a high-roller like Shure was to the Telluride airport and then by car down the San Miguel River Valley toward Norwood, there were ample opportunities for the subsequent steps of the process.

The "meeting" was supposedly a discussion between Shure and the "owner" of the property, and Shure rose to the bait like a hatchery trout to a stonefly.

Second, they isolated the target's vehicle from other traffic. They managed this with the expedient of two semis, one in front to block Shure's car and one behind to slow trailing traffic.

Third, they used a phony construction crew to route the target vehicle onto an isolated tertiary road. This was easy, given the lack of traffic between Placerville and Norwood, and, because the lead semi was routed as well, step four was expedited.

Fourth, they merely blockaded the target vehicle, front and rear, and extracted the individual of interest from it. To this end, the lead semi rolled to a stop, the back door rolled up, and the occupants of Shure's rented car found themselves staring at a rocket launcher held by someone wearing a black hood, sitting casually on a stool. There must have been a black curtain behind him, because there was nothing to be seen in the interior of the semi-trailer. Shure's driver immediately tried to reverse directions, but he discovered that a large farm implement—a combination hay rake and bailer, as it happened—was blocking the road behind them.

After that, it was simply a matter of negotiation.

Before Shure thought to telephone for help, someone was calling him. Surprised, because he thought his cell phone number was confidential, he pushed the Talk button.

"Yes?"

"Mr. Shure, my abject apologies for the inconvenience. First, let me reassure you and your driver that no one will be threatened in the least by this little delay. The, ah, device in

Excess Homicide
A Four Corners Mystery

the truck in front of you is merely to get your attention. We know your driver is armed, and we simply want you to understand that we hold the upper hand. All we want is to talk with you for a few moments."

"What is it you want?"

"If you'd walk past the truck in front of you, you'll find a most comfortable van in which we can conduct business. I'm sure you know that these cellular telephones don't offer much in the way of privacy. Your driver can remain seated. You can reassure him that you'll return, completely healthy and even well-fed, if you'd like, in a short while. We will maneuver the van so he can see it, and it won't be going anywhere."

"How do I know that I'll be safe?"

"You'll have to trust me, I'm afraid. Given the situation, surely you can see there's little choice." At this, the hooded person holding the rocket launcher waggled the tube. Shure realized that he must be listening to the conversation. Or maybe he was even conducting it, from under the hood. "I'll expect you in the van shortly." The phone went dead.

"I'm told I should get out and get in a van that's ahead of this truck, Walt. What do you think?" The driver, Walter Herrington, looked skeptical.

"I think I can't go anywhere, Mr. Shure, what with the truck in front, that equipment behind us, and these ditches on either side. Besides, that thing on that guy's shoulder is not something I feel like arguing with. But I don't like you getting out. What's the deal? What do they want?"

"He said, to conduct business. He also said I'd be safe."

"They just moved a van into view up ahead. See it?"

Shure leaned to the left, and there was a black, windowless van, sitting on the road ahead of the semi.

"What if we call for help?" Walt was clearly not comfortable with Shure's leaving the car.

"He mentioned that cell phone calls are easily monitored, and I think that was a sort of warning. I guess I'll just have to do this."

"Well, be careful. I'll sit tight, with my hands visible."

Shure opened the left rear door, and got out onto the road. He felt an overwhelming urge to run for it, but the hooded person in the semi loomed. So he simply walked ahead to the van. As he passed the tractor of the semi, he noticed that the driver was also wearing a black hood, as was the person sitting behind the steering wheel of the black van. The side door slid open as Shure approached.

"Mr. Shure, please, come in."

Shure saw a young man, curiously familiar, sitting in an easy chair in the van's interior. A second chair, on the other side of a small side table, sat empty. Shure climbed aboard and sat.

"Mr. Shure, my name is William Campbell. I'm an attorney representing the interests of a group that I believe you've heard of, the Aryan Rights Foundation."

"Have we met?"

"Yes sir, we have. Until recently I was employed in the legal office of UNELECO. I recall meeting you several years back when your company hired me right out of law school."

"And you quit working for us and went to work for this Aryan Rights bunch? What could have possibly motivated you to do this?"

Excess Homicide
A Four Corners Mystery

"Um, er, well, they made me an extremely attractive offer," Campbell was writing on his legal pad while talking, "and it seemed to have, ah, career potential on a faster track than what a large office like UNELECO's did." He tore off the paper and slid it across the table to Shure.

Shure read "They are listening. They blackmailed me."

"I see. Well, I certainly wish you the best. Now, I was given to understand that I would be meeting with the owner of certain timber and mineral rights that I was planning to lease. Normally, this would be handled by the heads of the appropriate UNELECO divisions, but the owner's representative was insistent on me. I now see why. But I don't see why the need for this cloak and dagger stuff. Surely, we could be having this conversation at that address in, um, Norwood that we were given?"

Campbell reached for his piece of notepad paper and began writing.

"Well, um, the Sen... Ah, that is, my understanding is that the Aryan Rights Foundation wants complete secrecy in its dealings with you at this stage." He handed the paper back, and Shure read "Show of force—Intimidation."

Campbell continued, "The purpose of this meeting is to follow up on the letter and the book that they sent you a few days ago. I was told to give you this computer CD." He handed Shure a standard CD jewel box.

"The CD contains images of the other volumes of your great-uncle's laboratory notes. The other volumes were 'borrowed' and scanned electronically. My clients are certain that you'll be able to read them."

"I'm afraid that I simply don't understand what this is all about. Why these people believe that I would be interested in all this is beyond me."

"I'm told to tell you that this will be made clear soon. For now, it's suggested that you return to your car and review the material on the CD at your earliest opportunity. That's all there is for this meeting." Campbell looked both nervous and apologetic.

"I think not. Someone owes me an explanation, and you, having taken the position of the Aryan Rights Foundation, or whatever these people call themselves, the position of their lawyer, you are the one to start explaining. First of all, who are these people?"

"I'm truly sorry, Mr. Shure, but I'm simply not at liberty to tell you that." Campbell was sweating heavily. "My clients aren't ready for you to know more. They will insist on doing things their way, I'm afraid." He took the paper back from the table, folded it several times, and reached across and slid it into Shure's jacket pocket.

"Now, Mr. Shure, as I said, I'm afraid this meeting is over. It would be best for both you and your driver if you were to return to your car."

Defeated, but with some understanding that the notes Campbell had passed meant more than he yet understood, Shure exited the van and walked back to his car. Inside, he reassured his driver that he was perfectly fine, and they both watched as the semi-trailer door rolled down. The van ahead of it backed down the road to a pull-out, reversed its direction, and sped away.

Then the door of the semi-trailer rolled up a couple of feet, and a body was pushed out. It flopped onto the roadway, right in front of Shure's car. The truck began rolling, and roared off in a cloud of dust.

Shure and Walt Herrington leapt out of the car and approached the body, which was lying face down in the

Excess Homicide
A Four Corners Mystery

gravel, a pool of blood seeping out from under the left cheek. They turned it over, and Shure gasped as he recognized William Campbell, now with a small red hole between his eyebrows. A note, pinned to Campbell's tie, scribbled on the same paper as was in Shure's jacket pocket, read:

We tolerate neither traitors nor incompetence.
Consider this an example of our ongoing efforts to clean up the gene pool.

Four

SOME CHARTER MEMBERS of SCREW were more action-oriented than others. One, who was completely inaction-oriented as well as not entirely trustworthy, was tolerated mainly for the controlled substances he could provide to enliven meetings. Another was too argumentative to include in tactical planning, so he was left out. A third had to work.

So SCREW's first operation was up to Steve Rutherford, Reid Tompkins, and Lolly Markham. They were the most appropriate conspirators for this one anyway, because they were the ones who had known Luke Begay best. A planning session, at Tompkins' house in Cortez, was in progress.

"So, the deal is, last September, Luke was found at the Four Corners Monument, shot in the back of the head, close range, with a soft-nosed .22 long-rifle slug. An execution. The only thing that anyone could have wanted him dead for was his politics. He didn't do dope, he didn't gamble, he didn't owe money. But he was into AIR in a big way. And he was working to get the forests back into Indian ownership." Steve had done quite a bit of homework to piece this all together.

Lolly had a far-away look in her eyes. "We went out a few times. He was a good guy. Not militaristic or anything. Kind of shy. But really committed to ending commercial

Excess Homicide
A Four Corners Mystery

exploitation of the lands of his people. That's why he was so involved in the Mother Earth Defense League, and in American Indian Restoration."

"Yeah, and it went beyond the tribal thing with him. He was Navajo, but he was working hardest on a project that would have benefitted the Utes. The latest thing was to keep some big logging company out of the San Juan National Forest over east of Dove Creek, north of the McPhee Reservoir. They were getting a lease from the Forest Service, I think it's called the Glade Mountain lease, and Luke was claiming it was invalid because those were really Ute lands, that the feds had illegally stolen them. He used to come into my office to talk about the legal aspects." Reid's day job in Cortez was with an environmental law firm.

"So," Steve drew the obvious conclusion, "Someone from the logging company doesn't like his advocacy and whacks him. Should we try to find out who, or should we go after the company?"

"There's one more relevant thing. Jake Colvin was working the same issue, from a little different perspective. He didn't care so much about the Utes, but he cared about the trees the logging company was going to destroy. So I think that he and Luke were actually working together. I remember seeing Jake at a MEDL meeting or two."

"I didn't know Jake, but I heard he was a big-game guide."

"Yeah, I went out with him a few times, too. Before he got married. What a hunk." Lolly had that far-away look again. "He guided because he couldn't do logging any more, and he needed the money. He was an old-school guy, it was in his family. None of this mechanized clear-cutting stuff. One tree at a time, carefully. The big companies really pissed him off."

"So maybe this company wanted to off both of them. How do we find out the name of the company? These killings were last fall."

"Forest Fiber Products, Inc. I remember from the conversations with Luke. Let me look 'em up." Reid walked over to the desk and sat down. He was by far the most well-equipped of the three of them to deal with the modern world and his computer system was even turned on already.

A few minutes later, he found what he was looking for. FFPI was a wood products company whose local installation was a lumber mill and a wafer-board plant, both over in Monticello, Utah, about 25 miles northwest of Dove Creek. According to their web site, FFPI was a subsidary of something called UNELECO.

The UNELECO web site, they discovered, was huge. And intimidating. To think that they were going to take on something of this magnitude was scary, especially to Reid. As a lawyer, he knew the power of a large corporation, with its regiment of highly paid legal counsel.

"This is a multi-billion-dollar international conglomerate. Jesus! How can we deal with something like that?"

"Hey, we're environmental warriors, remember? We start with the real culprit, the logging company. We hit and run. We don't get caught. They get SCREWed, pun intended. We can destroy their capability to carry out their destruction pretty easily, I'd think. And if we can find out where the executives live, we can get them personally. Really avenge Luke. And Jake."

Excess Homicide
A Four Corners Mystery

"Poor Jake. He was such a great guy. I really liked him. Let's give 'em hell." Lolly looked to be on the verge of tears. "But what do we do? Kill somebody?"

"Let's drive over there and scope out the operation. If it's a lumber mill like that one that was up in Olathe, I bet we could burn it down without too much trouble. Reid, why don't you see if you can identify the plant's managers? We can go after them individually."

"How do we know they're responsible?"

"Who else could it be? But, look, you're right. I'll do some more digging around. If it was this Forest Fiber bunch that's responsible for both Luke and Jake, there will be a way to find out. I'll ask around up at Cedaredge."

"I miss Jake. He was so, so kind. And considerate. And, and strong." Lolly was awash.

THE TWO VICE PRESIDENTS had been waiting for Shure's arrival at the Durango – La Plata County airport so long that they were becoming restless. Shure was late because his helicopter had detoured well to the south to get around turbulence over Wolf Creek Pass. UNELECO's Chief Executive Officer had a weak stomach, which was why he normally preferred his Gulfstream executive jet, but the hop from the roof of the UNELECO headquarters building to Durango was not worth the trouble of dealing with the Colorado Springs airport.

Even with the detour, Shure looked dyspeptic when Henry Abraham and Bill Morton boarded the Bell. It was being refueled for the next leg of their tour.

"Hank, Bill, glad to see you. Hope this wasn't too short notice. I want to talk where there's no chance of being overheard, and you know about the itinerary, right?"

H. P. Hanson

"Tina said that you wanted a tour of our current operations, Mr. Shure." Henry Abraham was the UNELECO vice president in charge of Forest Fiber Products, Inc., the lumber and wafer-board division. "So I assume that you want to head northwest to that lease of ours north of McPhee Reservoir."

"And Gretchen told me the same thing, so I guess that means farther north to Bedrock." Bill Morton was the UNELECO vice president for Mile-High Mining, Inc., UNELECO's division for all things underground.

"Right on both counts, plus another possible lease. We'll make a loop and come back down past Norwood, or just west of there."

The intercom crackled, and then said, "Whenever you're ready, Mr. Shure." Shure pushed a button by his seat.

"All set back here." He released the button. "Better belt up, guys. It's bouncy up there today."

Morton and Abraham fumbled for their seat belts as they heard the rotor winding up. Even with the extra soundproofing in this executive model, the ride was going to be noisy. Shure settled in and looked closely at his underlings.

"I had a strange and frightening experience the other day I want to tell you about. Remember our conference call about that possible lease on Hamilton Mesa? The owner wanted to meet with me personally, remember? And we talked about the potential of the property and you did some background research, right?"

"Well, as I recall, the board feet were on Hamilton Mesa, but the tailings were farther northwest, on private mining claims." Abraham's interest in those trees was palpable.

Excess Homicide
A Four Corners Mystery

"Yep. The story was that this guy had heard about our new reclamation process and wanted to get us involved in some of his old tailings. But we're not doing a flyover because I signed anything. I just want you guys to point out to me where the timber stands and these tailings are supposed to be." Shure paused and took a deep breath.

"See, what happened was that the so-called conference about the lease was really a setup." And Shure related to them the conversation with William Campbell and his murder, carefully leaving out references to the Aryan Rights Foundation.

"So after we discovered that Campbell was dead, Walt and I got the hell out of there. I've been waiting for the other shoe to drop, and all I've seen was a story in the Grand Junction paper, 'Lawyer found shot on country road' sort of thing. It looks like there's no ties to me or Walt or the car. But someone pulled a fast one on both of you to get to me."

"Jesus, Mr. Shure. I'm sorry." Morton was aghast. "I verified that the tailings are really there and that they're from an old uranium operation, so it seemed legit. It was kind of weird that they wanted to talk to you, yeah, but we have weird experiences with landowners all the time."

"Right. And there's lots of board feet up there, as we'll see when we fly by it. Someone went to a load of trouble to set this whole thing up. Why would anyone want to do this?"

"One of the notes that Campbell passed me, notes that got him killed, it seems, said it was a power play, to intimidate me. For what purpose, I'm not sure, but it worked. I've been wondering if either of you might have some ideas. Do we have competition that would do this sort of thing?" Shure looked back and forth at his two vice presidents.

They speculated on this and other possible motives as the helicopter made a wide circle, west and then north over a new federal timber lease north of McPhee Reservoir, then north some more and farther west past the large uranium tailings piles at the Department of Energy complex near Bedrock, then finally east again to the private land-holdings. Shure restarted the lagged conversation.

"My understanding is that the private timber lease is somewhere down there, on the west and south sides of the mesa below us."

"Yes, it's supposed to be about below us now. North of that road." Abraham had scouted the region by air when first informed of the opportunity and was now scanning the landscape below with binoculars. "Lots of board feet down there, for sure, but the access will be a real challenge. It's rough terrain."

Several buildings, including a huge log cabin, came into view as the helicopter drifted farther south. Abraham continued playing travel guide.

"Mr. Shure, those buildings are the X-S Ranch, and as far as we can tell, their holdings include most of Hamilton Mesa."

"So this X-S Ranch is the owner of the rights, including the mining claims?"

It was Morton's turn.

"We haven't been able to verify that for certain, but it looks like it, Mr. Shure. The problem is that the X-S is a privately held corporation, owned by a trust with layers of lawyers shielding the people in control, and what they control. About all we've been able to find out is that the

Excess Homicide
A Four Corners Mystery

person who lives down there is a Colorado State Senator, Jarvis Schoenfield. The X-S used to belong to him and his father before him. Then this corporation was set up with the provision that he can live there. He probably controls it, but we haven't been able to prove that. Yet."

Shure pushed the microphone button by his seat.

"Henry, let's head back up toward Norwood, to the north and a little east. Follow the main highway east from town a ways." He then turned to his two vice-presidents.

"I remember that we got stuck behind this semi on the hill that climbs out of the river valley up to the plateau here. Then there was this construction detour that had us turn left onto a gravel road. Let's see if we can spot where my little adventure went down." He looked pensive, and, after a pause, continued.

"Jarvis Schoenfield. That's a familiar name in Colorado political circles. I've met him a couple of times. He's one of the most senior members of the Colorado Senate, a real operator. And it looks like he might be behind my little adventure the other day, huh?" His vice-presidents were carefully non-committal as the helicopter began to skim along over a two-lane paved highway.

"Yeah, it was probably one of those county roads that head off south from the highway here. Not sure which one. Let's find out who owns these pastures and hay fields to the south of the highway. If it's the X-S crowd, I'll be pretty satisfied that they're behind this. Then we have to decide where to go with the information about the murder." Shure turned from looking out the window to his two vice presidents.

"Gentlemen, this has been a very interesting tour. I think for now we're going to proceed with this leasing business as if nothing happened, if possible. And I'll make arrangements to deal with Schoenfield as soon as you can confirm his control over these resources. I assume that you will be able to confirm this, one way or another?"

"Yes, Mr. Shure." They were almost in unison.

AFTER HAL'S CONFERENCE in Boulder ended, they headed home the long way. The second night, they stayed in a bed and breakfast in the forest just north of the little town of Divide. Their plan was to spend three nights there, with two full days of fishing the South Platte in Cheeseman and Eleven Mile Canyons.

Hal had managed to play hooky from the arid lands conference for only one day, to fish the Cache la Poudre north of Fort Collins, and it had been something of a challenge as the runoff had finally started. So he planned the trip home to include stops on rivers protected by dams. After the South Platte, they were going to head north and west, through South Park, up the Arkansas Valley, and over Independence Pass to the Frying Pan above Basalt. After that, a short day's drive would take them home through Delta and Ouray.

It was a honeymoon of sorts. After their marriage in March, they had both been too busy to take the time to get away, and the Boulder conference provided an excuse for a well-deserved break. Hal felt lucky that Annette liked flyfishing well enough that he could plan an itinerary such as this, and Annette felt lucky to be traveling with someone who knew the back roads and the off-the-track places to stay in the Colorado high country.

Not that obscure inns and B&Bs were their only choices. The first night, they had stayed in the Honeymoon

Excess Homicide
A Four Corners Mystery

Cottage at the Grand Lake Lodge, after a drive over Trail Ridge Road. The late spring had delayed the snow melt, and the highest through road in the country had just opened by the Memorial Day Weekend target date. Snow banks twenty feet high on the sides of the road caused flatland tourists to stop and gawk, and Annette, who hadn't been into Rocky Mountain National Park before, was awed by the scenery.

And she finally had a chance to see a yellow-bellied marmot, the foot-and-a-half long, high-altitude cousin of the woodchuck that had been adopted as the sports mascot at Frémont State. A particularly robust individual was sunning itself on some rocks near the Forest Canyon Overlook parking lot off Trail Ridge Road.

"That's your mascot? No wonder you guys don't win a lot of games."

"Hey, we won the NCAA Division II national championship in football a couple of years ago! Don't you remember our friends the defensive linemen? Besides, that guy's probably a victim of tourists with Cheetos. He probably weighs twice what he should."

"But it's just a big rodent!"

"Um, well, yeah. See, what happened was that when the teaching college became Frémont State University years ago, they had a contest for the students, to select a new sports mascot. And this was back when students had a collective sense of humor, unlike today's politically correct student body. And all of the real sports-like names were taken. Like, Adams State over in Alamosa is the Grizzlies, and so on. I don't think the athletic department has ever been able to get used to the Golden Marmots. They tried 'Mountain Marmots' at first, but that provoked too much satire. The word play against 'mounting marmots' and the resulting mental image of marmot sex, along with not a few black-market tee shirts, were just impossible to deal with. So we're the Golden Marmots, and proud of it." He struck an especially heroic pose, but the marmot on the rocks just belched and went to sleep.

On the west end of Trail Ridge Road, Annette was charmed by the Grand Lake Lodge, with its rustic accommodations and elegant dining room. They had after-dinner coffee on the front porch and watched the shadows lengthen on Grand Lake and Byers Peak.

After the relative hustle and bustle of Grand Lake Lodge, the small B&B in Divide was something of a relief. They drove into Woodland Park for supper, and settled in for an evening of reading and relaxing.

"I feel like I've been a paradigm of patience." Hal finally broke a comfortable silence. "Hmm. 'Paradigm of patience.' I'll have to remember that. Has a nice ring." Annette was giving him her cynical look. "Anyway, I haven't been bugging you about your future. But I am intensely curious, you know."

"Me, too, actually. This is one of those hard choices between two good things. I've pretty much decided to take Walter up on his offer of a leave of absence to try out the CBI. I'm really curious about these serial murders, and I can probably work with Derek Petersen well enough to make progress on the case. But I really don't know what I'll want to do in the long run. Thing is, joining up with a state government organization is opening a door to getting entangled in bureaucracy. I've learned to work whatever bureaucracy there is in Durango pretty well. But I bet the state one is a lot tougher. And the Durango office is attached to the western district office up in Montrose, and I don't know what autonomy I'll have. So the bureaucracy thing is a little intimidating."

"No doubt. That's certainly been my experience, whenever I have to deal with the educational bureaucracy in Denver. The bigger it is and the more layers there are, the worse it is to navigate. So what have you found out about all these killings? Anything interesting?"

"I made the rounds with Derek, like I told you last week, and we interviewed all sorts of people. A lawyer from Lakewood who was on his way to Boulder when the van got blown up, all of the police and other official people involved. Everyone's been cooperative. But there's just not much to go on. Even the local SCARAB supporters don't know anything. Of course, everyone who's in that camp has some kind of conspiracy theory or other, but that's no surprise. SCARAB is one of those groups that makes a lot of people mad, for sure. But not generally mad enough to do something like this."

Hal looked thoughtful. "I seem to remember that the Frémont State chapter was hell-bent on protecting prairie dogs, or something like that."

"Me, too, and I think they probably got that idea from the people in Boulder. Prairie dogs are almost a religious icon for them. But that sort of activism is more of a nuisance than a real threat. It shouldn't motivate murder. At least I don't see how."

"What about all the other killings? Are they linked together?"

"Derek told me that the more he looks into it, the more they appear to be. Everyone on the list had some connection to everyone else via a fringe environmental group called the Mother Earth Defense League, MEDL. They were all involved in other things, too, but that was a common thread. Thing is, we can't find out anything about this group. They're not officially chartered in Colorado, or anywhere else, apparently. It seems to be more organized than the thing called ELF, the Earth Liberation Front—you know, the ones who claimed responsibility for burning down that restaurant at Vail and some other such things. But MEDL's not organized enough to appear on very many radar screens. Anyway, it looks like some of the victims were bank-rolling these MEDL folks and some were actively involved with them. Um, you mentioned the other day that you were relieved that there wasn't a connection with the U this time. Well, brace yourself. Derek thinks that the Durango victim, Luke Begay, was the League's president and that he had an active chapter going, underground, at Frémont State."

"Lovely." Hal looked disgusted. "I'll have to get together with John as soon as we get back, to fill him in. Here we go again."

EVEN THOUGH DURANGO is not very big, it must be big enough that I'm used to the city lights. Damn, Steve Rutherford thought, it's *dark*.

They had waited for the new moon to carry out their raid. A couple of casual reconnaissance trips to the FFPI plant over in Monticello had persuaded them that it wouldn't be too difficult, really—a few cans of gasoline strategically placed and cigarette "fuses" would create enough of a fire to set FFPI, or at least this particular plant, back on its heels for a long while.

He and Reid Tompkins, dressed all in black, with soot smeared on their faces in artistic patterns by Lolly, had spent the better part of an hour shuttling between the rented

Excess Homicide
A Four Corners Mystery

Chevy Blazer and various parts of the FFPI facility, carrying two-gallon cans of gasoline. After they placed the cans, they'd gone back to light the fuses, and sucking on ten cigarettes to get them burning had been more than Steve had bargained for—he was now feeling light-headed from the nicotine. He almost jumped out of his skin when he felt a hand on his shoulder.

"I think I may puke." Reid was having a similar reaction to his cigarettes, apparently. "Let's get out of here."

They kept close to the buildings and stacks of lumber and made their way back to the car. Rounding the last corner, they stopped in horror, and shrank back out of sight. Lolly had moved the car when they had finished unloading the cans of gasoline, to the far side of the parking lot, near the lone street light.

And in the light they could read "San Juan County Sheriff" on the side of the white sedan parked just behind Lolly.

"Holy shit!" At least Tompkins managed to keep his commentary to a stage whisper. "We're dead meat! We've got to get out of here before those cigarettes burn down."

"Shhhh. Calm down. Lolly will handle this, she's an expert at dealing with men. What do you bet that guy is so busy looking down the front of her blouse that he's forgotten all about the rest of the universe. But why she parked under that light is a mystery." The individual leaning on Lolly's car, bending over to talk into her window, did indeed seem focused on the conversation. "We've got plenty of time. And he doesn't have his emergency lights on, so he probably hasn't called this in or anything."

"But cops always call in license plates. Always."

"That's why I borrowed the plates from that other green Blazer back in town. Wait here."

Three minutes later, Tompkins watched as the sheriff's deputy stepped back from Lolly's car and, from what Tompkins could tell, began talking into his shirt. Then the deputy tipped his hat to Lolly and walked back to his car, started the engine, turned all the lights on, including the emergency lights on the roof, and sped away into the night. Rutherford appeared at Tompkins' elbow.

"He left? Perfect. Let's get out of here." They sprinted for the car. On reaching it, Rutherford detoured to the power pole with the street light on it, for a last errand.

Two minutes later Rutherford was behind the wheel, carefully negotiating the back streets of Monticello via a different route from their initial approach to the mill. Except for the occasional street light at intersections with stop signs, it was as dark as before.

"What was that about, Lolly? The cop, I mean." Tompkins was in the back seat, cleaning soot off his face with a baby wipe. Lolly was working on Rutherford's face while he drove.

"He just wondered what I was doing there. Said he was on a routine patrol and asked if I was having car trouble. I told him I had a fight with my husband and needed to get away, to think. That we were on vacation and so on and got to arguing. I think it worked."

"What did you do to make him leave, Steve?" Tompkins spoke up from the back.

"I used the cell phone to call in a traffic accident on the highway south of town. I said I was a passer-by and that there was someone hurt."

Excess Homicide
A Four Corners Mystery

"You know, of course, that all cell phone calls are logged and can be located to the nearest tower."

"Yeah, and that's why I lifted this cell phone to use. This afternoon. I'm glad the owner didn't find it missing yet and deactivate it. I'm going to ditch it at the first opportunity. Which reminds me, we need to swap the plates back to the ones that came with this thing. So they match the registration in case we get stopped. Then we can get the borrowed ones back where they belong before morning."

"You should take the battery out of that phone, now, just in case they try to query its location." Tompkins heard a grunt of assent, fumbling noises, and a sharp "click." "And you got the note posted, like we talked about, right?"

"Yep, on the power pole with the street light, where Lolly was parked. Speaking of which, why in the world did you park there, Lolly? Christ, we were trying not to get noticed."

"Hey, ease up, Steve. I parked there because I thought it would be more suspicious in the dark. There sure weren't any other cars parked around there. And I wanted to read."

Rutherford looked in the mirror just in time to see Tompkins rolling his eyes.

They turned onto the highway back to Cortez, and Rutherford noticed something in the rear-view mirror. He watched for a few seconds and grinned.

"Houston, we have ignition, and liftoff."

Tompkins swiveled around to stare out the back. Several bursts of flickering light illuminated a patch of night sky on the near horizon behind them. As he watched, they grew and merged, as the inferno gathered strength.

Back where Lolly had been parked, in the flickering light of the flames, now bright enough to outshine the streetlight, a notice was tacked to the power pole. It had a picture of a large lag bolt on it, and it read:

> Dear Forest Rapists:
> Guess what: you've been SCREW'd! We hope it was as good for you as it was for us!

FIVE

TWO MORNINGS LATER, the story appeared in both the *Durango Herald* and the *Frémont Free Press*, and it was the talk of the campus. Hal was reading the *Free Press* version in his office when his boss, Provost John Martin, strode purposefully in.

"Morning Hal. I see you're catching up on the sensationalized version of this little affair. We need to talk."

Hal looked up, surprised. He had heard all about it from Annette the night before and read the *Herald's* version earlier, at home. He was not surprised that the *Free Press* played up the environmental angle and sympathized with whoever was responsible for the fire at the FFPI mill in Monticello. But the *Free Press* was independent of the university, so Martin's concern seemed odd.

"Uh, about what? This fire? What's it have to do with us?"

"I just got off the telephone with George Jepperson." This made Hal's expression even more surprised, as Jepperson was Frémont State's head legal counsel. "It seems that he received a call this morning from the legal office at Forest Fiber Products, Inc. They are asking for our cooperation in their internal investigation of the fire. Of course, the Utah State Police are on the case, but FFPI is doing some work on its own. They have the resources of their parent organization behind them."

"Who's that? I really don't know anything about any of this stuff."

"A multi-national conglomerate called UNELECO. Headquarters in Colorado Springs. Profits last year of about half a billion. A significant contributor to us, incidentally."

"So we cooperate. That's easy. But what's the connection to us?" Hal was partly playing dumb, hoping not to hear what he was afraid he was going to hear.

"They've concluded that there's a new environmental sabotage group responsible for this. It has to do with a note that was left at the scene. And because we're a hotbed for environmental groups, well, they think there may be a connection here. And, of course, the faculty with environmental leanings are in your college."

"Well, now, I'm not so sure about that. We have the environmental science disciplines, yes. But most of the environmental radicals on campus are in other departments, in other colleges. The most technical person I know who classifies as an environmental 'radical' is in the math department, for example. The environmental science faculty know too much about the scientific side of all this stuff to be radicals. They're all middle-of-the-roaders, as far as I know."

"What about that SCARAB outfit?" As provost, Martin was suspicious of student groups.

"Perfect example. They're a bunch of animal rights people. The local coordinator is a research assistant in sociology. And there's a more wild-and-crazy group I heard about from the grapevine, the Mother Earth Defense League, I think it's called. The leaders of that group are students, mostly in the fine arts, as far as I could find out. I try to keep up with this stuff, and I'm confident that my faculty aren't going around torching lumber mills."

"OK, I'll keep an open mind about faculty involvement. But I think we do need to cooperate with the FFPI investigation."

Hal stared at a corner of the ceiling, thinking about the implications of working with a private company in their investigation of a criminal offense.

"'Cooperate,' I guess I can go along with, as long as we don't violate anyone's rights here. 'Assist,' though, isn't something that I'm automatically comfortable with. Thing is, this is a criminal investigation at some level, and a private investigation could hamper the official one. Also, there's always the possibility that FFPI could mount a sham investigation to cover something up. Maybe they burned the place down themselves for insurance, or something like that, for example."

"That seems unlikely, given the company's profitability. But I suppose that this branch could be in trouble. Surely, you're not going to argue with the assertion that Frémont State is a hotbed of environmental activity?"

"No indeed. I will stipulate that this place is getting crazier and crazier in that regard. Want to hear the latest? I've got a TA who's plugged into SCARAB. She tells me that they're going to try to get the city council to outlaw the concept of pet ownership. So you won't own your dog, or cat, or goldfish, you'll just be their 'companion,' a companion with various responsibilities for their care and feeding. They even want to outlaw using the word 'pet.' It's too demeaning, they say."

"I heard about this happening up in Boulder, so I'm not surprised. Edith will be delighted. She's big on the animal rights thing. I'm continually amazed at how you can be married to someone for decades and not really know them. But doesn't this strengthen the argument that someone associated with Frémont State could be behind the fire-bombing?"

"In principle, but I know some things that you don't. Let me make a phone call." Hal picked up the handset of his desk phone and poked a speed dial button.

"Trieri, investigations."

"Hey, you've got to change that now."

"Oh, hell. I keep forgetting. Let me start over: Trieri, CBI."

"Much better. How's your day?"

"So far, so good. The FFPI firebombing is leaking more and more onto our turf, though."

"That's what I'm calling about. John Martin is here. Let me turn on the speaker phone, OK?"

"I hate those things because my voice sounds funny, but OK."

Hal pushed more buttons. "Annette? OK, like I said, John's here. He's under some pressure to cooperate with an internal investigation that FFPI's running. They think, apparently, that Frémont State might somehow be connected to the fire-bombing. And, of course, there is a strong environmental advocacy community up here. I don't know how closely you're likely to be involved in this, but maybe we could all share information. I mean, is it OK for me to tell John the stuff we talked about yesterday? And maybe he'll have information relevant to your involvement."

Excess Homicide
A Four Corners Mystery

"Hi, John. Normally, I'd have to be careful about this, because there's always the possibility that the victim isn't really a victim. But FFPI has been eliminated as a suspect. They're very profitable, and they just signed onto a new timber lease that will feed several million new board feet into the Monticello mill, or would have. And that mill had no problems, union-wise, or safety-wise, or anything-wise. So their investigation will be considered a friendly one by the people in Utah and, to the extent we're involved, by us. So whatever I tell you, you can tell them. But beyond that, this isn't going to be for public consumption, OK?" Annette was right: she sounded funny on the little speaker.

Martin cleared his throat. "Good to talk with you again Annette, and congratulations on your new assignment. I'll be extremely discreet, you can be sure."

"So, John—and, Annette, jump in here if I screw this up—the thing about the fire-bombing is, there's a suspect, with a description, and unknown accomplices. A San Juan County Deputy Sheriff on routine patrol just before the fire questioned a woman, early thirties, long blond hair, buxom, in a green Chevrolet Blazer with Colorado plates, near the FFPI mill. She gave him a story about a domestic argument, getting away to think, and so on. He was interrupted to respond to a 911 call about a traffic accident, which turned out to be bogus. But he got the license plates, which, it turns out, were stolen from a green Blazer in Cortez. Or at least that's the best guess. The Blazer they belong on hadn't been moved for weeks, it even had a flat tire, and there are indications that its plates had been tampered with. Its owner has an ironclad alibi. And the phone that called in the fictitious accident was a cell phone, stolen at the public library in Cortez. It hasn't been recovered. I guess the point is, all this suggests a more professional level of involvement than either students from here or even the pseudo-professionals in our environmental groups would be able to pull off."

"And, John," Annette spoke up, "we've heard that the reconstruction by the arson experts points to gas cans with relatively primitive fuses, but ones that can't easily be traced. Cigarettes folded into packs of matches, which lit a plain black-powder fuse into the gas can. This is a well-known guerilla warfare tactic. But the trick is the fuses. They can only be acquired by people with the right connections. And your run-of-the-mill environmental radical group is unlikely to have those connections."

"So we shouldn't worry, I take it. But I believe it would be irresponsible of me not to remind our officially recognized groups, such as SCARAB, that any illegal activities on their part will place their status in jeopardy." Martin was keenly aware of the university's legal exposure.

"By all means, John, do that. Worded as strongly as you'd like, with reference to the Monticello thing. But so far, there's no indication of a solid connection with anything at the U."

Hal piped up, "Of course, the suspect could work here, and there are any number of other possibilities. But nothing with an official connection."

"Guys? I'm going to have to go, got another meeting. We can talk more later if you need to, OK?" Annette disconnected.

"John, there's one more thing you should know about. Probably not related to this fire-bombing, but you never know. Annette's working a possible serial murder case that might possibly have a connection to us." And Hal related the tale of the dead environmental activists, their connection to MEDL, and the possibility of a campus chapter.

"But the only connection you know of to a campus chapter is the guy who got killed last September? If we haven't heard anything about it since then, maybe it dried up and blew away." Martin had enough to worry about that he wasn't going looking for trouble.

"We can always hope. And, of course, we can also keep our ears to the ground. I'll let you know if I find anything out."

STEVE RUTHERFORD, enjoying a late lunch at home, was also engrossed in the papers, delighted at the coverage. Then the telephone rang.

"Yeah?"

"Steve? Reid. We've got big trouble, on two scores. First, they've got a solid description of Lolly. You know that rose tattoo she has on her right tit? Well, it was just like you thought. That deputy was looking down her blouse, and she was playing him for all she could get. So he saw it."

Steve didn't, in fact, know about the tattoo. He felt a flash of heat just thinking about it, and then another of jealousy when it occurred to him to wonder just how Tompkins did.

"So, we'll just tell her she needs to keep her shirt buttoned up. What's the other thing? And how did you find this stuff out? It's not in the papers."

"I had an early lunch with the courthouse crowd today, and they're gossiping about all they've heard. The second thing is not good either. Sort of bad news and bad news. FFPI has announced that they'll be able to ship the logs from the Glade Mountain lease up to Moab until they can get the Monticello plant rebuilt. Which they plan to do. They're saying they can modernize it and improve their capabilities. So we may have actually helped them."

"Well, crap. We certainly didn't plan for that. But we can't change what happened. It seems to me that we need to do some damage control. To protect Lolly. And to fill the others in on what's happened, so that they aren't surprised by this. If the papers print the contents of the note, Dave and Aaron, and probably even Flip, will recognize what's happened. We ought to tell them first."

"Good thinking. I'll call Aaron and Dave if you'll get hold of Lolly and Flip. And get Lolly to dye her hair."

"But she had a wig on the other night. The cop saw blonde."

"Yeah, but she didn't have it on when we got together at my place. A third color will further confuse things. Maybe she can do some of that henna stuff, add some red highlights."

Steve was less concerned and had begun to think of the future.

"So what are we going to do next? I mean, we've got to lie low for a while, but there's a chance to gather momentum. What about a raid on the equipment they have up at the Glade Mountain lease?"

"What is it with you, man? Addicted to the rush of danger or something? Sheesh, we've got to do better than just to lie low. We've got to be invisible."

"All right, all right. But when things quiet down, let's talk about that equipment. OK?"

"Right. And, listen. Tell Lolly to keep her tits out of view, for Christ's sake. That rose will bring her down in a flash."

Excess Homicide
A Four Corners Mystery

The mere reminder of Lolly's chest made Rutherford's face hot again.

WHEN ANNETTE finally got home from her last day at the Durango PD, it was close to 10:30. She had spent most of the time since returning from her three weeks away catching up, and then she had a mountain of things to do to make a smooth transition to her CBI assignment. Her last day was exhausting.

By that time of night, she expected the house to be dark, or at least mostly dark, but it was lit up like a Christmas tree. The first thing she noticed was a smell of fireplace soot. The second thing was Hal.

He surprised her by coming down the stairs, carrying a long-handled landing net and wearing only thick gloves and what she was able to identify as his old fencing mask. She had run across it while cleaning up the attic a year ago, and he'd not been able to part with it, even after its 30-plus years of dust-gathering. Rather than let her get rid of it, he had put it on the mantle over the fireplace. A "conversation piece," he called it.

The odd combination, not to mention the brevity, of this attire took her a multiple double-take to get over being speechless. By then he'd slipped past her toward the kitchen, muttering something like "bat." She followed his naked backside through the dining room.

"Ummm, I'm sure there's quite a logical explanation for this, but I couldn't possibly think of what it is." He stopped and tilted his head back, apparently peering around the ceiling of the room through the screening of the mask.

"Bat, or bats. At least one, maybe more. I lost track of it, or them." And he was off into the kitchen. She followed.

"You mean the little flying mammals, not the ones in your belfry, I guess. I sure am glad I didn't bring the folks home to meet the new hubby."

By then he'd been confronted by himself in the full-length hall mirror. He struck a gallant pose, net held like a sword before him.

"I'd have to explain about our sex life, I guess. You know, how we dress up like this to spice things up."

"Uh, I'm definitely not going there. Where'd they come from? The bats."

"The chimney, I think. I heard noises in the fireplace and rattled the damper handle. Some soot fell out, so I opened the flue to let it out now, rather than be surprised by it next winter. And at least one bat zipped out into the living room.

"That was just about at dark. I couldn't find it, so I finally went to bed. And ten minutes later, there was a bat flying around the bedroom. I could see him in the glow of the streetlights, making circles over the bed. Remember those old Dracula movies? It was just like that. It's probably just trying to find a way out, so I thought I'd help."

"Somebody told me once, probably you, that bats navigate almost perfectly by their sonar, so what's with the mask?" By now Hal had begun prowling the house, watching the ceilings carefully.

"It's psychological. If I can find the thing, I'll try to get it with the net, but I could scare it. I thought about my eyes."

"Um, it seems to me that you have other, ah, sensitive parts exposed. Did you think of that?"

Excess Homicide
A Four Corners Mystery

"Yeah, but it's flying around the ceilings. Look, it's perched up there." He was pointing to a dark corner of the hall ceiling. He handed her the net.

"Hold this. I'll go get a stool to stand on and see if I can grab it. If it takes off, see if you can get it in the net. Gently. I really don't want to hurt the little guy. They eat their weight in bugs every night, or something like that."

Two minutes later, Annette was trying to ignore her eye-level view of Hal's rear end and thinking about the benefits of tanning salons. He was standing on a kitchen stool closing in on the bat with his gloves. It must have been worn out, for it only chattered at him as he carefully trapped it with both hands.

"Got it!"

"Now what?"

"Open the front door, and I'll let him go."

"You're going outside like that?"

"Well, make it the back door."

Hal stuck both hands out the door and launched the bat into the night, and it flew off, presumably in search of big juicy bugs, they figured. Then they retired to cups of tea in the kitchen, after Hal substituted a robe for his gloves and fencing mask.

"So why would we have bats in the chimney? Is this something that happens?"

"Probably the time of year. I heard enough noise that there must have been a colony of mothers and babies in there. Nursery colonies like that get established in the late spring, and the house was quiet while we were gone. So they took a liking to the chimney. It's got that cap, so the rain stays out. I'll read up on how long it takes before the babies can fly and then do something to discourage them, like smoke or noise."

"I've heard something about rabies."

"Yeah, it happens, but it's pretty uncommon. Skunks are worse. I'm all in favor of bats over bugs, but a colony would wind up producing quite a stink. Especially if we don't get rid of them and all their poop accumulates in the chimney. The first fire next fall could be..."

"Ecch.

"Right. So, you had a long day. Did you eat dinner?"

"Got a pizza delivered. Yeah, trying to catch up after three weeks and getting ready to go on leave is a lot of stuff all at once."

"Anything happen while we were out of town?"

"Not really, at least not anything that Fred can't handle. He seems like he'll do OK acting for me while I'm at the CBI office. The only thing we have pending is one of those CBI killings, the Durango guy who got killed over at Four Corners."

"When do you officially start?"

"Monday. Although I've sort of started already, given the amount of attention I'm giving to their list of dead people."

"Did I see that CBI's involved with that killing up by Norwood last month?"

"Oh, yeah, that's another one they've been handed. The locals up there don't have the resources, because it's obviously some kind of execution. A soft-point .22 slug between the eyes; body left out in the country on a dirt road. There's a witness who's talking about a small convoy of vehicles headed in that direction early the same day—a van, a couple of semis, a passenger car of some kind. It's not

Excess Homicide
A Four Corners Mystery

clear that it's connected with my list, though, yet, at least. We'll get the FBI to compare the ballistics with the slug from last fall, Luke Begay's killing. They're handling that case."

"From what you've told me, his killing and some of the other ones on your list look like executions, too."

"That bothers me, but it's also an opening. But, listen, I've been at this stuff since eight this morning. How was your day?"

"This is the time of year I get to do faculty performance evaluations."

"That says it all, I guess."

"Pretty much. Let's go to bed. I promise to protect you from bats, if there's another one in the house."

"Should I wear a garlic necklace?"

"Ooo. Sounds kinky. Can I wear my fencing mask?"

"I didn't know I married such a romantic—he wants to keep a metal screen between us in bed."

"Well, maybe just the gloves."

THE MEETING HALL outside Montrose had seen better days, first as a Grange chapter and later as a supper club that tried to be too fancy for the local folks. After the new highway bypassed it and the tourists couldn't find it any more, the place sat idle for years, slowly acquiring the sagging demeanor of abandoned buildings that eventually renders them picturesque and attractive to amateur photographers. Still, its original construction had been solid enough that it was yet weather proof, and the power company was only too glad to have someone pay them to turn the electricity back on. And electricity was important, because the

H. P. Hanson

sophisticated public address system brought in for the occasion needed plenty of power.

Out in the long-unused parking lot, the several dozen muddy, battered pickups ticked peacefully as they cooled. The weeds, those not smashed flat under parked tires, were gradually recovering in the cool twilight.

But inside, things were heating up.

It was dark in there, except for two spotlights centered on one end of the spacious, open room. They illuminated a large banner on the wall that read "Resources For Humanity." Behind a long folding table, also lit by the two spots, stood an imposing figure, tall, heavy-set, just beginning to work up a sweat. The sleeves of his white shirt were rolled up a couple of cuffs' worth, and his tie was loose. He held a black book in his left hand, and was gesturing dramatically with his right. Wet stains were growing under his arms. His voice boomed from the huge PA speakers.

"Now, whatever you folks think about the Bible, you'll have to agree that it's one of the oldest and most widely-read books in history. Far as I know, it's still on the perennial best-seller lists. And its philosophy provides the foundation for the beginnings of western civilization. You don't have to be religious, or take it as the revealed word, to understand that. Of course, for those of us who do believe that it's God's revealed word, it's all the more powerful.

"This isn't a revival meeting, so don't get the wrong idea. But I do want to take a minute to read you a little of it, *from its very first page*, from the Book of Genesis."

He help up the book, and grinned.

"For those of you who pay attention to such things, what I've got here is the King James Version." Then he

*Excess Homicide
A Four Corners Mystery*

settled his reading glasses down on his nose, cleared his throat, and opened the book. "Here's what it says."

> So God created man in his own image, in the image of God created he him; male and female created he them.
> And God blessed them, and God said unto them, "Be fruitful, and multiply, and replenish the earth, and subdue it; and have dominion over the fish of the sea, and over the fowl of the air, and over every living thing that moveth upon the earth."
> And God said, "Behold, I have given you every herb bearing seed, which is upon the face of all the earth, and every tree, in the which is the fruit of a tree yielding seed, to you it shall be for meat.
> "And to every beast of the earth, and to every fowl of the air, and to every thing that creepeth upon the earth, wherein there is life, I have given every green herb for meat," and it was so.
> And God saw every thing that he had made, and, behold, it was very good. And the evening and the morning were the sixth day.

He closed the book and looked across the crowd. Although he couldn't see them, out there in the dark on those rows of folding chairs he'd help set up, he knew the room was full.

"Now, like I said, this isn't a revival meeting. But I think that these words bear some thought. And their meaning is pretty unmistakable, really. I mean, phrases like 'subdue it,' 'have dominion,' and 'I have given'—this is

God speaking, remember—these are pretty unambiguous. Their meaning is clear.

"And this is the real message of Resources For Humanity. The earth is ours, for us to use and prosper with. With all due respect for our Native American brothers who believe otherwise, it's our heritage that the earth is here for our use and prosperity.

"Of course, there are lots of folks who seem to have some kind of inferiority complex, that they're not good enough to take advantage of all the earth's resources. Hell, there are some folks who think that prairie dogs are more important than people, that coyotes, for crying out loud, should be protected. Coyotes! Is that what you folks think?"

There was a sort of derisive growl from the darkness.

"I didn't think so. This same bunch of insecure tree-huggers is not only rich enough that they don't have to do honest work, but to make matters worse, they're trying to eliminate honest work for people who do. Like you folks. Y'all heard about that fire they had over in Monticello, I bet. The one that destroyed the Forest Fiber plant?"

The growl was louder, and decidedly affirmative this time.

"Well, guess who? That was sabotage, pure and simple, by some new bunch of environmental crazies. Hey, maybe they're well-meaning, but they sure are misguided. Turns out they put at least a hundred folks out of work. Maybe more, if they have to shut down harvesting the timber because there's no place to send it."

He could hear the growling continue, but he wasn't ready for the big finish, just yet.

Excess Homicide
A Four Corners Mystery

"I know, I know this is upsetting. I know it isn't fair. But that's what Resources For Humanity is all about. We're here to work to make it fair again.

"And I'll just bet y'all could use some good news, for once. Here's some now: we're not here to ask for your money! All we're here for is to ask for your support. Do we have that?"

Applause broke out, with a couple of cheers.

"Thank you. Thank you very much. I should tell you that I feel a little foolish standing up here with this microphone and these big speakers. Hope it's not too loud. But they're not here for me, really, they're here for a special guest, who's on the phone with a special message. I don't think he needs an introduction around these parts."

He chuckled, and fiddled with a box of switches on the table.

"I sure hope this works. It usually does, but once we somehow picked up one of those weird rap music radio stations. So-called 'music' by folks who have lots of rhythm but nothing else, no brains, no talent, nothing. Just a bunch of criminal bums, really. Yeesh." The audience joined his mirth. "Senator, you there?"

"I am, sir, I am indeed. And I'm honored to be able to talk with you folks a bit. I'm sorry I couldn't be with you tonight, but, as you know, I have responsibilities in Denver that I just can't get out of sometimes. If I'd been home, I'd be with you myself.

"Most of you folks know me, because you're in my district. There are probably some folks there from other districts, but, well, maybe you know me, too. I mention this because, like many of you, I'm a southwest Colorado native, third-generation native. Like so many of you, my great-grandparents came over from Europe over a hundred years ago and helped tame this wild land.

"And what's been happening lately is sad, truly sad. It makes me angry that it's happening to native Coloradans like you folks. What we have is outsiders moving here from far away, from New York, California, all sorts of places. Places where nobody appreciates our heritage. Places full of people who are concerned with 'lifestyles' rather than with good, honest work. People who are concerned with 'self-realization' and 'self-esteem' rather than with family and community. People who think that all cultures are equal, rather than people like us who know the value of our cultural heritage. And the worst of it is that these people are trying to take our world away from us. Eliminating our jobs. Preventing our use of our land. Imposing their foreign ways on us.

"Oh, I guess that 'foreign' isn't completely accurate. These are Americans, mostly. But their ways sure seem foreign. And there are even some that *are* foreign. People who come to this country and think they can take over. Immigrants. Some legal, some illegal.

"Now, my great-grandparents were immigrants. But that was back when there was room for new folks. I don't know about y'all, but I'm beginning to think that we're full. No more room for new people, whether they're foreigners from the coasts or from other countries.

"So that's why I'm calling you now. To support Resources For Humanity and to urge you to do the same. I think that you've been told that you're not going to be asked for money. At least you should have been told this. That's because Resources For Humanity is being supported by a private foundation. What you can do, however, is to provide support for the ideas and agenda of Resources For Humanity.

"One more thing. I bet you're concerned about that fire over in Monticello. Well, I am, too. And I'm going to use whatever powers I have to look into it. And to do something about it. Don't know what, yet, but those who know me will tell you that when I say I'm going to do something, well, I do.

"So that's the message. Support Resources For Humanity and their agenda to help hard-working, native Coloradans and to get rid of the environmental radical outside agitators. RFH is here to look out for you, and you can help by joining in.

"And, y'know?, I think there's something more. Y'all can stand up to those agitators. In meetings, like city council meetings and county commissioner meetings, stuff like that. You don't need to take their crap. You're Real Americans. Stand up for your heritage! Thanks for listening."

The speaker fiddled with more switches, and the room lights came up. As people in the audience were able to look around and see each other, they began to break out in hand shakes and applause. Applause that went on for some time.

Six

ABOUT THE TIME the meeting near Montrose was breaking up, Steve Rutherford's phone rang. He almost didn't answer it, being distracted. He'd set his computer up to spend the better part of the afternoon and evening automatically downloading images from one of his favorite porn sites, triple-d-cup.com, and was now browsing through the various pictures, trying to find one that closely approximated his fantasy of Lolly with no clothes on. The models, however, all seemed lots younger than Lolly and, well, levitated somehow. As if they'd been photographed in a zero-gravity environment. Must be silicone, he thought.

But the phone, right next to the computer, kept annoying him with its distracting rings, and he finally gave in to it.

"Yeah." He noticed his breathing was not quite even.

"Steve? Dave Wellington. Listen, you need to know about something I ran across the night before last. A meeting, in an old barn at a ranch west of here, between Del Norte and South Fork. Heard about it from some contacts in the logging world in South Fork. Managed to sneak in without being recognized. You there? All I hear is heavy breathing. Are you practicing to call little girls, or something?"

Excess Homicide
A Four Corners Mystery

"Huh? Yeah, sure, I'm here." And I wish she were here with me, Rutherford thought. Damn, look at those!

"OK, well, anyway, it was a meeting held by some wise-use group that I hadn't heard of before. Calls itself 'Resources For Humanity.' Most of the pitch was the same old same old. But this one had some subtle overtones of racism."

"Yeah? So? Most of these bozos are closet racists." Oho! Definitely not a natural blonde, this one.

"Maybe, but not as much as I bet you think. At least over here in the Valley. But the speaker at this meeting last night was treading very close to racism. These wise-use people always talk about 'family heritage' and so on, how ranchers and loggers have been here since ever and all that stuff. But this included references to 'Native Coloradans' and other such code words for white folks. And also there was a religious angle, subtle but unmistakable."

"So it was worse than usual." Holy hooters! Can those be natural? No way.

"Yep, but that's not why I called. The most disturbing thing was a phone call, or maybe it was just a taped message, from a Colorado state senator from out your way, Jarvis Schoenfield. He mentioned the little escapade over in Monticello and allowed as how he was going to use his powers to get whoever did it. And I looked him up and found that he's chairman of the Senate's Law Enforcement Committee. It oversees the State Patrol and the Colorado Bureau of Investigation. Hey! What the hell's going on over there? What's with the heavy breathing?"

"Uh, isometrics. I'm trying to get an early start on the ski season by doing isometrics for my quads. Sorry." Rutherford realized that he was going to have to concentrate

103

on the conversation. "I've heard of this guy. Been in the state senate forever, almost never opposed for reelection. I think he lives up around Norwood somewhere."

"Something like that. Wasn't he behind the head-bashing at the last Nucla protest a couple of years ago?"

"Oh, yeah. Before my time in SCARAB, but I remember hearing about that. Got the state cops to beat up some of our protestors at the prairie dog shoot. But it backfired on him. The publicity was so bad that they quit having them, at least they quit publicizing them."

"Right. And now he's talking about how native Coloradans should assert their rights, stand up to what he calls the environmental radicals, and so on. And how he's going to get whoever did the Monticello raid. I sure wish you guys hadn't gone off half cocked. I worry about Schoenfield's reach."

"Hmm. Well, we're going to lie low for a while. And I don't think that there's any way that any of us are going to be implicated. I mean, this is a Utah investigation, southeastern Utah, and they're not exactly rocket scientists over there. Buncha dumb Mormons."

"Yeah, well, just remember those dumb Mormons are as tenacious as bulldogs, and not real tolerant of the likes of you and SCARAB. Not to mention our new little enterprise. Gotta go. Later." He hung up.

Great, Rutherford thought. Something else to worry about. Well, whatever. Now, then. Let's go back and find the redhead with the feather boa. She looked a lot like Lolly. And she even had a tattoo.

He felt his face getting hot again.

Excess Homicide
A Four Corners Mystery

EVEN IN SUMMER there were meetings—administrative meetings, academic planning meetings, faculty development meetings, facilities improvement meetings, meetings to schedule yet more meetings. Try as he might, Hal simply couldn't avoid them, at least not all of them. He managed to delegate many of them to junior faculty—always providing memos of appreciation for them to show their department chairs the proof of their service to the college—but some meetings just needed The Dean in attendance. Too many, if you asked Hal.

Alice Swan, Hal's administrative assistant, knew Hal's aversion to meetings well, and she was particularly adept at keeping his calendar under control. As she edged ever closer to retirement, Hal's sense of the impending loss grew ever keener. Now, with only a couple of years to go, he was beginning to feel panic over how he was going to survive without her. He was reminded of this problem by the annual taste of it that he had to confront when Alice took her vacation, a benefit she seemed to resent.

This year, she had decided to take two weeks in June to visit her grandchildren in Virginia, so Hal was suffering through a temporary replacement, a young woman who not only could not deal with calendar scheduling at Alice's level but who didn't really care. And she chewed gum. With her mouth open.

Crystal's inability to schedule meetings to Alice's standard was why Hal was now sitting in his third of the day, with another to follow. All the way across campus from where he now sat listening to a discussion of new grading standards for student athletes, meeting number four was going to be the really important one. And, somehow, he had to work in an informal get-together with Provost

Martin, to bring him up to date on the implications for the campus of Annette's investigations. He would probably wind up being late, unless someone stepped in to negotiate a deal between the athletic department's representative, who was demanding a 2.1 minimum grade point average, and the chair of the department of English, who would settle on nothing lower than 2.25. As the senior academic officer present, Hal knew he would have to mediate this impasse.

"Time out, time out. Folks, let's calm down here. First, we're talking about a small difference, between just above a flat 'C' and just below a 'C+.' It seems to me that what we're doing is putting a lot of energy into arguing over pretty low standards. Like arguing over the difference between Walmart and K-Mart. How about raising our sights a little? What's wrong with a 'B' average, a 3.0?"

It looked as if Milt Grabowski, the athletic department's academic advisor, might explode, while Sadie Mickelstein, the chair of English, suddenly took on an uncanny resemblance to the Cheshire Cat.

"I know I haven't been at the earlier meetings," Hal continued, "and I'm sorry if this is ground you've covered. But why are we aiming so low here? Sadie?"

"Thank you, Dean Weathers. I've been advocating all along for something respectable, and a 'B' average would be more than respectable, I think. I've been unable to persuade my colleagues that this is appropriate."

She paused to take a breath and Grabowski jumped in.

"One reason is because we'd lose our ability to compete, in just about all of the varsity sports. Jesus, Hal, a 'B' average would eliminate almost two-thirds of our scholarship athletes. Even a 2.25 would eliminate a significant number. I mean, you've got to remember that the

Excess Homicide
A Four Corners Mystery

NCAA rules for us mandate only a 2.0 for fourth-year students, and even lower before that."

Hal feigned surprise.

"Well, we certainly want to maintain our standards well above the NCAA minimum, don't we? And do you mean to tell me that you offer scholarships, university scholarships, to individuals with GPAs under 2.25? *Scholarships* for students who can't even maintain a 'C+'? My goodness. I seem to remember that we approved what I considered to be a questionable curriculum, the one we call 'university studies,' for people who are, ah, challenged by our more traditional curricula. And you're telling me that this isn't good enough? That we're offering scholarships to people who can't even maintain a 'C+' in university studies? We do have accreditation to worry about, you know."

Grabowski's red face had become more and more crimson, and he opened his mouth to respond. Then he took a breath in preparation for a speech. Then he stopped short, apparently thinking better of it. That was all Sadie Mickelstein needed.

"Thank you, Dean Weathers, for supporting my position. In the English department, we have developed special courses for the university studies program, and, I have to say, calling them 'remedial' is to use polite terminology. I believe that similar comments apply to such courses in other departments." Hal knew that this was indeed the case in the earth sciences, but he also knew that he would be unable to maintain a hard line on this. The athletic department had substantial clout in the university president's office.

"Look, Milt. This is an advisory committee, and its job is to recommend, not implement. We have a responsibility to the university to uphold high academic standards, and, more than that, we have a responsibility to our student athletes to make sure that they are not shortchanged in their education. To let their grades slide too far is to cheat them—those NCAA rules, for example, are just pathetic. These kids bust their butts in practice, and they make the university lots of money in return by playing their hearts out. And they don't get paid for it, they just get NCAA rules stuffed down their throats. It's not as if a lot of Frémont State students go into professional sports, after all. Also, we need to let this committee save face. You may not realize how uncomfortable it makes faculty to think of a 'C' average as acceptable. But because the decision will be made in the president's office, we can recommend high with a clear conscience, and let them change it."

Grabowski, less red this time, went through the same process of starting to talk and stopping. Then he started up again.

"Probation at 2.5, but they keep playing above 2.0."

"2.5 in academic curricula, 2.75 in university studies." Sadie Mickelstein is definitely not someone with whom I want to negotiate, Hal thought.

"I'll have to check with the AD." Grabowski seemed beaten down. It's time, Hal thought, to be conciliatory.

"Milt, one thing that we can probably do is to help you with the tutoring program. I have a dynamite teaching assistant who can help with earth science courses. And I know a guy in chemistry who could help with that. If we start tutoring early, when it looks like someone might be dropping below a 2.5, or 2.75, maybe we can catch them before they go much lower. Then they can continue to play and also get off probation."

Excess Homicide
A Four Corners Mystery

"I'll check with Charlie."

"Thanks. And I've got to run. Again, I'm sorry to have missed the previous meetings." Right, Hal thought. "But I'm glad we've resolved this." And he stood, closing his notebook.

Now I get to sprint over to the student center, he remembered. Then I need to brief John Martin, if I can get in to see him. What fun.

MAYBE, ANNETTE THOUGHT, just maybe I'll get lucky twice in one day. Seems like I deserve it, at long last.

Her first bit of luck had been a phone call earlier. The FBI ballistics lab had called with the news that the slugs that had killed Luke Begay and William Campbell had come from the same gun. This physical evidence, combined with the similarity of the executions, provided the first real break in the portfolio of environmentalist killings. How Campbell fit into the whole thing was still not clear, but at least it appeared that the killings were related.

Lucky break number two would depend on a couple of things. First, Deedee would have to want to cooperate. And, of course, she'd have to be the creator of Lolly's rose.

"We're BAD!" hand-lettered in bright orange paint on the front window of Body Art by Deedee, a seedy storefront on North Main Avenue, announced Deedee's attitude to the world. Annette was glad to have had her several years of experience investigating all sorts of unsavory matters for the Durango police department, because she had developed an underground network of people who owed her favors. Deedee was about to have her favor called in, bad attitude or no.

H. P. Hanson

Inside, the walls were covered with flash, patterns for all sorts of skin-based self-expression, and the music was almost too loud for comfort. Some sort of heavy metal, distorted guitars accompanied by a screeching noise that Annette decided was supposed to be singing, was blasting from speakers on the ceiling, and it got louder deeper into the shop. Annette wandered toward the back and began to hear behind the "music" the buzzing noise that meant Deedee was at work on a client, who Annette soon saw was wearing headphones.

And what a client he was. Huge. Hairy, except for the shaved spot. And apparently scared out of his wits. Deedee, hunched over, working on something to do with the guy's right shoulder, didn't see her, so Annette watched in fascination. His eyes were clamped shut, his teeth were clenched, and he was sweating. She could see his massive hands clinging to the arms of the old barber chair. Looking over Deedee's shoulder, Annette could make out a snake emerging from the pattern of blood as Deedee blotted it off.

Finally Deedee noticed Annette and held up one hand, fingers splayed. She mouthed "five" in a question, and Annette nodded and went back out to the front room to study the art work. It was a sort of gallery, she decided, of the comic-book school.

A few minutes later, the music moderated and Deedee appeared, stripping off her latex gloves. She promptly lit a cigarette.

"Find one you like yet?"

"Ha. I'm too chicken. I hope I'm not interrupting too much?" Annette wanted to start off as politely as possible.

"No, not hardly. Snake back there needed a break. The guy I mean. You'd think someone that big and mean-

Excess Homicide
A Four Corners Mystery

looking with a nickname like 'Snake' wouldn't be bothered by a little prickling sensation. But he's really wimped out, probably more chicken than you. Wanted drugs... ah... but of course we've got none here. So he's got those headphones cranked up so loud that he can't possibly hear what I'm doing. But he's still freaked. Glad I'm almost done."

"I've seen the finished product, but not the process. It's bloody."

"Yeah, but it's just capillaries. You want these things to take, you've got to go deep enough to hit them. It heals fast. Now, what can I do for you, Lieutenant?" Annette decided not to bring Deedee up to date on her employment status.

"I'm hoping you can do me a favor, Deedee. We need to find a witness to something I'm looking into. We got a partial description of her, and she has a tattoo of a rose on her chest, upper right breast."

"And?"

"And I was hoping you might have done it and be able to point me toward her. We really need her help."

"You know how many roses on tits I do? It seems to be a favorite these days."

Annette had been anticipating this response, so she had driven over to Monticello to interview the deputy sheriff personally. That had been strange indeed, because, as a law enforcement officer, he was trying to cooperate and, as a devout church-goer, he was trying to maintain his sense of modesty. Talking about body art on a woman's breast, and especially how he had been staring at it, was not easy for him.

"Yeah, I was afraid of that. I do have a somewhat better description. This is a blonde, in her 30s, busty. The rose is

111

red, just a rosebud, on a long green stem. It's upside down and runs across and down, like this." Annette made a S-shaped stripe with her finger from near her right armpit down and across to her sternum. "And it didn't look like a new tattoo. It was faded and a little stretched-looking. Does that help?"

"Even if it did help, what makes you think I'd give out information about a client? People pay cash here, mostly, with good reason. They like anonymity."

"Deedee, we both know you're not exactly Chamber of Commerce material. But we also both know that you're a member of the local business community, and you need us. So when we need you, you ought to be there. Remember that little episode with the biker gang last year? And do you really need us to check into whether your supply of Xylocaine is legal?"

Deedee stared, first at Annette and then at a garish depiction of a bloody dagger with the inscription "Mother," while she smoked.

"So how many favors like this do I owe you?"

"I don't think of it as 'owing' so much as I think of it as a business relationship. You're the first person I refer people to when they ask me where they can find a good body-art shop. And I always put in a good word for you with the folks in vice."

Deedee stared some more.

"Well, like I said, I do lots of roses, but mostly recently. If you're looking for an older one with a long stem like you described there's only one I can think of. I did it about five years back, and gave a discount in return for getting her to agree to show it to girls who might be interested in one.

Excess Homicide
A Four Corners Mystery

Name's Billingsley, Louella Billingsley. But she's not a blonde."

Annette tried not to gloat. "Well, you said that was five years ago, and you know how things change. Thanks, Deedee. I won't bother you again about this. And I won't say anything about you to Ms. Billingsley."

This, she thought as she walked back to her car, is what we need to get this thing moving along. Wonder where we'll find Louella Billingsley?

IT HAD TAKEN over a month to get the text translated and analyzed, one of the most distasteful months in Wendell Ellison's career. Today, finally, was his big presentation up in the executive suite, and he could put this whole sorry episode behind him. The Biotechnology Division was still on the second tier among UNELECO's various ventures, so he knew he'd be going into the meeting with a slight handicap. But he also knew that Biotechnology had been selected by the CEO as one of the growth areas for the conglomerate's future, and this would give him an edge.

And he needed all the edges he could get, because he was not going into the meeting with good news. There was nothing of scientific value, not a shred, in Heinrich von Scheuer's volumes of laboratory notes.

He'd driven down from the UNELECO Biotechnology Laboratories in Boulder the evening before so he'd be fresh. Then he made a point of arriving at the corporate headquarters building early, so he could double-check the computer setup. He should have known, he told himself, that in the executive conference room it would be fine. More than fine, really, for they had only the newest and best up there.

So he was sitting near the front of the room in a side chair, trying to be inconspicuous while he enjoyed the view of Pikes Peak, as the assorted vice presidents and their minions began arriving for the 9:30 meeting. They studiously ignored him, an outsider in their *sanctum sanctorum*, a mere research scientist in their high-powered world of corporate executives.

He sat and watched the preening and the conversational cliques with interest. Even though he'd worn his best—and only, truth be known—suit for the occasion, with a new white shirt and conservative tie, he felt underdressed. The others also wore suits, of course, but they seemed to fit better, to look more elegant somehow. The difference between a tailored Armani and an off-the-rack from Foley's, he figured.

Then there was a commotion at the double doors, and in swept Charles Shure, followed by several attendants. Wendell recognized him from corporate literature, and he looked as impressive in person as he did there. The various vice-presidents sort of gravitated his way, and, even though no voices were raised, Wendell could tell that there were urgent attempts at communications being made. What a world to operate in, he thought.

He was surprised, astounded to see Shure headed his way, shaking off the clinging vice-presidents, walking around the big table, right up to where he sat, right hand extended.

"Dr. Ellison? I'm Chuck Shure, we spoke on the phone last week. I want to thank you again for that confidential report you sent me and all the help you provided me over the phone so I could understand its nuances."

Excess Homicide
A Four Corners Mystery

Wendell had stumbled to his feet and noticed how well Shure shook hands. Not the dead fish approach, not the usual western knuckle crusher; just right.

"Ahh, well, of course I'm glad to help, Mr. Shure, and very glad to meet you in person."

"And thank you for coming down from Boulder for this briefing. As I told you, there have been so many rumors about this whole thing that I want to get it out in public and behind us. Especially since there's nothing of use to us. One thing I didn't mention: I hope your presentation is a dumbed-down version of that report, dumbed *way* down. Some of these guys are not even up to my feeble level of being able to understand this stuff."

"I planned to keep it simple. And pretty short, really. There's really nothing much of interest. Um, have you considered my suggestion about donating the final volume to the museum?"

"Yes, and I'm going to announce it when I introduce you. And then there's going to be a press conference this afternoon. I hope you can stay around for it?"

"Anything you'd like, Mr. Shure. I'll think about what to say if someone asks me something."

"Good idea. But right now, we need to get this show on the road. This assembly of suits is costing me over fifteen thousand an hour." Shure's pleasant, business-like expression morphed into an impish grin. "Watch this."

He turned from Wendell and walked to the end of the conference table, stood for a short five seconds, and then snapped his fingers. The room immediately hushed, and, within another five seconds, everyone had taken a chair. Shure looked at Wendell and winked, and then turned to the assembled suits.

H. P. Hanson

"Thank you for coming on such short notice. We're here to gain closure on a strange episode that started in May, when I received a bizarre package. I know that there has been a considerable amount of rumor and speculation about this, and the purpose of this meeting is to present what we know, the facts, to you publicly. There will be a press conference about this later today, and you can feel free to pass the information along to the folks in your divisions as you feel appropriate.

"Now, I'm really not sure why I received this package, although I have a theory that I'll explain in a minute. But what I do know is that, after it had passed our security tests, I unwrapped it to find a book. It turns out that this book is an historical artifact, and nothing more, and we will be donating it to the appropriate museum this afternoon. It was hand-written in German, so we had it translated, and we also had the book itself, the cover and the binding and so on, analyzed.

"What I received turns out to be Volume 25 of a set of laboratory notes of a Nazi prison camp doctor. One of our researchers, Dr. Wendell Ellison," he gestured in Wendell's general direction, "will present a brief review of its contents shortly. The book, which we have stored in an environmentally controlled vault, is bound in tanned human skin, apparently taken from prison camp inmates." There was a collective gasp from the others in the room, and a murmur of comment.

"As I said, this is an historical artifact, and we'll be donating it to the Holocaust Museum in Washington at the press conference this afternoon. This is appropriate because they already have the first 24 volumes of the set of notes, not on display but in their archive."

Excess Homicide
A Four Corners Mystery

Shure paused and took a deep breath. He looked around the room slowly.

"As you can imagine, I've given a lot of thought to why this might have been sent to me. The only thing that I can think of is that my grandparents immigrated here from Germany after the war, and it appears that the Nazi prison camp doctor may have been my great-uncle, the brother of my grandfather Peter, who, as you know, was the founder of what's become UNELECO. I didn't know of this great-uncle until our research into this book. For obvious reasons, he wasn't someone my grandparents were proud of. I certainly feel no connection to him. However, donating this volume to the Holocaust Museum, along with a small endowment to assist their educational efforts, will help to ensure that that reprehensible chapter of our society's history is neither forgotten nor whitewashed over. Now, let's hear from Dr. Ellison."

Wendell, having heard most of this previously, was not nearly as shocked as the other occupants of the room, so he was ready.

"Can we have the lights, please? I think the most effective way to present this material to you is with pictures, some of which I'm certain you'll find disturbing." And he turned on the computer projector as the room lights dimmed.

Seven

First things first, Annette decided, so she started with the phone book. She had enough experience at this sort of thing that she wasn't too disappointed when she didn't find a Louella Billingsley. But there was a Richard Billingsley Realty, with an address in Pagosa Springs. She crossed her fingers and picked up the phone. There was a clicking noise that she recognized as the call's being forwarded.

"Hello? Rich Billingsley here." The signal was less than clear and she suspected a cell phone. Also, there was background noise, perhaps wind.

She decided that someone in the business community would likely be cooperative and that she could be straight.

"Mr. Billingsley, my name is Annette Trieri. I'm with the Colorado Bureau of Investigation. I'm calling you with the hope that you may know a Louella Billingsley. I need to reach her."

There was a long pause.

"Is she in some kind of trouble?"

"Not that I know of. We just need to talk with her."

"Oh. Too bad. And unusual, really. That's she's not in trouble, I mean. Listen, I'm with a client, and it sounds like I'm almost out of cell range. Can we talk when I get back to town?"

"You do know her, then?"

Excess Homicide
A Four Corners Mystery

"Oh, yes. But I'd rather talk about it when I'm back in my office, with a stiff drink and my feet up."

They set a time later in the afternoon for a follow-up. A stiff drink? Why, she thought, would he need a stiff drink to talk about this?

There was a knock on her office door—a real door to a real office now, one of the perks of her new position. Derek Petersen stuck his head in.

"Ms. Trieri? You said you wanted to go over the budget estimates?"

"Come in, Derek. And look, man, you've *got* to call me Annette, around here at least. Really."

He was still getting used to his new role as her combined second-in-command, chief-of-staff, and head expert on all things bureaucratic in the CBI. Somewhere in his middle forties, he was just beginning to acquire that mature look—thinning hair, a spare tire, and the slight squint that suggested he should have his eyes checked.

"Derek, I'm pretty much of a straight-forward person, and I'm not very good at maintaining hidden agendas. I want to accomplish two things around here in addition to all the stuff I mentioned in that little speech I gave last week." On her first day, she had held an all-hands meeting and outlined her vision for the organization.

"First, I want to parlay my good relationships with the counties around here into a coherent regional law enforcement system. That's really what I meant when I was talking about a strengthened southwest CBI office. And, second, Director Andersen and I conspired to put you into a position that would provide you with the experience you need to take over one of the division offices someday soon. He said what you need is more administrative experience. I hope that putting you behind a desk hasn't got you too upset with me."

"Uh, no, I was surprised and a little disappointed at not getting promoted, but Rod, that is, Director Andersen, called me and gave me a pep talk. And your reputation preceded you. To tell the truth, I'm going to be happy not to be on the road so much. Laura, that's my wife, could use me at home more. The kids are teenagers now, and she needs help. But I'm not sure I'm cut out for this administrative stuff. These budget estimates, for example, are, um, foreign territory for me. And no matter how hard I try, it's hard to get interested in them."

She smiled.

"Rule One: Delegate. You're used to working in the field and being pretty much on your own. Rod told me that Bob Weldon had become entrenched as a micro-manager, so the entire staff here, including you, are probably used to that style. I don't want to micro-manage you, and I think that you shouldn't micro-manage the others. So let the accountant, what's her name… ah, Cheryl, do her thing and get her in here when we talk about the estimates. These folks may take a while to adapt to bosses with a new approach, but most people like a loose leash."

"Don't forget that we're all state employees, used to dealing with lots of rigid procedures and silly rules."

"Yeah, but I bet everyone's got ideas about how to make those rules work in our favor, or how to avoid them. And I see that as part of your job—assimilating all those tricks. And teaching them to me. Now, since Cheryl isn't here, let's talk about something more interesting. We have the ballistics connection between the killing up by Norwood in May and the other one, same execution style, same gun,

Excess Homicide
A Four Corners Mystery

down at the Four Corners monument last year. You're the one with the field experience. What do you make of this?"

"Well, for one thing, the FBI is probably going to be a pain in the you-know-where. My experience with the local guys is that they need lessons in how to share information. They're sort of a black hole—stuff goes in but nothing comes out."

"That's what happened, all right. Last year, the day it happened, they called the Durango PD to get an ID on the victim down at the monument, Luke Begay, his name was. We told them what we knew and then didn't hear a word about it. My next smidgeon of information was in that assembled file I got from Rod's office, the one with all the dead environmentalists in it. What about the other one? That's the San Miguel sheriff, right?"

"Yeah, and he's also a little problematic. See, one of his constituents, a big player, is a state senator who lives southwest of Norwood. Senator Jarvis Schoenfield. Chairman of the Committee on Law Enforcement. Controls our budget. And controls Jim Nettleman, the sheriff over there."

"I met him, Schoenfield, I mean. Roderick took me to see him last month, just after I signed on. First thing he asked was when we were going to make an arrest for that murder. He said he wanted to be kept informed about our progress. And that he expected progress."

"This sounds in character. You were talking about micro-managing. He seems to think that because he holds sway over our budget he's our real boss. And Rod has to go along with it, pretty much. Same thing is true for the State Patrol."

"So, is it a problem?"

"Well, let's just say that we ought to be cautious. He's in something like his seventh term, really entrenched. Although, I have to say, with all the new folks moving into the vicinity of Telluride, his margins of victory have been less the last couple of times. But his power base includes some, how shall I say it, seriously right-wing groups. And he owns, or used to own, about half the county. Now I guess he's set up his ranch as some kind of non-profit trust. Gets him out of property and other taxes. Anyway, you can bet that anything that Jim Nettleman knows, Schoenfield knows."

"Yeah, but that's not much, right?"

"Right. Victim's ID, cause of death, and so on. That's about it. The funny thing is that no one in the area knows the victim, or will admit to it. He was from Colorado Springs. What he was doing out Norwood way, dressed in a business suit, is a mystery to everybody. The indications are that he was killed pretty close to where his body was found, given the amount of blood at the scene. And there's that witness report of the several vehicles. But that's it so far."

"What are the biggest unknowns?"

"I'd say just that, I mean what was a Colorado Springs lawyer doing in Norwood, and what's the connection with Begay? If we can answer those questions, we'll have a good start on the portfolio, I'd think."

Annette nodded. "That's my thinking. Y'know, Rod and I sort of set you up, to get administrative experience so you can take over a division some day soon. But I hope you'll be stay interested in case work, because I'll need the advice, and someone to bounce ideas off of."

Excess Homicide
A Four Corners Mystery

"I'm hoping to. Stay involved, I mean. This administrative stuff may be necessary, but I don't think it's my cup of tea."

"I know what you mean. Just remember Rule One. It's what kept me sane at the PD."

THE RIGHT REVEREND Dr. Michael Oswald was letting Schoenfield vent. His fancy titles and even his last name were not quite accurate, but being accurate was less important to him than making an impression. Jarvis Schoenfield, however, was not impressed.

"That ungrateful, Jew-loving son-of-a-bitch! Does he have any idea of how much trouble we went to to get him that book? Plus the copies of the other ones? And now he's giving it to the Jew museum? And he has the gall to pull out some so-called 'scientist' to tell everyone that there's nothing of value in the set. I think that scientist, what was his name? Ellison? I think he's going down for this."

"Now, Jarvis, calm down. You'll burst an artery or something. C'mon, you knew this business of enlisting Shure was a gamble. And I still think it might have worked, if your guys hadn't popped that lawyer, Campbell. I bet that's what scared Shure off, and this is how he's distancing himself from us." He let Schoenfield stomp around the porch for a while.

They were sitting on the veranda of the log cabin, looking out toward the southeast, watching the afternoon shadows lengthen on Lone Cone Peak, and Oswald couldn't help but think that Schoenfield had it too good. He was like a spoiled child, always wanting, and mostly getting, his own way. When he didn't get it, he had a tantrum. Like now.

"Look, Jarvis, let's just let go of this thing with UNELECO and move on. We don't really need them. And those meetings I've been holding around the region are going pretty well. We're going to wind up with a good-sized group of people interested in moving up to stage two. And the people who drop out aren't going to hurt us. I mean, I think the meeting over by South Fork last week was infiltrated, but even that's not a big deal. The message I'm laying on them is so bland that it doesn't matter who hears it. It's stage two where we have to be more careful. And the same thing's true with Shure. He really didn't hear enough to be a danger to us, right? Besides, Timmy's going to provide us with insider information about what Shure knows."

"The South Fork meeting was infiltrated? By who? I know that those meetings are for public consumption, but we need to make an example of this guy. If we're gonna get spied on, we're gonna send a message."

"I don't know who, but I'll find out and let you know. But, listen, Jarvis, we can't go around killing everyone. That report you got, along with Timmy's information, shows that the CBI is aware of what's going on, at some level at least, and we know the FBI's responsible for investigating that killing down on the Rez. We've got to be careful."

"I'll worry about the CBI, and the FBI's going nowhere. You worry about getting people enlisted. And Shure needs reminding to keep quiet about what he's heard. Another news conference, and he gets put on the hit list."

"Just as long as he's one of the 'natural causes' hits. He's too high-profile to have anything suspicious happen to him. And, Jarvis, I'd be careful about the others, too. People besides the CBI are going to start putting two and two together."

"Yeah, yeah. Where's that damned phone?" He was fumbling in the pockets of his jacket and eventually fished out the handset of a cordless unit. He punched buttons.

"Pickle? Can you come over to the back porch? The Reverend and I have some stuff we need to talk over." He put the phone away, in a different pocket. "It doesn't really matter who puts what together, because I've got control of everything that counts. The CBI—hell, even if Weldon is leaving, there's this new girl Andersen's putting in his place. She'll be easy to keep under control. And I've got the State Patrol running scared over their budget. Jim Nettleman and his crew at the sheriff's office owe me too much to give us trouble. And, besides, Pickle's good, real good."

ANNETTE CALLED right on time.

"Billingsley Realty, Rich speaking. How can I be helpful?"

"Well, if you've got your stiff drink and your feet up, you can tell me about Louella."

"Oh, yeah. Ms. ahh… Treery?"

"Trieri. Annette Trieri, Colorado Bureau of Investigation."

"Right. Sorry. I was out in the woods showing a parcel to this guy from Texas who's looking for a place for a summer house, and I didn't have a way to write it down. So you want to talk with Lou? Is she in some kind of trouble?"

"As I told you, I don't know. We need to talk with her about an investigation we're doing. But we don't know how to contact her."

"Well, if you have her name as Louella Billingsley, that's probably why. That was a long time ago. When we were married. I'm still paying for that mistake. If it weren't for these rich folks from Texas wanting to buy land up here, I don't know how I'd manage to pay her off."

"So you were married to her and now aren't?"

"Not by a long shot, thank God. Divorced four years ago."

"Do you know how we might contact her?"

"Well, I have the dubious pleasure of sending her checks every quarter, and she cashes them. So they must be getting to the name and address I'm sending them to."

"Which are?"

"Please tell me that she's going to be in hot water."

"Mr. Billingsley. I'm afraid we can't promise to act as your personal avenger. All we want to do is to talk with her. If it will make you feel any better, I imagine that it will make her nervous to have us contact her. Most folks react that way, no matter what." Annette had always been good at manufacturing little stories when they helped her cause. She certainly wasn't going to stop just because she changed jobs.

"Well, try to make her real nervous, OK? She's not Louella Billingsley anymore, she's Lolly Markham. Markham's her family name and Lolly is because she never really liked Lou. I think I made her actually hate it. So that's what I call her whenever I get the chance. Here's a phone number." He rattled off a string of digits, which Annette wrote down.

"I assume this is a home number, Mr. Billingsley. Would you know if she's employed?"

Excess Homicide
A Four Corners Mystery

"Yeah, and that's the best thing of all for me. She has to do something with her time besides sit around on her fat ass and spend my money. She's got a job at Carman's Western Art on Main Avenue." Annette thanked him and escaped. With relief. She turned to her computer.

What, she thought, is the name of the shortcut I made to the program that looks up drivers' licenses? Oh, yeah.

And within a couple of minutes she was looking at a screen-sized image of the Colorado driver's license of one Louella Markham, resident of Durango, required to wear corrective lenses to drive. Shoulder-length chestnut hair, if the picture could be trusted. Semi-attractive in a mid-thirties, used-hard sort of way. Not, from her face at least, thin.

Now, she thought, how do I do this? Copy the picture from that program to this other one, then send it as a fax over to the San Juan County, Utah, sheriff's office. She used the mouse and a graphics utility program, and finally the computer confirmed that the fax was sent. After they had Deputy Clean-Cut look at it, she should have a positive ID of the person he chatted up, and ogled, just before the FFPI fire. They'd owe her one, and maybe she could get a look at the file on the Natural Bridges Monument killing.

She looked at the clock. 4:45. When do you suppose these state employees go home?

She wandered out of her office and down the hall toward the receptionist, Sally Brigman. On the way she noticed that Derek Petersen was still in his office, working on a formidable stack of paper. Cheryl Trudeau, the head of the business-office side of things, was also still in, peering at her computer screen at what looked like a small-print spreadsheet. Damn, Annette thought, I've got to find out

H. P. Hanson

where that woman gets her clothes. She has the best sense of style I've run across in a long time.

Sally, behind her receptionist's counter, was staring at a calendar on the wall and talking through pursed lips into her headset.

"I appreciate your sense of urgency, Ms. Williams, but I'm afraid that public calls are always routed through me and assigned accordingly. And none of them go directly to our Director. I'm afraid that your high opinion of your Mr. Shure is not enough to make an exception. May I route you, and him, to one of our investigators?" She noticed Annette and rolled her eyes. Annette winked.

"Ms. Williams, I understand, but what I'm telling you is that I don't care who Mr. Shure is. We need to begin at the beginning and that's not with our Director... Well, if that's how you feel. Have a nice day." She ground her teeth and shook her head.

"That's not the way I like to finish up the afternoon. And if she has the clout that she says, you may be getting a call from Director Andersen in Denver. Sorry."

"Don't worry about it, Sally. If it's that important, Rod will understand, and so will I. You did admirably. Keep up the good work. And, look, it's just about five. Take off. Have a nice evening." Sally beamed. The idea of having a boss who wasn't a clock-watcher was a new experience. One she liked.

Annette strolled back to her office and was writing up the conversation with Billingsley when the phone rang.

"Annette? This is Rod Andersen. Sorry to bother you." Annette noticed it was 5:10. Whoever this Williams person is, she does indeed have clout, she thought.

"What can I do for you, Director Andersen?"

Excess Homicide
A Four Corners Mystery

"Ugh. Please, call me Rod, at least when we're not in front of the Governor. Or the press. Um, I just got a call that started with my Public Affairs person and then came to me. It's convoluted, but the bottom line is that Charles Shure wants to talk with you, about a case, it seems."

"Should I know this person?" Annette was far more familiar with the criminal world than the business world.

"You don't? Oh. Well, I wouldn't have expected your front office people to, and they did a good job of protecting you, I guess. Charles Shure is the CEO of UNELECO, a big conglomerate based in Colorado Springs. One of the top three business people in Colorado, and in the top twenty between the Mississippi and the West Coast. What you would definitely call a Big Cheese, at least in the business world. I take his calls so that the Governor won't call me and tell me to."

"Oh. Never heard of him. But I did hear that the company, um, FFPI, whose plant got torched over in Utah last month is a UNELECO division. Suppose he wants to talk about that?" Things were clicking into place in Annette's head.

"No idea. Could you call him? I've got a direct number. He's a workaholic, so he'll no doubt be in for a while."

"Be glad to. And, um, is there a list of people like this whose calls I should take? My receptionist would sure appreciate it. How should I handle this sort of thing?"

"I started my own list a long time ago and keep adding to it. Some are obvious, like the Gov, but others aren't. So just wing it. I don't think Shure is mad, or anything, I think he just wants to talk with you."

"I'll call him right back. Thanks, Dir... ah, Rod. Be talking with you."

I'll call him, she thought, but not this second. I don't care who he is, he's not jerking me around this much.

IT WAS JUST GETTING DARK as David Wellington eased his old Mazda pickup along the road behind the mill on the edge of Creede. He was, he noticed, barely on time. The 65 miles from Alamosa included the main streets of several small towns—Monte Vista, Del Norte, South Fork—and the propensity of the local constabulary to seek community income from people who played fast and loose with speed limits was well known to the residents of the San Luis Valley. He felt clever that he'd made it in an hour. And relieved not to have been caught by one of the various radar traps between the towns.

But he was also still a little pissed. Why in the world he needed to hustle over here on such short notice was a complete mystery. But the message on his answering machine had been insistent that he get himself up to the lumber mill at Creede by dark. He'd recognized the voice, sort of, if you filtered out the sneezes and the allergy-induced nasal tone.

The voice had said to park on this road behind the mill, right by the third pile of logs. He was supposed to pull off the road next to the pile, which was set back off the road a little more than the others. He idled slowly up to the spot and stopped next to a fifteen-foot wall of huge logs. Damn, these were big trees, he thought. Some of those suckers must be five feet in diameter. Old growth timber. Just the sort of rape and pillage activity that he and his friends in SCREW were trying to put a stop to.

Except for the fact that his fellow SCREWers were so impulsive, they might be able to accomplish something

Excess Homicide
A Four Corners Mystery

good. But that raid on the Monticello plant was too much, too soon. The risk of getting caught was way out of line with the payoff. So what if they burned down a lumber mill? It would just get rebuilt, newer and better.

That bunch seemed to think it was all a big game. Rutherford wouldn't take anything seriously, and, besides, he was obviously infatuated with Lolly. At least he spent a lot of time staring at her chest. And she was just too scatterbrained to be trusted, or useful for much of anything, either. The other two, Felterson and Tompkins, had potential, but they were old-school anarchists, hard to control. And Flip Chester was a danger to all of them, with his ever-present stash of joints.

Well, he thought, better a SCREWer than a SCREWee.

But Rutherford was right about one thing. When you assembled that list of their dead friends, it looked pretty clear: someone was systematically eliminating people involved in MEDL. Wellington felt his heart rate increase slightly as he remembered the circumstances over in Horca. He hadn't talked to anyone about it, but he'd been there, having breakfast with Holly and Jack Levine. They were on their way to Santa Fe to talk strategy with Roger Colgate and his buddies—Roger was dead, too, Wellington remembered—and he'd driven down early to meet them at Horca. They had discussed Wellington's idea to develop a new MEDL chapter at Adams State College in Alamosa. The students there tended to be more conservative than over in Durango, but there was still a strong environmental consciousness. And water issues in the San Luis Valley were one thing that got them involved in a flash. Whenever one of the big Front Range cities hatched another plan to grab San Luis Valley groundwater, the students at Adams

State got hopping mad, some of them mad enough to take direct action.

He and the Levines had eaten a pleasant breakfast at that little restaurant at Horca—Rosalita's? Rosella's? Rosa's? He couldn't remember—and he'd left them lingering over a last cup of coffee. It wasn't for another day that he heard about the car bomb and their deaths.

Let's see, he thought. Holly and Jack. Roger. That arrogant bastard down by Taos, the one with all the money. The Mayers up in Boulder. And, of course, Luke Begay over in Durango and Jake Colvin up in Cedaredge. That Park Ranger over in Utah. And Jodie P. down in Flag. Damn.

He tried to shake off his gloomy mood, but the gathering darkness didn't help matters. Where, he wondered, is that jerk who left me the message? And, goddammit, I've got to take a leak. Well, there isn't anybody around, at least that I can see through these dirty windows.

He opened his door and got out, standing in the middle of the gravel road to look around in the gloom. Seeing no one, he walked around the car, to stand between it and the log pile for some privacy. At least he could get more comfortable. The smell of freshly-cut conifer reminded him of the back woods. He took a deep breath.

He unzipped and let fly at the logs on the base of the pile. Looking up, he noticed the stars coming out. Creede, he thought, doesn't have the light pollution of Alamosa. How beautiful. But that's strange. That top log looked like it moved.

He looked down and flexed his neck around in a circle to loosen it up and to clear his head. Then he looked up again just in time to see the top-most log on the pile, a four-footer, rolling off the top and falling down toward him. It did its job so well that he didn't see the next dozen or how effectively they flattened his truck.

Eight

"**He's coming down here** this week to give us a formal statement. I guess I should be impressed, although I'm cynical enough to think of it more as ass-covering."

"Charles Shure himself, eh? Well, he *is* one of those hyper-busy corporate executives who values his time. Think this will help you move ahead on the portfolio?"

Annette and Hal were having a relaxed breakfast on the summer solstice, sharing bagels and the newspaper. Her new job had been playing havoc with their joint schedule, and they took every opportunity to spend time together.

"Well, we can't place this guy Campbell with the others in the environmental movement, but he was killed by the same gun as one of them. So, we'll see. On the other hand, that lead to the woman at the Monticello FFPI mill the night of the fire is getting interesting. I got a call-back last evening that the deputy sheriff over there places her at the scene just before the fire, based on her driver's license picture. A Durango citizen named Lolly Markham."

"So now what?"

"We'll pick her up for questioning and get one of the Utah investigators over here to be in on it. She was sitting behind the wheel of a car with stolen, or at least 'borrowed' Colorado license plates, and that's enough of an excuse to ask her some pointed questions. And the cell phone

Excess Homicide
A Four Corners Mystery

someone used to get the deputy away from her was stolen, hasn't been recovered. Stolen from the library in Cortez. So these are both Colorado crimes and belong to me. Meaning I can pick her up and question her, and we don't have to fool around with extradition just yet. If it turns out she was connected with the firebombing somehow, well, we'll share."

"But Shure's coming down to talk about the murder, not this?"

"That's what he said on the phone. He has information about it, including something in writing and, he said, a videotape of a press conference that's related somehow. So I don't really know details. He did say that he can't identify any of the players beyond the victim."

"Interesting. When the FFPI thing went down, John and I called you the next day, remember? He was wanting us to cooperate with their internal investigation because they're such big contributors to the U. But now there's a second connection, not to the university, exactly, but to Shure and UNELECO."

"From what I understand, their internal investigation focused mostly on whether it may have been worker sabotage, and they concluded that it was not. They're assuming that there's some new enviro-radical group that's responsible, probably called SCREW, based on that note."

"Yeah, I remember you told me something about a clever note. I wonder if they're connected with that other shadowy organization you mentioned. The Mother Earth Defense League. I've been poking around, carefully, and whatever connection there is at the U is so clandestine as to be invisible. The closest thing is the SCARAB chapter—Students and Citizens for Animal Rights and Biodiversity, remember?—and they're mostly animal rights oriented. But their publicity talks about 'opportunities' for involvement at all levels, without being specific. I suppose they could be a front, or entry-way, or something, for a more radical group. Or groups."

"Any way to find out?"

"Well, I probably can't. Being a Dean means lots of people who might know don't trust me for anything. But let me ask a couple of folks who do trust me. Maybe they can find something out. You remember Gil Taylor, right?"

"You bet. My friend with the chemistry lab that's got all the fancy analytical equipment. Does analyses for the PD."

"And just about everyone else on campus. Including, sometimes, students with concerns about purity of certain substances they manage to obtain. He's worried about safety and does some screening for poisonous impurities."

"So he's plugged into the dope-smoking, enviro-hippie, tree-hugger crowd?"

"Uh, well, 'plugged-in' is probably overstating things. I think he just doesn't want any of the kids to get their brains permanently fried by toxic stuff. After he analyzed those bogus designer drugs for you, and those joints that had PCP in them, he started to worry about what the kids are getting into. So he talked to me about quietly putting the word out that he'll do discreet analyses. He's being careful. For example, he's not screening for purity, just toxic impurities."

"Meaning he's not telling folks if the coke they just bought is cut, unless it's cut with bad stuff?"

"Right, and even then he's not telling cut how much. Just if it's dangerous. That is, dangerous in unsuspected ways, given that most of that stuff is dangerous in some

*Excess Homicide
A Four Corners Mystery*

sense even if it's pure. Uh, he talked all this over with me and I gave him a thumbs up. I figured the chemistry department owes the community a favor."

"But you didn't tell me."

"Um, well, you remember that business of whose jurisdiction is where and how the campus is really outside the city's purview? Well, I used that to rationalize that it's none of the Durango PD's business." He was wearing a sickly grin.

"Right. But now I'm CBI and the campus, being state property, is my jurisdiction, no?"

"Oh. I hadn't thought of that. Yet. But now you know, so it's OK, eh? Please?"

"I think I'll have to go have a chat with Gil."

"Oh, crap. Now I've got him in trouble."

"Gil? How could he be in trouble with me? He's a friend of mine, and he's been more than helpful on several occasions. I think I should just talk with him about this, that's all. Because I know about it, he needs to know that I know, and all that."

"Yeah, but he'll be pissed that I told you."

"I won't tell him that, so don't worry. I'll let him think that I found out some other way. And, look, I view this as a sort of public service, kind of like handing out disposable syringes to help prevent the spread of AIDS. And I bet he's got some kind of anonymous drop-off system set up, so he doesn't know who's giving him samples. So don't worry."

"I see a Machiavellian gleam lurking in your eyes. What sneaky thing are you planning?"

"Innocent li'l me? Well, I did have a thought. Perhaps I can talk Gil into helping with the serial murders, assuming that's what they are."

"By spying on the environmental community, you mean?"

"Well, maybe just by asking a few questions in the right places around campus. You know, places you can't really go and get straight answers, Mr. Fancy-Dan Dean."

"That's why I love you so much. It's that sass."

GIL TAYLOR will just have to wait until tomorrow to hear from me, Annette thought. With the Shure interview and tracking down Ms. Markham, I'm going to have a full day. Especially since that late start. And what a worthwhile late start it was—one of these days, I guess the honeymoon will be over, but I'm quite happy that it isn't yet. Mmm-mmm. Thank you Dean Fancy-Dan.

She pulled into the parking lot at the downtown station of the Durango PD, and smiled to see Fred Winders' car in her old spot. There was no real reason to expect trouble with Lolly Markham, but backup wouldn't be a bad idea. And, Annette thought, I can get my pals from the PD involved. That would be both politic and fun.

Twenty minutes later, she strolled into Carman's Western Art, which turned out to be a tourist-oriented gallery and high-end souvenir shop near the train depot downtown. She'd planned this earlier and dressed for the occasion, in jeans, her western riding boots, Indian jewelry, and a cheap straw cowboy hat, pushed back on her head. Although a bit pumped up for the occasion, as she always was on a bust, she made a point of playing the role of the bored shopper, looking for the perfect treasure to take back home to Toledo, for that special place on her knick-knack shelf.

"May I help you? All items are twenty per-cent off today."

After another critical look at the statuette, Annette turned and, at a glance, took in the name tag reading "Sondra" and the disparity between this person and the driver's license picture she'd seen.

"No, thank you." Smile. "I'm waiting on my husband to finish up at the fishing store down the block. I thought maybe I'd browse around and see if I could find something for my mother back in Ohio. Thanks." Back to the shelves.

She worked her way around the shop and finally came to the check-out counter. The person behind the cash register wasn't Lolly either. Time for plan B.

"Excuse me, I'm looking for someone. A friend of mine said I should look up Lolly Markham here, to say hi. Is she here?" The person with the name tag reading "Denise" looked surprised.

"Lolly? Sure. I think she's in the back. I can get her."

Annette smiled. "No rush. I'm looking for just the right thing for my mother back in Ohio, and I have plenty of time. Once my husband gets talking about fishing, there's no stopping him." She went back to the displays and pulled out her cell phone.

"Fred? Listen, I'm here at the Western Art Gallery, and I'm just about finished. Are you going to be much longer?"

"Hey, Annette. All set?"

"Just about."

"We'll move in."

In short order, Fred Winders wandered into the shop and worked his way toward the back, near the "Employees Only" door. He'd worked for Annette for years, and now he was acting in her old position at the PD, so he knew the drill: he studiously ignored her. Annette noticed another official-looking person standing outside the front door.

When Lolly came out from the back looking for Annette, the rest was easy.

With Lolly safely, although perhaps not comfortably and certainly not happily, in the detention center awaiting the arrival of the Utah investigators, Annette turned her attention to the day's other appointment, the meeting with Charles Shure, CEO of UNELECO. And, according to the message that awaited her in her office, his attorney, his driver, one Walter Herrington, and *his* attorney. The southwest office of the CBI was about to experience a sort of corporate takeover, she supposed. She went looking for her chief-of-staff.

"Derek, can I tear you away from all that paperwork?" They both recognized her question as rhetorical. "Have you read the file on that killing up by Norwood last month?"

"For sure. I don't have time to get out and investigate things, but I make time to read up on them. If I'm going to do the budget and all this other stuff, I need to know what's going on."

"Good thinking. I have two people, apparently, coming in to provide statements related to it. We should question them separately. Want to take one?"

"You bet. Got to keep the hinges oiled somehow. But I'm swamped. Which one will be quicker?"

"The driver, probably. We'll start out together to see what they're going to ask for. They called us to volunteer to come in and make a statement, so I doubt that they're going to confess to murder. They probably know something that they think is relevant. Maybe they were part of that convoy of vehicles that's in the report. But if they're bringing lawyers, they'll probably have a set of conditions they'll want to discuss."

"Like immunity, no doubt."

"No doubt. But I expect that their only real vulnerability is waiting until now to talk with us. Leaving the body there instead of calling in the local sheriff immediately. So immunity could be a good deal from our perspective."

"Assuming they have anything to contribute."

"Right. We'll see. And we can use all the help we can get with this one, especially because of its possible connection to the others I'm supposed to be clearing up. I'll call you when they get here. We can all meet in the conference room, and then we can use a couple of the rooms across the street." The county detention center had video cameras ready to roll. Annette had called her old friends over there and arranged to use the facility. Never underestimate the value, she thought, of having a personal contact network.

"SO, AFTER WE COMPARED NOTES," Annette was talking around a mouthful of the lasagna that Hal had concocted for dinner, "we found that their stories are completely consistent. Aside from not reporting the killing right away, we have no reason to think of Shure or his driver as suspects. But the really interesting part is the rest of Shure's story, the part that the driver, Herrington, didn't know about. Or at least didn't talk about."

"Why they were there and so on?"

"Right. The connection with this racist group, the Aryan Rights Fund, or Foundation, I guess. Apparently, this was the second contact, the first being the package with the book that I mentioned."

"But Shure was supposedly there to talk resource leases."

"Yep, on private land associated with the X-S Ranch. Of course, most of the private land around Norwood is part of the X-S. But it's hard to believe that there's not a connection between this Aryan group and the X-S. I mean, why drag Shure all the way over to Norwood? They could have concocted potential leases closer to the Springs, like in the Wet Mountains or somewhere."

"After we talked this morning, I did some Internet sleuthing. That's the nice thing about the campus this time of year. It's quiet and there's time for this sort of fooling around. I found out that one thing that Shure's company has done is to develop a new method of reprocessing mine tailings waste, doing it profitably and, from an environmental perspective, safely, at least so they say. So maybe whoever set this up thought that all the tailings up by Uravan and Bedrock would be an extra added attraction to Shure."

"Shure mentioned something like that. But they were originally supposed to have the meeting in Norwood, in an office at the X-S headquarters building, or the business office or whatever it is. I guess that they could have just picked that out of the phone book, but it looks like there's a potential, one that's too big to ignore, for a connection between the ranch and this Aryan group. Oops. I smell garlic bread burning." She jumped up to rescue it from the oven.

Her voice continued from the kitchen. "I looked up the ownership of the X-S and found out that it belongs to some non-profit trust called Resources For Humanity. Then I ran out of time." She returned, with a basket full of well-toasted and quite fragrant pieces of bread.

"I seem to recall something about the X-S, vaguely. There's a reservoir south of Norwood that I fished one time, can't remember the name. And there were no-trespassing signs all over the countryside, saying X-S Ranch and displaying a logo, or maybe a brand. A stylized 'x' with one leg curved to make a sort of 's.' That was years ago."

"Anyway, Resources For Humanity could be anything. Sounds like maybe one of those 'feed the world' foundations, but maybe not. It's probably going to be hard to show a connection between them and the Aryan group, though. Shure said that the Aryans were very secretive, lots of hocus-pocus."

"And this book he talked about was really from a Nazi prison camp?"

"Apparently. Shure's people examined it thoroughly, and we have their report, quite solid-looking with all sorts of high-tech analyses. Get this: The book was bound with tanned human skin. Shure donated it to the Holocaust Museum in Washington. It turns out to be part of a set of lab notes on medical experiments on prisoners."

"Why would they have sent it to Shure?"

"The letter they wrote talked about how the guy, the prison-camp doctor, who wrote the notes was Shure's great-uncle. And it appears that they, the Aryan group, were trying to recruit Shure. He showed me this letter they wrote him. Pretty weird stuff."

"And you said that the meeting in Norwood turned out to be more of the same. The lawyer who got killed gave him copies of the other volumes of lab notes?"

"Right. The discussion of leases didn't come up. The lawyer, Campbell, passed notes to Shure talking about how the whole thing was supposed to be a show of force, to further intimidate Shure. Strange way to do recruiting, but this group seems strange all around."

"Where to from here?"

"Shure's going to contact us if this ARF group contacts him again, and we'll figure something out. He doesn't know how to contact them, though, so all we can do is wait. Meanwhile, tomorrow we're going to try again on that woman who was at the Monticello fire. Lolly Markham."

"Try again?"

"Today all she did was weep and demand her attorney. Who is in Cortez and couldn't get here today. So tomorrow, it'll be the Utah guys and me versus Ms. Markham and her lawyer. If the lawyer's got any sense, he'll work some kind of deal. The Utah deputy sheriff has her in the car with the stolen plates when the fire was actually being set, so she's not one of the principals. Just a driver."

"Why would she have a lawyer from Cortez? This town's crawling with them. And she lives here, doesn't she?"

"Yeah, and I don't know why. Asked myself the same question. But, hey, we're not going to screw this up on a technicality, and letting her choose her own representation is easy for us." She bit into another slice of the garlic toast.

ACROSS TOWN, Steve Rutherford was once again becoming emotionally involved with his two-dimensional facsimile of Lolly, the one on the computer screen, when the phone rang with news of the real one. Bad news.

"Picked up? In custody? CBI? Jesus!"

Excess Homicide
A Four Corners Mystery

"And she wants me there when they question her. I'm really worried about this one, Steve." Reid Tompkins seemed to be blaming Rutherford, for some reason.

"Well, that's good, isn't it? That way, you can keep her from giving the wrong answers."

"Ha! What if she slips up and talks about 'we this' or 'you that'? That'll implicate me. She's such a ditz. I don't trust her not to slip up."

"Can't you talk with her first, alone, and sort of rehearse what she should and shouldn't say?"

"Of course. And I will. But I'm worried that if she gets rattled she'll blow it. And, look, I'm an officer of the court. I can't afford to be implicated in this. I'd be disbarred!" Tomkins' worry was palpable.

"Calm down. For one thing, you're not really a criminal lawyer, right? Can't you pass this one to someone who is? Then the potential for slip-ups would be less, wouldn't it?"

"But she asked for me and I sure don't want to piss her off. She'd have to tell another attorney what this whole thing is about, and he'd want to cut a deal. She's not who they're really looking for. That's us. And if she's pissed at me, or you, then she could just give us up."

"So you go with her and get her to stick to the story she gave that cop originally. The fight with her husband and so on."

"Right. And they'll ask where this 'husband' was, what motel or whatever, and then we're screwed."

"Well, you can't have it both ways. Either go represent her or don't. I think it would be better for you to work with her than to try to avoid all this."

"Yeah, really, so do I, I guess. But I also think we're awfully close to completely busted. You need to lie low, really, really low. And the others, too. Why don't you call them and warn them?"

"OK. But I can't seem to get hold of Dave. I was trying last night and today, to talk about something else. You heard from him lately?"

"No, but he goes off camping a lot."

"Yeah, I know. I'll leave him a message to call me right away. And I'll call Flip and Aaron tonight. Let me know if there's anything I can do to help with Lolly."

"Bail money, for one thing. Find some." And Tompkins hung up.

Bail money, eh? Rutherford thought. Then Lolly would owe me a favor. A big favor. The least she can do is to let me see that tattoo.

Aaron Felterson wasn't home, so Rutherford left an urgent, albeit cryptic, message. Flip Chester was home, sort of.

"Who? Oh, yeah, far out, man. 'S-happenin'? Want some more weed? I got a new stash, better than ever."

"Flip, listen up. This is important. You remember the conversation we had about that fire over in Monticello?"

"Right on, man. You dudes really did a number on those lumber guys. Good deal."

"Yeah, well, Lolly's got herself picked up by the cops. CBI no less."

"Bummer, man, major bummer. CBI? What's that?"

"Colorado Bureau of Investigation. Not just the Durango fuzz or the sheriff. These are the heavies. Lolly's got herself a real problem, and, hey: She's gonna need bail money. Can you help out?"

"Whoa, man. Bread? Like, how much, man?"

Excess Homicide
A Four Corners Mystery

"Don't know yet. But you've always got a lot of cash, and this is a friend in trouble. It'll only be a loan, until we get her out of this mess she's in."

"Yeah? How are you gonna do that, man?"

"Reid's a lawyer, remember? It'll be cool. So can you help with bail money? We'd help you."

"Depends on how much. But I can help, some. Let me know."

"I will. And, listen. We've all got to be careful just now, right?"

"Hey, man, I'm always careful. Gotta be, right? But you're the one who's gonna be in trouble for this one, not me." He giggled. "But I'll be careful. Extra careful."

Maybe it was because he'd been talking with Flip, the perennial outlaw. Maybe it was because he couldn't get Dave Wellington on the phone. Maybe it was because he didn't entirely trust Reid Tompkins. Whatever it was, paranoia took over Rutherford's thought processes.

The first thing he did was to turn off all the lights, room by room. The computer screen, grandly displaying a busty young woman wearing only a pink feather boa and a smile, lit the apartment with an eerie glow. Then he carefully, slowly, eased the living room curtain back to peek out at the street below.

Just the usual cars were sitting out there... except for that one. Across the street, facing his way. Jelly-bean shaped American sedan of some sort, generic features, some dark color or other. Was that a glow, a cigarette, from the front seat? Somebody in there watching? Oh, shit.

He stepped back from the window, glad he'd at least turned out the lights behind him. What now? Ignore it? Wait and see if the car goes away?

H. P. Hanson

He settled on going for a walk to see if the car would follow him. At least he didn't have the worries that Flip would, a stash of contraband. Oh, double-shit. There was that stuff in the kitchen, in a jar with the other jars of spices.

He walked, as calmly as he could under the circumstances, into the kitchen and, with the lights still off, fumbled in the spice cabinet. Trips back and forth to the light of the computer monitor to see labels made the process drag on and on. Finally he found the one labeled Roma Oregano. Then, staying near the wall, he crept into the bathroom, and emptied the jar into the toilet. From the glow of the computer screen in the living room, he could just make out that... it was floating! One flush, wait. Two flushes, wait. Three flushes... there, that should do it. He let out his breath. Then he crept back to the living room curtain, and gently drew it aside.

The car was still there... but here came a young girl, high-school age, it looked like. Bouncing out of the house that the sedan was sitting in front of. Leaning into the driver's side window. Getting in the other side. Driving off.

Triple-shit! That was nearly a whole ounce, of that $500 North Coast Hybrid from Flip, no less. Shit, shit, shit.

On the computer screen, the Lolly-look-alike, proud of her silicone adornments, just kept smiling.

CONFLICTING SCHEDULES meant that the next day Hal couldn't get in to see Provost John Martin until 4:30, and by then Hal was meeting'd out. Earlier, he had acted as the facilitator—the latest fancy word for referee—in a meeting on a reorganization plan for the social sciences and humanities college.

Excess Homicide
A Four Corners Mystery

The hang-up was sponsored research. As in the natural sciences in Hal's college, there was a variety of potential funding sources for research in psychology, anthropology and archaeology, and sociology. Not so in the humanities departments. The cultures of the two sides of the college were drifting apart, and they had a mandate from the provost to stop the drift by reorganizing. Reduce 'tribalism,' a term the anthropologists derided as racist. Increase a sense of 'community,' a term that the comparative theology faculty felt smug about. And it was Hal's job, as a favor to John Martin, to chair their meetings, keep order, and maintain whatever little momentum they were able to generate. It was an exhausting task.

"The sun's over the yardarm, Hal, in the Midwest, at least, and I'm going to celebrate." Martin opened a panel in his bookcase, revealing a highly illegal cache of expensive liquor bottles. He reached for the Laphroaig.

"As I remember, you have soda and ice over here in the 'fridge." Hal was familiar with the provost's liberal interpretation of state laws about liquor on campus. "Want some to go with that?"

"Tonight, it's neat. Now, what brings you here at this hour? I thought you tried to go fishing on these long summer evenings."

"What's got me here instead of in the river is our patron in the state senate, Jarvis Schoenfield. We may have a problem. And I know you like plenty of warning about possible problems, especially ones of this magnitude."

Martin was staring through the amber liquid in his glass at the maple trees outside.

"And now for the bad news?"

"I'll have to tell Annette about this, of course, because I thought of it today. Last night, she told me that there's a connection between a murder in San Miguel County and the X-S Ranch. Charles Shure, the UNELECO CEO came down to provide a statement about his knowledge of it. He seems clean, but it appears that the X-S may be involved. And today, I finally remembered where I'd heard about it. From our connection to Schoenfield. The X-S is his place, isn't it?"

"Used to be. He still lives up there. What's the story?"

As Hal told him, Martin sank deeper into his chair, and finally got up for a refill on his Laphroaig.

"Actually, this isn't the end of the world. He's the ranking member of the Senate Committee on Education, but he's not the committee chair. There's some rule about being chair of only one committee at a time and he's chair of something else, law enforcement, I think. But you're right about his being our patron. We're his baby. Especially since we've been doing so well in football."

"So if this business with the X-S involves him, somehow, we may lose an important political ally."

Martin took another sip of the scotch. "Yes, but I don't think it'll be the end of the world. I have a kind of bad feeling about him. Ever since we won the national championship three years go, I've wondered about him. I remember he was congratulating me at some meeting or other, and then he launched into a monologue about how it was too bad we had to use all that imported talent and couldn't win with students from around here. The big, strong ranch boys, he said. He also implied that we were somehow forced by political correctness, the diversity issue, to import all the non-local talent. So he was treading very,

Excess Homicide
A Four Corners Mystery

very close to issues of race, and it seemed like he was on the wrong side. It's bothered me ever since."

"I imagine you didn't come to the defense of our diversity program."

"Not hardly. You know that I don't like to go looking for trouble. But, anyway, if he takes a fall of some kind, I'm not going to panic. Hmm. I think I will make a point of finding out who's the second-ranking person on the education committee, however."

"So, if he doesn't own the X-S any longer, who does?"

"I'm not sure. He told me, kind of bragging, about how he set up a trust, gave the ranch over to it as a tax deduction, and has a deal to live there. He was talking like he ran the thing but that no one could really prove it. There's some kind of foundation that gets the income from the ranch. He didn't go into detail, and I probably wouldn't remember it anyway. But, look, like I said, I think he's chair of the law enforcement committee. Which would oversee the CBI. Seems like that would have some implications, to say the least. Does Annette know about this?"

"The foundation part. It's called Resources For Humanity. She didn't seem to know about Schoenfield last night, though. I'll fill her in." Hal poured himself a touch more soda water.

"So she told you that Shure talked about some white power group, or something like that?"

"Aryan Rights Foundation, I think it was. It's been in contact with Shure, apparently trying to recruit him. And they seem to be behind the murder of that lawyer that Shure met up by Norwood."

"Which means that if the X-S is involved, Schoenfield is probably involved in this Aryan thing and maybe the murder. I think I'll have a chat with President Black and see if we can start to distance ourselves from him. Having a right-wing patron is one thing, but having a racist one, who's involved in a murder to boot, is another." Martin was looking off into space, thinking, evaluating.

"Right. If that bunch I was just meeting with were to find out, there'd be hell to pay."

"Bunch?" Martin's eyebrows went up.

"The SS&H faculty. You asked me to facilitate their reorg, remember? These folks are the stewards of political correctness, even more than the arts faculty. They'd rather see the U go belly-up than to have a white power group's support."

"Well, for once I may just agree with them. But my job is to make sure that we can stay solvent without that support. Since you mentioned it, though, is that SS&H reorg making progress?"

"Oh, about what you'd expect. I think I have them convinced that combining their talents and leveraging resources is more likely to be productive than back-stabbing. But don't expect any major changes in the college's structure, like new departments or anything like that. They'll probably agree to form some kind of joint planning committee, though. Maybe that'll make things work."

"I'm grateful for your doing this, Hal. The acting dean has his hands full, and we need to get our house in order before we do a search for a new dean. My job will be to find the right candidate to put the final touches on what you're starting."

"And, right now, my job is to get home and put together dinner. Annette likes her new assignment, but she sure has a weird schedule."

"Which won't get better if Schoenfield really is involved in all this stuff. Good luck, Hal."

SOUTHEASTERN UTAH, being big and mostly empty, breeds people who think nothing of a 200-mile drive for lunch. It was therefore not surprising that the investigators from the Utah State Patrol had decided to commute rather than to stay over in Durango. What was surprising was that Reid Tompkins, Esq., agreed to postpone until afternoon the joint interview involving Lolly Markham, himself, the CBI, and the Utah crew.

Normally, Lolly would not have stayed in custody for so long without being charged with something. Annette was prepared to do that, but her best shot at the moment was pilfering license plates. She was therefore pleased that Tompkins had asked for the afternoon session.

What she didn't know was that Tompkins needed the extra time to prepare his client. And what *he* didn't know was that his client wasn't her usual pliable self.

"Lolly, we don't have a lot of time, so we really need to put it to good use."

She had been pacing about the private interview room and now stopped, leaned over the table toward him, and looked daggers his way.

"Up yours, Tompkins. I'm the one who's been stuck in this rat hole. Get me out of here!"

"I can do that, and will. After they question you. And we need to be ready."

"Ready for what? I think I'll just tell them what happened!"

Tompkins took a minute to suppress the fear surging through his nervous system. Lolly, he saw, was staring at him defiantly. Definitely looking her age, and then some. Bedraggled and, well, puffy. He'd brought lunch, but she was apparently on a hunger strike. Not that losing a few pounds would hurt her.

"Lolly, there's no reason to do that. You're just as committed to what we're all trying to accomplish as I am. And we have to stick with our story, or our whole effort will be ruined."

He paused and summoned up a sincere expression. "And you know that I'm still in love with you. I won't let them hurt you."

She had been staring out the window, arms crossed against her ample chest. Then the magic words had their effect, and her icy defiance began to melt.

He stood up, walked around the little table, and wrapped her in hug.

"It'll be OK, I promise. Look, why don't you eat something. I got all this stuff from the deli. And let's talk about how to handle these people."

"Reid, it was so lonely and cold here last night." Sniff. "You feel so warm. Mmm. Oh, what's happening here, you naughty boy? Do you want to warm me up? Hmm?" She sank to her knees in front of him and began fumbling with his belt buckle.

"Here? Lolly, we don't have any time for this right now."

"Oh, c'mon, Reid, it never takes you much time." Maybe she was on the slippery slope toward middle age, but

Excess Homicide
A Four Corners Mystery

she still knew that playing the coquette would push his buttons. He stepped back, embarrassed by his reaction to her.

"Lolly, we've got to be ready when those CBI people come in. Look, I'll take you to the Strater tonight, after we get you out of here, OK? Then we can take as long as we want. With champagne and oysters." He sat back down on the other side of the table.

"Getting older, baby? Need oysters these days?" She licked her lips, showing more tongue than was really needed.

"Lolly! Get with it, OK? Now. Tell me again what they told you when they picked you up yesterday."

Now she was pouting.

"Well, just that she was with the CBI and needed to question me. I asked what about and she wouldn't say. We got down here, and I was scared, so I started asking for you. They told me they would provide a lawyer if I needed one, but I kept asking for you. And I asked what are we waiting for and they told me that you couldn't get here right away. That's all I know."

"OK, well, here's what I know. Remember when you were in the car over in Monticello, and that sheriff's deputy was talking to you? He saw your tattoo, because I heard that there was a description of it being circulated. And I'm certain that before he got out to talk to you he called in the license plate number. That's standard procedure. So they know about the stolen plates and probably found you through the tattoo somehow. I think that the thing to do is to stick with the story you told the deputy. About getting away to think after a fight with your husband."

"Except I don't have a husband."

H. P. Hanson

"Right. OK, so he becomes a boyfriend. You told the deputy that it was your husband because it's Utah and you wanted to sound respectable, OK?"

"OK. And his name is ordinary, like, like, Robert Jones, OK? Uh, Bob. Right?" She was beginning to get interested in creating the story.

"Sure. Now, they're going to ask where you were staying, I mean, what motel. You had a fight and had to get away from him. So you left him somewhere. A motel. Has to be a motel because it was, what, three in the morning?"

"OK. What motel?"

"I checked, and there's a Super 8. They'll find out, probably, that there wasn't a 'Robert Jones' registered, though. So tell them that you think that maybe he registered with a fake name. Because you're not married and it's Utah. That's consistent with the boyfriend thing. And consistency is what we need."

"What about the stolen license plates?"

"It was Bob's car and you didn't know they were stolen. Just that he lives in Cortez, you met him at a bar, pick your favorite one here in Durango, and you went away for a few days together. To Moab. To go camping. Got it?"

"Uh, I think so. New boyfriend, met him in a bar. Robert Jones, from Cortez. Went camping in Moab, in his car, that green Blazer. Stayed in the Super 8 in Monticello because it was too late and we were tired. He told me he was using a fake name, because it's Utah, but didn't tell me the name. Had an argument, about sex, why not?" She winked at him, and his body tingled. "Went for a drive to think, and the deputy stopped to talk to me. That's all I know."

Excess Homicide
A Four Corners Mystery

"Great! Lolly, you sure do a good job of hiding your smarts sometimes. And, listen, if they ask you anything you have a concern about answering, don't answer. Look at me. I'll be right beside you, and I can guide you. This is what they expect anyway. I'll whisper in your ear."

"Blow in my ear and I'll follow you anywhere, lover." The tingle returned, and he began wondering how much time they really had.

But then there were noises in the hallway, several people, with keys.

H. P. Hanson

NINE

ALTHOUGH THE REVEREND was part of Schoenfield's inner circle, he wasn't privy to everything. The final planning meeting for the ambush in Boulder involved only the Senator and his operatives Pickle and Mad Dog.

"We're all set, Senator. Equipment's ready and in place, all tested and everything. But I have to keep telling you, I don't think there's much of a chance for accuracy with this set-up."

"And like I keep telling you, Pickle, don't sweat it. Just the event will send our message. Go over this one more time for me, willya? I need to hear the details again."

"Well, Senator, like I've told you, this all started with an opportunity we heard about. There was this article in the paper about how the White House announced a visit by the President to NCAR, in Boulder. And how NCAR was going to get all fancied up for the visit, including refurbishing some of its educational displays. They have a bunch of old scientific instruments, and some newer displays, in their lobby, and school kids and the public just love it." Pickle squirmed in his leather chair, trying to get more comfortable.

"So," he continued, "it seems that one of the displays is this old telescope, originally invented by one of the NCAR scientists to look at the Sun and to record something about it

Excess Homicide
A Four Corners Mystery

I don't understand. Sunspots or something. This guy, the inventor, he's retired now. But NCAR asks him to polish up this old telescope for the President's visit. There was another newspaper story about this, in the *Denver Post*, one of those human interest things. So they pack it up and the guy works on it in his garage. When you expressed interest in making your statement, well, I figured this was an opportunity not to pass up. So we, ah, worked with this old guy to help him polish up his telescope. That's how we got the equipment installed. The rifle is inside the telescope tube, mounted so that it can fire down into the main part of the lobby from the balcony it's sitting on. It's completely hidden, so no one will find it unless they completely disassemble the whole thing. The camera is also inside the tube, but the lens is on the outside. It looks just like it's supposed to be part of the instrument."

Schoenfield was staring at the ceiling, trying to find flaws. "And so it's in place and all you have to do is use the remote controller to turn it on and watch for the target. What's the plan for your cover? The remote doesn't have lots of range, I expect."

"Pest control. We've got signs and uniforms to make the van look just like a pest control truck. It'll need paint, too, but that's easy. That way, we can park in the subdivision down the hill from the laboratory and be inconspicuous. That's within the range of the transmitter. Then we wait, trigger the rifle when we see a chance, and drive away while there's still confusion at the laboratory. Then we'll take the signs off the truck, probably down in the parking lot of that big shopping center at the base of the hill, change clothes, and head back here."

"Right. And this old guy. The retired scientist who first invented this, this telescope instrument you got access to?"

"Well, he's decided to take a long, long trip to a remote place. Left in a big hurry. No one knows his itinerary." Pickle didn't succeed in looking innocent.

"Sounds solid. And you got that special message on the bottom of the controller box, right? It'll be amusing, and it'll confuse things further."

"All set."

"Great. Now. How are you coming with plans to deal with Mr. High-and-Mighty Charles Shure?"

Pickle looked uncomfortable, and Mad Dog's eye wandered more randomly than ever.

"That's going to be a tough one, Senator. See, he's got this driver, the same one who was up this way last month, who's really more of a body guard. And he's using an armored car these days. You said you wanted an accident, and so we've been trying to fix some kind of traffic deal. But I don't know."

"Hmm. Let me think some more about it. I don't guess there's any real hurry. In fact, if we wait, he'll become less and less concerned and maybe ease up on the security a bit. Stop using that armored car, drive himself, and so on. Or maybe we can think of another kind of accident. He must fly places. How about some kind of airplane accident?"

"He has a corporate jet and a helicopter. And he flies commercial a lot. I'm not sure I could get a commercial plane down, though. And, anyway, remember that all aircraft accidents are investigated by the feds, right? And, of course, airport security is a tough nut these days. Isn't there some other way we could get back at this guy?"

Excess Homicide
A Four Corners Mystery

Schoenfield, although autocratic, also knew when to listen to advice, especially from an expert such as this.

"Got something in mind, Pickle?"

"Well, do we really need a hit? I mean, couldn't we get him through his company, or something like that? From what you've told me, his company is his life."

"Yeah, well, I own stock in that company, and I sure don't want to shoot myself in the foot."

"So sell it. Divest. Then we could call Timmy and see if he has any ideas."

A smile materialized on Schoenfield's grim face, little by little becoming an intense, evil grin. His left eye twitched a little.

"Timmy. Sure. I hadn't thought of him. He does good work, doesn't he?"

MOSTLY, Hal's habit of coming in around mid-morning in the summer worked fine. He could get some work done in the peace and quiet of home, and nothing much was happening up on campus anyway.

On the other hand, sometimes, there was.

He arrived at about 10:00 the next day, looking forward, for once, to the budget meeting he had scheduled with the provost at 11:00. He was going to be able to present John Martin with some good news: his college was going to finish the fiscal year with a slight surplus. And there was nothing else on his schedule.

But then he walked into his office, into the ante-room, Alice's little domain. And there on the couch, nodding, presumably, to whatever was emanating from his headphones, was a young man, a student by his age. Coffee-colored skin, fairly well muscled, far too tall to fit comfortably on the couch—his knees were practically touching his chin—probably a student athlete. At least he should be, Hal thought. The basketball team could use all the help it could get.

"Morning Alice."

"Good morning, Dean Weathers. This is Jamal Washington. Here to see you." She raised her voice a few decibels. "Mr. Washington? MR. WASHINGTON?"

His eyes opened, and he smiled and began to unfold himself from the couch. The process went on for some time, and included his pushing a button on the gadget the earphones were plugged into and removing them from his head. Finally, he was standing, towering over Hal by about a foot.

"Mr. Washington, this is Dean Weathers. Dean Weathers, Mr. Washington tells me he was sent over here by the Athletic Director to discuss tutoring."

Hal's synapses clicked into place. Feeling short, he extended a hand, in an upward direction, to the student.

"Nice to meet you, Mr. Washington. Come in to my office. I think I have a chair that will fit you better than this couch."

They settled themselves—Hal's side chair was still far too small—and Hal guessed that the young man would be shy.

"So Charlie, I mean, the Athletic Director, sent you over to talk to me about tutoring, hmm?"

"Yes, sir. He wants my grades up so I'll be eligible to play this fall."

"Play..."

"Play ball. Basketball. I've got a scholarship, but my grades are, um, too low."

Excess Homicide
A Four Corners Mystery

"What about you? Do you want your grades up? I mean, sure you do, so you can play. But what about besides that?"

"Well, my Momma would sure like that. And I guess I would, too. But the science course I signed up for looks pretty tough for me. And I don't know about the computer course."

Hal smiled, a friendly smile, he hoped, and looked out the window.

"Jamal Washington. Now why does that name ring a bell? Do I remember your name from the all-state team?"

"Well, I was on the all-state team. On the Parade All-American Team, first team, too."

"Right! That's right. And you took a scholarship to come here, huh? How come? I mean, you must have been recruited by the big-time schools, Duke and Arizona and so on."

"My Momma, she wanted me to come here. My brother went here, and she was real impressed with the school."

"Your brother..."

"Radford. He played football. He graduated a couple of years ago."

"Radford Washington? Oh, yeah. Defensive lineman when we won the national championship. I met him a couple of times. A good guy. Big, but not as tall as you. Fast. And smart. He always seemed to know if a play was going to be a run or a pass. Sacked a lot of quarterbacks that way. Let's see. He went to the Bears in the second round, right?"

Jamal was clearly impressed with Hal's knowledge of Frémont State sports. "Yeah, but he busted up his knee in training camp. But, see, what impressed my Momma so much was that he got a job in the Bears' front office, on

163

account of his education here. So here I am. Also, it's a lot closer to Denver than Duke and some of those other schools that offered me scholarships. And my Momma, she wasn't going to let me go up to Boulder, no way."

"I don't remember you from last year's team, so this is going to be your first year?"

"Well, I was here, red-shirted so I could get my grades up. Also so I could put on some weight. Coach, he says that I'll get knocked around out there and I need to be stronger. So I've been trying to bulk up and get my balance improved, stuff like that. Anyway, I thought I was doing OK with my grades. But then some committee changed the rules."

"Oh. Right. Well, it's appropriate that you're here, because that's my fault. I was on that committee. We raised the requirements earlier this month. Sorry."

"It's OK. I just have to get 'A's—in that Intro to Natural Science course I'm going to take this summer and that computer course, and I should be OK to play. Before, 'B's would have been good enough."

"Are you worried about the courses?"

"Well, they look hard, but no. Um, mostly, no. But I don't know about an 'A,' especially in that science course. That's, like, something different for me."

Well, normally a 'B' in that course would be something to be proud of. We designed the course to be challenging."

"What's covered?"

"Just what it says, 'Introduction to Natural Sciences.' A little geography, geology, weather and climate and some oceanography, some ecology, and so on. It's the first third of the elective sequence for the general majors, like that university studies program. Are you in that?"

Excess Homicide
A Four Corners Mystery

"No, I'm in theater and dance. I figured the dance part would help my moves on the court. And I kind of like acting. What are the other electives?"

"Two other courses in the departments. You pick based on what you're interested in, like a geology course and an ecology course."

"You said weather, huh? Maybe I'll take that one. People are always asking me 'How's the weather up there?' and I need a snappy answer."

"Hey, get interested in it, combine it with theater training, and become the world's tallest TV weather guy. In the meantime tell them that it's OK but that the contrails make you sneeze."

"Say what? Uh, sir?"

"Contrails. You know, those stripes of clouds that are made by jets, condensation trails. Someone asks you how the weather is up there and you hit them with that one. A snappy answer that will shut them up. When it gets worn out, we can think up another one. The more absurd the better. Unless you like being asked that kind of thing."

"Well, no, I really don't. It makes me uncomfortable."

"I don't blame you. Hit 'em with something like that contrail answer, though, and I bet they stop asking."

"Uh, I'll think about it. But what about the weather guy thing?"

"Sure. You're good looking, you speak well, especially for your age, and you said you like acting. Learn some weather stuff and get a job with a TV station. After your basketball career, I mean. But first we've got to get you to an 'A' this summer. Let me make a couple of phone calls and we'll set you up with a tutor. And you can always come and see me if you need a second opinion, like another explanation for confusing things. Like the Coriolis force."

"What's that?"

"It's what makes weather systems spin, you know, like you see on satellite loops on TV."

"Coriolis? That some foreign word?"

"A guy's name, who first figured it out. I think. Anyway, a famous weather guy from a hundred years ago, or more, I guess. Point is, the Coriolis force gets everyone confused the first time through. If you can't understand it well enough to explain it to your teammates, come see me and I'll help you with it."

"Well, thanks. I don't think the AD was expecting a dean to tutor me, though."

"Probably not. But it's summer and I have the time. Besides, it'll make the basketball season that much more interesting for me. And we can also help you find a computer tutor, if you need one."

"Cool. I appreciate it. I'm good with computer games but, uh, I kind of think that the course will cover other things. I'm sure I'll need help."

"That's why we're here. We'll help and try to make this as interesting for you as we can."

"SO, THAT'S HER STORY and she's sticking with it, huh?" Derek Petersen was amused, in contrast to Annette's disgust.

"Yep. It's always remarkable to me that people believe they can conjure truth from fiction. And consider the contrast between Charles Shure and his driver the other day and this Markham person. The story they told left us satisfied, like dinner at a four-star restaurant. The story told

Excess Homicide
A Four Corners Mystery

by Markham and her lawyer was more like scrounging appetizers from a dumpster. And they expect us to believe it."

"Has she identified this boyfriend?"

"That's our next step. She's shielding him, for now. The lawyer, this guy from Cortez, Tompkins, I think, was whispering in her ear the whole time. Actually, it was surprising. He seemed more nervous than she. I checked on him, and he's not really a criminal attorney, just an environmental lawyer. Sues the Forest Service a lot, on behalf of advocacy groups. So why he's representing her is another interesting question. She insisted on him."

They were sitting in Derek's cluttered office catching up on each other's work load. As much as she was bored with it, Annette knew she needed to stay informed about her budget and other administrative matters, and she had quickly learned that Derek appreciated being kept up to date on the progress of investigations. As Annette was staring out the window trying to talk herself into a better mood, Sally Brigman walked in.

"Oh, here you are. I was just going to ask Mr. Petersen if he knew where you went. This fax just came in for you." She handed Annette a sheaf of papers.

"Thanks, Sally. Hmm. Five pages from the Mineral County Sheriff. You know him, Derek?"

"Sure. Ralph Wertlinger. Under-funded, under-paid, over-worked. Mineral County is one of the poor ones. Good guy, but stuck in a lousy situation."

"Says here his guys found a corpse. No, some lumber mill guys found it and called Ralph's guys. Let's see. Looks like an accident, sort of. White male carrying the Colorado Driver's License of one David Wellington, of Alamosa, crushed beneath a collapsed log pile. Along with his car. The body looks like the CDL picture, as much as they can tell through the damage and decomposition."

"A lumber-mill accident? Not unusual, although they don't happen nearly as often as they did in the old days."

"Except that they have questions." Annette began ticking items off on her fingers. "Like, what was the victim doing there? Why did the pile collapse? Why was he out of his car? Uh, he was found between the crushed car and the center of the pile. It says his pants were unzipped so they're speculating he was taking a leak. And when did this happen? Looks like it was several days ago, but they don't know exactly, yet."

"They asking for help?"

"Not here." She had shuffled rapidly through the paper. "They're just letting us know what they have. A note here says that we'll see it in the paper, but they wanted to inform us officially."

"Protocol. You'll find that some of the counties are better than others. Like I said, Ralph's a good guy."

"You've met him, then?"

"A couple of times. Talked on the phone a few times, too."

"Maybe we could call him and you could introduce me. On the speaker."

"I hate those things. But, yeah, that's a good idea. Is there a number on that fax?"

She shuffled through the paper some more, and he dug around on his desktop, looking for the speaker phone. She found a number, and he found the phone.

"Sheriff's office, Darla speakin'."

Excess Homicide
A Four Corners Mystery

"Darla, this is Derek Petersen, CBI over in Durango. We just got a fax from you folks. Is Ralph around?"

"Did you get all five pages? I never trust this thing."

"All five, nice and clear."

"Great. Here's Ralph."

"Derek! How are ya? I hear you got stuck behind a desk."

"I did indeed. Think I'm already gaining weight. Ralph, I want to introduce you to Bob Weldon's replacement, Annette Trieri. She's here on a speaker phone."

"Sheriff Wertlinger, nice to talk with you. I'm planning to get over your way as soon as I get the chance, so I can meet you personally. I'm sorry that I've been too busy getting my feet under me to make it over there yet."

"I understand completely. Don't think of it. Nice to talk with you as well, Ms. Trieri. We've heard a lot about you. Good things. I bet you're calling about that fax we sent your way."

"Indeed we are. I'm impressed with how complete it is, given that you just found the body this morning."

"Well, superficially, it's transparent. Guy's hanging around a pile of logs that collapses and squishes him. And his car. Naturally, we're looking beyond the superficial. And that's not quite so transparent."

"My thoughts also."

"We found out a little more about him since this morning, assuming he was carrying his own driver's license. He was an environmental activist from Alamosa. Worked at Adams State College, in the admissions office. I'm told he was trying to get a student group started, probably modeled on one of the groups over your way, at Frémont State."

"Are there specific indications that this wasn't an accident?"

"Well, that's one of the things we're looking into. Ya see, this happened some days ago, maybe a week. The guys at the mill finally figured out something was wrong by the smell. Nobody noticed it before because the log pile looked just like all the others."

Annette looked at Derek Petersen, puzzled. "Huh?"

"Well, see, this pile of logs collapsed and squished this guy, but it collapsed into the same size and, uh, configuration as all the other ones, their usual stack of big logs. So that means it was different before it collapsed. So maybe someone set this up, by re-piling the logs in that pile in a way so that they'd collapse back into the original configuration. And then they pushed them over on this guy Wellington."

Annette looked startled and sat down, carefully, in Derek Petersen's side chair.

"Sheriff? One reason I was hired here was to tackle a case, or set of cases, that haven't received much publicity. Over the past year or so there have been nine or ten suspicious deaths, some definitely murder, of people active in environmental issues. All here in the Four Corners region. A couple in New Mexico, one in Arizona, one in Utah. All with very clean crime scenes, and a couple possibly accidental. Your crushed guy sounds like he could be part of this pattern."

"Well that sure puts a different light on things."

"The other Colorado cases are all over the place. A double murder, a car bomb, west of Antonito; an execution—bullet in the back of the head—at the Four Corners Monument; a car accident over by Cedaredge;

Excess Homicide
A Four Corners Mystery

another double homicide up in Boulder. And, just last month, another execution over by Norwood, with the same gun as the Four Corners Monument one. One of the two in New Mexico could have been an accident, guy fell off the Taos bridge into the Rio Grande Gorge. The other one, and the ones in Arizona and Utah, were definitely homicides."

"Ma'am, could I put you on hold for just a second? I want to call my guys over at the scene and tell them we've got a homicide on our hands, probably." They heard the clunk of the receiver's being set down and then a jumble of background noise, including mumbling sounds that could only have been instructions.

"Hello? You folks still there? Thanks for holding on."

"Would you like us to send a forensics team over? Uh, I don't mean to suggest you folks can't handle things, you understand. It just seems like we should offer." Annette was treading carefully. Her relationships with the sheriffs of the counties around Durango were solid, but she hadn't dealt with Mineral County before. Getting off on the right foot seemed wise.

"Well, I don't know that it'd be worth the effort. I mean, thanks for the offer and all, but I don't think there's much here. We'll take the car to our garage and go over it carefully, and it'll be there if you want to have a look at it. So there's no hurry there. And the scene was pretty well disturbed by the time all the logs got moved off the body and the car. The guys from the mill are saying that it looks as if the logs were moved about a week ago, they were looking at cuts on the bark and so on. Which would fit with someone fixing that pile so it would collapse easily. That, I mean moving the logs, would require machines, but all of the mill's big machinery has been in use ever since. So there's not going to be anything there to find. We'll do an autopsy, of course, but I don't think anything remarkable will come from that. This guy Wellington was squished by the logs, pure and simple. And we're already working with the folks in Alamosa, looking for anything at his residence. Maybe there will be something in his files or in his mail, or something like that."

"Well, if there's anything we can do, please do call us in. I'm told it's our job to help and not to grab headlines or credit from you folks. And it seems like that's the way things have been done, according to the sheriffs I know from around here. It'll sure be the way I'm going to run things."

"Tell you what, Ms. Trieri. You take the headlines and I'll take the credit. If I get in the papers too much, nobody around here is going to vote for me no matter what. Anyway, we'll keep you up to date on what we find out. And we'll yell for help if we need it, you can be sure."

"Don't hesitate. Nice talking with you. I'll get over your way as soon as I can."

TIMOTHY LANGER WAS FRUSTRATED, stage four in the evolution of his emotions. He was finding the process of trying to hack his way into the UNELECO servers to be an emotional roller-coaster. At first he'd been surprised and amused that he couldn't work his way in via the usual back-door security holes. But they were all patched, some by means of algorithms he'd never heard of, never even dreamed of. Then he was outraged that the sophisticated tricks he knew of to gain access via the UNELECO web site didn't work—they always did, *always*. But UNELECO's web site, the interesting part, had some kind of triply

Excess Homicide
A Four Corners Mystery

circular firewall system, and getting through that required use of two separate one-time-only passwords. After that, when his personal bag of e-mail tricks failed him, he was simply in awe. Now, while waiting for a brute-force attack to have its inevitable success, he was getting frustrated. Bored from waiting and frustrated from failure.

Normally, he'd simply find something else to do while waiting, but he was under no little pressure. This particular client, unlike others, was not interested in excuses, no matter how valid they might be. He wanted results, yesterday. Because the brute-force attack simply could not be rushed, however, Timothy was forced to wait. And wait. And hope that his client wouldn't call to check on progress.

It made him feel better that it was only this first time through the firewalls that would require patience. Once inside, he would set up a hidden login account, probably piggy-backed onto an existing administrative one, and in the future it would be trivial. But for now, patience was more than a virtue, it was mandatory. There was simply no choice.

With the waiting, he had time to think. It occurred to him that he really didn't have a plan once his attack succeeded. Of course, there would be the usual housekeeping to be done, associated with creating his hidden login and so on. But his instructions were simply to snoop around and see what kind of system UNELECO had and what its vulnerabilities might be. This, he realized, reflected merely the computational naïveté of his client, because he knew that he wouldn't be finding one system but rather a network of all sorts of systems, each with its own peculiarities and vulnerabilities. Once inside the UNELECO firewall, these vulnerabilities would be unprotected,

Timothy figured, at least if his experience with other corporate and governmental local area networks was any indication.

Remembering his experience made him smile. The worst was that server at the state police headquarters. Of course, they were cops, not computer jocks, but, really, there was no excuse for that sloppy level of security. He'd had no trouble at all tapping into their files. This had made his client very happy indeed. On the other hand, the best security so far was at Microsoft. Maybe because they developed their own operating system, they knew how to keep it secure. Or maybe they were all just afraid of Uncle Bill. Others that should be solid really weren't, like at the CIA and some of the other three-letter agencies in Washington. But they were pretty good, he thought, and that would keep everyone out but experts like himself.

He wondered if the UNELECO network would include its classified servers as well as all of the other ones. He'd seen from their public web site that they did a lot of work for the military, and their job postings talked a lot about ability to get and maintain security clearances. Classified systems were always a little more challenging than open systems, so he was hoping he'd be able to find some to try to get into. He liked challenges.

He was startled from his reverie by the ringing telephone, his cell phone making tweedling noises.

"Hello? This is Tim."

"Timmy, my boy. How are things going? Making any progress?"

"Oh, hello, sir. So far, it's not the kind of progress I'd like, but it is progress. I found out what won't work. Now

Excess Homicide
A Four Corners Mystery

I'm trying what will, but it's a slow process." Tim hoped his nervousness didn't come through in his voice.

"I thought you told me it would be finished by now."

"Ah, well, sir, I told you that I hoped it would be. But it turns out that these folks have quite solid computer security. And now all I can do is work my way in by brute force."

"What does that mean?"

"Well, I found the names of various accounts on their systems by looking carefully at the UNELECO web site. Now what I'm doing is trying to access one of those accounts by using passwords in sequence, the computer does it from passwords from in a dictionary, sort of. So it just takes time."

"What if they notice all the failed attempts?"

"This is always an issue, but what I'm doing is rotating among login names rather than using the same one all the time. And I set it up so that it will look to their computer as if these attempts are coming from different places, so they shouldn't notice anything strange. See, this kind of thing happens to big systems all the time."

"How long?"

"I really can't say precisely. It's never taken longer than three days with other systems, though. Uh, sir? One thing I thought of is that I really don't know what to look for when I'm in there snooping around. Could you give me some guidance?"

"What I want you to do is to get established on the UNELECO network without arousing suspicion. Then we wait a few days to let dust settle and let you figure out what their network is like, what kinds of computers and all that. I remember when you set up your access on the state patrol and CBI system that it took you some time to figure out its layout. UNELECO's is probably lots bigger and more complicated. So when you get in there, check out the layout, and then I'll get back to you in a few days. But first you've got to get in. Is there some way to speed up the process?"

"Well, I could use a more powerful system than this one I have here at home."

"Why aren't you doing that already? You know I'm in a hurry. And you know how I dislike waiting." Langer shuddered at the implied threat.

"I could use one of the systems at the university, but that would increase the risk, some. And I know that you want this to be done carefully."

"But you know I'm in a hurry. Why would it increase the risk? And how would it speed things up?"

"A more powerful computer, like a real workstation, could run lots of my scripts in parallel, try lots of logins simultaneously, sort of. But sometimes the systems people watch processes and someone could notice what I'm doing. That's never happened to me, but it could."

"Timmy, you know I'm in a hurry. Let's pick up the pace, OK? After all, I'm paying you quite handsomely for this, aren't I? And I'm also keeping quiet about our little secret, aren't I?"

"Yes, sir, Senator, you are, on both counts. And I appreciate it, I really do. I'll speed things up as much as I can, I promise."

"You do that, Timmy. I'll give you a call tomorrow to see how things are going."

"Yes sir. I'll give it everything I've got, to get into that system."

Excess Homicide
A Four Corners Mystery

There was the sound of a telephone receiver being clunked down on the other end, but Timothy was shaking too much to hear it.

H. P. Hanson

TEN

THE STORY FINALLY APPEARED in the next morning's papers. "Alamosa Resident Crushed at Creede Lumber Mill" led into the *Durango Herald's* subdued treatment, in which the facts were reported along with remaining questions, and a brief biography of David Wellington served as an obituary. The *Frémont Free Press*, true to form, played up the industrial accident angle and declared Wellington to be a hero with its headline "Environmentalist Martyred at Mill." The story talked of conspiracies spun by the logging industry, of Wellington's valiant fight to preserve old-growth forests, and of the day in the future when trees would be accorded the same rights as people.

Steve Rutherford's heart was with the *Free Press*, but his head was with the *Herald*. It was clear to him that there were unanswered questions, but surely, he thought, they would be the object of an investigation, if not by the sheriff over in Creede then by the timber company. He knew some of the people who ran the mill there, including the owners of the mom-and-pop outfit calling itself Upper Rio Industries, and there was no way that they were part of a conspiracy. The *Free Press* was full of it. But, still, there were some strange inconsistencies.

If this weren't bad news enough, it appeared that his friends in SCREW had taken the name of their organization

Excess Homicide
A Four Corners Mystery

a little too literally. Tompkins had called, from Lolly's place, according to Rutherford's caller ID, at 7:00 this morning. He wanted them all to get together to discuss how to deal with Lolly's legal predicament. It seemed that the CBI was insisting that Lolly produce this boyfriend with whom she'd been staying in Monticello. Plan A, Tompkins said, was for Rutherford to play the part. On his drive over to Lolly's, Rutherford was working hard on formulating a Plan B. For one thing, he wasn't going to just play at being Lolly's boyfriend while Tompkins was actually enjoying being her boyfriend. For another, he had already thought through the down side: how would he explain to the CBI and the Utah cops about those license plates?

He pulled up in front of Lolly's small bungalow on the west bluff. The neighborhood had undergone a renaissance over the past couple of decades, with most of the small houses, originally built by the coal company for its workers, having been remodeled and upgraded to modern standards. Lolly had mentioned wanting to remodel her house but, obviously, this hadn't happened yet. It needed new siding and a roof, and window upgrades seemed in order. The yard was also neglected compared to the neighbors.

Rutherford gathered his thoughts as well as the newspapers. Tompkins hadn't mentioned anything about Wellington during the earlier phone call, and they all needed to discuss that one as well as how to play Lolly's story, so he'd brought reference material.

As he was getting out of the car, he heard a noise from the house and looked up to see Lolly hurrying down the walk toward him. Wearing, well, not much. A lightweight summer bathrobe over a nightie. Both pretty transparent. Damn, he thought, they *are* big.

H. P. Hanson

"Bobby, baby, I thought you'd never get here! I'm so glad to see you!" She waltzed around the car to where he was standing, threw her arms around him, and planted her mouth squarely on his. He felt her tongue insinuating itself between his teeth.

After a long time, at least what felt like a long time, during which she ground her body into his, she stepped back and batted her eyes at him.

"C'mon into the house, honey. Have I got a surprise for you." She waggled her backside, which made the rest of her waggle in syncopation. Why, he wondered, was she talking so damned loud? Then she practically hauled him up the walk to the front door.

Once inside, it all changed.

"Whew!" She was out of breath, and blushing. "Steve, I'm sorry for that, but we thought we should put on a show for those cops out there. Maybe they got some good pictures. Excuse me, I've got to go put some clothes on." And she dashed down the hall, her bottom in sublime motion beneath the filmy fabric, and closed a door behind her. Rutherford stood, dumbfounded, staring down the hall.

"I don't think it'll win any Academy Awards, but maybe it'll help." Tompkins' voice from the living room behind him made Rutherford spin around, his anger rising as his erection fell.

"What the hell was that all about? I thought we were going to discuss this whole thing, but now you've got me up to my eyeballs in it. Goddammit! There's no need to keep getting in deeper with this. All we have to do is stand on the story that we have. Putting me in jeopardy isn't going to make things better!"

Excess Homicide
A Four Corners Mystery

"Steve, Steve, calm down. The CBI wants this boyfriend for questioning. Lolly's dead meat unless we produce him. It's got to be you."

"No it doesn't. She can claim she doesn't know him well enough. You gave them a name, right? A name she was supposed to say she thought was fake, right? Just stick with the damned story, man! Except now it's too late."

Tompkins tilted his head to the side and stared.

"Hmm. Maybe not. I think maybe we just increased our options. Thing is, they released Lolly on recognizance while they check out her story. Said they would probably want to talk with her again and that they wanted to find this boyfriend. We didn't promise to produce him, though. Maybe we could stick with the story. It would make her out to be something of a slut, though. Going off for a weekend with a guy whose real name she doesn't know. I mean, the story so far is that her boyfriend is 'Bob Jones,' who probably registered at the Super 8 with a fake name. But 'Bob Jones' could also be a fake name. We, I mean, Lolly, already told them that she'd met this guy only recently."

"She called me 'Bobby' out there, man. If the cops were listening... hey, what cops? I didn't see any cars out there with people in them. Who was that show for?"

"I was watching. Across the street and three cars down. They ducked when you drove by. But they were watching the performance. And it sounded to me like 'Baby, baby,' so our options are still open."

"Well, let's exercise those options. Better she should come across to the cops as a slut than have me questioned about the license plates and everything else. The more people we have trying to tell the same lie, the more likely we're going to screw up."

"Who's a slut?" Lolly emerged, wearing jeans and a tee shirt, both opaque, to Rutherford's simultaneous disappointment and, because he really didn't need the distraction, relief.

"Nobody, at least not here. What we were saying is that maybe we can avoid producing your boyfriend, this Bob Jones character, by just letting them think you are. What if 'Bob Jones' turns out to be a fake name, too? You don't know where he lives, or his phone number. You just met him in a bar and then went off for a weekend in Moab with him."

"I guess that would make me kind of a slut, wouldn't it?"

"But who cares what they think, as long as this all fades away? It's like this: They let you go, you stay around and act cooperative, and this Bob Jones character never calls or anything so you don't know how to find him. He's a jerk, love 'em and leave 'em, wham-bam thank you ma'am, all that. You're pissed at him for not calling. But since he hasn't, you can't put the cops onto him. Does this make sense?" Tompkins had bought into the story completely, to Rutherford's relief.

"It sure makes sense to me. Lolly can kiss me any time she takes a notion to, but we've got to quit embellishing this story, or we're dead." Rutherford was watching Lolly as he said this, and he was gratified to see her blush again. It made him tingle.

"Well, I guess so. I guess I really don't care what the cops think of me. I mean, who are they to judge? So, I just sit tight and wait for them to call me?"

"Sure. Life goes on, things are normal, all that."

"Right. And I'm not the boyfriend of the story no matter the little charade out there. Now. Did you guys hear about Dave?" Rutherford plopped the newspapers on Lolly's coffee table.

The plopping noise, transmitted cleanly through the single-pane picture window in Lolly's living room and picked up by the ultra-sensitive directional microphone aimed at it, made the two undercover officers, one from Utah and one local, wince. In unison, they removed their headphones and griped, the Colorado officer with the more colorful language. Consequently, they missed the part of the conversation inside the house about Wellington's connection to SCREW and whether the Creede sheriff would bring the others into his investigation.

But the tape machine didn't miss anything.

EVEN THOUGH it was something of an emergency meeting, it needed to be formal, very formal. Hal had therefore asked Alice to have Jamie McFarland wait for ten minutes and then to call him on the intercom. He disliked using such intimidating tactics, but sometimes they were for the best. He needed Jamie to be off balance for this one, even if the wait did make her a bit angry. When Alice finally buzzed him, he asked her to send Jamie in.

"Come in, Jamie, please sit down. Sorry to keep you waiting." Hal was sitting behind his desk, in the Power Seat, and the chair he indicated for Jamie was across from him. Annette sat off to one side of Hal, also in a position of superiority.

"No problem, Dean Weathers. What did you need to see me about?" She didn't appear to be overly nervous, Hal noted.

H. P. Hanson

"A telephone call that found its way to me this morning. We have a problem with our systems." Jamie, the computer systems administrator for the natural sciences college, instantly went on alert.

"Why would someone call you about a systems problem?"

"The nature of the problem. The fact that the call got routed to me via Provost Martin's office is a clue to its severity. Another clue is sitting here. Let me introduce Annette Trieri, Colorado Bureau of Investigation. She's the director of the CBI's southwest office here. The reason I asked you to come in is that we need your help. It seems that someone has been using our systems to try to hack into the computers of UNELECO, some of which are military classified systems. UNELECO has a whiz-bang computer security shop and they traced the attempts to our systems." Hal was holding back the bombshell for now.

"Uh, what's UNELECO?"

"A conglomerate based in Colorado Springs. They got their start in electronics and they still do a lot of R&D work for the military. But they're also involved in a lot of other things. For example, the outfit that ran that mill over in Utah that got burned down last month—remember?—that's a UNELECO division, Forest Fiber Products. But this computer attack was on their corporate server network, which includes the military R&D. Their computer security people have been watching this hacker trying to weasel his way in for some time. Initially, it was happening slowly, the attempts, I mean. Then last night, it picked up and that's when they were able to trace things back to our systems. Before, the attempts were routed through faked-up accounts on a variety of those freebie e-mail hosts floating around out there."

"Our systems, hmm? Well, I can do a process check and see what's been happening for the past couple of days. But I haven't noticed any unusual activity, not that I've been really watching for any."

Time for the bombshell, Hal thought.

"Well, Jamie, one thing that you should know is that this hacker has been using your login account for his attacks."

"What?! How can that be? I have a truly random password, and I change it all the time. And the system root password changes every time. And only I and Bill Brooks have the list. It's not Bill, I'm certain. And of course it's not me. I've got far better things to do. Maybe I have a hidden account on our systems, one that I don't know about."

"Hidden account? What's that?"

"Well, it's possible, if you get system access and know the right tricks, to set up an invisible user account that sort of piggy-backs on a real user. Everything that this piggy-backer does looks as if it's being done by the real user. So someone must be piggy-backing on me and trying to get into these UNELECO computers that way."

Annette cleared her throat gently.

"Ms. McFarland, because I don't know you at all, I'm a neutral observer in this. Dean Weathers, of course, knows you and is therefore biased. I'm sure that you can see that, from a neutral perspective, you'd be under some suspicion here?"

"Naturally. And the best way for me to deal with it, I assume, is to help you, and UNELECO, figure out just what's going on. I infer from what's been said that the hacking attempts have not been successful so far, is that right?"

"That's our inference, too, although I'm not sure that the UNELECO computer people would tell us if they were successful. Whatever the case, it would be nice to catch whoever's doing this. Using state property, that is, your computers, for this is potentially a felony."

"Especially if there's an attack on a military system. That could be a federal felony, I suppose. Normally, what I'd do in a case like this would be to rebuild my login, or the login of whoever's being piggy-backed on. That would wipe out the hidden account. But I guess we need to stick with this and figure out who it is and how they're getting access to our systems."

"Say, I bet it's via an incoming phone line. UNELECO told us that the attack was slow until last night. There could be a phone connection to those floating e-mail hosts. But a phone connection to our systems would allow lots of attempts to be created and run in parallel, right, Jamie?" Hal was confident that Jamie wasn't behind the attack on UNELECO, and he wanted to enlist her help immediately.

"Could be. We've upgraded our modem pool to have caller ID automated and logged, so if that's the case, we should be able to find who's doing this pretty easily. But then what?"

Annette was ready for that one.

"You ID this person and we'll take it from there. I'll call Charles Shure, he's CEO of UNELECO, I know him from something else, and find out if they want to press charges or what. If you can provide documentation from your system's logs of this person's activities, we have him, or her, for misuse of state property, at least. And if

Excess Homicide
A Four Corners Mystery

UNELECO wants their pound of flesh, well, we can get it for them as well. And if UNELECO's secure computers, the classified ones, are involved, well, the FBI may want a piece of this fool."

Jamie's indignation finally spilled over.

"Hey, *I* want a piece of this fool! I say we stick his head on a pike for all to see. If we make a big enough example of him, maybe others will take their hacking skills elsewhere."

"If it's a student, I have a better idea." Hal knew an opportunity for free tutoring help when he saw one.

STAGE TWO was by invitation only. Because there would be fewer people attending, stage two meetings were to be held in central locations, and the first, the kick-off meeting, was held in a church basement in Cortez. Invitations had gone out to people in all four states, and a good turnout was expected despite the dominance of Indian Nations in the immediate vicinity. The church—the Temple of Jesus Our Savior—didn't really know the purpose of the "prayer meeting" that the Right Reverend Dr. Michael Oswald had organized, they just appreciated the color of his money.

Oswald checked off names from his invitation list as the men—and all were men—came in through the side door. Farmington and Aztec, New Mexico; Bluff, Blanding, and Monticello, Utah; and a variety of small towns near Cortez in Colorado was represented. Notable for its absence was Arizona, but the northeast corner of Arizona is the land of the *Diné*, and this meeting was not for Native Americans, nor anyone else of non-Aryan background.

After all of the names were checked off, Oswald closed the doors and strolled to the front of the big meeting room.

He faced the crowd, a big smile on his face, and waited for the various conversations to subside.

"Evening, everyone. Glad to see y'all here, glad you were able to come. I expect that you've had a chance to look around the room, to check out the others here. I see that some of you know others—I hope that you have a chance to get to know the people you don't. And I hope you appreciate that you're among people you can trust. Every one of you got an invitation to be here, because we know you are with us. We're all starting out on the same page here, and the purpose of our little gathering is to turn some pages together and wind up at the end of the same story. This make sense?"

There was reluctant nodding, a murmuring of agreement in the audience.

"Great!" Oswald was familiar with how long it takes to get a group, especially a new group, worked up.

"Now," he continued, his voice warming to the oration, "Y'all were at one or the other of our first set of meetings, what we refer to as our 'stage-one' meetings. This is stage two. By invitation only. That's because we're going to discuss some things that require trust. If we don't trust each other, well, there's potential for trouble. So we've got to have agreement that what's said in here stays in this room, OK?"

Again, the murmuring, but this time a hand shot up, from near the back.

"Got a question? In the back, there? How about introducing yourself, OK?"

"Uh, yeah, I'm George Sm... Uh, George, from uh, Utah. What about people I trust, people who aren't here that I'd like to bring in to this?"

Excess Homicide
A Four Corners Mystery

"Right. Great question, actually, because we need more recruits. Let me make a suggestion and see what you think of it. Eventually, we want to bring as many people into this as we can. We'll figure out how to do that as we go along. But now, at first, we need to develop trust among ourselves, and we need to keep this whole thing pretty close, so that it develops a strong foundation. I worry that if we start bringing in too many people too soon, we run the risk of weakening that foundation. So, is it OK to keep things within this group here for now? What do you think, George?" Oswald was staring directly at the nervous individual standing in the second row from the back.

"Uh, sure, OK, sounds good." And he sat down abruptly, obviously relieved. To be under Oswald's close scrutiny gave him the willies.

"Good. Thanks for the question. Now. You'll recall that we have behind us the resources of an outfit called Resources For Humanity. This organization is privately funded, so there aren't any of those stupid restrictions on it that the government has. And it, I mean Resources for Humanity, wants to return the use of the land to the people who live on it. Us. For us to use and prosper. For us to be able to raise our families the way we know is right. Right? Remember this?" He knew they did, so he plunged ahead.

"So what we're here for now is to decide how to make this happen. How to reach these goals. It's pretty clear that what we need to do is to figure out how to get the roadblocks out of our way, the roadblocks that are preventing us from using the land to help us prosper. So. What does that mean? Well, we have to ask what those roadblocks are. Anybody got any ideas?" Oswald was wondering just how long he'd have to wait to get someone from the audience to volunteer an answer. Not long, it turned out.

"The damned feds!" The audience mumbled agreement with that sentiment.

"Yeah, the Forest Service."

"And the EPA!"

"The tree-huggers!"

"Colorado Department of Wildlife!" The noise level had increased enough for Oswald, so he held up his hands to calm things down.

"This is wonderful. You guys obviously know what I'm talking about. And how to get rid of roadblocks like those is a good question. Even the tree-huggers are pretty damned tenacious. Some of you probably remember the old days, when we used to just beat the snot out of them. Right, I think it was pretty funny, too. But that's not so effective any more. First, the media gets hold of the story and blows it way out of proportion. Second, they get lawyers. And, of course, the feds and the state guys are even worse—some of them *are* lawyers, and the others are almost cops.

"I don't know how many of you guys remember your high-school English classes, but I bet the name William Shakespeare rings a bell. If you do remember him, it's probably because of Macbeth or Hamlet. But he wrote lots of other plays as well. And in one of them, there's this line where one guy says to another guy 'First, let's kill all the lawyers.' You've probably heard that used. What's not so well known is that he said this in the context of destabilizing an existing government so they could take it over. By getting rid of the lawyers, the government would be destabilized and ripe for the plucking." Oswald looked around the room to make sure everyone was following his logic.

"So what if we apply this strategy to our situation? Well, think of this. What's driving a lot of the efforts of the feds and the state guys is the tree-huggers. They lobby, they hire lawyers, they elect soft-headed liberal politicians. So how do you suppose we could fix this?"

The voice from the third row was unequivocal.

"Kill all the tree-huggers!"

"You got it. And you know what? I've heard that there have been several of these tree-hugger types biting the dust lately. Not that I know anything much about it, mind you, heh, heh. But there sure have been a lot of them dying mysteriously lately. Like that guy over in Creede, got squashed at the lumber mill." The murmuring was both astonished and confirmatory.

"So, what's the next step? Well, maybe we're ready to take the feds on. Let's talk a little about where things could go from here..."

H. P. Hanson

Excess Homicide
A Four Corners Mystery

Part II: The Days After

H. P. Hanson

Excess Homicide
A Four Corners Mystery

ELEVEN

THE MEDIA, print and broadcast, but especially broadcast of course, had a field day. News stories on the Fourth of July weekend were normally about kids, fireworks, and picnics, but the adventure at NCAR provided fodder for real reporting. The only thing that could have been better would have been a *successful* assassination attempt, not that anyone at the networks would have admitted, at least publicly, to wanting *that*.

As it was, the interviews with Joe Loughlin and his wounded *gluteus maximus* played well enough to sell lots of advertising time, and the background footage of the picturesque NCAR laboratory and its herds of tame deer gave photographers plenty of opportunities to exercise their artistic talents.

Despite advice to the contrary, the President discussed the matter willingly, praising the response of his Secret Service detail and referring to his perceptions of the whole thing as its having reminded him of some kind of bad fraternity prank.

"I heard somebody shout 'GUN' and the next thing I knew I was at the bottom of a football scrum. Thank God that no one was killed. And Mr. Loughlin has my everlasting gratitude for his vigilance, and for being between me and that rifle. I'm glad he wasn't hurt worse."

The networks' best footage was of the President shaking Joe Loughlin's hand, smiles all around. It was a grand hospital photo-op that drove the medical staff crazy.

Naturally, NCAR management was mortified. How could such a thing happen on their turf? They announced that the laboratory would be closed for a week and sent everyone home with the admonition that they be on-call for interviews with the Secret Service investigative team. The interviews started immediately with the security staff, even while the forensics team was going over the lobby centimeter by centimeter.

There were two important results from this initial investigation. First, they were able to dredge up video tapes from the security system of the two individuals who had delivered the solar telescope several weeks back, after its refurbishment. Unfortunately, the retired scientist whose job it had been to polish it up had disappeared. Second, they found the .30-06 slug that had sliced through Joe Loughlin's right hind cheek.

The FBI had also investigated the shooting of Arthur Powell at Natural Bridges Monument back in December. A junior G-man was assigned to hunt around the parking lot until he found the slug that had cut Arthur down, which slug then went into their database. So they found a ballistics match to Joe's slug within a few hours.

The forensics team also quickly deduced that the transmitter for the video camera could have had only a very limited range, and a canvassing of the Table Mesa neighborhood below the laboratory quickly uncovered the fact that a yellow and tan van with pest control company markings—Bug-Be-Dead—had been parked on Vassar Drive during the time frame of the assassination attempt.

Excess Homicide
A Four Corners Mystery

Further questioning of residents uncovered a morning jogger who had seen the van—it was described as looking like some kind of box-elder beetle—and was able to place one of the individuals shown on the security tapes in it. Another resident, who had been shopping down the hill at the Table Mesa Shopping Center, had seen two guys removing some peel-off signs from a yellow and tan van. Unfortunately, no one had noticed a license place number.

All this, of course, caused quite a lot of excitement, both in Washington and in Boulder. The investigative team decided to keep their findings as quiet as possible, and so the media weren't informed of the ballistics test results nor of the descriptions of the suspects. They were told merely that the assailant had escaped. All of the Boulder residents interviewed had been admonished to keep quiet about this, in order to avoid sabotage of the investigation, so all there was to report was a "massive manhunt" being conducted by the FBI and the Secret Service.

But what was really happening was nothing. After the initial flurry of success, the investigation stalled. The van and its well-described occupants had vanished. There was still more work, of course—the company that had made the magnetic signs would be found; the parts, and fragments of parts, from the rifle setup would be traced; Bug-Be-Dead, Inc., would come under serious scrutiny. But there was going to be no instant gratification here.

IN THE LAW ENFORCEMENT COMMUNITY, bad news travels fast, and Annette heard about the assassination attempt by noon on Friday. She called Roderick Andersen in Denver, but all he could tell her was to be available if the feds asked for help. So, with question on question rattling around in her head, she rearranged her Friday schedule so she would be in her office if a call came in.

The rearrangement meant that she would not be serving the arrest warrant they had obtained for one Timothy Langer, 19, student at Frémont State University, full-time Durango resident and native of Placerville, a hamlet just down-river from Telluride. UNELECO had been most willing to lodge a formal complaint against whomever was trying to hack into its systems, and Jamie McFarland's ire had motivated her to find that "whomever" within a few hours of her embarrassing conversation with Dean Harold Weathers. As nice a guy as Hal thought himself to be, his being dean caused folks to think otherwise.

So early Friday afternoon, Annette was sitting in her office. Fidgeting. Tapping pencils, shuffling papers, staring out the window in annoyance at the fine day out there, and generally being impatient. When her telephone rang, she jumped about a foot in the air and landed with her hand on the receiver.

"Treiri, CBI."

"Hey, did you hear about the doings up in Boulder? Damn, it sounds like a close one."

"Hi, Hal." She paused and drew a deep breath. "You know, I'm glad you called. I've been going nuts waiting for the other shoe to drop. I'm supposed to be on call if the feds need any help, but they're not calling. And I've got a team out picking up our UNELECO hacker, a guy named Timothy Langer, and waiting for them is also tough. Maybe talking with you will calm me down. And, yeah, it did sound close. Apparently the President is fine, though, and the NCAR guy just got a flesh wound."

"So Jamie came through, huh? Was it a student of ours?"

"Bingo."

"Great." Hal sounded disgusted. "Just what we need. Well, catching him on such a fast time scale will help us look better, I guess, given that we helped. Actually, I'm sort of glad it was a student, because I'd rather have students hacking into our computers than outsiders. Strange as it may sound. Keeps it all in the family, sort of. What's going to happen?"

"We have an arrest warrant, kind of a vague one based on misuse of State of Colorado property, and my team is bringing him in for us to question. If he was just doing this, I mean trying to get into the UNELECO computers, on a lark, like lots of these computer hackers, then we'll probably just put the Fear of God into him and let him know he's on a probationary status with us. I presume you'll want to discipline him as well?"

"Hmm. Well, I think I'll follow your lead. We should probably send him up before our computer ethics committee, and they'll give him a really hard time. It's a peer-pressure sort of thing. Depending on how things go, I've also got another idea, sort of in the mode of community service. Want me to come down for your interrogation? I can be a real Mean Dean when I put my mind to it. And if I talk with Jamie first, she could probably put me in just the mood. She's pretty pissed about this whole thing. Especially because this guy used her login."

"You mean the old, never fail, 'Good Cop, Bad Dean' interrogation strategy? I suppose that might be effective, depending on this guy's personality. They should be back in an hour or so if you want to come down."

"Let me talk with Alice about my schedule. Actually, I need to talk with her about that thing in Boulder. Tell her that I've talked with you and found out that there's no new information. Yet. For some reason, she thinks the world of this President. Maybe it has to do with his father, or something like that. Anyway, she's been in a real tizzy."

"Well, you can tell her that the manhunt is on, but there are no results yet."

"OK, so after that I'll head over your way. Since I'm going to be down on your side of town, maybe we can go out to dinner somewhere down there. Have you got anything else happening?"

"What I should be doing is going over a transcript of a meeting between Lolly Markham, her lawyer, and another guy who seems to be a friend of theirs. Guy named Steven Rutherford. Works in the sociology department at the U as a research assistant of some kind. Know of him?"

"Well, crap. Steve Rutherford is the coordinator, or something like that, for the local chapter of SCARAB. Remember Whitney Bradford, the guy who got killed in the Rock Creek Tunnel explosion? Rutherford took over for Bradford. So I have yet another FSU connection to weird things going on in your world."

"Well, it gets weirder, a little at least. Remember that news item about the guy who got killed over in Creede at the timber mill there? Well, he was from Alamosa. And, as part of the post-mortem, the Alamosa County folks checked out his apartment, and found messages, three, they said, on his answering machine, from Rutherford. Rather urgent messages. 'Call me as soon as you can, it's really important' sort of messages. So squished guy, David Wellington, was connected with Rutherford, and therefore Lolly Markham, somehow."

"Squished guy? Is that some kind of medical terminology?" Hal was laughing almost too hard to talk.

"Ah, well, I picked that up from the Mineral County Sheriff, Ralph Wertlinger. He said that's what happened, that Wellington got squished, and who am I to dispute a first-hand account?" Now she also was laughing. Must be the tension, she thought.

"Hmm. So Markham, Rutherford, and the squished guy could have been involved together in the FFPI mill arson in Monticello, is that what you're thinking?"

"And I'm betting the lawyer is in on it, too. He's not a defense lawyer. He seems like a friend of Lolly's. But I've got this transcript I should read. We taped them talking the other day, and the surveillance team told me that there's stuff there that bears on Markham's story. So, uh, where did you want to take me to dinner? There's not much in the way of quality food down this way, you know."

"Not in town, unless you want to go back to Fanny's Saloon for old times' sake."

"Right. For old time's sake, or so you can ogle all those girls with no shirts?"

"OK, OK. How about a nice drive up to the lake? It's Friday and we deserve a date."

"I need to be available for this assassination thing, if someone needs me. But I can take a phone and be available that way. So it sounds fine, as long as you know a place to eat up there."

"I'll ask around. And I'll see you in a couple of hours. Maybe between us we can get some information out of Mr. Langer."

"I sure hope so. Just once, it would be nice to have someone in here who actually wants to tell me the truth."

"Good cop, bad dean. Just remember that. See ya."

PICKLE AND MAD DOG had been listening to the radio, the all-news stations especially. The news, or, rather, the lack of it, was frustrating.

"What's with these guys? Why isn't there more news?" Pickle was the worrier of the two.

"Ya know, it's strange that there's not more information." Mad Dog, wandering eye or no, was a keen observer. "It must be that the feds are keeping a tight lid on this."

"Yeah. Good thing we did all that planning. Let me know when you want me to drive."

After peeling the magnetic Bug-Be-Dead logos from the van, and discarding the stolen license plates that no one had seen, they had headed east to an automatic drive-through car wash at an Amoco station, where the day before they'd purchased a deluxe wash, wax, and dry. The van entered the wash bay sporting the insect-like, two-tone, yellow and tan color scheme of other Bug-Be-Dead vans. After a few minutes it emerged—out the back, where no one who saw it go in would be likely to see it again, they'd checked— black. While the wash was cycling, they'd changed clothes in the back of the van and stuffed the fake Bug-Be-Dead uniforms, along with sunglasses they'd had on and the radio controller, in a garbage bag for later disposal.

Then they headed farther east and then south toward Denver International Airport, Pickle driving and Mad Dog fussing with a battery-powered shaver, removing the moustache and goatee he'd been working on for the past six months. Both were wearing latex gloves, and had been since the beginning of the operation.

At DIA they drove into the far back reaches of the east parking garage, where they swapped vehicles. The now-black van was parked in the spot formerly occupied by a Jeep Grand Cherokee, bought used, for cash, which had been waiting for them for the past two days. It had twenty extra gallons of gasoline in cans in the back. This time, Mad Dog drove, and Pickle worked loose the shaggy moustache that was glued to his upper lip. His next step was to eliminate his sideburns with the shaver.

They headed west and then south, and, on reaching the end of Peña Boulevard, southwest on I-225. When they reached I-25, they turned north, back toward downtown, and then west on Hampden. This took them through the western suburbs toward the foothills, and, along the way, they found a dumpster behind a supermarket, into which went the fake uniforms, radio controller, sunglasses, latex gloves, and the shaver. By 12:30, they were on their way up US 285, in Turkey Creek Canyon, homeward bound. Through the foothills, South Park, and down the Arkansas Valley; over Monarch Pass and down the Gunnison Valley to Montrose; over Dallas Divide and up to Norwood, they'd be home to Raven's Roost for a late dinner, if all went well.

"So, what do you think? How's the Senator going to take it? I mean, the fact that we missed." Pickle always had something to worry about.

"Well, he said several times that he really didn't care if we hit the guy, that he just wanted to put a scare into him."

"Right. 'Send a message' was what he cared about. Well, I guess we did that. What's the message? Any ideas?"

H. P. Hanson

"Naw, hell, I can't figure out what the Senator's trying to accomplish with this. I understand that he's pissed about all those blacks and browns and women in cabinet positions. But, Jesus, how this little episode is going to send a message about that is beyond me."

"Yeah, and what's this got to do with all those other jobs we've been doing? Things are getting too complicated. Simple jobs are so much better, ya know? Like that hit on the park ranger. Or the car accident we helped that guy up in Cedaredge have. All these complicated plans are just trouble waiting to happen. Sooner or later, someone's going to see something we don't want them to, and we're dead meat."

"You got that right. Like the last time we were up in Boulder. Or that job down in Flag. I didn't think that one would even work at all."

"Right. We got lucky on that one, estimating the height of the wire right and all. The others, though, and even that one, all worked because of good intelligence, good advance information. I'm sure glad we had that relaxed schedule, so we didn't have to rush things. Like that guy down in Taos who we had to watch for a week before we figured out the thing with the bridge." Pickle's pucker twisted into something resembling a grin. "He sure hollered when you dumped him over the railing, didn't he?"

"I liked the one in Santa Fe. Man, you hit that guy perfectly. Stuck him to that tree like pin the tail on the donkey."

"I'm glad this is the end of it for a while. The Senator says we're supposed to head up to Idaho after we check in with him."

"Yeah, and we probably do need to lie low. But what's up there?"

"Well, I'm going fishing. But he said something about meeting up with a group up there, somewhere north of Coeur d'Alene. Start linking together, I guess. But I want to take some time off, go fishing."

"Time off sounds good. I'm behind on my poetry. Maybe northern Idaho will be inspirational. I want to start on an epic, maybe a series of sonnets. But first we've got to get home. Damn, this thing handles good. I'm going to have to watch the speed."

Pickle knew better than to say anything about poetry. With at least seven hours of driving left, he surely didn't want to get Mad Dog started.

TIMOTHY LANGER turned out to be an innocent, terrified of what was happening to him and not hiding his terror, guileless in his responses to even the most leading questions. The "Good Cop, Bad Dean" strategy wasn't necessary, because he opened right up. It quickly became clear that he had no particular reason to pick UNELECO for his hacking attempts, so Annette asked the obvious question.

"Who put you up to this, Mr. Langer?"

His response was their first hint that someone had scared Langer more than the CBI or the Dean of the College of Natural Sciences could ever hope to. He shivered, sat up straighter, thought for a minute, and drew a deep breath.

"I have to take full responsibility for this. It doesn't matter who put me up to it, I'm the one responsible. There's no point discussing anyone else. I can't go there, period. I did the hacking, and I have to take whatever punishment is coming."

"Hmm. You sound like this is not negotiable. Is he paying you?"

"I just can't talk about this."

"Is he blackmailing you? You know, blackmail is in itself illegal. More illegal than what you did. We can help you with that. The best thing to do with blackmailers is to call their bluff."

"No comment."

"You know, when we got the arrest warrant, we also got all records for you, public ones and others, too. The sheriff over in San Miguel County, where you're from, was very helpful. Did something happen when you were working on the ranch one of those summers?"

This question disturbed Langer so much that Annette knew she was on to something.

"Ah, n-n-no, what ranch, anyway? I didn't work on any ranch. I grew up in town, in Placerville."

A major slip, Annette thought. Maybe I should gamble a little.

"You know, Mr. Langer, the reason we're interested in who put you up to this thing is so that we can believe your story. There's no reason for you to have attacked UNELECO on your own. Telling us will provide credibility, rather than implicating this other person. You're right, it's your fall to take; you did the hacking, and this isn't going to get this other person into much trouble, really. It's not really that big of a deal, hiring someone to do a job like this. Especially in this case, because the Senator's already in a lot more trouble than this could ever cause."

Bingo! Langer was shaking with terror, unable to speak.

Excess Homicide
A Four Corners Mystery

"One thing you can tell us, Mr. Langer, is why the Senator would want to attack UNELECO. What's he got against UNELECO, anyway?"

But he was incoherent. They decided that an extended break was in order, and Langer was taken back to a holding cell.

"What happened there? Where'd that question about 'the senator' come from? What senator?" Hal didn't get to observe Annette's interviewing technique very often, and he was amazed.

"Senator Jarvis Schoenfield. Sort of intuition and sort of a gamble. I called Jim Nettleman, he's the San Miguel Sheriff, about Langer, and he talked about a teen-age trouble-maker who had worked on 'the ranch' during summers in high school. You saw Langer's response to that. And also my blackmail question got a rise out of him. I remembered that Shure had commented on something that Campbell, the dead lawyer, had almost said. A couple of times he almost said 'The Senator' but then caught himself. And Nettleman said 'the ranch' not 'a ranch.' Up that way, '*the* ranch' is probably the X-S spread, which used to belong to Senator Jarvis Schoenfield. All this sort of came together in my head and I decided to gamble with a question. Obviously scared the hell out of the kid."

"That's for sure. I remember about Campbell and Shure's sort-of kidnapping, but I didn't know about the slip. But this is a connection that I don't understand. It must be that Schoenfield was trying to get Shure to do something that he refused, so now Schoenfield is trying to make trouble for Shure's company."

"Shure talked about an organization called the Aryan Rights Foundation. Said he was getting mail from them, including that Nazi prison-camp diary. He went public with the book a few weeks back, and if Schoenfield was behind the recruitment, I can see that Shure could have made an enemy real fast with that stunt." Annette stared off into space, thinking.

"Right. And if that's what's going on, this hacking business is more than an illegal use of state property. It's harassment at the least."

Annette was nodding. "And if it's connected to Campbell's murder, well, it's murder and possibly attempted murder. And remember that Campbell was killed with the same gun as Luke Begay, last September. Trouble is, this guy Langer is obviously more scared of Schoenfield than any scare either of us can put into him."

"I think you're right about that. I've never seen anyone so terrified. Do we need him for anything else?"

"Well, explicit confirmation of Schoenfield's involvement would be nice. Hmm. I wonder if Langer has hacked into any other systems for Schoenfield. Maybe I should talk to my boss about this."

"Probably wouldn't hurt. Say, you said something earlier about a transcript about the FFPI firebombing. Read it yet?"

"Yeah, while I was waiting for Langer. Very curious. It proves that Lolly Markham is lying about her presence in Monticello, and it shows that her lawyer and this other guy, Rutherford, are in on the lie. We can't use it officially, because it'll fall under attorney-client privilege. But it's information that we can use to guide us. And it also had some other stuff, about something called 'SCREW,' which would mesh with that cutesy note found at the scene of the fire. It's not clear what it's about, but it seems to involve those three and the dead guy over in Creede. And someone called Aaron Felterson over in Pagosa Springs, and a local pot-head whom I've known for years, Flip Chester. SCREW must be the name of some new organization. No idea what it could stand for."

"So what are you going to do?"

"Continue to watch them, see what happens next. Of course, things are a little distracted right now, at least potentially, if the feds want help with the Boulder thing. And there's the Schoenfield matter to clear up as well. No rest for the wicked. Speaking of which, I seem to recall something about dinner up by the lake. Anything wicked up there to eat? Like, a big steak maybe?"

"Oh, yeah. Big and rare, with a lake view. Ready to go?"

THE PROBLEM, Annette thought, with driving up to the foothills for dinner is that Hal remembers he needs to go fishing. *And here I am, stuck in the middle of two investigations and a potential emergency.*

Their dinner, at Virginia's Steakhouse, with great steaks as well as the promised view of Lake Vallecito and the San Juan high country beyond, had been lovely. But Hal spent the drive up watching the Los Piños River, and Annette knew he'd be off trying out a new batch of trout flies today. So the next morning she worked off some of those beef calories on the ski machine and then headed in to the office. But the only thing to be done on a Saturday was paperwork, unless something happened.

Two hours later, something did, in the form of a telephone call.

"Trieri, CBI"

H. P. Hanson

"Ms. Trieri? This is Todd Sweeney, from the Durango Field Office of the FBI. I bet you can't guess what I'm doing today."

Annette laughed. "Oh, let's see. Mail fraud, I bet that's it."

He laughed back. "I'm calling about ballistics. You folks sent us a report on a .22 slug that killed a lawyer up in Norwood, remember? We found that it matched one found in the head of a Luke Begay, who was killed, execution-style, at the Four Corners Monument last September. I remember calling your office at the Durango PD about that case."

"Right. Fred Winders told me. I was in the hospital at the time. But that case has never been cleared, no?"

"No, indeed. Crime scene was completely clean, we couldn't find any reason for someone to want to kill the guy. There was no indication of involvement with any of the usual stuff that gets you executed. Drugs, stuff like that. We found out that he was involved in some flaky organization at Frémont State, some kind of Indian rights group, but that wouldn't get you shot in the head. At least I don't think so. So the case just flat stalled out. Anyway, I've got an even stranger ballistics match for you. The .30-06 slug that hit that guy in the butt up in Boulder yesterday is a match with one that killed a National Park ranger over in Utah last December. I figured you'd be interested because of the other match in your area. And I thought maybe you'd made some progress on the other one, that lawyer."

"Nothing firm. But the .30-06 match is really interesting. Let me think, that Parks guy was Arthur Powell, right? A black guy, I mean, an African-American guy, that the NPS had assigned to Natural Bridges. Talk about a fish out of water, a guy with his background in rural southeastern Utah. But what's interesting is that he's one of a portfolio of about eleven people in the region who have died in suspicious circumstances in the last year, all of them connected with some facet of the environmental movement. Begay's organization, the flaky one, was called American Indian Rights, known as AIR. But he was also involved in an environmental group, the Mother Earth Defense League, appropriately known as MEDL. And Powell, of course, was a Park Service ranger. I have six other of these cases, and there are three in Arizona and New Mexico. All environmentalists. Campbell, the guy up by Norwood, is a little outside this box, but the ballistics on that .22 slug tie him in. And now this whole package is tied in with a Presidential assassination attempt? Wow. This is really too weird."

"How are the others tied together?"

"Well we really don't know they are, for sure. It's a hunch. They're all environmentalists. But other than that, it's thin. For that matter, some might be accidental. For example, there was a guy up in Cedaredge who died in a car crash, but there's an indication that he could have been pushed a little. And another guy, just a couple of weeks ago, who was crushed by a pile of logs at a timber mill. It was definitely supposed to look like an accident, but there are some strange things that haven't been explained yet. Others were obviously murder, like a car bomb, a guy with a crossbow bolt in his throat in downtown Santa Fe, stuff like that. But the thing is, these folks all seem to have been tied in with this Mother Earth Defense League organization. It's as if someone's going around killing them off. And to have the incident yesterday tied in with this is, well, like I said, too weird."

"Especially since the President isn't exactly known as an environmentalist. Although he might like people to think that, they don't. But you said the Norwood lawyer wasn't either."

"Actually, he was a Colorado Springs lawyer who just happened to get whacked up in Norwood. That's one of the puzzles. To make things stranger, this lawyer, Campbell, was working for something called the Aryan Rights Foundation, some kind of white supremacy group, apparently. He used to work for a big company in the Springs, but this other group made him an offer too good to ignore. This ARF outfit is another shadow organization, espousing how white folks are naturally superior and all the usual crap, but not really existing in a formal sense that you can grab on to. It's doubtful that they have anything to do with the environment, though. If they do, it's probably like those wacko outfits up in Montana and Idaho, white supremacists and tax evaders and mountain men who don't bathe."

"Real solid citizens, those folks. I'm glad we haven't had any confrontations around here like the ones up in Montana. I'll work the Rez any day."

"I'm kind of surprised you haven't been under a lot of pressure from the Navajo government to make progress on Begay's killing."

"Well, we have, some. But he seems to have alienated a lot of his own people. He was working on stuff that would have benefitted the Utes, and those two groups are not exactly best of friends. And a lot of his people thought he'd sort of 'turned white.' He lived here in Durango, he worked on those Anglo-type environmental causes, all that stuff. Same thing for Powell, in a way. If he'd been a civil-rights activist, we'd be under incredible pressure to do something. But he was a park ranger, not something that African-Americans feel particularly close to, it seems."

"Well, maybe we'll eventually get somewhere. Thanks for the information about the ballistics from yesterday."

"And there's more that I didn't get to. It's not for public consumption, but we have solid descriptions of two suspects, from the security people at that lab in Boulder. And a description of a vehicle. I'll fax you sketches. And one more thing, quite strange. It rings a bell with me, but I don't know where. Like I read a report about it but can't remember details. Anyway, the assassination attempt failed because they were using a remote control on the rifle, which was fixed on a tripod and couldn't really be aimed. They had a little TV camera sighted along the rifle and a transmitter with a radio controlled triggering device, and they could only shoot at what walked through the sights. All the electronics for this was in a box, a box that was rigged to melt down. But there was a message on the bottom of the box. And this isn't for public consumption either. It said 'Dear Mr. President: You've been screwed,' spelled capital S-C-R-E-W-apostrophe-little-d. Like SCREW is the name of something."

Annette was certain that he heard her gasp.

"Todd? What are you doing for lunch? We need to talk in person."

Twelve

ENTHRONED BEHIND his huge desk, Jarvis Schoenfield, back to the room, feet up on the window sill, was staring out at the incredible view but not really seeing it. Instead, he was reviewing the debriefing with Pickle and Mad Dog, searching for vulnerabilities. He was thinking hard, tapping his fingers on the arm of his chair and jiggling the pointed tip of the cowboy boot on his right foot.

They had arrived, exhausted, about 9:00 the previous evening, and he had postponed their discussion until this morning, so that they would be fresh. Then, over a breakfast that ended up lasting all morning, they had discussed every detail of Friday's events, going over some of the details three and four times. Schoenfield repeatedly assured them that they should consider their mission accomplished, even though they had shot the wrong person. To tell the truth, he was just a little disappointed that they hadn't been successful, but, well, he'd said all along that the message was the more important thing.

Pickle, flushed with success, had the audacity to ask "What *was* the message, Senator," but even that act of insubordination had not been enough to dampen the high spirits of the meeting. He'd even passed them envelopes stuffed with bills, despite the indiscretion.

Excess Homicide
A Four Corners Mystery

"Well, Pickle," the Senator had been feeling generous, and forgiving, "You've heard me gripe about how this new President of ours has loaded up his cabinet with people I don't exactly approve of. He seems to be trying to please everyone, all the special interest groups, instead of doing what's right, what he was elected to do. And then he goes and visits this think-tank where they spend our tax money on this global heating horseshit. So I wanted to let him know that not everyone approves of him, including people with spine, not just those limp-wristed Democrat liberals. And that we can express our disapproval even when he's in a federal research facility. That he's not safe anywhere. Think he got the message?"

"The last part for sure, but the Secret Service probably tells him that all the time. I don't know about the rest. We fired the rifle as soon as we saw all hell break loose. Some guy, maybe the guy we shot in the ass, because he sure wasn't a Secret Service guy, saw the rifle and pointed it out to an agent, who dove for the President. We fired, they fired, and the TV camera went out. Then we got the hell out of there."

"That was the right thing to do. I saw the son-of-a-bitch on TV last night, shaking that guy's hand, in the hospital. All smiles for the TV cameras and the public. But I bet he's pissing in his pants about this whole thing. I think we've succeeded. We'll be able to get what we want—what we deserve—from him in the future."

Schoenfield was confident that last night's conversation had dealt with Pickle's curiosity. Now, the question that was keeping Schoenfield from enjoying the view was whether the job had gone smoothly enough that he could keep his two operatives around for a little longer before sending them off to northern Idaho. That other job Timmy was supposed to be doing had unraveled completely—word was that Timmy had been picked up and was now in custody. Schoenfield needed advice, so he reached for the phone.

"Find the Reverend and send him up here, willya?"

It took about ten minutes, during which Schoenfield continued to stare at the scenery without seeing it. Even after the knock on the door, the command to enter, and the seating of the new guest in a chair with a view equal to his, Schoenfield continued to stare.

"God's country out there, sure is beautiful, isn't it Senator? Makes me feel blessed to live out here." Oswald was gazing with rapture at the scenery Schoenfield wasn't seeing.

"Come on, Mike, you know that crap doesn't work on me. What are we going to do about Timmy? He's in custody down in Durango. CBI's got him."

"For what?"

"I don't know for sure, but the university caught him using its computers for that job on UNELECO I mentioned to you.

"The one that was Pickle's idea, yeah. But we both know that Timmy won't talk."

"Not directly. But they'll question him over and over, and he's likely to slip up at some point. We've got to do something."

"I don't think I want to hear where you're going with this."

"You've got to. He's your responsibility, too."

"He's my nephew, yeah, but you're the one controlling him." Oswald was looking increasingly nervous.

Excess Homicide
A Four Corners Mystery

"Right. And my concern is that he's out of my control just now. If he is in custody, they'll need to charge him formally, then he gets the phone call, and so on. I presume he'll call you. If he does, I need to hear about it. And we need to find him the right lawyer. Obviously not you, you're too close to him." He stared at Oswald, and his left eye twitched.

"Seems like that fella Bill Campbell would have been perfect."

"Don't razz me, Mike! And besides, Campbell was a corporate lawyer who didn't know criminal law. Anyway, we'll find someone, and we'll get Timmy out on bail. Then I need to get him back under control. I was thinking of keeping Pickle and Mad Dog around for a few days, before they make that run up to Idaho we discussed."

"Oh, no, you're not going to send them after him, are you? Jarvis, Timmy's *family*!"

"Yeah, well, even family needs reminding of the state of things once in a while. I'm not going to have Timmy hit, just reminded, OK? So calm down. In fact, why don't you stay here and talk with Pickle and Mad Dog about this with me? Then you'll see we're not going to hurt the kid." He reached for the telephone.

"Send Pickle and Mad Dog up again, willya?" He turned back to Oswald. "So, how are the stage two meetings going?"

Oswald was now the one staring out the window, trying to compose himself. He shook his head and took a deep breath.

"Well. Every time we have a meeting, I get a couple of questions about letting other people into the circle, but so far I've been able to deflect them, to keep the circle unbroken. I've received lists from the first two meetings, in Cortez and in Alamosa. Got a total of two dozen names, of feds, of State of Colorado people, of tree-huggers, that we could do without. The next step will be to set up teams of new people to handle the hits, in a cell structure where no one knows about everything. Most of the hits, of course, will be set up as accidents. Like we've talked about, this needs to be done carefully, without anyone except us knowing everything. Pickle and Mad Dog just can't handle all these new hits, and the new people are going to make mistakes, unlike our two pros. But we'll set this whole thing up to look like a grass-roots revolt, so whoever gets caught won't be linked to anyone else. The tactic of using someone from one cell to direct an operation in another cell will also keep the level of secrecy high."

"I like it. You're doing a great job. Can I have a look at those lists? Maybe I can help prioritize them. We've gotta be sure to avoid making such big splashes with the first ones that we scare off the others."

"I'm planning to sit down with you and do just that, when we get the lists from the other three meetings. Sometime next week, probably."

There was a knock on the door.

"Yeah, come in."

Pickle and Mad Dog entered and sat in their usual two chairs.

"Wanted to see us, Senator?"

"Yep. I need you two to hang around for a few days. Not go up north right away. Got another job, an easy one." Schoenfield opened a drawer in his desk and took out a bottle of Jim Beam. He poured a generous three fingers into an old-fashioned glass and took a large gulp.

Excess Homicide
A Four Corners Mystery

"Well, OK, Senator. But don't you think we should make ourselves scarce, just in case they've got descriptions ready to circulate?"

"Yeah, I've been thinking about that. But you guys were wearing shades, you've both shaved. And now that you've had a chance to clean up completely, your hair is a different color from yesterday. I can't see how you're likely to be identified. Maybe if you were hanging around Boulder, but not out here. I think it's pretty safe, as long as you don't get busted or something like that."

"If you say so, Senator. What's the job?"

"Timmy Langer needs the Fear of God put into him. The Reverend and I are going to chat with you about just what this means." He smiled an evil smile and took another gulp.

A WORKAHOLIC like Charles Shure, Annette thought, would surely be in the office on Saturday. Let's see if that number he gave me is really his own private line. She punched buttons on her desk phone.

"Shure here."

"Mr. Shure? This is Annette Trieri, Colorado Bureau of Investigation."

"Ms. Trieri. How nice to hear from you. What motivates you to call me on a Saturday?"

"The possibility of progress, not much, but a little. Have your computer security people briefed you on the hacking attempts that were directed your way?"

"Well, we get lots of those all the time. That's why I have such good computer security people. What's especially amusing are all the foreign operatives, what I mean by that is basically spies, who think they can find stuff on our web site and then get into our systems and find more. I usually don't hear details, though."

"This little episode has been going on over the past week or two, and your people traced it to Frémont State."

"Oh, right. I did hear about that one."

"We got the guy, dead to rights. He's a student there, and he's admitted to trying to break into your systems, although he won't tell us why. Yet. We're thinking the most appropriate thing is to twist his arm into telling us and then working a community-service deal. Lots of times these hackers can be turned away from the Dark Side, to use a hackneyed metaphor. But I thought I should talk it over with you."

"My computer security people are almost all ex-hackers. Maybe I should offer him a job."

"That's part of what I want to talk with you about, indirectly. First, though, I wonder if you'd mind if I go over some of that statement about the incident up in Norwood. I want to verify my memory and the transcript."

"Ahh, should I get my lawyer in on this?"

"You can, but there's no need to. You're not under any suspicion of anything. In fact, you're about our most valuable witness to something that just seems to keep growing. I can't tell you details, especially over the phone. I promise to some day, though. Anyway, I just want to check a couple of things."

"Sounds OK with me. I still remember most of that weird affair."

"Good. So it all started with that package containing the letter and the book. Then there was this so-called appointment to negotiate some resource leases, right?"

"Right. And they insisted on having the meeting over in Norwood, at a bank, the First National, as I remember."

"And you flew to Telluride and drove to Norwood and were hijacked on the way. And met with this lawyer, who passed you notes and then, after the meeting, got dumped out of the truck in front of you with a bullet between his eyes."

"Scared the hell out of both me and my driver. We got out of there as fast as we could."

"I don't blame you. Now, here's what I'm interested in. You reported that this lawyer, Bill Campbell, said he was representing this Aryan Rights Foundation outfit. But you also reported that he slipped up in referring to who he was working for and started to say something else. But he caught himself."

"Right. He said 'The Sen...' and then reverted to this Aryan Rights bunch. And, like I told you, we had done some background work related to these leases. It turns out that the board feet are on property that's part of the X-S Ranch, and the tailings we were going to process are from mining claims owned by the X-S also. And, until fairly recently at least, the X-S Ranch was owned by Senator Jarvis Schoenfield, whom you know. It had been in his family for generations, until he turned it over to a private foundation. Since the incident, we've found out that the foundation is something called Resources For Humanity. This RFH is a non-profit that seems to fit in with the other so-called 'wise-use' organizations, but it's hard to be sure."

"Do you think what Campbell almost said was 'The Senator'?"

"Well it would sure all fit together, wouldn't it? Although there's a missing link, between Schoenfield and the Aryan Rights bunch."

"Say, something just occurred to me... but it's probably stupid. We have the Aryan Rights Foundation. A-R-F. And we have Resources For Humanity. R-H-F. A-R-F and R-F-H. If you say them, you know, like acronyms you can pronounce, you know, 'arf' and 'rfh,' they are pretty similar. At least they're both like noises dogs make. I wonder if they're linked and someone made the linguistic equivalent of a Freudian slip somewhere? Hmm, well, like I said, it's probably stupid."

"Hmm, indeed. You know, though, that it isn't trivial to come up with names for organizations. Most of the obvious ones are taken. A Freudian-like slip could be possible. But I guess I'd have to say that this probably wouldn't fly in court."

"You don't think so?" She was giggling. "Yes, Your Honor, we, the people, assert that these two organizations are really one and same because they both sound like doggie noises. Wow. I think I need a vacation."

"If you do get to that point, I mean, in court, please invite me for the day. I'd like to see that one. But, seriously, I'd think of it as more of a hint than a coincidence. Really. If you get enough hints like this one, something will come together eventually."

"As I said, there are some things that I can't talk about just yet. But here's one thing that I can. This student that was trying to hack into your computers. I suggested to him that he was put up to this by someone, and he got all high-and-mighty about how this was his doing and how he'd have to take whatever punishment there was. I pushed things a bit and eventually dropped the phrase 'The Senator' into the conversation. At that, he almost had a heart attack. It definitely pushed buttons with him. Point is, I sort of think that Senator Schoenfield may be behind the attack on your systems."

"I guess that wouldn't surprise me. If he is behind the ARF, then I probably made him quite angry by going public with that prison camp book. I'm pretty convinced, not in a way I could prove it in court, mind you, but convinced, that he's behind that hijacking episode. Which means he's behind the ARF. And, presumably, the RFH. Say, you know? The more those two things get used together, the more they do seem linked. You've got good intuition, madame."

"Well, thank you sir. And I promise that I'll invite you when we present that evidence in court. Anyway, thanks for verifying the solid information and for all the hints. They'll be quite helpful."

"If there's anything else I can do, let me know. I'd like to see this bastard's hide nailed to the barn. He's the person to go after, not this student."

"Oh, if this all comes together, nailing his hide to the barn will be the least of it. Thanks for your help."

SHURE ISN'T AFTER HIM, and prosecuting him for illegal use of state property is a waste of time. Community service, Annette thought, is sounding more and more appropriate. And last night Hal was talking about how he needed to find a computer science tutor for some athlete whose grades are on the edge. Subtle, the man is not. But that could work. After all, it was the university's computers that were the property being mis-used.

Maybe I should pay Mr. Langer a conciliatory visit.

After polishing off the last of the week's paperwork, she headed over to the county detention facility, where the state contracted to have its needs for short-term incarcerations met. It took her longer to get through the socializing than anything else. She knew these folks well, from cases in years past. Eventually she was in an interview room, sitting across from Timothy Langer. She'd brought a bag full of Burger King lunch, having called ahead and ascertained that he'd not been eating. It was clear that the smells wafting from the bag were having their effect on Langer.

"Mr. Langer, this is not a social call, but neither is it meant to be as adversarial as our discussion yesterday. I heard you haven't been eating, so I brought this in case you get hungry. Hope you like burgers and fries."

"So, are you going to charge me formally, or what? Don't I get a phone call and all that?" He was eyeing the bag carefully.

"I'd rather not do that, because it puts in motion a lot of paperwork that's hard to stop. What I'd like to do is to accomplish two things. Yesterday, you admitted that you've been trying to access the UNELECO computers without authorization, and you stated that it's your responsibility to take whatever punishment is appropriate. So, the first thing I'd like to do is to get that resolved. If we can reach an agreement about this, and that's part two, I think the appropriate payback is for you to tutor in computer sciences at FSU. And if you do that well, you know, take it seriously, be conscientious, and so on, it may just be that the UNELECO computer people would like to interview you

Excess Homicide
A Four Corners Mystery

about a job. I hear their compensation package is extraordinary."

"Why would they want to hire me?"

"The UNELECO CEO, a guy named Charles Shure, told me that a lot of his computer security people are ex-hackers. It was he who suggested that they might hire you." Stretching the truth was something Annette did often in these circumstances.

"OK, well, what's part two? This agreement you want."

"Yesterday, it was obvious that you don't want to talk about who put you up to this. The agreement is this: I'll stop asking about that, give up on it completely, if you'll provide me with information about other computer systems you've hacked into for this person. And for anyone else, as far as that goes. The idea here is that you go straight before you get in real trouble. And that we see if there's any hacking damage you might have done that can be reversed."

"You don't want to know who I'm working for?"

"What I want to know is what systems you've hacked into, besides the ones at the U and the attempts at the UNELECO ones. That's it. Well, I also want to know that you're committed to going straight, that you'll do as good a job as you can with the tutoring, and stuff like that. But we'll leave your employer, or benefactor, or blackmailer, or whatever out of it completely. And, of course, you won't be charged with anything."

"When can I go home?"

"Well, I think I'd like the list first, and some way to verify it. Give me that and it'll start the process of my trusting you. Then we can take it from there. How's that sound?"

"What's in the bag?"

H. P. Hanson

"Like I said, a burger—a double Whopper—and fries. And a Coke."

He reached for the bag and dug in.

"So, how do I know I can trust you?" She was surprised he could talk with his mouth so full.

"I won't be charging you, like I said. Give me the list and you're out of here. And I won't ask about who put you up to this. I'll also call off others who might. If someone does, then you can go back to hacking. Of course, we'll catch you again, eventually. See, by giving me something tangible, this list, then I can start believing that you'll keep your promise to go straight. On your side, I'm not making promises for the future, I'm doing things now. Like getting you out of here. I figured the food would be a nice gesture."

"Got some paper, and a pencil or something?"

THE LENGTHENING SHADOWS on Lone Cone Peak held Schoenfield's attention, not because they were different from other days, but because his mind was now at ease, at least relative to its earlier level of heightened concern. The half-bottle of Jim Beam he'd consumed since mid-afternoon also helped. Oswald was captivated by the scene, too, and this time he wasn't even going to try pseudo-religious platitudes. But now it was his turn to be concerned, unlike before.

"Senator, I know you don't like to be second-guessed. I hope you realize that the concerns I express here, in this room, are meant to help you in your decision-making."

"Aw, hell, Mike, everyone's got to have people to bounce ideas off of. And you help a lot."

"Well, the stuff I talk about with you here stays here. In public, I back you one hundred per cent, all the time."

Excess Homicide
A Four Corners Mystery

"That's the word I get." No harm in letting him know he's being watched, Schoenfield thought.

"I appreciate that you told Pickle to go easy on Timmy. I agree, he does need reminding. But that's the thing with computer hacking. It's hard to stay ahead of everyone. I'm not surprised he got caught. After all, he's only a kid."

"He hasn't called you yet, right? That's my main concern now. If he was arrested, he should be making a phone call for help."

"Well, he knows the drill. If he's caught, he's just a college student snooping around on the Internet. Maybe they're questioning him and that's it. He didn't tell you that he got into the UNELECO systems, right? He got caught in the process. He's a student, so probably the university will have some process to deal with the transgression."

"I sure hope that's all." His left eye twitched, twice.

"Me, too. Senator, there's something else I'd like to ask about. I don't mean to offend you with this, but I'm just too curious to stay quiet. Did you have anything to do with that little affair up in Boulder yesterday? I noticed that Pickle and Mad Dog were gone all day and got back late."

A wide grin spread itself across Schoenfield's face, and he leaned back in his executive chair and put his feet up on his desk. Staring at the ceiling, he chuckled to himself.

"Well, now, Mike, what makes you think that I'd have something to do with an assassination attempt? I mean, it's just flat unpatriotic. And you know me to be a true patriot."

"I do. And I've also heard you rant and rave about this particular President. And I've heard you say good things about the Vice-President. With your two hit men gone, things just started to add up. Besides, that shit-eating grin you're wearing tells it all."

"Can't fool you, Mike. That's why I put you in charge of RFH, you're good. Yeah, well, we didn't expect to succeed, we just wanted to send a little message." He proceeded to fill Oswald in on the details of his antipathy toward Presidential politics.

"Forgive me, Senator, but that seems a little thin."

"Yeah, well, it was good enough for Pickle."

"And Mad Dog, too, no doubt. But you don't really expect it to be good enough for me, do you?"

"No, I don't, and never did. We kept you out of the loop, though, for two reasons. First, I figured you'd try, and try hard, to talk me out of it. Hell, even Pickle did. I just didn't want to argue with you about it. Second, the fewer people who knew about it, the better. Especially you, because you've been doing those stage two meetings and knowing about this could have influenced your presentation, maybe even made you slip up. But now that it's over with, and it looks like we did it cleanly, that's not an issue."

Schoenfield got up from behind his desk and began pacing about the room.

"And it'll fit in with what we're trying to accomplish. When these stage two guys find out—and we need to work out a plan for how they find out—when they find out that their leadership pulled something like this off, that'll solidify our power base, don't you think? And that's only part of it. After Pickle and Mad Dog have their little conversation with Timmy, I'm sending them up to Idaho. Partly to get them away from here and whatever investigation is going on, but mostly to get them in touch with some groups I know up there, groups with the same agenda as ours, more or less. Groups that want to do the same thing, successfully, I mean take out the national politicians, and haven't been able to."

He stopped pacing and stared directly at Oswald, something that made the Reverend shiver.

"When they hear that it was us that did this Boulder thing, well, that'll put us in a leadership position, won't it? None of those other groups have pulled something like this off. They talk about it a lot, but that's all it is, talk. But we've actually done something, so we're going to come out of this as the leaders of the movement. And then we can exert some leadership and begin to consolidate all of the groups that think alike on these matters. You can start having RFH meetings up there, and getting to stage two will be easy. This will put us lots of steps closer to getting a critical mass together."

"So far, we've been small and invisible. Don't you think that consolidating all these groups will make us big, and potentially visible to the feds? Then we'd be in for trouble, for sure. Don't you think so, Senator?" Oswald looked uncomfortable.

"I'm using the word 'consolidate' loosely. We've done a lot with very few people. If other groups take the same approach, just think of the impact. Hell, the tree-huggers do it. You've read about these people who call themselves the Earth Liberation Front, ELF. They claim there's no central organization, no one knows what the other people are doing. If those damned hippies can do this, so can we. We adopt their tactics and wipe them out in the process. Along with other such groups and certain people in the government who are in our way. Then we can get the land back to the landowner. Use it to prosper and all that other stuff you talk about."

"You mean you actually listen to my message? Senator, I'm flattered."

"Far as I'm concerned, you don't go nearly far enough. But, I know, I know, you've got to go easy on the masses. I'm being patient, don't worry. But eventually we've got to start getting the message across that we Aryans are the folks that run the show. The others can hang around to work for us, or go back to the cities on the coasts, to their ghettos. But the inter-mountain west is our turf."

THE ATTEMPTS BY THE FEDS to keep a lid on the investigation had worked for the Saturday papers, largely because of timing. Given the 36 hours between the Big News Event and the Sunday deadline, they had no such luck with the Sunday papers. Of course, the networks had been providing as much coverage as they could justify to their advertising departments, but both Hal and Annette craved analysis, such as would be available. So Hal went out early and came back with bagels and accoutrements and an armload of Sunday papers, including the *Denver Post* and the *New York Times*. The *Durango Herald* had plenty of wire coverage, but Hal knew Annette would be starving, for news as well as for breakfast. Even if the stories were just repeats, this was a day for more pages than the *Herald* offered.

They settled themselves on the deck with the papers, the food, a toaster oven, plenty of coffee, and telephones, just in case someone called. It was like moving, a little.

"Did you plan to feed an army? Two bagels I can manage, but there are at least a dozen here."

"Didn't know what flavor you wanted," Hal was stringing an extension cord to a plug on the house, so that they could keep the coffee warm and toast the bagels. "So I got lots of choices. Also, we might be having company."

"Company?"

"Well, you told me yesterday that you were going to release Tim Langer after he gave you a list of the places he'd hacked into. And I want him as a tutor. So I may call him in a while and ask him over, and maybe the student I want him to help, too. Get them acquainted in a sort of social setting rather than the formality of my office. So pick your favorite flavor, and we can offer what's left to them."

"Poppy seed, two of 'em. Toasted, with butter and some of those raspberry preserves. That'll do me. What are you going to have?"

"Sesame seed, with cream cheese and lox."

"Oh, *very* Durango. I'm sure that will impress Tim. Probably the only thing they eat up in Placerville. Along with knishes and piroges."

"I'll be done by then. Sure you don't want some?"

"No, thanks. The preserves will do nicely." Annette rather liked raw fish, especially fixed the Japanese way, but not for breakfast.

"So, uh, was there anything interesting on the list Tim gave you? Can you tell me?"

"Well, it's not for public consumption, but there were some familiar organizations. Most familiar is us, the CBI and the State Patrol. I promised Tim I wouldn't push him to tell me who he's been doing this for, but I'm really tempted on this one. And another organization, familiar because it's in the news just now, NCAR, up in Boulder."

"You think it's Schoenfield?" He fiddled with getting hot bagels out of the toaster.

"Probably. See, I don't think that Tim was free-lancing, doing these hacking jobs for lots of people. I think he has one client and it's Schoenfield. Tim's reaction to the mere mention of Schoenfield, not even by name, just by title, suggests that Schoenfield has some hold on him. So I'm going to ease off. I already told my boss that we need to reprogram the computer system, though. I don't know if Tim was supplying Schoenfield with information, or if Schoenfield is computer literate enough to have his own secret login."

"Would it be fair to ask Tim? Not who, just how?"

"Hmm. I'd have to be careful how I asked, but maybe I could."

"Thing is, if Tim's supplying the information and it suddenly stops, Schoenfield is going to be suspicious. The other way is to use this whole setup against him, pass him information that he could only find out via a clandestine link to the CBI system and then use it against him."

"Boy, for a stodgy academic, you can be quite diabolical. Machiavellian, even."

"Is there anything on your system that would be damaging if Schoenfield had it?"

"Well, there are reports on the Campbell investigation. And, say, the entire file of the environmentalist portfolio is there, too. Of course, all that would tell him, the Campbell file, too, is that we're not making progress."

"I assume you informed Andersen of this. I'd sure want to know."

"I told him about the hacking but I'm holding back on my suspicions on Schoenfield. That's a real bombshell, politically. It's real touchy." She took a bite of raspberry-covered bagel.

Excess Homicide
A Four Corners Mystery

"Well, if you trust him, you ought to tell him your suspicions. At least I think so. Like I said, I'd want to know. In a way, it's a damage control thing."

"Let's talk with Tim first to see how the information was getting passed."

"Sure. It's your call, anyway. Are you finding anything new in those articles?"

"The *Times* got to the NCAR guards. Hmm. Says here that they remember the guys who delivered that telescope. Reporter must have suggested they blew it. But the security tape is in the hands of the feds, and the guards were told to keep quiet, they say. Well, actually, they're saying that the feds want all communications to go through them. So the NCAR guys aren't talking much to the *Times*, or anyone, it seems. There's a comment in the story that the guards were unresponsive to questions about people's right to know and ability to help find the suspects." She looked up and grinned.

"Here's one you'll like, from the *Post*. I guess they put a whole team of local reporters, people who know Boulder, on this. They went door-to-door in the neighborhood below the NCAR lab. Found a guy the feds missed, apparently, who seems to like to talk. He saw a yellow and tan van from a local pest control company—he remembers a logo in the form of some kind of bug but can't remember the company name—this van was parked out in front of his house Friday morning between about 9:30 and 10:15. He remembers it because the guys in it never got out. He figured they were on a coffee break and he didn't want them in his yard, so he was watching them. And the *Post* people found out that NCAR contracts with a pest control company that has yellow and tan vans, outfit called 'Bug-Be-Dead.' Calls to them weren't returned."

"Interesting. I bet the *Post* reporters don't know how close they are. If the feds had let it be known that the rifle was radio controlled, people would be camped outside Bug-Be-Dead. But, you know, this could open the flood gates. Todd Sweeney, the local FBI guy, told me that his colleagues were trying to get all of the folks they interviewed to be absolutely silent about this, like the way the NCAR guards were behaving in this *Times* story. But now one guy has talked, and that'll probably get everybody talking, probably anonymously. I bet tomorrow's stories are even more interesting."

Thirteen

After an hour or so of torturous persuasion at one of their meetings, Steve Rutherford had finally convinced his fellow members of SCREW that they needed an outing, something to break the tension, get them outside, accomplish something goal-oriented. He knew of a land-clearing operation, a new subdivision going in on the edge of the National Forest north of Pagosa Springs. The contractor had all sorts of heavy equipment sitting out there in the woods, there were survey stakes galore, and surely no one would be working on Sunday of the Fourth of July weekend. Time for some monkey-wrenching.

Reid Tompkins begged off with the excuse that he had real cases to catch up on—all the time he'd been spending on Lolly's legal situation had put him behind. The consummate diplomat, he didn't mention the amount of time he'd been spending on Lolly herself. But Flip Chester and Aaron Felterson were willing and ready, Flip giggling at the prospect of the fun they were about to have and Felterson righteously indignant at the thought of yet another subdivision of forty-acre ranchettes ripping up the landscape, disrupting elk migration routes, destroying habitat.

Preparations were pretty simple, really. Lolly made a picnic lunch for all of them and was proud to drive her new car. She had saved enough from her ex-husband's alimony checks for a down-payment on a Dodge Neon, the sporty edition, in purple. Felterson provided local information—maps, in particular, because this new subdivision was definitely off the beaten track. Flip provided his usual contribution, and Rutherford had made up another clever message, complete with pun, for the contractor to find. The three Durango residents drove to Pagosa Springs, getting higher and higher as Flip kept rolling joints. Down in town, they picked up Felterson and headed back west up the hill to the turnoff onto Piedra Road, the county road that provided access to a variety of subdivisions, including the new one, and to the eastern reaches of the Weminuche Wilderness.

It took a few miles, about to the end of the pavement, to persuade Felterson to lighten up and get high with the rest of them, but he finally caved in. Yes, everyone agreed that their work was important and that these subdivisions were the blight of southwestern Colorado. But, come on, they could still have fun, couldn't they? Geez.

A few more miles down the gravel road, about half-way through their second joint since Pagosa Springs (Rutherford had lost count of the ones since Durango), they came around a curve and over a little rise, into a huge meadow, pasture for about 500 head of cattle. And about halfway across the meadow, they found most of those cattle walking down the road. There were three fellows on horses—cowboys!—keeping track of strays and generally moving the cattle along.

"Steve," Lolly was appalled, "You told me that the road was slippery because of mud, because it must have rained. I don't think so. Look at that." She was pointing toward one

Excess Homicide
A Four Corners Mystery

of the steers just ahead of the car, who was making his personal contribution to the road's slick surface.

"Steve, this is my *new car*. And it's going to be all covered in cow shit!" She was in tears, but she had the presence of mind to tap lightly on the horn. The cattle parted to let her pass.

Normally, Rutherford would have been appropriately solicitous about Lolly's feelings, maybe even offered to wash her new car for her. He, however, was not normal, nor were the car's other two occupants. As a result of their particular abnormality, their response to Lolly's tears, and especially to the coating on her new car, was hysterical giggling. Uncontrolled, can't-get-your-breath giggling, which soon evolved into rolling-around, pounding-on-the-seats belly laughter. And because Lolly was not normal either, it didn't take too long for her to switch moods and join in. All the while, the two-tone purple and brown sports-edition Neon was easing its way toward the front of the herd and the open road beyond.

Meanwhile, Red Collins was having a great day. He had won the coin flip and was riding point, ahead of the herd as its guide and, most importantly, on the gravel road in its pre-slippery state. Much less fragrant up front. The weather was dandy, the cattle knew what was happening—this early July change of pasture meant new, sweet grass—so they were cooperating, and what better way to spend a Sunday than to be atop his bay mare Sweetheart riding in the high country? Besides, he had a date for the annual fireworks display later. His boss, Archuleta County Sheriff Ron Grange, had given him the evening off so he could go out with his fiancée. Maybe, he thought, Sweetheart here is only the first filly I'll be atop today.

He wasn't really paying attention, because the noise of the cattle, the warmth of the day, and his thoughts of the coming night had lulled him into reverie. But then there was this strange noise, a sort of toot-toot-tooting. He swiveled around in his saddle to see a little purple car, the sides streaked with brown, inching its way through the herd, almost on top on him. He edged Sweetheart over to the right side of the road.

As the car passed him, he automatically waved, and the occupants waved back. Then he caught the familiar whiff of burning contraband. At the same time, he saw that the people in the car were laughing hysterically. He pulled a cellular telephone out of his shirt pocket and hit a speed dial button.

"Hey there, Zelda. This here's Red. Hey, I'm doing this cattle drive up Piedra Road, right now we're right about at Ant Hill. And, listen, a car, a new Dodge Neon, purple underneath the cow shit, Colorado plates, just went by northbound, full of dope-smoking hippies. They're so whacked out I don't see how they can drive. Y'all got anybody up this way today? Ron's up here? Aw, hey, that's perfect. Let him know, will ya?"

THEY DECIDED to invite Tim Langer over first, ahead of Jamal, to have a chance to talk with him alone. He was initially reluctant, but Annette reminded him of their deal and promised food. Nothing like food to entice college students, except maybe beer, but Langer was only 19 and it was Sunday morning. Hal and Annette were still absorbed in the papers when the doorbell rang. Annette stood up to get it, and shortly she returned with the reformed computer hacker in tow.

Excess Homicide
A Four Corners Mystery

"Good morning, Tim. Want some breakfast?" Hal wanted to start things out on the right foot.

"Uh, good morning, Dean Weathers. I am kind of hungry. Um, this sure looks, ah, domestic. Do you both live here?"

"Oh, you didn't know? I guess we didn't say anything the other day. We're married. Domestic, huh? Yeah, you're right. This is our Sunday-morning-after-the-assassination look, newspapers everywhere. What kind of bagel do you want? And should I toast it? And what on it? Welcome to the Eighth Street Deli."

"I'll try this one," he was pointing to an "everything" bagel, covered with all sorts of different things. "And, uh, what's that pink stuff on the plate there?"

"Lox. Smoked salmon."

"Looks raw."

"Almost. Not as raw as sushi. And not as smoked as the smoked salmon in those packages at the store, the Alaska kind. Want to try it?"

"Raw fish for breakfast? Um, can I just have it with butter, or cream cheese, is that what that is?"

"Fine with me. I'll try the raw fish out on Jamal. He's from Denver, maybe he's had it before."

"Tim, while he's playing chef, burning your bagel," there was a good-natured "Hey!" from Hal in the background, "I want to ask you something about the hacking you've been doing for the people on that list you made up yesterday."

Langer was instantly on alert, eyes narrowed suspiciously.

"Don't get upset, I'm not going to ask you who you were hacking for. I promised not to go there, and I'm not going to. But there's something I didn't think of yesterday, and it relates to how—not for whom, but how—you were doing this hacking. Did you go into these systems you compromised and find information and pass it to whoever it was, or did you get them access so they could find their information themselves? The reason that this is important is this: if you go straight, like we discussed, you won't be passing information any more, and that could get you in hot water with whoever you were working for, right? And we'd like to avoid that."

"Oh. You're right. I didn't think of that either, but that's because I haven't been passing the information. I've been setting up logins, the secret kind like I had on the FSU system. I don't know what kind of information is of interest to, well, you know. And I don't want to know, actually."

"OK, thanks. Now, Jamie, the systems person who caught you once we knew someone was using the FSU systems without authorization, Jamie said that the secret login you were using was sort of piggy-backed onto something she called 'root.' Are the others like this?"

"Yeah, they're all the same. See, I get in, there are different ways to do that, and run a script that sets this secret login up, then I turn it over to, uh, the others, and don't go to that system again. Except I didn't do that with the FSU system because I needed it for myself, as a fast host."

"OK. I'm not a computer guru like you are, but I don't need to know details. One thing I'm curious about, though, is how you get into these systems in the first place. You said there are different ways."

"Several. And there's a book that describes a couple, and other ways are discussed on hacker Internet sites. Once

Excess Homicide
A Four Corners Mystery

you know the IP address of a computer, that's like an Internet phone number, then you try a couple of things that tell you what kind of computer it is. There's a utility called 'ping' that works on most systems. Once you know that, you can see if the systems people there have plugged up known security holes for that kind of system. If not, you're in. If so, well, then my next step is to find the web site of the organization and see if it has any security holes that are vulnerable. Most web sites of organizations have e-mail links to people there, and these links give you addresses. There are e-mail security holes on some systems that are worth trying. Finally, there's the 'brute force' method, where you take e-mail names, assume that they're login names—they usually are—and just try to guess passwords using a dictionary, a special dictionary. That takes a while, and it's risky. The systems people for the system you're working on see all these attempts from the same user and wonder. I imagine that's how I got caught."

"Excellent. Thank you. No more such questions. So you'll know, the UNELECO people told us that they were watching your brute force attack, but they had discovered you before you started that and had been watching for a couple of days. They wouldn't go into details. And it looks like our deli chef has got your bagel ready. Coffee?"

"That'd be great. Black. Hmm. Sounds like those UNELECO people are good. So, I have a question, Dean Weathers. Who's this athlete you need me to tutor? And what's his situation, grade-wise?"

"Basketball player named Jamal Washington, a real super-star, at least by Frémont State standards. Seems sharp. He'll be a second-year student this fall, his first year they had him on 'red-shirt' status, meaning he was here but didn't lose a year of eligibility. He's taking two courses during the second summer term that starts in a couple of weeks, a survey course in natural sciences and an intro to computers course. He says he's got to get 'A's in both, to maintain the GPA he needs to play. That's my fault, partly, because I'm on this faculty committee that's recommending raising the minimum standards. Hence my involvement."

"What's his major?"

"Theater and dance, interestingly enough. He said he likes the acting and wants to improve his coordination on the basketball court with the dance. I can just imaging him doing ballet lifts. His partner would get nose bleeds from the altitude. And, listen, both of you, don't make any 'tall' jokes. He's sensitive. And, as you'll see, tall."

"I didn't take the intro course, so I'll have to find out what's covered. But it shouldn't be too hard. Where's he from—oh, you said Denver, didn't you? What high school?"

"East High. Pretty good school, as inner-city big schools go. His brother, Radford, was here a couple of years back, and he graduated in four years with honors. So either it's a smart family or a good high school, or both."

The doorbell rang again, and this time Hal got up to do the honors.

LOLLY, the one person in the SCREW crew with first-hand experience, was able to say with authority that the Archuleta County lock-up was not up to the standards of the La Plata County lock-up, although the view out the little barred window was better. Neither Rutherford nor Felterson had any reason to be experienced with the legal system. And, despite his potential for such experience, by some miracle

Excess Homicide
A Four Corners Mystery

Flip Chester had managed to avoid it, even with his reputation in Durango's police department.

It was not pleasant, for any of them, experience or not. How quickly a fun Sunday outing had degenerated.

The Neon had a reasonably good HEPA filter on its air conditioning system, and the stronger odors of the cattle herd began to seep into the car's interior about half-way through the teeming mass of bovines. The car's stoned occupants had quickly opened the windows, only to find the outdoor air to be even more fragrant. As they made it past the herd, waving gleefully to the cowboy leading it, they all stuck their heads out of the car, like dogs on a ride, for fresh air.

It took several miles for the car to begin to smell fresh—there was a lingering scent from the brown streaks—and just about the time they were breathing freely, their world ended.

"Oh shit, oh Jesus." Lolly, driving carefully in the fuzz of her cannabis-impaired senses, was the first to see the sheriff's SUV parked across the road ahead, lights flashing, uniformed officer standing impassively with his hand in the "STOP" gesture.

Rutherford, in the front seat with her, had less charitable thoughts. At least the car was aired out pretty well, he thought, and the cow shit should hide whatever other aromas there might be, especially incriminating ones. That, however, turned out not to be the case, because Sheriff Ron Grange, having been raised on a ranch, had no difficulty distinguishing between cattle fragrances—the sweet smell of money—and the odor of dope smoke.

At least he was nice about it, the sheriff. He had them sit on the ground, on a soft patch of grass, with red Indian paintbrush and columbines, plastic cuffs on but with their hands in front, while he searched the car. Flip, on seeing the SUV, had divested himself of his stash, so Lolly would be held responsible for the baggie of vegetable matter that Grange found wedged behind the rear-seat arm rest. Felterson had brought several rolled-up maps in a day-pack, and one of these had a circle drawn around an area in which Grange knew a new ranchette subdivision was being developed. There were several containers of strange substances in the trunk, including bottles of Karo syrup and cans of lapidary grit, and some long-handled bolt-cutters.

And in Rutherford's shirt pocket, he found a folded-up note that piqued his interest.

Sheriff Ron Grange, being a modern sort of sheriff, read everything he could from his neighboring sheriffs' offices and from the CBI, so he was well up to date on various ongoing investigations in the region. And, with what he was finding, he knew just what phone calls to make when he got back to town.

So, as the SCREW crew was adapting to their new accommodations, Grange was on the phone. Annette and Hal were cleaning up after their breakfast/brunch/lunch marathon when a telephone rang from under a pile of newspapers. Annette recognized it as hers and went digging for it.

"Trieri, CBI"

"Ms. Trieri, this is Ron Grange, over in Pagosa Springs. How's your Sunday, nice, I hope?"

"So far so good, Ron. How are things over your way?"

"Well, interesting, I guess you'd say. I'm calling because of that, actually. Got some folks in my detention facility who might just be connected with that fire over in

Excess Homicide
A Four Corners Mystery

Monticello at that lumber mill I heard you're investigating along with the Utah State Patrol folks."

"No kidding? Well, that would certainly brighten my day. Who?"

"Four people, caught them with various strange substances, including marijuana, in suspicious circumstances. Let's see. Car owned by and driven by one Louella Markham, Durango address, said she's 32 but her license suggests she's 38. Passenger number one is Steven Rutherford, 27, Durango. Passenger number two is Aaron Felterson, 29, Pagosa Springs. I know this guy. He's a local activist and general pain in the ass. Passenger number three is Phillip Chester, 39, Durango."

"I know passenger number three, he's a local pot-head. If you found some grass, it's his, 99% probability. He's pretty harmless, small-potatoes sort of guy. And I know Ms. Markham, too. She's out on a personal recognizance bond during pre-trial maneuvering. She was spotted near the mill in Monticello, but all we have her for is driving a car with stolen Colorado plates. And this guy Rutherford is connected with her somehow, maybe with the Monticello thing also. What strange substances, besides the pot?"

"Couple gallons of corn syrup. Some really fine sand, like lapidary grit. Maps, and Felterson had these, showing the location of a new subdivision—and they were on the road toward it. I figure they were going to mess up some construction equipment."

"You going to charge them?"

"Well, I'm not sure it's worth the hassle. The dope wasn't much, way under an ounce, and it was stuffed in her car behind the rear-seat arm-rest. I figure that one of the guys in the back seat, probably Chester, according to what you just said, put it there when I stopped them. Can't imagine Markham carrying it around in a new car, especially if she's out on recognizance just now."

"Unless it was left over from before her adventures with us. She's kind of an air-head."

"Maybe, but they were all higher than kites. One of my deputies smelled dope smoke when they drove by him up the road a piece. He called them in and I collared them. Anyway, I can book her for DUI and probably conjure up some kind of disturbing the peace thing for the others, if you want me to hold on to them."

"Did they make their calls?"

"Markham did, to a lawyer in Cortez, ah, some guy named Reid Tompkins, according to our version of caller ID. She got his answering machine, and boy, was she pissed."

"Did you do the roadside test on Markham?"

"Yeah, and she fell flat. I mean literally, during the one-foot part. Good thing the turf underfoot was soft. With that and the stash, I could cause her lots of headaches, but you know how these cases are."

"Yeah, not worth the hassle. But because she's out on recognizance just now, this is an excuse for me to see if I can get it revoked. I'll work that end, and we can figure out how to get her out of your hair. And I'll leave the others to you. I guess it would be pretty hard to get them on 'intent to sabotage' or something just for having that other stuff, though."

"Yeah, but there's one more thing. It's what made me think of the possible Monticello connection. Rutherford had this piece of paper in his pocket, folded up. Printed on it was 'Dear Developers: SCREW [and it's SCREW in capitals] you! Stay out of our forests!'."

"Oh. Well. That's interesting indeed. More interesting than I'm supposed to tell you, unless Todd Sweeney has talked with you."

"Sweeney? The FBI guy over your way?"

"Yeah. Well, hell, I'll just tell you anyway, but keep it secret, OK? You called me because you read about the SCREW note in Monticello, right?"

"Right. And because of the connection with sabotage."

"Well, the secret is that there was a SCREW note at the scene of that assassination attempt up in Boulder on Friday."

"What? No shit? Uh, excuse the French. But, really? I mean, from what I've been reading, that was carefully done, the perps got clean away. I can tell you, there's no way that this bunch could have pulled that one off. These people remind me of the Three Stooges and their girlfriend."

"I've been thinking the same thing. The Boulder note is probably a misdirection. The feds know about the Monticello note, I talked with Sweeney about it. He agrees that they're probably not connected, but they're looking into it. I'll mention this one to them as well. So, anyway, I'll get Markham's bond revoked and come pick her up. Anything else I can do?"

"Yeah. Figure out what to do with her car. It's stinking up our holding lot. But that's a long story."

ANNETTE WAS RIGHT—after the interview on Sunday, the flood gates opened. Monday's papers were full of "unnamed source" interviews, sound bites, and hearsay about the mysterious Bug-Be-Dead van and its two occupants.

Although less precise than the descriptions from the NCAR security tape, the public perception of the van's occupants was taking form. The *Denver Post* reporter who summarized the variety of eye-witness reports described that form for his friends as "Those Las Vegas comics, Penn and the short guy Teller with a corncob up his ass." And the radius of their sighting was increasing—someone had seen the van drive into a car wash on the far east side of Boulder, over a mile from the shopping center where its occupants had been seen taking the signs off.

The car wash information was new to the Secret Service and FBI teams, and they were not amused to be scooped by the news media. The news media, of course, rubbed this in with gleeful abandon.

Pickle and Mad Dog, however, were too busy to read the Monday papers, for they had chosen Monday as the day to lean on Timothy Langer. They drove down from Norwood quite early and staked out an apartment building where he was supposed to be living.

About 9:30, Langer left the apartment building in the company of two other people, and they all climbed into a beat-up, older model Ford Bronco and headed off toward the campus. Langer was let off in front of a building with a sign that said "Streak Willoughby Athletic Dormitory," and, before Pickle and Mad Dog could do anything, he disappeared inside. They debated what to do next, and finally settled on following him into the dorm. Langer would recognize them on sight, of course, but they would be careful.

After spending a half hour trying to find a parking place that wouldn't get them towed—even on the Monday holiday, the public spots were mostly full—they walked

Excess Homicide
A Four Corners Mystery

back to the athletes' dorm and strolled in through the open front door. They found themselves in a large lounge area, full of couches and easy chairs, study tables and bookcases. There was a television in a far back corner, tuned to the Cartoon Channel, from the looks of it. After their eyes adjusted to the relatively dim lighting, they recognized the back of Langer's head, over in a corner in front of two open windows, sitting with a group of very dark-skinned young men. One had his leg in a cast, propped up, crutches leaning against his chair. Another, quite tall, was leaning over a table, paying close attention to Langer. The third, a tall, bulky fellow, was sitting in an easy chair, reading a newspaper, nodding off.

Following a brief consultation, Pickle walked toward the corner where the group was sitting, and Mad Dog held back, leaning casually against a column in the middle of the room.

For his part, Tim Langer was surprised at how fast everything was going. The Sunday meeting with Jamal—and man, this dude was *tall*—went better than he'd expected. For one thing, there was no communications gap. Tim had sort of expected to have to get used to hearing ghetto slang, but that wasn't the case. In fact, Tim was finding himself speaking with more care than he usually did, so as not to sound like a dullard to Jamal. For another, Jamal seemed both interested in learning about the technical background behind the tool that he had learned to use in high school and adept at picking technical issues up quickly. So they had agreed to start on the tutoring first thing Monday, which turned out to be at 9:30, in the dorm where Jamal lived and generally hung out with his fellow athletes.

H. P. Hanson

Tim was a little late, but no one really cared. Jamal was waiting for him in the main lounge, with two of his pals, Freeman Williams, the football team's star right tackle, and Abdul Moustafa, a running back who was recovering from getting his knee 'scoped. The poor guy had blown his medial collateral ligament during a springtime pickup game—a flag football game, to his embarrassment. Having read about these football stars in the paper, Tim was learning the pleasure of consorting with celebrity. Basketball season, he thought, will be a lot more interesting this year.

Just as he was finishing going over the outline for the Intro to Computers course—Tim had spent the evening before surfing the Web—he felt a tap on his shoulder and saw Jamal looking up at someone. Tim turned to find his nemesis Pickle standing behind him.

"Hey, Timmy, listen, I need to talk with you. Could you step outside? C'mon now." Pickle had taken hold of Tim's left shoulder.

"Excuse me." Jamal's voice was silky smooth. "We're in the middle of something here, something that is really important to me. Something that we have an appointment for. We won't be much longer. Please take your hand off *my friend*." The very notion of a middle-aged guy, especially such an *ugly* one, grabbing Tim offended Jamal to the core.

"Hey, pal, I suggest you stay out of this, if you know what's good for you. Timmy and I have a little business to discuss."

During this exchange, Tim had begun to tremble; this, combined with his pallor—white as snow, a remarkable contrast to the athletes he was sitting with—made it clear to Jamal that something was amiss. So he stood up. By the

Excess Homicide
A Four Corners Mystery

time he was finished, he was hovering a good 18" above the top of Pickle's head.

"Excuse me again, sir, but I'm not your pal, and I would appreciate it if you would take your hands off my friend."

Then Pickle, whose head was tilted way back to see who was talking to him, heard a deep, sonorous rumbling from behind him.

"Don't think you're anybody's pal around here, buddy. You heard the man. Let the little dude go."

Pickle turned, only to see another very tall individual standing staring down at him. This one, however, was much, much wider than the first one.

As if by magic, a knife appeared in Pickle's right hand.

"OK, fellas, back off. I can take care of the kid here and slice you both to ribbons before you can say jigaboo." He looked surprised, apparently realizing what he'd said just a fraction of a second too late to stop saying it.

"Before we can say *what*?!" Jamal and Freeman were almost in unison. But Pickle didn't have a chance to answer. There was a sharp cracking noise, and Pickle squealed in agony as his right wrist broke from the blow by one of Abdul's aluminum crutches.

"Aw, it bent!" was Abdul's only comment, referring to his crutch, as Pickle's knife went skittering into the corner.

"Time for you to fly, friend." The rumbling resumed briefly as Freeman grabbed Pickle by the shirt collar and the belt, picked him off his feet, swung him back and forward and let him sail out the open window.

In itself, this wouldn't have been catastrophic for Pickle, for this was the first floor and they had come up only a few steps from the ground at the entrance to the dorm. His wrist, of course, was broken, but he could have landed on the grass with little additional damage. However, outside the window was a robust hedge, green and healthy, thick and hearty, of carefully pruned hawthorne. The pruning administered by the grounds keepers over the decades seemed to have enraged the otherwise placid bush, because it had grown its thorns much longer than one would usually expect.

Pickle's first ever solo flying lesson ended with a landing in the hedge. He sank in a foot or so, felt himself being stuck as if he'd become a pin cushion, and wriggled so much that he became completely entangled. The pain of his wrist was a secondary problem now, and the wailing sounds he was making were easy to hear inside the dorm.

Back inside, Mad Dog had sprung into action, but he was just a tad late to save his friend from flying. He took out Freeman with a blind-side rabbit punch, and kicked the cast-encumbered Abdul off his chair. Then he was facing Jamal, who had come out from behind the table and was standing between Mad Dog and Tim, who had backed into the corner.

"Stand on the knife, Tim, but don't pick it up. Fingerprints. There's going to be police involved here, sometime." Although calm, Jamal seemed ready for trouble. He was also fascinated by Mad Dog's wandering eye, which was doing double time in its random walk around the room.

"You, boy, are in bigger trouble than you know."

"Jigaboo? Boy? Man, what planet are you two guys from, anyway? Listen, whoever you are, you can sucker punch and kick people in leg casts, but you've got more than you can handle with me. The folks over there are calling the cops. We've got witnesses. Your friend isn't going anywhere without hedge clippers. You might as well just sit down and be quiet and await your destiny. It's inevitable. Unless you want to get hurt, white boy." Jamal had taken just enough theater training in his first year at Frémont State to have access-on-demand eloquence.

With a growling noise, Mad Dog rushed the taller, lighter basketball player, but Jamal simply stepped aside and gave Mad Dog a kick in the pants, which helped accentuate his crash into the bookcase on the wall. Mad Dog turned, truly worthy of his name now, and began a slow, careful stalk.

But Jamal stood his ground, balanced on the balls of both feet. When Mad Dog was just under two meters away, it happened, almost too fast to see. Jamal jumped, executing a double pirouette with remarkable speed and even grace, and, on the second revolution, he thrust out his left leg a long, long way, landing a back heel kick with his Doc Martin boot squarely on the point of Mad Dog's jaw. There was a sort of crunch, and teeth flew from Mad Dog's mouth. He toppled into a heap on the floor, sliding under the study table.

"Holy Moroni!" Tim was the first to speak. "Jamal, what in the world was that move? I've never seen anything like it, even in the movies!"

"Well, I took karate at home, in high school. Now I'm taking ballet. I sort of improvised."

The rumbling noise was back.

"Abdul, you OK? Good. Hey, guys, I was reading in the paper about how the President was almost assassinated by two men, a big one and a little one, and the little one had a funny, puckered mouth. What the hell, let's call the FBI."

"I've got a better idea." Tim was smiling so wide his nose was stretched. "I know this lady who runs the _C_BI, the

Colorado Bureau of Investigation, down here. She'll know what to do."

Excess Homicide
A Four Corners Mystery

Fourteen

"He said what?"

"He said that he was going to send me two season passes for basketball. He claims that it's because I started things in motion, I guess he means the tutoring, things that wound up with all the great publicity. He figures that all the home games will sell out, and probably away games, too, because we have this ballet-jumping, karate-kicking center playing for us. Of course, I think it's all a way to get me to make sure Jamal's grades are good enough. And we already have season tickets, even though we haven't used them, so I'll give the new ones away. Hmm. Unless they're better than ours."

Annette and Hal were once again in the middle of a long breakfast on the deck, home-made muffins this time, discussing Hal's conversation with the Frémont State Athletic Director. His call was the most recent fallout from the "Rumble at the Streak," as the *Frémont Free Press* called it.

From Hal's perspective, the fallout was good news. The students had reacted appropriately, if exuberantly, to a clear threat, and the threat had been mitigated in the least damaging way possible. The university fared well in the press reports.

The fallout was also good news from Annette's perspective. For one thing, the feds now owed her, big time, *biggest* time. She had turned over to them, with no fanfare or expectation of credit, their two main suspects in the assassination attempt. And she'd done it in relative secrecy. More importantly for Annette, having Pickle and Mad Dog off the streets had opened Timothy Langer up, and she now had a much clearer picture of Schoenfield's activities than before. Tim was still afraid of Schoenfield, so he wasn't going to be testifying. But Annette knew enough to develop strategy.

Although still afraid of Schoenfield, Tim considered the fallout to be good news, too. He had a new set of friends, his first ever, practically—friends with celebrity status on campus, no less. He had season tickets to both football and basketball. He wasn't afraid of getting caught hacking any more. And girls were noticing him.

About the only people for whom the fallout was bad news were Anthony J. Mercer, also known as Pickle, and Morgan L. David, aka Mad Dog. Mercer's wrist was in a cast, and some two hundred small puncture wounds, many as deep as two inches, had been tended to. David's jaw was wired together, *sans* three molars, two uppers and a lower. From a medical perspective, the only good news for these two was that David's eye had stopped wandering. He was delighted and would have talked Mercer's ear off, the one with the four little holes in it, if he could have talked more than just to say "Mrrph."

From a legal perspective, there was no good news at all for these two. Because the NCAR security guards had positively identified them as the two Bug-Be-Dead workers who had made a service call to the laboratory the morning

Excess Homicide
A Four Corners Mystery

of the assassination attempt, the feds were holding them without bail. And the ballistics match that showed their involvement in the assassination attempt implied their involvement in the murder of Arthur Powell at Natural Bridges Monument. Annette had her suspicions about other murders as well, and their incarceration on federal charges would give her time to sort all of those out.

And, to add insult to injury, Bug-Be-Dead, Inc. had announced that it was going to sue them for defamation.

"Does this mean that we're going to the basketball games this year? And can you pass the peanut butter?" A basketball fan ever since playing on her college team, Annette had been wanting to go, but something always came up.

"Well, it makes a difference, knowing one of the players. You remember how we enjoyed football more after we met the Twin Towers, no matter the circumstances. And, hey, this basketball player could be a gas to watch, if he's on your team. I mean, anybody messes with him is asking for trouble, and the opposing players know it. This could be fun."

"I'm glad it all worked out so well. If I'm right, these two thugs are responsible for killing a lot of people, very well, I might add. The clean crime scenes, for example. They must have had brain lock to get themselves in the situation in the dorm."

"I bet they weren't thinking it would be an issue. I mean, it's a college dorm. They go in, find Tim, use their adult ways to intimidate the students, and spirit him out of there. They didn't figure in running into Jamal and his friends. The flying lesson was especially good. Who'd think those hawthorne hedges would be so useful? They were planted years ago, you know, when the old college needed a way to keep the boys out of the girls dorm."

"I didn't know. But I do remember college, so it isn't surprising. Anyway, that chapter seems to be closed. The issue now is nailing Schoenfield and there still isn't solid proof of much of anything. Even if Tim agreed to testify, he would get torn to shreds by a good defense lawyer. He's got some real animosity toward Schoenfield that he isn't talking about, but it would come out in court. His testimony wouldn't hold up."

"Is there evidence that Mercer and David work for Schoenfield?"

"Formally, they work for the X-S Ranch, Incorporated. The X-S is owned by the non-profit corporation Resources For Humanity. Its board, the public board, is a bunch of community leaders from around the region, but everyone recognizes that it's run by Schoenfield. But that's hearsay. So, if asked, Schoenfield will say that these two renegade X-S employees, whom he hardly knows, went off and did these Bad Things without his knowledge, oh dear, oh dear."

"But if Mercer and David testify against Schoenfield, and Tim does too…"

"There are possibilities there, but I don't think Mercer will. David's not talking just now. And getting Tim to testify is more than I'm willing to push for. What I really want to do is to get Schoenfield red-handed. Somehow. But I'm optimistic. Events, she said ominously, are in motion," she said, ominously, despite her grin.

"You were talking the other day about a computer sting. That's probably the best part about getting Tim to stop worrying about whatever he was worried about."

"Yep. I think he was worried about Mercer, as controlled by Schoenfield. He'll talk about it eventually."

"Well, I'm thinking that the U will come out of this in pretty good shape, unless our guy Steven Rutherford turns out to have killed somebody."

"Probably not. I expect he was part of the Monticello arson, but that's it. He's not talking about that, but he's talking about other stuff, being pretty cooperative. I think he's pissed off that Mercer and David used that SCREW note up in Boulder. But he's also worried, I think. The guy who got killed over in Creede, the squished guy—remember?—was a friend of his. Rutherford thinks he may be next on some hit list. There was talk between them of a sort of revival meeting for Resources For Humanity. Wellington, the squished guy, thought it was just a wise-use group thing, but he talked to Rutherford about racist overtones. So that's another possible connection between RFH and Schoenfield's outfit, at least I think it's Schoenfield's, the Aryan Rights Foundation.

"Anyway, we've managed to scare the bejesus out of those environmental people, and they're actually starting to cooperate. I had a little chat with the lawyer, Tompkins, about the lay of the land, and he's been pretty reasonable. I'm not sure about him, though. There's more there than I've figured out." She popped a piece of muffin smothered in peanut butter and honey into her mouth.

"Anybody ever figure out what SCREW means?"

"I think Tompkins knows, and I'd bet the mortgage that Rutherford knows, but they're not talking. Probably worried about incriminating themselves."

"At least, if you're right, with Mercer and David off the streets, Rutherford doesn't have to worry about being next."

"Yeah, but we don't have to let him know that. I like keeping him off balance."

BOTH HAL AND TIM LANGER had ulterior motives in seeing that Jamal's grades were up to par—good basketball games—so they were meeting often to keep on top of the situation. When Annette heard about this, she designated Hal as a sort of de facto probation officer for Langer. This merely gave Hal an excuse to discuss computer hacking issues with Langer, in particular, those related to Langer's former client, as they had come to refer to Schoenfield. Annette's ominous reference to events in motion had piqued Hal's curiosity, so that afternoon he broached the subject with Langer during one of their meetings.

"It's pretty clear to everyone that Mercer, I mean, Pickle, is just a fall guy, an operative, for whoever's in charge of all that was going on."

"Oh, yeah. He was an enforcer, and if his enforcement didn't work, Mad Dog would take over. I can't tell you what a relief it is not to have to worry about them."

"They were looking for you, but why?"

"Probably because I wasn't getting the job done, the job on UNELECO. Because I got caught by you guys."

"Your name was kept out of the papers, I think. At least I didn't see it. Do you suppose that you could still succeed at getting into UNELECO? I mean, tell your client that you've done what he wanted?"

"But I haven't. And he knows I got caught, I think. At least he knew it if it was on the CBI computer, and it probably was."

"Oh. You mean that he wouldn't buy a story about how you were questioned and released and are being disciplined by the university. But then you went ahead and hacked into UNELECO anyway, just because you wanted to do a good job?"

"Uh, I don't think he'd buy that, no."

"Hmm. Well, I was thinking of helping Annette set up her sting."

"What kind of sting?"

"As I understand it, the idea is to plant information somewhere that he can get to only if he has unauthorized access to where it's planted. The information would be about something that the CBI thinks he's done, something shady. It's false information, of course, but designed to make him act on it, but only if he's really involved in the shady stuff. Then they have him stung."

"So what do you need UNELECO for?"

"With all due respect to the CBI people, I think UNELECO's computer systems jocks are better, they could do a better job on the sting. Also, your client doesn't know his way around on those systems so well. If the CBI makes changes to catch him, he might notice something fishy."

"Right, he might. He's not real sophisticated, though. If they want to make changes, a good way to do it would be to make it public, like it's a normal part of systems upgrades, or something. Put out a flashy MOTD for all to see. Then, the changes to catch him wouldn't be so suspicious to him."

"Uh, MOTD?"

"Message of the day. It tells people, when they log in, what new stuff has happened on that system, that sort of thing."

"Hmm. I know Annette got her boss to stop big changes on the CBI system, like—what did Jamie call it?—

rebuilding the root login, I guess it was. That would apparently wipe out your secret login, right?"

"Yep. And, of course, he'd wonder why he couldn't get in and probably try a lot and be real frustrated and mad, but that would be the end of it. Keeping that login alive is the first step toward getting him."

"So what's your position on this. Want to get him?"

"You bet. With him as well as Mad Dog and Pickle out of circulation, I'd be breathing a lot easier. I mean, as things are now, he could hire a couple of new thugs and I'd be back to where I was a week ago."

"You have a unique combination here, you're knowledgeable about this, and you're motivated. And, since this is summer, you have time. Jamie knows what to do, I think, but she's mostly upset with you, not your client. And I guess the UNELECO people are out of the picture. Annette is working the sting from her own angle. But the more angles we get going, the better."

"So, if you don't mind my asking, Dean Weathers, what's your motivation in all this?"

"Oh, a couple of things. I want Annette to succeed, of course, but she'll do that with or without me, I'm sure. But I also want to get who's really behind all this, at least if he's responsible for the portfolio."

"Portfolio? Of what?"

"That's right, you may not know. Well, over the past year or so, someone has been killing off people associated with the environmental preservation movement. Mostly, it's been pretty radical environmentalists that have been killed, all with some connection or other to some shadowy group called the Mother Earth Defense League, MEDL. But not always. I forget how many, but it's around a dozen. As much as I'm a centrist on these issues, it offends me that someone's going around killing people. And everything we know, which is admittedly not much, points to Senator Schoenfield."

"I heard my uncle give a speech once, where he talked about how the tree-huggers were preventing people from using their land, the resources God gave us, for their families. He's a sort of bogus preacher, and he brings God into everything when he can."

"Your uncle? Would I have heard of him?"

"Michael Oswald. He calls himself 'reverend,' but that's just his ego. He's really a lawyer. I heard he got disbarred for something or other. Now, he spends his time drumming up support for Resources For Humanity, the outfit that the Senator set up as the front for his ranch and for his other thing, the Aryan Rights Foundation. What a crock that one is."

"Does Annette know about these connections?"

"Um, I think so. I don't remember if I talked about them with her. But I think so."

"Is it OK for me to tell her what you just said, in case she hasn't heard it?"

"Uh, sure, but I'm still scared of going to court or anything."

"She isn't going in that direction at all. But better yet, why don't you just give her a call? Volunteer to set the sting up for her. That would really rehabilitate you in her eyes."

EVEN THOUGH they all knew each other, they were supposed to pretend they didn't. Instead, they were assigned numbers, and the operation began to sound like a parody of a bad spy novel, "Number One" this, "Number Two" that.

H. P. Hanson

But those were the rules. To make matters even more ridiculous, they had to wear hoods, black ones that were intolerably hot during the day, when they were practicing. During the real thing, at night, the black hoods would help disguise their lily-white skin. But no one thought to suggest white hoods for daytime practice. Even tan and green camouflage ones would have been better than black.

Number Three, known to the rest of the world as Gerald McTeague, was sweating so much that he couldn't see. He'd been using the hood to sop the sweat from his eyes, but it was saturated by now and so were his sleeves. But he needed to see, for his role in the operation was to be the signal relay. A flashlight was going to send him the "go" signal, and he would use a flashlight of his own to relay the "go" to Number Two, who in actuality was Gerald's best friend Bob Roy, down the way. Bob Roy, er, Number Two, would cut a climbing rope with his razor sharp axe, which would let the rock go, pulling out the support under the main timber of the little bridge over Lime Creek above the Spar City site, which would collapse the bridge just in time for the Forest Service truck, on its rounds bedding the camp grounds down, to fall into the creek and be swept over the falls just below, killing the meddlesome rangerette with the big hooters in a way that would look like an accident. The flashlight that Gerald's sweaty eyes were supposed to see was to be triggered by the pickup's passing a certain tree just up the road from the bridge.

Of course, during this practice run, the pickup wasn't the rangerette, it was Number Five, the only one of them that no one knew, the ringleader. He was from Cortez. And, naturally, Number Two wasn't going to cut the rope, he was going to whack a log instead. In theory, it was easy, but

Excess Homicide
A Four Corners Mystery

with the sweat and the daylight, Gerald had his doubts about whether he was going to see the flashlight. At night, of course, it would be a snap. But Number Five insisted on practice, and he was a real taskmaster. Plus a real asshole.

The latter personality trait had come out during planning meetings. The distances involved, a few hundred yards, would allow the use of those cheap walkie-talkies, or even whistles, so why not use them?, Gerald had asked. We thought of that already, came the condescending answer: Because they use open radio bands and anyone can hear, and because we need to keep quiet. But if someone just said "Go," well, so what if it's overheard? Smarter people than you thought this up and this is the way it's going to be done, with flashlights, was the answer. If you don't want to do it the right way, then we'll find someone else and you can get yourself off the "A" list.

Was that it? Or was that a glint from a car window on the road? Shit, this is impossible. Just to cover his ass, Gerald turned and blinked his flashlight in the direction of Bob Roy, who must have seen it because there was the whacking noise, right on time. OK, great, exercise over, I'm getting out of this goddamned hood. Gerald stripped the dripping black cloth off.

"Number Three, you're out of uniform." The booming voice seemed uncannily close. "That'll be ten demerits. You also screwed up the operation with a false signal. That's about it for you, soldier. We don't tolerate mistakes or incompetence. You want to play with the real men, you've got to do it the right way, our way. Otherwise you might just as well head for Boulder and hang out with those limp-wristed faggots up there. Ten demerits for being out of uniform is a hundred push-ups. In uniform. Now! And screwing up the exercise means you clean out the latrine tonight! On the ground. Now!"

It didn't help that Number Five, whom Gerald had turned to stare at, was only about 5'1" tall, a little bantam rooster puffed up with self-importance. Well, he needed to play the game, and that meant getting past this test.

"My apologies, Number Five. I saw a blinking and thought it was the signal. It must have been sunlight off the window of a car. And I signaled Number Two, he responded, and I thought the exercise was over. These hoods are hot in this sun." He put his hood back on and started on his push-ups.

While he was busy humping the ground, Numbers Two and Four arrived from their appointed positions, seeking approval from the leader. Number One was on station near the bridge and had pretended not to hear the whacking noise. His job in the operation was to untie and retrieve the rope from the keystone rock, eliminating evidence that this all wasn't an accident. During the practice, however, he was sitting in the shade with his feet in the river, listening to the gurgling water and thinking about cold beer. His hood was wet, too, but with cool river water instead of sweat.

"Whoa. What's Ger... um, Number Three up to, Number Five? I saw his light and did my thing. We done now?" Bob Roy's drawl from under his sopping hood was unmistakable, no matter what Number he was pretending to be.

"He's being disciplined for being out of uniform. And he gave a false signal anyway. We've got to do this all again."

"Aw, hell, Number Five, it's too damned hot for this fooling around. We can pull this off just fine without any more practice. The main thing is to get that Rube Goldberg contraption set up right, so the whole thing actually works when I cut the stupid rope. I don't see why we don't just blow the damned bridge anyway. I've got some TNT up at my mining claim."

"I've had just about enough of your questioning my authority, Number Two. That'll be ten demerits for you, too. On the ground. One hundred push-ups. Now!"

Because he didn't have Gerald's motivation, with a muttered "To hell with that. I'm out of here!" Bob Roy stripped off his hood and stalked off in the direction of the pickup, *his* pickup. He roared off in an indignant cloud of dust.

Gerald was up to fifty-two when he heard the truck go. Great, he thought, it'll be as long a walk for asshole Number Five as for the rest of us assholes.

"WELL, TIM," Annette was gazing out her window at the top of Smelter Mountain, "I appreciate your wanting to help. Really. In fact, you may be the best chance we have of pulling off a successful sting operation using computers. But, look, I promised not to require you to testify, and I want to keep that promise. You've been as helpful as you could have been, even telling me about Senator Schoenfield, but the more you get involved with this the greater the likelihood that we'll need you to testify."

Tim Langer squirmed in his chair, evaluating his next move. He knew she was right.

"What I'm afraid of is that I'll testify and he'll get off anyway and come after me."

"You've told me that he's behind all this stuff, at least as far as you can see, but you haven't told me what his hold on you is. Is it through your uncle somehow?"

"My uncle doesn't know, I don't think. He's kind of the Senator's front man, but he's always treated me like family." Tim squirmed some more. "See, when I was in high school, my uncle got me a job up at the Ranch, wrangling horses. I used to help out with the pack horses when the Senator went on hunting trips. And on this one trip his wife died. The county coroner ruled it an accident, but what happened is that she fell off her horse because the saddle wasn't tight enough, and she broke her neck. And I'm the one who saddled that horse. And the Senator knows all about it, so if he tells the coroner the case will get reopened and I'll get accused of being responsible for her death, maybe even charged with manslaughter. At least that's what the Senator says. I know I saddled that horse perfectly well, so I really don't know how it could have happened. But it did and she's dead and the Senator's got me under his thumb."

"So if you don't do what he wants, he'll get you for her death? Surely it's just your word against his?"

"But who would believe me? On the other hand, people would believe him. He's a senior member of the Colorado State Senate, for God's sake."

"Hmm. Well, you're probably right, there's no point in poking at that particular hornet's nest. But, look, you told me you set up computer access for him to various sites, including the CBI one. And you were going to set one up for him on the UNELECO system, right? But you also said he was pretty unsophisticated when it comes to computers, right?"

"Right, on both counts."

"Hal said he talked a little with you about the sting idea. It seems to me we ought to be able to work something out, since you've done this work for the Senator already."

"I was thinking about a practical way to get to him. But what we could do to get started is just turn the tables on him. Hack into his system."

"What? Oh. Of course. Well, Mr. Langer, you get a Gold Star. But how?"

"Well, he's probably heard that Pickle and Mad Dog have been arrested, or he will. So he'll be accessing the CBI system to try to find out why and what you people know about them, right? I could set up a script to detect when he's logged into your system and then to access his system, do things like download his directory structure. The next time, we could start downloading his filesystems, the data files, to see what's on there and what he knows. We could even write to his system, plant things to make him look bad."

"Planting things isn't what I want to do, because it could backfire. But, look, doesn't hacking into a system take time? And he's not permanently connected to the Internet, right?"

"No, he uses dial-up access. But it won't take time at all, so that's not an issue. I guess I understand about not planting things on his system. But we could plant things on your system and wait until he finds them and downloads them, right? And then he'd be caught."

"Right. And if those things motivated him to act in some way, to do something else illegal, well, then we'd really have him. But, look. I don't understand why it won't take a lot of time to hack into his system."

"Well, because it won't really be hacking. I'm his system administrator. I know the logins and passwords."

EVEN WITHOUT THE HOODS, it was still hot, but at least they were bare-headed. It helped to be able to see.

After Bob Roy had set them afoot, the remaining Numbers had grumbled and argued and grumbled some more about what to do next. Number Four's cell phone wasn't getting a signal, so they couldn't call his wife to come and get them. There was little hope that hitch-hiking, this far up in the watershed, would be productive. Bob Roy was probably sitting in a bar, sipping a cold one, and he sure wasn't going to reappear.

To make matters worse, at first Number Five had insisted that they continue to wear their hoods. The first priority was to keep their identities secret, he said. Finally, some not-so-gentle and persistent persuasion had succeeded in changing his mind. After all, if someone should see four people walking down the road in black hoods, well, wouldn't that be just a tad suspicious?

The breeze was pleasant, and the babbling noises of Lime Creek, over to their right in the trees, was soothing as they walked along. If they got too thirsty, they could drink stream water, giardia or no, but at least they wouldn't get dehydrated. Number One was complaining about being hungry, but he needed to lose some weight anyway.

Gerald figured it was at least ten, maybe twelve, miles back to Creede, and it would be well past dark by the time they arrived. They would all be hungry by then. But the time involved would also mean that things would be cooling off. He and his fellow Numbers could have used one of those summertime thunderstorms today.

Excess Homicide
A Four Corners Mystery

Gerald was thinking that this Number business was about the dumbest thing he'd ever been involved in. Number One, real name Billy Henderson, rather liked the hocus-pocus involved, but that was no surprise. A rocket scientist Billy was not. Playing at being soldiers of fortune in the woods was a welcome break from his real job, mucking the stable at the Three Rivers Dude Ranch. Even wearing a black hood in the hot sun would be an improvement over that.

And Number Four, Jonas Alberts, was unemployed, so anything to do was good news to him. The alternative, hanging out in what passed for downtown Creede hitting up the tourists for spare change, had a tendency to attract the sheriff's attention. Jonas had done that once too many times to want it to happen again.

So Gerald and Bob Roy were really the only reliable members of the team, aside from Number Five, whom none of them knew well enough to trust. They had all speculated on how this "exchange program," as the Reverend had called it, would work out. Now, Gerald thought, they were all probably wishing that Will Johnston had not been exchanged for whoever this jerk Number Five really was.

All the while, Number Five was continuing his authoritarian ways, enforcing a fast pace in single file, and silence. At least it was downhill. And, after Gerald straggled once too often, Number Five stopped leading and began following so that he could berate them from the rear. Gerald took pleasure in scuffing up as much dust as he could for Number Five to eat. Number Five responded to this by acting even more like a drill sergeant, so Gerald got to watch Number One's large behind marching in double time just ahead of him.

Then Number One stumbled, and Gerald hopped aside to avoid him. But Number Five didn't, resulting in a rear-end collision of the sort when a motorcycle runs into a dump truck. Number Five bounced into the ditch, and Number One lurched into Number Four, who toppled with him in a tangle. Gerald had to work hard not to laugh out loud. What a bunch of pathetic losers!

About that time, around a curve ahead, coming up the road their way was one of those powder-puff green Forest Service pickup trucks, driven by none other than Rangerette Adams, she of the hooters. It rolled to a stop next to the chaotic little parade.

"Hey there, fellas. Out for a hike, eh?" She was obviously trying just to be pleasant, and they all had little choice except to be nice in return. But no one seemed inclined to respond, and Number Five was even trying to hide his face. Finally, to avoid letting Number Five make too much a fool of himself, Gerald decided to speak for the group.

"Ah, no, ma'am, we're on our way back into town. Car broke down up a ways. We'll get a tow truck and come back for it tomorrow."

"Hiking into town? Geez, it must be ten miles. Want a ride? I've got time to take you in."

Gerald didn't care what Number Five might think of this. He just didn't want to walk.

"You bet. I'll hop in, these guys can get in the back. C'mon fellas." It appeared that steam was coming from Number Five's ears, but what could he do but climb in?

"Good work, Ginny, and just keep pretending you don't know me." Gerald was buckling himself in as he muttered

Excess Homicide
A Four Corners Mystery

this under his breath. Then, more loudly, "We all sure appreciate this, ma'am. My name's Gerry."

"And I'm Ranger Virginia Adams. Nice to meet you." She stuck her head out the window. "You guys all set? Hang on back there." And she jockeyed the pickup around to head back down the hill.

As they rattled down the dusty road, Gerald kept up a running monologue, interspersed with appropriate comments of encouragement from the ranger. He rattled on and on, in a louder voice than he needed to, about how he and his friends had been fishing—catch and release only—and their car broke down, about the weather and how nice it was with no storms to worry about, about what beautiful country the upper Rio Grande Basin was, about what a tough job Forest Service rangers must have.

All the while, he was writing notes on the back of the top piece of paper on the clipboard he'd found on the seat between them.

H. P. Hanson

Fifteen

The only good thing about it was that, with Lolly stuck in jail because her bail had been revoked, Reid wouldn't be getting any. Everything else was bad; no, everything else was horrible. Steve Rutherford, released on a recognizance basis, could only go about his life as best he could and wait for the other shoe to drop.

It finally did when he received a summons from Dean Harold Weathers of the College of Natural Sciences—routed, for reasons of protocol, through the Dean of the College of Social Sciences and Humanities and then through Rutherford's boss, the Chair of Sociology—to appear in Weathers' office at 10:00 AM on Tuesday to discuss the status of SCARAB as a student organization. It seemed that Weathers had responsibility for oversight of student groups with ties to programs in his college, and biodiversity was one such tie.

On Tuesday morning, Rutherford found his way to the natural sciences building—an unfamiliar location to him—and sat himself on the couch in Dean Weathers' waiting room. The little old white-haired receptionist was polite, if distantly cold, and she persisted in giving him what he could only interpret as the Evil Eye. Little did he know that Alice held SCARAB at least partly responsible for the death of her son. So his five-minute wait for Dean Weathers to finish a phone call was not at all comfortable.

Inside Hal's office, he and Annette were finishing a cup of coffee and discussing strategy, the five-minute wait for Rutherford having been calculated in advance.

"So you don't think we should even bring up the SCARAB business I concocted? Just hit him right off with MEDL and the portfolio?" Hal had thought to sneak up on the real reason for the meeting by putting Rutherford off guard.

"Well, like we discussed, we can use the threat of scrutiny of SCARAB as a trade-off for him. If he doesn't want to cooperate on MEDL and so on, SCARAB gets audited, or whatever you folks do here at the U. If he cooperates, we don't even have to talk about it. Surely he'll be a little relieved if we don't even bring SCARAB up."

"Probably. And I have this idea he should be pretty willing to cooperate. I mean, we have him tied to a Presidential assassination attempt, for heaven's sake. Wouldn't he want to get as far away from that as he can?" Hal picked up his phone and buzzed Alice. "Hi, Alice, go ahead and send him in. Did you offer him coffee? ...No? ...Good. Neither will we. Thanks."

There was a tap on the door, and it opened to admit a sheepish looking Steve Rutherford, dressed in his usual summertime sociology research assistant uniform of polo shirt and jeans. Hal and Annette were seated in their Power Seats, and Rutherford had little choice but to aim for the chair across the desk from Hal.

"Good morning, Dean Weathers. You wanted to see me?" Despite not wanting to act it, Rutherford was intimidated, and it showed. Upon recognizing Annette, his intimidation level ratcheted upward several notches.

"Mr. Rutherford. I believe we met briefly at the student-group orientation meeting last fall. Do you know Ms. Annette Trieri of the Colorado Bureau of Investigation?"

"Yes, I do. Ah, may I ask why she's here?"

"Of course. As you know, Frémont State University is a State of Colorado entity, and the Colorado Bureau of Investigation has ultimate jurisdiction over legal matters on state university campuses. So her presence is entirely appropriate when legal matters related to university organizations are being investigated. However, she has an additional reason for being present at this meeting as well." Hal turned to Annette.

"Glad to see you've been keeping your nose clean lately, Steve. I want to talk about the Mother Earth Defense League." They watched as he looked surprised and sat up straighter. "And I particularly want to talk about this list of people. How many of them did you know?"

She handed him a sheet of paper, which he took only after hesitating. He read it, blinked several times, and read it again.

"Ah, ahem, ah, I thought you wanted to talk with me about SCARAB, Dean Weathers."

"He did, and does, maybe, but I'm first. Here's the deal, Steve. So far the feds don't know about the note you had in your pocket when Sheriff Grange picked you and Lolly and the others up over by Pagosa Springs." Annette had no problem lying to suspects when it suited her. "They do know, of course, about a similar note found up in Boulder, in the debris of that assassination attempt on the President. What do you suppose they'd want to do with you if we told them about your note?" She paused for rhetorical effect, and Rutherford shifted in his chair, trying to get comfortable. It didn't appear to work.

"Now, I think that whoever was involved in the thing up in Boulder was just copy-catting your Monticello note, as a misdirection, or maybe as a joke. But the feds won't think that, at least not for a while. So what we're here for is for you to persuade me not to talk to the feds about your note and for you to persuade Dean Weathers that we have more important things to talk about than the irregularities in the SCARAB bank account. And you can do that by talking to us about MEDL and that list of dead people." This time her pause was long enough that Rutherford felt he need to respond.

"They *are* all dead, aren't they? I made a list a while back, too, and I was surprised at how many there are."

"Friends of yours?"

"Mostly. Not all. Are you investigating their deaths?"

"That's the general idea, and that's why we want to talk with you about MEDL and them. Not because you're a suspect, mind you. In fact, if you knew they're dead and some were friends of yours, I think I now have a motive for your arson at the FFPI mill. So now you really do need to talk with us."

"Why? Are you arresting me? And what do you mean, 'my arson'?"

"The FFPI arson was over in Utah, so I can't arrest you, not for that. Of course, I could tell the guys over in Utah about the motive and the note we found on you, couldn't I? But what I really want is information from you about MEDL and those dead friends of yours. We know they all have some connection to MEDL, but the more details we have, the better the chance we'll be able to find who killed them. And that's what you want, too, no?"

"I sure do. A couple were close friends. So, what do you want to know?"

Hal had been listening passively, but now he leaned forward.

"Well, the first thing I'd like to know is what SCREW stands for. I'm mostly just curious."

Rutherford looked smug. "Southern Colorado Radical Environmental Warriors. My idea, actually. Kind of clever, don't you think? And there's, I mean there was, only six of us, now there's only five. Dave Wellington is the last name on this list."

Annette nodded. "And the others in SCREW are you, Lolly, Aaron Felterson, Reid Tompkins, and my old friend Flip Chester. Which one of them was with you and Lolly at the mill?"

"Tompkins." Rutherford had no reason to protect him. "Are you granting me immunity, or what?"

"Probably 'what.' We'll see how cooperative you are. But I think you may be able to help us get a ways down the road of clearing all these cases, Steve. Maybe you can help me find a solid connection among all these victims."

BACK IN HER OFFICE, Annette was assembling the information from Rutherford in context of what she already knew, when her phone rang. That meant that Sally, the receptionist, was putting a call through directly, per instructions. Not that Annette didn't want to talk with Sally; rather, Annette was trying hard to change some of the culture of bureaucracy she'd run into at the office.

Excess Homicide
A Four Corners Mystery

"Trieri, CBI." Her new greeting was coming more naturally, after about six weeks.

"Afternoon, Annette, this is Ralph Wertlinger over in Creede. Got some information for you."

"Good to hear from you, Ralph. How are things up your way?" Annette was glad she'd taken the day last month to drive over to Creede, to meet the Mineral County Sheriff, even though his county was in a different CBI district. For one thing, the personal connection would pay for the investment in time. For another, she hadn't ever been to the spectacular valley of the upper Rio Grande, and she hadn't realized what amazing country was on the north side of the San Juans.

"More interesting all the time, actually. You remember that guy that got killed here at our lumber mill back at the end of May?"

"You bet. One of what we're calling our environmentalist portfolio."

"Huh? Oh, yeah. We talked about that when you came over for the visit last month. Well, like I told you then, we have a couple lines of inquiry going, in cooperation with the folks in Alamosa. One of them is following up on some information we found at Wellington's—he's the dead guy—at Wellington's place".

"I remember your telling me something about notes concerning some meetings that Resources For Humanity was holding."

"Right. Well, I called in a favor and got an informant to go to their next meeting, and he's managed to get himself on the inside of what they're doing. Seems that they have this tiered system, where the first set of meetings, like the one Wellington went to, is pretty open, but then they have a second tier, where only a select group is invited."

"And that's where things get interesting, I bet."

"You got it. What's happening in this second tier is that they're talking about killing people in the Forest Service, the state Division of Wildlife, and other such organizations."

"You mean talking about as in conspiracy to murder?"

"Pretty much. They don't plan specific hits at these meetings, but they talk about it in general. Then they form small teams, local people led by someone from another part of the region, someone the team doesn't know, to do a specific hit. My latest information is about a plan to kill a Forest Service ranger here. We're going to prevent it, of course, but without showing our hand."

"Good strategy. Maybe you can follow the information up the chain of command."

"We hope so. And it should be pretty easy. My guy says that their plan probably won't work anyway, because the team is sixty per cent losers. The leader, a guy from Cortez, is a little Napoleon, more strut than skill. But one reason I called is to alert you. They have some kind of exchange program. They brought in this guy from Cortez to lead the operation here, and they sent a local guy over to Cortez, or at least over your way, to lead another over there."

"Any particulars?"

"Just that his name is Will Johnston, nothing about what the job is. I know Johnston, so I can send you a description and so on. But their system keeps the information about the different jobs compartmentalized, so my guy doesn't know anything else."

"You said they were going to hit a Forest Service ranger?"

"Yep, Virginia Adams. Nice girl. They're going to try to rig a sort of accident, put her pickup into a creek so she'd drown, I guess."

"Interesting. What started as hits on people in a pretty radical environmental group, hits by pros who were very careful, is expanding to hits on regular folks. Hits by amateurs, sounds like."

"Good way to put it. And that means they can expand the operation by getting more people involved."

"Right. Just what we need to deal with. What's your next move?"

"Well, like I said, we're not going to let anyone get hurt. But we want to watch these bozos and see what they try next. I think we have enough to get them on a conspiracy charge now, but I'd like to catch more than just the little fish."

"Me, too. Let's keep in touch. And if you send me information about this Will Johnston guy, we'll keep an eye out for him."

"Will do, Annette. Nice talking with you again."

THE NEXT ITEM on Annette's agenda was the weekly CBI status-report conference call. She called in at the appointed time and listened to everyone else saying hello and how's it going and so on, then introduced herself one more time. Not everyone had become used to her new appointment yet. After hearing several district reports, she had just finished a report on activities in the Durango office when Sally walked in and slid a note across her desk. "Todd Sweeney, FBI, my line, says it's urgent." With glee, Annette excused herself and punched buttons.

"Todd? You rescued me from a conference call. Good work!"

"If you think that's good, wait 'til you hear this. We've got the Bug-Be-Dead van from the Boulder assassination attempt! It was parked at DIA, in the far reaches of one of the garages. It's black now. And guess who owns it?" Sweeney sounded triumphant.

"How in the world did you guys find it at DIA?"

"Well, it's about time we got a break in this thing. I mean, the reporters beat us to several important tidbits of information, like that car wash, and the two primary suspects were apprehended, for crying out loud, by a bunch of college students, jocks, no less, the ones who called you."

He took a deep breath and continued. "But we really didn't find the van either. It was the DIA parking security guards, rent-a-cops, who did. They noticed a black van parked in a normally empty section of the east parking garage, because one of its back tires was flat. It had picked up a nail and had a slow leak. It sat long enough, accumulating $12 per day charges, that it finally got tagged and then eventually towed. The guards remembered the news reports about the wanted Bug-Be-Dead van that was seen entering a car wash in east Boulder. And they're bored out of their minds, way underemployed, so they decided to play amateur detective and dust the steering wheel and gear shifter and door handles for prints. It puzzled them at first when they didn't find any. Then they called us. We got a make and model ID from one of the Boulder witnesses and then went to work on the thing. It seems the car wash it went through wasn't completely thorough. And neither was whoever wiped the thing clean. So we found some yellow paint that matches the Bug-Be-Dead color and some latents. And you didn't answer my question. Who do you think owns the van?"

"It had plates?"

"Stolen ones, it turns out. But we traced ownership through the VIN."

"OK, you got me. Whose prints did you find?"

"Not the owner's but someone who probably works for him. Anthony J. Mercer and Senator Jarvis Schoenfield, respectively. Actually, the title is held by the X-S Ranch, Inc., J. Schoenfield, Proprietor. Must be dated before he divested himself of the place, and they forgot to transfer the title formally." He laughed.

"Interesting. We knew about a connection between Mercer and Schoenfield, of course, but this cements it. But, look, Todd, a good lawyer will tie you up in knots. The paint is helpful but not enough. There's no crime in parking in a parking garage, even for a long time with a flat tire. And maybe Mercer's just an anal compulsive who likes a clean vehicle."

"Yeah, we know. This is just another link in the chain, not the smoking gun or anything. But it does confirm what you've been telling me about Schoenfield's possible involvement."

"He's still got deniability, though."

"Sure does. But less than before. Anyway, since you got Mercer and David for us, I thought you'd like to know."

"I appreciate it. We've got two possible tie-ins with a black van, one to a murder up in Norwood and one to another in Santa Fe, for which the only lead at all is an eyewitness report of a black van with New Mexico plates.

And I think I told you the Norwood murder was connected to your murder on the Rez last September. So things seem interconnected. Anyway, look, we're hatching a plan to get Schoenfield as well." Annette filled him in on the connection to Tim Langer's skills with computers. "What we need is information that we can put on a system that Schoenfield has clandestine access to, maybe the central CBI one, that will make him act. Got any suggestions?"

"Hmm. How about something related to the van? Doesn't have to be true, of course. Something that connects him more tightly to it. And it to the NCAR thing."

"Right. Of course, if he's the owner, he's tied to the van pretty well. But he can always claim that it was stolen, but he just didn't report it. His prints and stuff like that won't work, because he'll know better. Hmm. Say, how are you holding Mercer and David? Can they communicate with Schoenfield?" An idea was beginning to take shape in Annette's mind.

"Indirectly, through their lawyers. But their lawyers are avoiding Schoenfield."

"Didn't you tell me that the rifle that took the shot at the President was radio controlled? What if we put an inventory of the van on the CBI computer and say that we found the radio controller, or least parts of such a thing? That would be a link to the assassination attempt that would scare Schoenfield."

"I assume it got ditched somewhere, of course. Probably along with the stuff they were wearing and so on. But, look, he can still say the van was stolen, and so anything in it isn't his responsibility." Sweeney was skeptical of her plan, Annette could tell.

Excess Homicide
A Four Corners Mystery

"What if we say there are prints on the controller parts that we can't match to the others in the van, but we're trying to get a match through the NCIC?"

"I'll see if he's in there. If so, that could put a scare into him. But I think you need additional bait on the CBI computer."

"I've got another idea as well. But for this one, could you write up a summary about this and e-mail it to me? I want to use as much of the truth as possible."

"Glad to. What's your other idea?" His curiosity was obvious.

"It's not completely figured out yet, but it involves something completely different, a couple of things, actually. I'll tell you about it when I get the i's dotted and so on."

"OK. I'm interested. See ya later."

She hung up the phone and considered her next move. Should I get back on the conference call? I sure don't want to. Let me think of one good reason I should... oh, yeah, I need to learn all I can about the CBI. Well, how about two good reasons? Nope, there's not another one I can think of. Whew.

SHE CALLED CHARLES SHURE'S private line instead of returning to the tele-conference. It rang about six times and then she heard it transfer somewhere, so she stuck with it.

"UNELECO, Mr. Shure's office," came a professional-sounding voice.

"This is Annette Trieri, Colorado Bureau of Investigation. Mr. Shure gave me this number as a way to reach him."

"Yes, it's his direct line. Unfortunately, he's out of the country and we can't forward things automatically."

"Is there a way I can reach him for a short conversation?" Annette was wondering if the voice would ask her whether the call was important.

"I have your number here, and I'll let him know to call you as soon as he can, that it's urgent. I'll send e-mail and leave a message where he's staying. I hope this helps? Excuse me a moment please?" The line went into telephone limbo. Annette was impressed nonetheless—it had been a while since she had encountered this sort of efficiency.

"Ms. Trieri? You're in luck. Mr. Shure just called in with an answer to a question I sent him a while ago. I'll transfer you." Before Annette could offer thanks, she heard clicking.

"Annette? Glad I happened to call in. What can I do for you?" Shure sounded a long way away, unlike most long-distance calls in Annette's experience.

"I guess I'm lucky today, Mr. Shure. Can I ask where you are?"

"Indonesia. The phone system is, ah, less than completely modern. And, listen, this is our fourth or fifth conversation. Please, call me Chuck."

"Chuck?" Annette thought. He seems more like a "Charles."

"Thank you, I will. Indonesia? Geez, it must be the middle of the night there. Ah, Chuck, I'd like to ask if you'd mind a little subterfuge on my part. Involving information related to you. It's to try to catch whoever it was that killed Bill Campbell, the lawyer you saw murdered."

"You mean, catch Schoenfield?"

"Well, right, if it's indeed him. We've found out that he has a surreptitious computer login on the main CBI system. Those hacking attempts on your system were to have provided him with a similar login on your computers. What we want to do is to plant some false information where he'll find it, information that will make him do something, force him into action. Then we can nail him."

"What did you have in mind?"

"Two things. See, I'm going to set up a bogus file and have several false leads in it. One will have to do with an FBI case. And I'd like to use something related to Campbell's death, I don't know exactly what. But what I really want to ask you about is that Nazi prison camp journal you got. I know you've said in public, in that press conference, that there's nothing of use in there. But what if we pretend you were just lying for public consumption, that there's something in there that you're going to pursue actively, through your biomedical people, or something? That's what he wanted to happen, wasn't it?"

"That's what he thought, yes. He gave me a bootlegged copy of the other volumes of notes for that purpose. But it's all just garbage, of no scientific value at all. I see what your strategy is, though. What kind of results are you going to make up?"

"Well, I was sort of hoping you'd be able to suggest something. You've heard the pitch for this Aryan Rights thing, and I haven't. What would push his buttons, make him act?"

"There was talk of cleaning up the gene pool. I guess that connects with the Nazi agenda of eliminating what they saw as inferiors. And, well, the latest biomedical research has to do with gene splicing, related therapies, and so on. Of course, a lot of this was simply not part of the body of scientific knowledge in World War II. But I guess that Schoenfield won't realize that. Anyway, this Aryan Rights bunch, the doggie-noise outfit ARF," he actually giggled, "seems to assume that they're the ones with perfect genetic structure, or at least preferred structures. What if we pretended that the Nazi journals had information to the effect that the Aryans were actually inferior to the others, at least in some ways?"

"You mean, pretend something like the journal has information showing Jews to be, oh, I don't know, say, the intellectual superiors of Aryans?"

"Yeah, or maybe that gays are genetically more artistic, or that Asians are harder workers. Genetically, I mean. Or that Africans are genetically more athletic." She heard him giggle again. "Or, better yet, that Africans have more sexual prowess. You know, stuff that provides genetic confirmation of Schoenfield's Aryan stereotypes. Think Schoenfield would buy it?"

"Maybe. Most of these racist types are basically hung up on various inferiority complexes. But what can we say that would make him act? So we can catch him, I mean."

"How about something like this: UNELECO is seeking ways to introduce these qualities into dietary supplements, so that everyone can benefit from them. Of course, we would really never do this, but we could put that out there on our computers for Schoenfield to find."

"Ah, well, I can't guarantee that he won't go public with this information. And it could put UNELECO in a bad light, you know, with horrible publicity."

There was a long pause, almost long enough that Annette thought the connection had been dropped. It was Indonesia on the other end, after all.

Excess Homicide
A Four Corners Mystery

"You're right. But, look, it's my company. And I have all these highly paid PR people who thrive on challenges. And I really, I mean *really*, want to get this guy."

"So you're OK with it?"

"Absolutely. Give me your e-mail address and I'll send you something in writing, along with some specific ideas about wording. At least I will as soon as I can. The technology here is, um, strange. And, tell you what, I'll also get in touch with Wendell Ellison, one of my senior scientists in the Biotechnology Division. I'll tell him to help you with absolutely anything you need."

"That would help a lot. Meantime, I'll work on getting something going. And, thanks, Chuck. I'll keep you informed. Especially when it gets fun."

TIM LANGER was feeling liberated, more than he would have thought. Also, horny. He was feeling liberated because he was finally doing hacking with full authorization—is it still "hacking" if it's authorized? he wondered. It was not as much of an adrenaline rush as his earlier, clandestine work, but it was a good feeling. And feeling horny was a puzzle he'd have to work on. A lot.

Jamie McFarland had been gracious in accepting his apology for piggy-backing on her login, but it didn't surprise him that she was still a bit distant. For one thing, she had a good five years on him. He usually didn't go for "older" women, but she was too much to ignore. Smart. A better systems person than he, although probably not a better hacker. Athletic, even, unlike most of the female computer jocks he knew. Sophisticated, too—she played classical music while she worked on code.

And then there were those cantaloupes she had hidden in her shirt.

Jamie had agreed to Hal's request to set Tim up with the necessary equipment, and access, to help Annette with her little scam, but Jamie had extracted some concessions. The main one, having Tim help with plugging all of Jamie's systems' security holes, was Tim's favorite. It required that they work together. So he'd apologized as abjectly and profusely as he could, and now he was trying to decrease the distance between them. But that was tricky, because he was sure she'd see through him and just laugh. And if she laughed at him, poof, no more horny.

For her part, Jamie was amused that Tim was acting like such a love-struck schoolboy. The fact that he was trying not to let her notice that he was staring at her chest was hilarious. She thought about wearing something that would show cleavage just to see if his eyes would actually pop out. As much fun as that would be, however, it would probably also lead to complications. For one thing, they'd have trouble working together as well as they had been.

But he was kind of cute, in a boyish sort of way. And so polite, and eager to please. Very different from the guys her age who tried to hit on her.

Plugging the security holes had actually been pretty easy, so Tim was now working on an automated program—what his computer world called a "daemon"—to put on the CBI computer. When Schoenfield logged in, it would go to work and do two things. First, it would monitor and record all of Schoenfield's activities, down to the last keystroke. Second, and simultaneously, it would download information—the entire directory tree, during its first activation, plus as many files from certain key directories as

Excess Homicide
A Four Corners Mystery

time allowed—from Schoenfield's computer. Then it would transfer the information to Jamie's computer, clean up after itself on the CBI system, notify Tim, and the second part would modify itself to wait for Tim to decide what it should do next.

He also needed to figure out how to ensure that Schoenfield would find the information that Annette wanted put on the CBI system. Schoenfield, he knew, was pretty computer illiterate, at least by Tim's standards. Tim fully expected to find, probably on his second raid on Schoenfield's computer, a file with all of Schoenfield's logins and passwords, listed by what computer they worked on. This would be most helpful in discovering if Schoenfield had anyone besides Tim setting up clandestine accounts. It would also be useful to Annette as evidence, he figured.

But with Schoenfield being such a computer dolt, Tim was going to have to get cute. He wandered off to find Jamie.

She was in the middle of reviewing usage on the college's number-crunching computer when Tim knocked on her door. Here he is again, she thought, coming to practice his x-ray vision on me.

"Jamie? Got a couple of minutes?"

"Come in, Tim. What's up?" He was staring at the screen of her new LCD monitor, not her. How different.

"Well, I want to see if you'll let me try out a new alias in the user list. A sort of simplified grep. Like, grep for dummies."

"Isn't there something called 'whereis' for that purpose?" Oh, right. Her new screen saver, the three-dimensional hyper-cube drawing, had kicked in. And it did indeed look way cool on this new monitor. Hmm. Was that just a tiny twinge of jealousy that she felt because he was looking at it and not her? Get a grip, McFarland.

"Yeah, but this is for a different system, and I want a new alias so I can announce it and everyone will see it. I've got to get someone pointed at some information but have him think he found it himself."

"So you just want to create a synonym, basically, for 'whereis?'"

"Yeah, although I'll simplify the syntax. I'll call it 'findme' or something like that and have it search for filenames and directory names as well as file contents. And it will make a global search automatic, or at least a global search within the user's permission space. And I won't require logical syntax for the search string. I'll announce it on the MOTD, with a pointer to a new man page." He was referring to putting a new page in the online user manual that described system commands.

"Why are you asking me?" She shrugged and wiggled her shoulders. That did it. He was practicing his x-ray vision on her again. She felt an unexpected surge of pleasure. What is happening to you, McFarland? she thought. Leave the poor kid alone.

"Well, I'd like to try it out on the physics department server. It's the same version of Unix that's on the machine I need to use it on."

"Use the physicists as experimental subjects? Experiment on the experimenters? Sounds like poetic justice to me. Mail me the code and a new man page, and I'll put it up." She smiled and, just to have a little more fun, licked her lips. Almost! His eyes almost popped right out.

Excess Homicide
A Four Corners Mystery

WILL JOHNSTON, who had introduced himself as "Bill" to this little group, was on the very edge of losing it. They just didn't want to follow the Plan.

"Now, look, Bill. We're all from around here and you ain't. We know most of the folks in these parts and you don't. Let's just go do it our way, and we can stop this stupid arguing."

"I keep telling you, Jim," Will suspected that "Jim" had another name on his driver's license, "All I'm doing is following the plan we discussed at the meeting with the Reverend. He insisted that we do things his way, because it's part of something bigger."

"Well then, tell us about this bigger something so we can understand what this is all about and where we fit in and why we should do things your way."

"It's not my way, it's the Reverend's way. We agreed to this at our stage two meeting, didn't you guys?"

"Sure, but we were talking about operations that were supposed to take out people. You're talking about a little-bitty firebombing job. I think we should just shoot 'em all." This was from "Roy," no doubt another stage name, Will thought.

"Guys, guys. I'm here on this exchange program, and some guy from here is over my way leading an operation over there. I have no idea what that is, but I hope he's having an easier time than I am. What I understand about this is that we're just supposed to put a serious scare into these folks. The deal is that they're little more than hired guns. What the Reverend told me is that we're saving elimination for people who truly believe in what they do. He said that people like these lawyers just aren't worth the risk of a real hit. So we're just supposed to scare the shit out of them. Understand?"

"We understand, Bill, but, hell, there are other points of view in this thing. And since we live here, we know these people better and we know what it's going to take to be effective."

"Well, now, look here, uh, what'd you call yourself, 'Jim?'" The fourth person there, a large, quiet fellow, had finally stepped forward. "I agree with Bill here. And you know me well enough to know I know the people here at least as good as you do. And one of 'em is a pretty good guy, underneath it all. So I think we should just do things according to the Reverend's Plan. OK?"

Will let his face relax into a smile. "Thanks, uh, well, thanks. I appreciate your support in this. I want to do things according to the Plan, that's all."

"You're welcome. And my name's Rudy. My real name." He looked daggers at the other two.

"And, believe it or not, my real name's William." Will smiled even bigger. "So, look, Jim, Roy, this isn't supposed to be a democracy, the Reverend was real clear on that. But even if it was, we'd be tied. Doesn't that suggest we should go with the Plan?" Jim and Roy were grumbling, looking at their shoes. But they were also nodding, reluctantly.

"So what is the Plan, anyway? I mean, the schedule and everything." Jim was apparently going to make the best of it.

"Well, like I said, a firebomb in their offices. And that, of course, is where you guys are indispensable. Like you've been saying, you're from here and you know the turf and the people. I don't know squat, even where the offices are. Or much at all about them, for that matter."

Excess Homicide
A Four Corners Mystery

Roy piped up, "They have offices, what they call a professional corporation, over on Fourth Street, a half block north of Main. In an old converted house. Kind of Victorian looking."

"Landscaping?"

"Lots of bushes, lilacs and so on. Big trees in the yard. Got some Mexicans who come and tend to it."

"They keep regular office hours? You know, nine-to-five sort of thing?"

"Seems like, except every now and then someone's there in the evening. Sometimes until late. Uh, see, I know about this because I drive by there a lot. And I notice things like this, especially about assholes like those folks."

"If it looks Victorian, it's probably wood siding, a frame house, right?" Roy was nodding at Will's question. "So that means we can torch it easily. I wonder if it's been upgraded with fire sprinklers inside and all that kind of stuff."

"Probably not." Jim seemed eager to show off his knowledge now. "The city code requires them for new commercial structures, but old buildings like this can be grandfathered in, so they don't need sprinklers. Probably has alarms and all that, though."

"So we want a fire that's hot and fast, to burn as much as possible before the fire department can respond. I don't suppose any of you have been in there?"

"I have." Rudy stepped forward again. "Just offices, with office furniture. Wood, as far as I could see. Even the file cabinets. All very impressive, but wood. Probably burn like hell, if we get the thing started right."

Will smiled again. "Well, I happen to have just the ticket. Any of you guys remember napalm? What we do is to set off several ignitions outside the house, around the base of where the wood siding is. And we get additional ignitions in through the windows, as many of the windows as we can. We set up the outside ones to ignite about fifteen seconds after the ones through the windows go off. The place will go up like a torch."

"With four of us, how do we do more than four windows at once?"

"Got it covered, as long as you guys can throw a softball accurately. I mean, the house has only four sides, right?" Will's smile was grim, now. "So tell me. What's in this place that the Reverend's so eager to burn up, anyway?"

"You don't know? These people are an environmental law firm. They file lawsuits to stop logging operations and stuff like that. They're funded by rich tree-huggers, so they're like the hired guns the Reverend said they are."

Sixteen

JARVIS SCHOENFIELD couldn't stand it any longer, so he finally opened up the armoire and turned on his computer system. Because the armoire was a family heirloom, he found a coaster for his glass of Jim Beam on the rocks.

"Timmy, you little son-of-a-bitch," Schoenfield had begun talking to himself in the days since Pickle and Mad Dog had been incarcerated, "I sure I wish I knew where you are. And this thing better still work, or I'll cut off your balls and fry 'em."

The entire system was controlled through a surge-protecting power strip, so it all turned on and the boot-up process proceeded. Eventually, Schoenfield was looking at the familiar screen, a single instance of the X-S brand as wallpaper with several desktop icons superimposed. He found the one labeled "CBI" and clicked it, and then found the one labeled "Logins" and clicked it. While the computer accessed the CBI computer, the text file with his logins opened, and he reminded himself of the one for the CBI computer.

Eventually, a large window opened itself, and large block letters, formed by clever groupings of standard text, spelled out "CBI," followed by "Colorado Bureau of Investigation, for official use only." This was familiar territory, so Schoenfield grinned with pleasure and took a long sip of his Jim Beam. Then there was the usual warning that was more explicit than the "official use only" declaration, how unauthorized users would be prosecuted and so on. Finally, and Schoenfield actually clapped his hands, there was the single word "Username:" followed by a pause. He typed in his name and then responded to the password prompt, holding his breath. He finally let it out when the system began printing lines of text on his monitor:

> **Notice:** New filesystem protocols in effect. Evidentiary files to be cataloged in subdirectories via suspect last name and files with case. Restricted to qualified users.
> **Notice:** New search utility in effect. Do "man findme" to learn about simple global searches.

After that was the thing Timmy called the "prompt," a simple "CBIMain:" statement and a pause. Well, he thought, your wish is my command. He typed "man findme" as requested.

How convenient, he thought. It even gave clear examples, unlike some of the other man pages he'd tried, including an example on how to send the results of the findme command to a file for later printing.

He took a deep breath and typed "findme schoenfield", and then set about finding Timmy's instructions on how to move files from the CBI system to his own. Soon, the prompt was back, and, just to preview the results, he typed "more findme.out", which would show the first several lines of the output file from the search on his name.

The files that began with labels like /etc/cases/evidence/schoenfield/bouldercase/... got his

Excess Homicide
A Four Corners Mystery

attention. And then the first of the login notices popped back into his head.

"Shit! This better not mean what I think it means. Now how the hell do I find that file? Oh, yeah, the change directory thing, ahh, 'cd'." He tended to talk to himself more when under stress, and he drank more, too.

He changed to the bouldercase directory and found several files, including one called "van" and one called "radio". "What in the world is all this? Jesus H. Christ, I hope Pickle didn't get careless."

The command "more van" produced a distressing result:

Boulder: cross reference Mercer files on same case.
Unsuccessful assassination attempt on the President (an FBI case) still open. However, vehicle used has been recovered and is linked to J. Schoenfield via hard evidence (ownership, among other things). Cross reference: .../schoenfield/bouldercase/radio. More to follow.

He was almost too afraid to look at the "radio" file, but finally did.

Boulder: cross reference Mercer files on same case.
Cross reference: .../schoenfield/bouldercase/van
Contents of van owned by J. Schoenfield suspected as used in assassination attempt included parts identified as radio-link components (rifle in attempt was radio controlled). Several latent fingerprints suggest that individuals apprehended (cross reference: Mercer, David files) are not matched. NCIC search in progress. More to follow.

"Christ! Didn't that idiot wipe the radio off? Did I even touch it? Oh, yeah, back in March or sometime, when he was putting it together." He could feel the sweat on his forehead. "NCIC? What's that? Oh, yeah, the national database for prints. Geez, am I in there? My Army record, maybe?"

If someone had asked him later, he would not have been able to recall his actions, but they were quite calm and calculated, under the circumstances. First, he returned to his home directory to download the findme.out results. Then he printed them on his home system and erased them from the CBI system. After that, he spent several hours systematically downloading each file that had his name in it, even the ones that referred to him only because of his role as Chair of the Senate Committee on Law Enforcement.

It was about 3 AM when he was finished with this task, and then he faced a dilemma. Timmy had told him that he could erase anything he found on the computer. However, most things could be recovered from backup tapes, and erasing something would tell the CBI people that someone was hacked into their system. Files he created himself, of course, should be erased, like the findme.out one. But how could he just leave all of that damaging information there? But if he erased it, it would be recovered and they'd know.

Besides, this wasn't evidence, it was information about evidence. What he really needed to do was to acquire and destroy the actual evidence. Maybe not the van, but surely those radio parts. But the FBI had the evidence. How could he get it from them?

The computer kept itself busy during his hours of work. Even if he had known to pay attention, though, he probably wouldn't have noticed all the extra activity on his hard disk, or how slow his downloads were. He was just too distracted and worried. And drunk, toward the end.

IT WAS ABOUT 3:30 AM when Steve Rutherford finally ran out of energy. He had driven over to Cortez, to Reid Tompkins' office, and they had been discussing strategy, alternately arguing and agreeing, since about ten the previous evening. About midnight, in need of strong coffee, they'd retired to the kitchen of the converted Victorian, now an interior break room used for coffee and snacks. Tompkins had lapsed into semi-consciousness an hour earlier and now was snoring peacefully, and Steve had retrieved a laptop computer from Tompkin's desk so he could type up his version of the agreement they had hammered out.

Just as he finished up his notes and felt himself slipping into a nap, he heard a crashing noise from upstairs, like a window breaking. Then, in quick succession, there were a dozen more crashes. The commotion even woke up Tompkins.

"Huh? What's that noise? What time is it?"

"Welcome back to the living. Sounds like someone, or several someones, don't like the look of your windows." Steve walked to the nearest door and looked out.

"Holy shit! That office is on fire!" He ran across the little kitchen to the other door and opened it a crack. "The waiting room is, too! Move it, Reid, we've got to get out of here." He looked around the kitchen, frantic to find another exit. Tompkins remained seated, still too groggy to comprehend the problem.

"Reid! Get with it! The building is on fire and we're in the middle of it." Steve spotted a fire extinguisher and grabbed it. "Come on! I'll see if I can put the fire down with this so we can get out of here. Come on, move!"

He took the extinguisher back to the first door and peeked out. The office, on one of the building's corners, had two broken windows, and it was an inferno. He knew at once that escape through there would be hopeless. By the time he made it back to the waiting-room door, Tompkins was standing, but still clearly half asleep. He was looking helpless and confused. Steve had the distinct feeling that the temperature was rising.

Steve opened the waiting room door a crack and saw that the fire there was confined to an interior corner. Something had set the Victorian couch ablaze, and flames were creeping up the wall behind it. An end table, covered with magazines, was in flames, and the fire had spilled onto the floor as well. Steve readied the extinguisher and motioned to Tompkins to follow. He dashed into the room.

It was only when he reached the front door that he noticed its window was smashed. A thought flickered through his mind that this must have been where the fire in this room came from. He also noticed that the large covered wood porch was burning, flames licking up the columns to its roof.

He tried the door. The knob turned, but it wouldn't open. Must be a deadbolt, he thought. Looking down, he saw that the locking mechanism required a key. He turned to Tompkins.

"What the hell kind of place is this? We're locked in!"

Excess Homicide
A Four Corners Mystery

Tompkins looked sick. "We worried that someone would break the glass, reach in, and just unlock the door." He patted his pockets and looked ever sicker.

"Shit! My keys are on my desk. I remember leaving them when I came in earlier." He ran to a door in the wall to his right.

"Wait! Feel the door!" Tompkins laid both hands flat on the door and jumped back as if shocked.

"It's too hot to touch."

"Then we're not opening it."

There were windows on either side of the door, and Steve could see the burning porch through each. But the one on the left appeared to have more fire showing, so he looked more carefully out the one to the right. Maybe, just maybe they could make it that way.

"Help me!" He was struggling with a large easy chair. Tompkins hustled around to the other side of it and stooped to pick it up.

"We're throwing it through the right-hand window, right?" Steve was sweating not only from the exertion and stress—it was becoming downright hot in the little room. "On three!"

They picked up the chair and swung it back and forth toward the window, letting it go with an extra heave. It broke the lower pane of the double-hung window, but it was far too big to fit through the opening and so it bounced back into the room, blocking access. Unbelieving, they both just stared at it for a few seconds. The fire had spread into about half the room, and their return to the kitchen was now impossible.

"Move that damned thing!" Steve rushed to a straight-backed side chair and picked it up.

Tompkins, with more strength than he knew he had, heaved the easy chair aside, and Steve smashed the side chair into the window, shattering the remains of the bottom pane as well as the top pane and the wooden frame. Then he ran the legs of the chair around the frame, clearing out hanging shards of glass. The window was clear, but flames from the porch came licking inside the room.

Steve looked around for the fire extinguisher, found it by the door, and began blasting the flames on the porch outside the open window with its white fog. They responded grudgingly, backing away from the powder when it hit them, then recovering and regaining ground almost immediately. The noise from the porch included the whooshing of the fire and a considerable cracking and groaning of the structure itself.

"We're going have to run for it. Follow me as close as you can!" Steve blasted the flames just outside the window and stepped out onto the porch. As quickly as he could, he sprayed a path toward the side of the porch, where the flames were less intense. Just as he reached the railing, he heard a scream behind him.

Turning, he saw that Tompkins had broken through the burning and weakened floorboards. One foot had punched through, and he was up to his knee in the porch, fire licking at his crotch. He tried to pull free, but the weight on the other leg put it through, and he was suddenly up to his waist.

There must have been fire under the porch as well, because the draft created by the hole Tompkins made caused a chimney effect, and Steve was suddenly looking at a human torch. Even though Tompkins' mouth was open, there was no more screaming. But Steve probably wouldn't have heard it anyway, as he was mesmerized by the terror in Tompkins eyes.

He was staring in shock at his rival for Lolly's affections, thinking that no one deserved this, when one of the roof beams gave way with a loud snap. His world went black.

TIM LANGER'S FIRST TASK each morning was to check for messages from the daemon he'd installed on the CBI computer, and he was finally rewarded. Even though the message was coming from himself, and its contents were therefore no surprise, he felt a thrill when he read "bait taken, trap sprung." He changed to the directory he had set up to receive the files from the Senator's computer and was astonished to see how many there were. The Senator, it seemed, was using his computer far more than Tim would ever have thought.

Then it dawned on him. As an unsophisticated computer user, the Senator didn't do computer housekeeping. Files were stored where the computer wanted to store them, and, because these were all simple text and word processor files, the computer wanted them all in the same place. So, instead of differentiating among files by directories and subdirectories, the Senator was forced to use increasingly complex names. But that meant that it should be possible to find the interesting ones, or at least for Annette to. He decided he should call her, even if it was still early.

But Annette was in her office, having been rousted out of bed about 5 AM by a courtesy phone call from the Chief of Police in Cortez. A fast-moving fire, probably arson, had completely consumed some legal offices, and there were two casualties. Although they were both burned beyond recognition, the positions of the bodies suggested that they were killed trying to escape the burning building. And if the fire was found to be arson, the deaths would become murder. Identification of the victims would require dental records.

So when her telephone rang, she thought it would be more information from Cortez. Tim Langer's voice surprised her, especially because of the excitement it conveyed.

"Annette! You're in. I thought I'd be leaving a message this early. Guess what? Last night we scored! Uh, I mean, the Senator took the bait and now I have copies of lots of files from his computer."

"Good morning, Tim. Great work. Does this mean that he's found the information we wanted him to?"

"Um, I don't know yet. The first thing I looked at was what got downloaded to me, from his system. Ah, let me look—where is it?—at the activity log from his session. Here. Ah, yes, it looks like he took it hook, line, and sinker. He used the search alias I set up to find files involving his name, and then he grabbed all of them. I can replicate his actions exactly to see what he got besides the stuff we put there."

"And you say that you now have many of his files? I mean, files from his system? How did you know where to look? And what to look for?"

"A hunch. There are a couple of default directories where computers like his store things automatically. I figured he wouldn't be smart enough to save files in special places. So I just had your system get everything in these default directories while he was logged in and looking at the stuff we put there. There are lots of files, some with pretty weird names. Like this one, I'll have to spell it out: r-f-h-underscore-o-p-s-2, numeral two. Or this one: a-r-f-underscore-i-d. Others are easier to figure out, though."

"Is it easy to open these files and read them? I mean, easy enough to do one now?"

"Sure. They're mostly plain text files. He didn't like fancy word processors. But a couple are Word documents."

"How about that r-f-h whatever one?"

"Sure... um, it's a list. It starts out with a bunch of stuff under the heading 'priority,' then has another heading called 'chronology.'"

"What's on the 'chronology' list?"

"It says 'Cortez, law firm,' then 'Creede, ranger,' then 'Montrose, DOW office.' And more stuff like that."

"DOW office as in d-o-w?"

"Right."

"Tim, this is incredibly important. What information about these files did you get from Schoenfield's computer?"

"Well, the file contents and directory information, the usual stuff."

"One of my programs tells me when files were last modified, probably because I set it up that way. Do you have this information about Schoenfield's files?"

"What I did was to capture a long listing of the complete contents of his hard drive. It's listed one line per file, so it goes on and on and on, lots of pages. But it's all there, including all the system files and the executables and so on for the programs he has."

"But you downloaded only some of his text files, his data files."

"Right. Why's this so important?"

"First, can you tell me when the file you read from was changed last?"

"Ah... it looks like a couple of days ago."

"Thank you. That particular file may just be evidence of Schoenfield's being part of a murder conspiracy. That's why it's important."

"What murder?"

"It'll be in the papers tomorrow. Last night, it looks like someone torched a law firm's offices in Cortez, and two people were killed in the fire. Don't know who yet. But if it's arson, the deaths are murders. And Schoenfield has it on what appears to be a planning list. And he had it there two days ago."

"Wow. So we've got him?"

"We will have got him when he's behind bars without bail. But this is another step in that direction. Can you bring all that stuff over? Or would it be easier to e-mail it to me?"

"If you're using a CBI system, I'd rather not e-mail it. If he finds his own stuff somehow on a CBI system, it's all over, and I bet I can find more next time if we don't get him suspicious."

"You're right. Well, I've got one of those new, high capacity Zip drives on a system that's not on the network. Will that work?"

"I'll be over to see you later this morning."

ANNETTE HADN'T TOLD TIM the name of the law firm that had been burned, because it wouldn't have meant anything to him. And, really, it didn't mean anything to her, except that it connoted environmental law. EarthLegal Associates just didn't sound like the usual small-town divorce and

Excess Homicide
A Four Corners Mystery

probate group. She knew that Reid Tompkins worked for an environmental law firm, but the connection was tenuous.

She'd just have to await the results of the identification process. Maybe the victims were the arsonists, after all. Sheriff Wertlinger had described the Creede operation as being composed of losers. Maybe the Cortez one was also. She made a note to call Wertlinger to let him know that his ranger was next on the list.

What did Tim call that file? She thought hard. Was it "rfhops"? "rfh" then "ops". As in operations, no doubt. But the "2"? Did that imply a "1" on another such file? What would that have in it?

She was snatched from her musing by a knock and the appearance of Derek Petersen in her doorway.

"Annette? You wanted to spend some time on the budget today, right? Is now a good time?" And it occurred to her that it was a better time than most, actually.

Two hours later, she was feeling much better about her understanding of the workings of the CBI budget process and how her office received its allocation. But, after two hours of budget minutiae, she was also ready for something else.

Tim showed up just in time. He waltzed into her office and, with a big grin and a flourish, pulled a Zip disk from his shirt pocket.

"Did you know that, way back when, twenty megabyte hard drive packs, the removable ones, were about the size of a sofa cushion? And that the gizmos you put them into, the drives, were about the size of an easy chair? Now we have more than ten times the storage on this little thing, and the drive itself is smaller than a portable CD player. Ta da." He laid the disk on her desk in front of her.

"Amazing. I mean, that miniaturization, plus it's amazing how easy it was to get this information from Schoenfield. Um, where else is it? His computer and yours, I know. Any place else?"

"Well, I had the CBI computer erase all this from itself after it transferred the information to the computer that I'm using at the university. It's not really my computer. And I found a file where the Senator keeps his logins and passwords, organized by what computer they're for, and there aren't any FSU computers on it. So, yeah, the only places where this information is are this disk and the two systems, his and the university's."

"How much have you looked at it?"

"Not much. That file with the logins. The file I read you. The directory with the file names."

"I'd feel better if you didn't look at it any more. In fact, it would be better to erase it from the university system."

"Well, are you sure? Then there would be only the Senator's computer and that disk. I know that people with systems experience like me are pretty paranoid about backups, but it's for good reason. Computers die and stuff gets lost."

"I'll copy this disk onto my non-networked computer and then make a copy of it onto another Zip disk. Is that good enough?"

"OK. Just keep the two Zip disks in separate places."

"OK. And you'll erase everything from the university computer? Is this one of Jamie's systems?"

"Yes and yes."

"Look, Tim, I know you're probably curious about all this stuff from Schoenfield's computer. But as someone with systems experience, you should know that curiosity isn't a good enough reason to go snooping into someone else's stuff, even though you're able to do it. And this particular stuff is like dynamite, it could blow up on you. Even though it's just information, Schoenfield seems to have quite a network of operatives. You got lucky with those two a couple of weeks ago. The people in Cortez last night didn't get so lucky. The less you know about all this, the better off you'll be. So I want you to go back to the university and erase all of this, or at least all of it that isn't needed to get more information next time. I guess you'll need to keep some in order to look at the directories, huh?"

"There's so much stuff and I'm so busy now that I really don't have time anyway. But, you're right, I do need some of it. I'll erase the rest, promise."

"And I'll get right on examining this. You've done us a great service with this, Tim. I think Hal, that is, Dean Weathers, will consider you to be rehabilitated. Well, this along with the tutoring. How's that going, by the way?"

"Great. Jamal's a natural. Which reminds me, I've got an appointment with him. Got to run."

Smooth kid, Annette thought. I think I'll call Jamie McFarland and make sure that stuff really does get erased.

IT WAS NOT UNTIL MID-AFTERNOON that Jarvis Schoenfield finally woke up. It had taken him another hour and an additional half-bottle of bourbon to get to sleep, but then his body's defenses kicked in and kept him asleep for a good ten hours. He woke up groggy but, to his relief, not hung over. He also woke up worried. It took him only a few minutes to return to his computer and the problem of the information in the CBI files. He started making notes.

Four hours later he called downstairs for a meal to be brought up, and he also asked for the Reverend. Michael Oswald was down in Norwood, but he would be summoned and available within the hour, he was told.

Schoenfield was just finishing the food when there was a knock.

"Yeah?"

"You asked me to come up, Senator?" Oswald looked peeved, but Schoenfield ignored it.

"Have a seat, Mike. Pour yourself a drink, and get me one, too. We've got trouble, real trouble. We need to talk."

"Now what? And, say, I heard that the Cortez job went off great."

"Yeah? That's right, it was supposed to happen last night, wasn't it? I was up most of the night and slept all day, so I haven't heard anything. What happened?"

"Burned to the ground. I've heard they found a couple of bodies, not identifiable, but all our guys are accounted for. Cortez cops are clueless so far. Keep your fingers crossed."

"Wonder who it was. Well, no matter. Anyway, we've got to talk about the information I got last night. Remember how Timmy set me up with a way to get into the CBI computer? Well, I've been staying away from it since Timmy got away from us. But last night I finally called it up. They have a new set of files with evidence information that I found. About me. It concerns that Bill Campbell hit and the thing in Boulder. For that one, it looks like the FBI has evidence implicating me."

"How's that possible?"

Excess Homicide
A Four Corners Mystery

"They found the van and traced ownership. Some idiot forgot to transfer the title to the foundation. And there's something about prints on parts for a radio controller."

"Hmm. Well, the ownership isn't any more of a problem than Pickle and Mad Dog are—you know, rogue employees and all that. They took the van and you didn't know. But prints on controller parts are different. Did you ever handle any of Pickle's stuff?"

"Hell, I don't remember. I mean, sure, some of it. But I don't remember about radio parts."

"Well, look, we can take the same approach with this as with the van. It's part of the ranch, you live here, you use it occasionally. One time there was this stuff in it and you had to move it to put, well, whatever you were putting, say furniture, in it. So you must have touched it without knowing what it was. Then these rogue employees went off and did all this stuff that you know nothing about. This isn't really any worse than having Pickle and Mad Dog picked up."

"Yeah, I thought of this angle, too. But the FBI worries me. Anyway, we'll figure out how to get through this. But there's other stuff I want to talk about, stuff I found on the CBI computer. For one thing, it looks like that bastard Charles Shure was scamming the public, and us, when he had that press conference about his great-uncle's journals. According to what's in the files, there's valuable information in there after all. Information he's going to use to make tons of money, the little weasel."

"Like what?"

"Like, Heinrich von Scheuer discovered that there are certain genetic traits in different populations he was working on. The CBI information is sketchy, but apparently von Scheuer provides hints about isolating these traits. With modern technology, you know, gene cloning and all that stuff, it should be possible to develop pills to let people change themselves. Or for parents to custom-make their kids. Or for bureaucrats to put stuff in the water supply to control the population."

"What was all this doing in the CBI computer? And what's the connection to you?"

"Well, the connection to me is just that my name was there, because I gave, or they think I gave, Shure the journal. So I found the computer file by doing a computer search on my name. And why it's in there seems to be that the CBI is concerned about misuse of these genetic supplements, or whatever they're called, about unauthorized experiments and so on. It's really an FDA problem, but CBI's worried because it's in Colorado."

"So, what kind of genetic traits are we talking about here?"

"There's not a lot of detail in the files. But, look, von Scheuer was at a prison camp and so he had lots of Jews to work with. One of the things mentioned is mathematical abilities. Everybody knows that Yids can do interest rate calculations in their heads. And look at all those physicists that invented the atomic bomb. And even Einstein was a Jew, right?"

"Well, I have to say, Jarvis, that it wouldn't hurt the American people to have better math skills. I mean, I get the wrong change all the time in stores because people don't know how to add and subtract, even."

"And you want the government to go putting Jew genetic supplements in our water supply? I may have to

Excess Homicide
A Four Corners Mystery

shoot you right here, Mike." Schoenfield picked up his glass of bourbon and swirled it thoughtfully.

"I didn't say that, Jarvis. Geez, you're uptight these days. Look, all this sounds pretty speculative. It's not clear that there's anything to be done about it right now. We should probably just keep our eyes open. You've got access to the CBI computer, right? Well, if they're worried about this, they will update their information regularly. So just keep up with their latest stuff, OK? Or did you have something more in mind?"

"Well, I was thinking about a stage two operation of some kind."

"Against UNELECO? Whoa. They have security, good security, remember? And all we have are little groups of civilians who are playing out their ninja-wannabe fantasies."

"Yeah, you're right. Well, how about kidnapping Charles Shure again?"

"What would that accomplish? All we could do is get a ransom, and we don't really need money."

"What if the ransom was to make them go public with this gene supplement stuff?"

"Hmm. Now that has possibilities. Let's think about this more."

Seventeen

"THANK YOU for these breakfasts." Annette was trying to be as sincere as she could, but she was sure it sounded corny, or silly, or just plain stupid. They were again sitting on the deck, basking in the glow of the late July morning sun and of *huevos rancheros*, among other things, finishing the papers, and waking up with the summer morning.

Hal looked up and smiled in his mischievous way.

"You mean, as opposed to that lovely pre-breakfast interlude, or to dinner, or what?" She wadded up her paper napkin and tossed it at him.

"No, I mean thank you because otherwise I'd be at the office already slaving away. And we both know I put in enough hours as it is, without going in early. Besides, I probably do better work this way."

"Well, you sure did better work about an hour ago..." She was looking around for something else to throw, so he continued in order to distract her from throwing her fork.

"I know what you mean. I figured it out for myself a long time ago. Aside from going to work more relaxed, starting mornings slowly gives me time to think about the day ahead, so when I get there I'm ready for action. I hate it when John or somebody else calls an early-morning meeting."

Excess Homicide
A Four Corners Mystery

"Sometimes, I guess like today, I also use it as an excuse to put off what I really don't want to do. Today I get to talk with Lolly Markham."

"Lollipop? She of the now-decimated SCREW? How is she, anyway?"

"I'm told she's not so good. Her lawyer hasn't called for some days, of course. I guess she doesn't know that his was one of the bodies found in that arson fire last week."

"So you get to tell her?"

"That's the plan. And I also get to tell her about the other one, that FSU assistant Steve Rutherford we talked with a while back. Remember?"

"Rutherford? He was there, too? I guess I didn't know that, or if you told me I forgot." Hal looked shocked.

"I just found out yesterday. It took some time to ID the bodies. We're talking very well done, here. Really crispy. But we know who's responsible, except for some of the small fry. When we bring in the leaders, we'll get them, too."

"Steve Rutherford, damn. Well, I guess he just got himself in too deep. I wonder how they'll take this in the sociology department. Maybe I should call someone." He shook his head and took a deep breath.

"So, yeah, you talked about that operations list you found on our esteemed Senator's computer. I guess that'll help you get them. What about that next job, the one over in Creede?"

A wide smile emerged on Annette's face.

"It fell on its face, largely because we knew it was coming. They, I mean, another of these little bands of losers, were going to try to kill a Forest Service ranger by sabotaging a bridge. She was supposed to drive over this weakened bridge, fall into the creek, and drown. Unlike the arson in Cortez, this was supposed to look like an accident."

"A Forest Service ranger? Why?"

"Well, apparently she's been pretty active in her spare time on behalf of preservation groups. So this bunch of crazies decided to make an example of her. Although if it had succeeded in looking like an accident, I don't know how that would have worked. Anyway, that was the plan. The sheriff over in Creede, Ralph Wertlinger, had an informant planted, though, so he knew about it. And on the appointed evening, the ranger, her name is Virginia Adams, I think, just stopped her truck at the bridge and waited while the band of crazies was rounded up by the sheriff's guys. I'm told that they were all wearing black hoods, and one of them, a short guy, started yelling 'Shut up number one' when one of the others started trying to explain. It seems they were calling each other 'number one' and 'number two' and so on. Talk about losers." She shook her head.

"Sounds like what we used to call going to the bathroom when I was a kid." Annette burst into a fit of giggles, so he went with it.

"You know, stuff like 'Excuse me number one, but I need a bathroom break.' 'You do? Number one or number two?' 'I'm number two but I need to do number one.' 'But I'm number one.' Like that old Abbott and Costello 'Who's on First' routine. Wish I could have been there."

She finally got control of herself. "That's why I love you so much. You make me laugh."

"Yeah, well, it's a good thing you're a pushover. But I'm glad. So, you've got everything under control except for the Big Fish. What's your strategy with them?"

Excess Homicide
A Four Corners Mystery

"We're letting some seeds we planted grow. Tim Langer's been getting great information for us, and Schoenfield seems to be snapping up everything we put there for him to find. This means that he's aware of the FBI's interest in him, and our interest in him, too. Which means that he'll be keeping his nose pretty clean, I expect. What we want to happen is for him to get interested in the UNELECO information we planted. It's supposed to push his Aryan Rights buttons. We'll see." Annette shrugged.

"John and I have been talking about how to live without the guy, and we've decided it'll work fine. He's the ranking member of the Senate's Education Committee, but the guy behind him is even more sympathetic to our needs. He's from Greeley, and he thinks that the big schools, CU in Boulder and CSU, get too much state funding, that the small schools like UNC in Greeley, and us of course, should get more."

"Should they?"

"Well, I'm not unbiased, of course." Hal, in fact, positively oozed bias, and he grinned. "But I can tell you that we, and UNC and the other smaller universities, spend a lot bigger percentage of our state tax support on teaching, instead of subsidizing research so much. So if the taxpayers want instructional bang for their tax bucks, we're a good choice for them. But do you think you can get both Schoenfield and the other guy, Tim's uncle?"

"Oswald. Michael Oswald. Pretend preacher who's really a lawyer, a defrocked lawyer it turns out."

"You defrock preachers. Lawyers get disbarred."

"Yeah. Whatever. But he's been leading these Resources For Humanity meetings and planning sessions, according to an informant. And so far the plans coincide with the stuff on Schoenfield's computer. And that is now murder one caliber stuff, as well as a lot of conspiracy stuff. Not to mention a link to the Presidential assassination attempt. Oh, and I bet I didn't tell you. I finally figured something out from the information we got from Schoenfield's computer. Tim told me about a file with a weird name, RFHOPS2. It has that Cortez fire and the Creede thing with the ranger in it, along with lots of other things. But I figured that there should be an RFHOPS1 file as well, but there wasn't. So I kept looking at these files, there are hundreds of them, and finally ran across what I was looking for. It was called PHASE1OPS, and it hadn't been changed since late last April. It has a list of all the deaths in our environmentalist portfolio, plus a couple we didn't know about. It looks like those two guys, Mercer and David, who the FBI has on the assassination charge, were responsible for all of them, and that Schoenfield was the mastermind."

"Was there a file about the assassination attempt?"

"Oh, right. Called PREZOP. Plus a big long essay about why the President deserves to die. Plus other essays on how Aryans are superior; well, no, actually they're about how non-Aryans are inferior. He really slanders Latinos. This guy's way over the edge."

"So why don't you just arrest him? It sounds like you have enough information to charge him with all sorts of stuff."

"There's concern about the admissibility of the information. Even though Tim was the system administrator for Schoenfield's computer, it wasn't really formal, so it may not have been kosher for him to download all of Schoenfield's files. Also, because we got them over the

Internet, it's not clear that we can actually prove they're Schoenfield's. So we're going to try to catch him actually doing something. Hence the business with UNELECO."

"What's going to happen?"

"Good question. Right now, I've got to get off to work, finally."

ALONG WITH THE USUAL PAPERWORK, Annette's main task for the day was the visit to Lolly Markham. Lolly, according to Annette's information, had been demanding to see her lawyer, but Reid Tompkins was, of course, no where to be found. Lolly had been offered the services of other attorneys, but she was set on Tompkins.

In order to make her visit with Lolly as productive as possible, Annette decided to have someone from the Durango Public Defender's office accompany her. She called Mimi Olive, whom she knew from an earlier case. Mimi was a good advocate for her clients, but she also had a pragmatic outlook. She briefed Mimi on the phone and they agreed to meet at the county lockup after lunch.

Mimi and Annette were waiting when the guards brought Lolly into the interview room. She looked, Annette thought, at least ten years older than she had just a month ago, when Annette first arrested her. But she also looked defiant. Kid gloves time.

"Lolly, you know the drill here. Everything is recorded and video taped. I want to introduce you to Mimi Olive, from the Durango Public Defender's office."

"I don't want a new lawyer, I want my lawyer, where the hell is he?"

"I know you want to be represented by Mr. Tompkins. You don't have to be represented by Ms. Olive. I asked her to observe this interview to ensure that your rights are protected."

"Great. Fine. Really. But where's my lawyer?"

"As you know, I've talked with Steven Rutherford about the organization you folks formed, the thing called SCREW. It started with six of you. You know that David Wellington was killed back in the middle of June, right?" Lolly, still looking defiant, was nodding, so Annette forged ahead. "Well, now fully half of the original members of SCREW are dead. Both Steven Rutherford and Reid Tompkins perished last week in an arson fire at Reid's legal offices. It appears that they were attempting to escape the fire but didn't make it. Whether their deaths were intentional or accidental, in terms of the arsonists intentions, isn't clear. This is why Reid hasn't been to see you. Understand?"

Lolly's defiance had evaporated, and she looked completely deflated, sagging, pale, slack. And even older. Then she collapsed in tears.

"Reid! Dead? N-noooooo..." Annette and Mimi let her grieve, and someone on the other side of the one-way mirror had the empathy to bring in a box of tissues. Finally Lolly looked up, pleading.

"We were going to be married. I'm going to have his b-baby."

Annette turned to Mimi. "I didn't know this, FYI." Then she turned back to Lolly.

"Lolly, now that you know where things stand, I want to urge you to cooperate with us. Perhaps we can use information you have, even if it's information that you don't think may be important, to convict Reid's killer or killers. Mimi, of course, will advise you to look to your own situation and your own defense first, and that's appropriate advice. And you certainly don't have to tell me anything. Also, Mimi doesn't have to represent you. But she's here if you'd like to talk with her. We can move you both to a private room—no cameras or windows or microphones—if you'd like to talk with her."

"They were burned to death? Oh, dear God. Do you know who did it? Have you caught them?"

"We have an idea of some of the people involved, and we know where to find them. We'd like to get all of them at once. That's where you might be helpful."

"What do you want to know?"

Mimi jumped in instantly. "Now, Lolly, you don't have to say anything at all, now or ever. Maybe it would be in your best interest for you and me to talk privately about this. Ms. Trieri has told me that you were originally charged in connection with a fire in Utah, and now that you're here because of a minor marijuana charge while you were out on a recognizance bond. And for some driving-related charges. This is all small-potatoes stuff, and if she wants information from you, we should be able to get you immunity. At least it's worth a try." She looked at Annette, eyebrows raised, questioning. Annette kept her poker face intact. Lolly's face brightened perceptibly.

"Is this true? Could I get out of here if I cooperate?"

"I'm not empowered to make deals. All I can do is to put in a word with the right people, and they can try to influence the District Attorney." Annette was, of course, understating her ability to influence matters. Mimi knew this and just looked at the ceiling, shaking her head gently. But Lolly was not at all aware of how things really worked, so she took the bait.

"Please. I'll do anything, I'll cooperate fully. I need to be out of here. All I've got now is Reid's baby, and I need to take care of myself, to get healthy, for him. Or her." She smiled and patted her tummy. Mimi, however, wasn't finished.

"Ms. Markham. Your attention, please. There's a right way and a wrong way for you to do this. If we do it the right way, your ability to be a good mother will be enormously enhanced. OK? First, you need to ask me to represent you." She paused, waiting.

"Oh. Well, will you please represent me?"

"Yes, I will. Now then," she turned to Annette, "Ms. Trieri, my client, Ms. Markham, will cooperate fully with you in return for full immunity for everything for which she is now charged, and for other matters in connection with these charges, and in return for her immediate release. She will agree not to leave the region and to be available to you for information and testimony if required. We need to reserve the right to protect her in the case of testimony that might lead to a dangerous situation for her. Also, if you find that she is not cooperating fully, you may consider this agreement to be abrogated. Further, this agreement does not apply to her future behavior. Because this is all on tape, I consider it as binding as a written agreement." Again, she raised her eyebrows in question.

Annette smiled. "You work fast. Lolly, do you understand all that?"

"I think so. Um, Ms. Olive, what do you mean by this agreement being abrogated?"

"I mean if you don't hold up your end, by cooperating fully, the deal's off and she can put you back here. It's the price you pay for getting out of here and having charges and so on dropped."

"Oh. Well, it sounds OK with me."

"OK. Done." Annette looked up at the mirror and gave a thumbs up to the camera she knew was there. "Let me ask one quick question now, and then we'll get you out of here. You were driving a car in Monticello, Utah, the night of the lumber mill fire. Did Rutherford and Tompkins start that fire?"

"Yes, but it was Steve's idea. Reid wasn't in favor of doing something so drastic so soon."

"Thank you. I'll pass along to the Utah State Patrol and the San Juan County Sheriff's office that we have eye-witness testimony that the fire was started by two individuals who are now deceased. That will let them close the investigation. We will, of course, have questions for you. One more question. Was that Flip Chester's pot that was found in your car?"

"Absolutely, the scumbag. He must have ditched it when the sheriff stopped us. I'm never having anything to do with him ever again."

"I thought so. We'll deal with him appropriately. And, Lolly?"

"Yes?"

"Good choice going with Mimi. She's top-rate, and she's free. Anyone else would have charged you $500, minimum, to make this deal." Amazing, Annette thought, how Lolly didn't look quite so old any more.

FOR COMPLETELY DIFFERENT REASONS, Tim Langer was also amazed. Astounded even, for Jamie McFarland had

H. P. Hanson

actually asked him out! They were going to walk downtown for dinner tomorrow.

But this meant he'd need a wardrobe upgrade. Baggy pants and over-sized tee shirts, with beat up tennis shoes, were OK for hanging out, even for his tutoring job. But this was different, it demanded something more sophisticated. So he'd borrowed a car to drive down to the mall to go see what they had at Mervyn's.

The parking lot, as usual, seemed to be full, so he had to park on the wrong end of the mall and walk. But his mood was so ebullient that it didn't matter. He kept thinking to himself about how he should act—be very cool, was his mantra—and where a dinner date might lead. He was so absorbed that he didn't notice the car that had pulled up beside him as he walked through the parking lot.

"Hey, Timmy! Long time, no see. Where ya been lately?" said a sadly familiar voice. He turned in surprise and fear.

"Un-uncle Mike! Ah, I've been around. Haven't seen you lately, either. What's happening."

"We need to talk. Get in."

"Get in? Oh, well, I'm on my way to something important, so how about some other time?"

"Timmy, don't make me stop the car and get out. Just walk around here and get in. Right now!" Even though his instincts were shouting at him to run, Tim went on autopilot and got in the car next to Michael Oswald.

"Good job. I could tell you were thinking of running on me, but this was the right thing to do. You understand why, don't you?"

Excess Homicide
A Four Corners Mystery

"I wasn't going to run, Uncle Mike. Honest. I was just surprised to see you, that's all. I haven't seen you for a long time."

"Not since before you got caught trying to do that job for the Senator, I think. How did that work out? Did you get in trouble?"

"Well, um, yeah, of course, some. But it's OK. I told them that I was just curious about that company. UNELECO, that's it. Because they do so much stuff with computers and military stuff. They caught me because I was using a university computer. I had to, Uncle Mike, because my computer network connection at home was just too slow. The UNELECO computer security is really, really solid, and I needed a fast connection. So they caught me."

"What'd they do to you?"

"Aw, just a slap on the wrist. They made me promise not to do it any more and they're making me tutor this guy who needs help with a computer science course. An athlete who needs his grades up."

"Well, the Senator needs your help more than ever. Did you learn enough about the UNELECO system before that you can pick up where you left off? Without the university computer? This is really important to the Senator, Timmy. And to me. And you owe him, and me. Pickle and Mad Dog are in jail because of you."

"Hey, that's not fair, Uncle Mike. It wasn't me, it was the guys at the dorm. They didn't like the way Pickle was treating me, and they stood up for me. And Pickle and Mad Dog just got in over their heads. These guys are athletes, and they don't take shit from anybody. Say, where are we going? I have to go shopping and then do some other stuff."

"We're going to drive around until I decide to take you back to your car. Don't worry, I'll get you back there. But I need to get you to agree to help the Senator get in to the UNELECO computers. It's lots more important than it was before." Tim knew he shouldn't agree too easily, but he didn't want to spend any more time than absolutely necessary with Oswald.

"But I'm out of ideas, Uncle Mike. That's why I needed the university computer, for its fast network, so I could get into the UNELECO systems by brute force. That takes a lot of bandwidth."

"Oh, I'm sure you can find some new ideas, Timmy. You're a bright kid. That's why the Senator's been paying you so well. And keeping your little secret."

"Uncle Mike, I wish you'd believe me. I didn't have anything to do with that. Someone tampered with her saddle."

"Timmy, Timmy. Who should I believe? My nephew, who I remember as a little kid always telling lies? Or Senator Jarvis Schoenfield, pillar of the Colorado Senate, owner of the biggest ranch in the Four Corners? Hmm?"

"I know, I've heard this before. So it's do what the Senator wants or I'm blamed for her death, right? I don't know if I can do it, but I guess I have to try."

"Good thinking, Timmy. I'm sure the Senator will be most pleased." To Tim's relief, he noticed that the car was headed back in the general direction of the mall.

"Well, all I can say is that I'll try. Does the Senator have a timetable I need to know about?"

"This one is urgent, Timmy. As soon as possible."

"OK, but you've got to buy me time. I'll start the brute force attack and work some other angles also. But it'll just

Excess Homicide
A Four Corners Mystery

be slower because I can't possibly use a university computer again. OK?"

"Results, Timmy, that's what the Senator wants. And you want to please him, don't you?" He slowed the car, in more or less the same place that he'd picked Tim up.

"I sure do, Uncle Mike. Can I get out now?"

"You bet, Timmy. Stay in touch. OK?" The smile reminded Tim of a shark's.

He breathed a sigh of relief as the car drove slowly away. Then he headed for the nearest telephone.

BINGO! was all Annette could think of when she and Tim were finished with their phone conversation. She immediately dialed Charles Shure's direct line and was surprised to hear his voice after only two rings.

"Chuck? Annette Trieri. I think we got him. Schoenfield, I mean. He's asking our guy, our computer hacker, to go back to trying to get into your computers. It must mean he's fallen for that strange information we posted about the Nazi journal."

"Ha! Wonderful, just wonderful. We'll cooperate in every way we can. Hang on a second." Annette heard various computer-generated telephone noises, and then a new voice came on the line.

"Peters, computer security."

"Phil, this is Chuck Shure. I've got Annette Trieri, Colorado Bureau of Investigation, on the line with me. Annette, Phil is head of our computer security group. Phil, remember that hacker we caught using the Frémont State computer systems trying to brute-force his way in a while back?"

"Sure do, Mr. Shure. As I recall, you told us not to worry about it because it would stop, and it did."

"Yep. Annette was involved at the time, and she's why it stopped. What's happening now is that it's going to start again. But this time, Phil, I want you to work with Annette, or whoever she has talk to you, her computer person, and let the hacker succeed this time. Maybe we can even help him out. OK?"

"Uh, Mr. Shure? This is pretty irregular for us, and raises lots and lots of questions, particularly with respect to our classified systems. Can we talk about this?"

"Mr. Peters? You and I should talk about this first, because I think there's far less here than you may imagine. And I bet there's nothing for you to worry about. Then you can take up Chuck's time if you really think it's really necessary." Annette wondered if her use of Shure's first name would have any effect on his employee. But she didn't have the chance to see.

"She's right, Phil. I'll give her your number and you can expect to hear from her. Thanks."

"Yes, Mr. Shure. Uh, nice talking with you, Ms. Trieri." And he went away. At least, she thought, he got my name right the first time.

"Annette? I'm sure that Phil will cooperate. His job is to be paranoid, though, and he's good at it. Being paranoid, that is. Well, his job, too."

"He's also right, especially because of your classified systems. But I think all we need to do is to set up a way for Schoenfield to snoop around in a little area we set up for him. He doesn't need access to the whole system, like he has on our CBI computer."

"He has access to your entire system? Geez."

Excess Homicide
A Four Corners Mystery

"Well, it got set up in the real hacker mode, with a login with root privileges. That's jargon I've learned, and I'm rather proud of it, thank you. It means that the login has system administrator powers. They're turning me into a computer nerd. Anyway, we don't need that for your system. All we need is a login that gets Schoenfield where we want him to get. And Phil can set that up quite easily. In fact, I bet that Phil has an old, stand-alone workstation or something that he could set up to look like the main UNELECO system and fool Schoenfield completely. Then he wouldn't be getting into your real systems, just a dummy one. A dummy system for a dummy."

"Damn, you're devious. And good. How much are they paying you, anyway? Want a job? Oh, let's talk about that some other time. We've got to get Schoenfield first."

Annette was surprised at this offer of employment and almost tempted to talk about it now. But he was right—nailing Schoenfield was the first priority.

"We will. We know he downloaded those genetics clues we gave him, so he's motivated to get into your systems. And because he's never been into your systems before, he doesn't know what to expect, so it should be pretty easy to set something up to fool him."

"Then what?"

"Well, he gets in, looks around, and finds things that rattle his chain. Your guy Wendell Ellison gave me some great ideas, so we should get him in on this. He seemed amused by the whole thing, quite ready and willing to help."

"Wendell's a good guy. I think he was pretty disgusted by that journal. Which probably motivated him to be helpful. And so we've got Schoenfield's chain rattling.

Then what?" Annette could see why his company was so successful. The guy at the top liked to think things through.

"At some point we have to start playing it by ear, and this is probably that point. If we put the right stuff on your systems for him to find, then we should be able to motivate him to act, and to act in a way we can predict. I mean, suppose we put information there that talks about specific ingredients needed to produce the dietary supplements we talked about. Then he might try to hijack shipments or corner the market or something. Uh, that sounds pretty lame, but do you see what I mean?"

"You're right and I do. But his real weapon against this supposed dietary thing would be publicity, wouldn't it? So we should make it clear in the bogus information that UNELECO considers this a top-secret project. Seems like that would really push his buttons. Maybe he'd try blackmail or something."

"And you said I'm devious. Welcome to the club. He's already blackmailing at least one person, our hacker, actually, so it's in his genes. Or something. Anyway, it sounds like a plan to me. And if you think of anything more devious, be sure to let me know. I'll call Phil as soon as I can."

"You know, this is all great fun, more fun than I usually have at work, I can tell you. Is this what you do all the time?"

"This is what I do for fun. All the time is paperwork. I'll be in touch."

LATE THE NEXT AFTERNOON, just as he was getting primed for his date with Jamie, Tim Langer's phone rang. Oh, no, he thought, she's calling to cancel.

Excess Homicide
A Four Corners Mystery

"Tim Langer? This is Phillip Peters. I'm the head of computer security at UNELECO." Tim suddenly knew the physiological meaning of the "fight or flight" syndrome, and his immediate reaction was to do the latter. Even the guy's deep voice was intimidating.

"Uh, yes, Mr. Peters? What can I do for you?" His voice just barely worked, and he noticed he was trembling.

"I've been talking with Ms. Annette Trieri." That helped Tim relax a little. "She tells me that you're under instructions to resume trying to hack into our systems again." That didn't.

"Uh, well, it's been requested of me, yes. I talked with her and she put me on hold. Told me to wait a day."

"That's what I'm calling about, to get you off hold. She and I have a better idea than having you try to hack in again. I have to say that it probably wouldn't work anyway, and if it did, we'd find out and come and get you."

Tim's trembling made it hard to hold the phone, and his voice failed completely. But it didn't matter, because Peters was continuing.

"I've got a login and one-use password on a special system for you. Got a pencil?" He rattled off codes and a telephone number. "Now, this system is stand-alone, and I've set it up specifically for you to be able to access. Its start-up screens look exactly like our main UNELECO systems do, so, if I wasn't telling you this, you'd think you were into our central system. Also, I've cloned parts of our web site onto it, and it has a network address." He rattled off more numbers. "It's set up so that you can create special web pages available only via that dial-up number, pages that will look just like our regular web site, our insider web site.

H. P. Hanson

And the login I gave you has admin privileges, so you can set things up to do whatever you need done."

"I think I understand. And it sounds like it's just what I need. So I won't be trying to get into your real systems again. OK?"

"OK indeed. I must say, before you tried the brute force attack the other time, your attempts were most sophisticated. We were all impressed. I understand you're in your second year of college. Let me know when you get your degree."

"Uh, thanks, and I will. Um, can I ask a couple of questions?"

"Ask away."

"Well, I don't know how much Annette talked to you about. What I've been asked to do is to set up a login on your systems so someone can poke around for information he's interested in. This stand-alone system is perfect, because I was real worried about your classified partitions. Anyway, he'll probably expect to see a UNELECO network, with at least different systems for different divisions. I think he'll be most interested in your biotechnology division. What I need to know is whether it's OK for me to set up this stand-alone system to look like a network, and if I can grab stuff from your other systems to make it look authentic."

"No sweat. This stand-alone system is all yours. And I've heard about the biotechnology angle, too. We have one of the scientists in our division, Wendell Ellison, working on some material for you. He's going to e-mail it to this login, so don't be surprised when you get something from him."

Excess Homicide
A Four Corners Mystery

"That will help a lot, because I really don't know enough to invent that sort of material. And, uh, it would help if I had another login to your real network. I mean, to get first pages and so on that the public doesn't see. To make it authentic. If I have to make it up, it won't be, I don't think."

There was a long pause, and Tim began to tremble again.

"I understand. But I don't think that would be a good idea. However, I can tell you that all of our first pages, the login startups and so on, are identical with one exception. When you access the system, you'll see a screen with text symbols and so on, and one line says 'UNELECO Gateway.' All of our other systems are identical, except they say stuff like 'UNELECO Biotechnology Division.' See what I mean? Oh, and the classified systems have a line in big letters that says 'Classified Use Only' and 'Need to Know Codes Required for Access.' So you could create some dummy systems on your dummy network to make it look to this guy as if he's found us for real. I can't imagine that he'd expect you to hack into our real classified partitions."

"Well I can probably persuade him that I can't go there, and he wouldn't want to himself because it could bring the CIA down on him, or something."

"No comment. Do you need any help setting this dummy network and so on up?"

"No, I think I can manage. I like this sort of challenge."

"I thought as much. As I said, we were quite impressed with your creativity."

"So, were you serious about calling you when I graduate?"

335

"Absolutely. In fact, if you were in school here at Colorado Springs, I'd be talking with you right now about an internship. But Durango's a little far away for one of those, I'm afraid."

"I understand. But what if I transferred to the University of Colorado there in the Springs next year?"

"Then we can talk about this again. Let me know."

"Thanks again. I will. Is there anything else I can do for you?"

"Just keep your nose clean. You need a Top Secret clearance, at least, to work for us."

"How do I get one of those?"

"Oh, we'll get it for you, but you've got to have a clean nose."

After hanging up the phone, and unconsciously rubbing the dirt off the tip of his nose, it took Tim quite some time to regain his equilibrium. An almost job offer, no less. And a way to deal with the Senator. He looked down at himself. And I didn't even wet my pants. Man what a scare that guy was.

He heard a thup-thup-thupping on the wall of his cubicle.

"Tim? About ready? I'm starved." Her voice came from right behind him, and he nearly jumped out of his chair.

Damn, he thought. Almost a job offer, a way to deal with the Senator, and a date with a real woman, not just one of those college girls. All in the same evening. Tim, old buddy, don't make a fool of yourself. He turned to her with a big smile.

But when he saw that Jamie was wearing a tank top, he knew he was in big trouble.

Eighteen

It was finally time to brief Rodney Andersen about the whole thing, so the next morning Annette took the early flight to Denver. She promised Hal she'd be back in time for dinner.

The short ride was actually smooth, because the daytime convection hadn't become established yet. After negotiating the DIA terminal—it helped not to have to wait for baggage—she found a taxi willing to take her downtown. By 10 AM she was in the CBI office, waiting for Andersen to finish up a telephone call. Finally, Sandy McStain's telephone buzzed. She listened to it and told Annette that the Director would see her now.

"Annette! Good to see you, sorry I took so long. Sometimes I can't get away from the telephone. That was Senator Jarvis Schoenfield, wanting to talk about some new, exotic security systems he thinks the state needs. Strange call. He doesn't usually get involved in such things."

The mention of Schoenfield's name naturally put Annette on alert, all warning lights flashing.

"Um, Rod, I wonder if I can ask for more information about that call? You'll understand in a while, I promise."

"Huh? Well, sure. You know he's the Chairman of the Senate Committee on Law Enforcement, that he controls, or at least has strong control of, our budget. So I'm always nice to him when he calls. Like I said, this was strange. He said he heard that this company in the Springs has developed some new, high-tech security system components that he thinks we should look into. I didn't want to say that we really don't have a need for high-tech security, well, not much. So I encouraged him. I even volunteered one of our experts to look into details, but he said he'd do it for himself. He just wanted to run it by me, to sound me out. Something about having a way to verify that he's serious if he needs to make an appointment with the CEO of the company."

"What company, may I ask?"

"I think I remember talking with you about it. UNELECO. Oh, yeah, Charles Shure, the CEO wanted to talk with you a while back. I never heard how that went. Anyway, Senator Schoenfield is going to look into these security gadgets. What's your interest in all this?"

"Well, that's actually what I came up to talk with you about. I need to brief you on an extremely sensitive issue that involves Senator Schoenfield. And, interestingly, Charles Shure. You said that the Senator may be trying for an appointment with him? I'd like to call Mr. Shure, if I may."

"Annette, that's fine, but what's this all about?"

"That's what I'm here to talk to you about, but there's a timing issue. Let me make a call first, please." He nodded, and she headed for his desk.

"Is the outside line nine?" He nodded again and she poked buttons.

"Chuck?" She was amused when Andersen's eyebrows arched in surprise. "Listen, this is quick. I just found out that Schoenfield may be calling you for an appointment, on

Excess Homicide
A Four Corners Mystery

the excuse of talking about security equipment for the state government. He may suggest you call my boss, Rod Andersen, for confirmation... Right. Why don't you tell him that you'll be in Durango and offer to meet him there, at some public place. Maybe a restaurant? ...OK. Let me know... Yeah, I think this may be it. Talk to you later, bye."

She smiled at Andersen. "Now I bet you're really curious."

"No kidding. 'Chuck?' Nobody else I know calls him 'Chuck.' And you just dialed and got him? Even the Governor can't do that."

"Uh, right, well, we're working together on this thing. It involves, like I said, Senator Schoenfield. Um, is this room secure? From eavesdropping, I mean?"

"Tighter than the Oval Office. Pray proceed."

"Well, it also involves that environmentalist portfolio that we talked about when you were recruiting me, remember?" He was nodding yet again. "And, believe it or not, the assassination attempt up in Boulder the Friday before the Fourth." If he looked surprised at her relationship with Shure, now he looked flabbergasted. "And, um, it also involves the arson fire in Cortez last week. Did you hear about that?" She thought his head might come loose from the nodding. Time to let him say something, she thought.

"Ahh, that's all? No plans to nuke Denver? Are you telling me that Schoenfield's involved in all this stuff? I sure hope you've got all your ducks lined up straight."

"I've been waiting to brief you until we do. Now, we aren't ready for a collar yet, which is why Schoenfield was able to call you. But his appointment with Shure is probably just a way to trick Shure into meeting with him. For a different purpose. But let me start at the beginning."

H. P. Hanson

"Please do. I'll take notes and try to save as many questions as I can for the end. And, um, let *me* make a call." He walked over to his desk. "Sandy? Listen. Cancel the rest of my morning and that lunch appointment... Yeah, I know, there will be hell to pay. But I've got to do this other thing. And please get the deli downstairs to bring us some sandwiches around noon." He looked a question at Annette.

"Ham and cheddar on rye, mustard, no mayo, no onions. Chips. Diet cola."

He repeated it to Sandy McStain and continued, "And I'll have a tuna salad on wheat toast, Coke, chips. Take it out of petty cash, this is definitely a working lunch. And, Sandy? Absolutely no interruptions unless the building's on fire. Thanks." He looked up at Annette, took a breath, and walked over to the conference table where she was sitting.

"So, you were going to begin at the beginning."

"I will. You know about the environmentalist portfolio. The next thing, chronologically, is where Shure came in..."

It took until 2 PM for her to tell it all and for him to get his questions answered. Somewhere in there, lunch happened, then coffee. He personally drove her back to the airport, and she even made it home in time for supper.

Aside from questions, all pointed and pertinent, his only comment was, "I've always wondered if that son-of-a-bitch wasn't crazy as a loon. Of all the stupid reasons for wanting to kill the President of the United States, this one's the stupidest I've ever heard."

THE TROUBLE WITH POLITICIANS, Annette thought, is that they're by nature gregarious. They meet people and remember them for the next time. The fallout from this was affecting her now, for she had been forced to come up with

Excess Homicide
A Four Corners Mystery

people who had never met Schoenfield or been present at small gatherings with him.

She needed the help, because Shure had taken her recommendation literally. Too literally, now that she thought about it. He'd suggested, when Schoenfield called for the meeting supposedly on security devices, that they have lunch at Oliver's, in the Hotel Strater, on Main Avenue in downtown Durango. Fortunately, there was a three-day lead time, so Annette was able to find people whom Schoenfield would not recognize, mostly from the police force in Durango. She was also able to work with the restaurant staff and reserve about half the restaurant for her help. The other half was already reserved by the public, and she couldn't risk so many cancellations. The resulting scene would tip off Schoenfield. But she would be able to treat much of the Durango Police Department to an elegant luncheon, at least by PD standards.

She decided to wait in the kitchen, with a view out the door to the dining room, because of the probability that Schoenfield would remember her from their brief meeting. Besides, the radio headset she was wearing would look suspicious. Charles Shure was wired for sound, playing his role with glee. With a room full of cops backing him up, what could go wrong?

They had ordered lunch and were making small talk over drinks—an iced tea for Shure and a large, probably a triple, Manhattan for Schoenfield. Then Annette spotted trouble. There were Tim Langer and a young woman she recognized—Jamie, Jamie McFarland—trying for a table. Annette grabbed a waiter, pressed a five dollar bill into his hand, pointed out Tim, and had the waiter tell him to meet her in the back of the lobby. She worked her way through the bustle of the kitchen to the other door, all the while listening to the insipid conversation on the headset.

"Annette! What are you doing here?"

"Getting you and Jamie the hell out of here. Schoenfield's in there, having lunch. It's all going to go down shortly, and you two don't want to be here, I promise."

"The Senator's in there? Well, they told me they were booked. I was trying to pay Jamie back for dinner the other night with a fancy lunch."

"Well, there are other choices. Get out of here and pick one. I'll call you later."

She worked her way back through the kitchen to the dining room door. It sounded as if lunch was arriving at the table she was eavesdropping on. She peeked out, and saw Shure and Schoenfield in quiet conversation, arranging food, responding to the waiter's questions.

Then, out the street window, she noticed Tim and Jamie in conversation with someone she didn't recognize. It appeared forced, out of kilter somehow. Then the three walked off together. She returned her attention to the dining room. The meeting was about to begin.

"Now, Senator, I believe you wanted to talk about some of our new security gadgets?"

"Well, Chuckie, I can call you Chuckie, can't I?" He was smiling, and his voice seemed lower than Annette would have expected. He continued in the same menacing tone.

"Just keep smiling, Chuckie, because if you don't, I'll blow a big hole through you, just below the table here, with this beautiful antique derringer I'm holding. It's not much for accuracy, but you're close enough. And it's a .60 caliber

Excess Homicide
A Four Corners Mystery

soft lead ball, which would punch quite a hole in your guts. Maybe even get that poor bastard sitting behind you. So keep calm and keep smiling."

Shure's voice was surprisingly steady, under the circumstances.

"Smiling I can do. Calm I can only try for. I guess I should have brought some of our new gadgets with me, hmm?"

"No smart remarks, you Jew-loving son-of-a-bitch. What's going to happen is that we're going to walk out of here best of friends. I'm going to leave a fifty dollar bill on the table, and we're going to just walk out quietly and calmly, OK? And this lovely little derringer is going to be on you the whole time."

"Um, we walk out of here, OK, then what?"

"We keep being best friends, of course, and we get in a car together. Got it?"

Annette could see the smile was strained, but intact. The two diners arose, and Schoenfield laid a bill on the table. She could just make out the snout of the derringer concealed in his large right hand.

She keyed her microphone. "All personnel. Schoenfield's got a gun. No one move."

The conversation in her headset resumed as they walked out, with Annette following as discreetly as she could.

"So tell me, Senator. What in the world does my affinity in your mind for people of the Jewish faith have to do with anything?"

"You know damned well what. You want to pollute the pure genes of good, red-blooded Americans with your filth."

"Huh? Excuse me? You think I'm trying to pollute people's jeans? You mean, like Wranglers?"

"Don't goad me, Jew-lover. And keep smiling. Here. Get in."

Suddenly Annette's reception waned markedly. Must be in a car, she thought. But Shure's voice still came through.

"Lovely vehicle, Senator. And it even comes with a driver."

"Let's go, Mike. Oh, well, hello Timmy. And a little chickie, too. Well, maybe we can have a party. Move it, Mike."

She reached the sidewalk just in time to see a large SUV turn the corner and disappear down the side street. But the voices in her ear didn't disappear.

"Annette? I sure hope you're still getting all this. We just turned north. White Ford Expedition. Uhh." There had been a slapping noise.

"You wired? You bastard. You BASTARD. I'll probably have to kill you for this. Where is it? Ah, got it." There was a crunch and the sound stopped.

It occurred to Annette that a chase wouldn't happen. The single car outside watching the restaurant was facing the wrong way in traffic, and her contingent of officers was still in the restaurant. Well, she thought, I guess they won't get lunch after all.

"TOO MANY CIVILIANS." Annette was explaining once again her decision not to prevent the kidnapping, this time in a conference room at her CBI office the next morning. Rod Andersen was hearing it again, this time in person. Todd Sweeney from the FBI was there, as were Fred Winders, her replacement, and Walt Jankowski, her previous boss at the

Excess Homicide
A Four Corners Mystery

Durango PD. Representatives of various sheriffs' offices from neighboring counties were also present, with Jim Nettleman, from San Miguel County, conspicuously absent. Even Hal was there. His computer systems person and one of his students had been kidnapped, after all.

"Too many civilians, and he had a cannon. A short-range one, to be sure, but it was too dangerous to move in at the restaurant."

"And you didn't have the street covered." Sweeney wasn't trying to be nasty, but it came out that way.

"We did, actually, but we weren't expecting that vehicle. Schoenfield arrived in a cab. I expect that the driver of the SUV escape vehicle was Michael Oswald, Schoenfield's second-in-command, or something like that. But he wasn't familiar to any of us. And our observer was not able to deal with the traffic and follow them. Of course, most of the PD was in the restaurant. I called the State Patrol, and they set up roadblocks to no effect. We have a report from local air traffic control of a helicopter taking off from a field on the north side of town and heading north, so that was probably them. There's a white Ford Expedition parked at a car parts store close by, a rental."

"Where'd they go?" Walt Jankowski was ever practical.

"I'm certain they went to the X-S Ranch headquarters, a cluster of buildings and cabins southwest of Norwood called Raven's Roost. It's where Schoenfield lives and the only place he'd feel comfortable and safe."

"Well, then, hell, let's just go get 'em." Ralph Wertlinger, Mineral County sheriff, was still put out that Schoenfield and company had tried an operation on his turf.

Rod Andersen stepped forward.

"We will, sheriff, but we've got to be careful. The hostages are our main concern at this point. Schoenfield isn't going anywhere, and this other guy, Oswald, is not as much of a concern. We'll get him sometime. As far as I'm concerned, Ms. Trieri handled this thing entirely appropriately. We're just dealing with a very clever individual who was willing to expose himself rather than maintain his previous façade of innocence. I never would have predicted that Senator Schoenfield would have behaved this way. So this is still Annette's case, as far as the CBI is concerned."

"The FBI has a call in this too, Director Andersen. We want to question him about the assassination attempt."

"I understand, and you'll get your chance. But that was an attempt, and we want to question him about something like a dozen actual murders. I suggest that this will work best if we all work together. And, like Ralph said, let's just go up there and get him."

Wertlinger, no wallflower, spoke up again, "Say, where's Jim Nettleman? It's his turf up there. Shouldn't this be his show?"

"Ralph, there is information that Jim isn't entirely objective when it comes to dealing with Jarvis Schoenfield. On orders of the Governor, the State Patrol is relieving him of duty, temporarily, for the duration of this operation, as we speak." Rod Andersen was trying to be diplomatic about Wertlinger's friend and colleague, but it was a thin attempt. "Annette?"

She stepped forward again. "This may be my show, but I need all the help I can get. And it's clearly in all our best interests to work together. Furthermore, the last time I tried

Excess Homicide
A Four Corners Mystery

a collar out in the woods, I almost ended up dead." She looked at Hal and smiled.

"Fortunately for me, Superman there came along and saved me." Everyone turned to look at Hal, and he blushed scarlet.

She continued, "But it seems to me that all we can do is to marshal forces and truck up there with the appropriate warrants. If they decide on a stand-off, well, then we use standard hostage-situation procedures. Now, let me show you some pictures. Can someone hit the lights?"

She stepped back, turned, and pulled down on the cord of a screen, yanking at it several times in the eternal hassle of getting the thing to stay down without rolling up with a snap.

"This slide is an aerial photo of Raven's Roost. We took it yesterday afternoon, late, as you can see by the shadows. We used a search-and-rescue helicopter and got shot at for our trouble. This large building is a two-story log cabin, Schoenfield's house. These out-buildings are the usual sort of thing for a ranch, garages, barns, equipment sheds and so on. Over here is what we think is a bunkhouse, and out here by the gate is another house, probably for a gatekeeper sort of person. The property, of course, is much larger than the area in this photo, but it should be possible to drive up to this gate without incident."

"A ranch this big has staff. Where are the hands?" It was too dark for Annette to see who was asking, but it sounded like Sweeney to her.

"On furlough just now, at least the ones we know of. This morning, we got records from the business office, down in Norwood, and contacted everyone we could. It turns out that relatively few employees live here at Raven's

Roost. There are at least two housekeeper/cooks and a sort of major domo type person. Two other people who used to live there are, fortunately, being held in the sumptuous accommodations of the FBI. They'd be dangerous to encounter, so I'm glad you guys have got 'em, Todd.

"What we're planning to do is to move in with a contingent of State Patrol SWAT officers and set up for a siege. We have phone numbers for the place, so we'll be in contact with whoever wants to talk with us. I think, because there are only a few hostiles in there, that we can move some people under the cover of darkness, if need be."

"Where are the hostages?" This sounded like Walt Jankowski to Annette, and she asked for the lights to be turned on.

"We're not sure. Most likely in the main house, where Schoenfield and Oswald can keep an eye on them and where the staff can feed them. But maybe somewhere else, like the bunkhouse." She paused. "Any other questions? ...No? Fred?"

"You said someone took a shot at the helicopter. Any idea where it came from?"

"We think it was the main house. It was some kind of large rifle, probably. We got lucky, because it hit only one of the landing struts. Blew a big hole in it, too. This wasn't your average high-powered hunting rifle. Any more questions? ...Well, thanks for coming, especially you folks from the around region. I know you're all interested in getting these guys behind bars, and we're going to do it. And we're going to do it without hurting any of these hostages. I know all of them, they're friends of mine. We're going to get them out safely."

Excess Homicide
A Four Corners Mystery

HAL TRIED NOT TO POUT, but he was certainly disappointed. Annette finally persuaded him that he had no business being part of the assault team. He argued that he'd been there to save her once, a year ago, and maybe he should be there to help again. But he had to agree that she made a valid point that this time there would be a couple dozen State Patrol officers with her and reinforcements could be called in as needed.

What really worried him was that there would be no cell phone availability up there. Raven's Roost was out of range of any cell towers. This meant that Annette would have to use a radio patch through the State Patrol office in Norwood in order to talk with Schoenfield. And, if she got in trouble, she would have no way to call home.

So, after Annette's morning briefing, Hal went to work and tried to accomplish something besides fiddling nervously. He knew he had failed, when, on about his sixth trip out to Alice's front office, she looked up at him, over the top of her reading glasses, with that quizzical expression that meant she was wondering what was going on.

"Is something wrong, Dean Weathers? You seem, may I say, not your usual calm self this morning."

He sat down and explained what was going on and was surprised by how much better it made him feel.

Annette, meanwhile, had assembled her team and was approaching Raven's Roost. She had six State Patrol officers with her for visibility, all looking sort of bulky due to the kevlar vests under their uniforms. Another twenty had been deployed earlier, SWAT members dressed in camouflage, around the perimeter of the Raven's Roost compound. There were warrants galore, so, technically, no one was trespassing.

Annette, riding with the lieutenant in charge of the Norwood office, was leading the column of six patrol cars, all with lights flashing, up the gravel road to the compound. As they came around the last curve, they saw the gateway, a huge, imposing structure made from logs at least two feet in diameter bridging the road. The gate under it was closed.

Someone was standing behind the gate, dressed in jeans, a long-sleeved white shirt, and a western hat.

"I believe that's Jim Nettleman. What do you suppose he's got himself into?" Tom Ayala, the lieutenant, knew the local law enforcement community well. In fact, he had the sad task yesterday of relieving Nettleman of duty.

The little caravan of patrol cars rolled to a stop spanning the road in front of the gate three abreast, two deep. Annette and Ayala got out while everyone else remained seated. She and he had agreed to let her do the talking.

"Mr. Nettleman, I believe? I'm Annette Trieri, CBI. I'm in possession of warrants for the arrest of Senator Jarvis Schoenfield and Mr. Michael Oswald, and for complete searches of all buildings on this property."

He ignored her completely, not even looking at her. His gaze, full of disdain, was on Ayala.

"Hey there, Tom. Thought I might see you today. Sure y'all know what you're doing out here?"

"Talk to him." Annette was surprised at how calm she was.

"Morning, Jim. Sorry about yesterday, but you know it was just orders. I do what the Governor says. And, like I said, it's only temporary. That is, unless you got yourself into something here that will make it permanent. We've got lawful warrants, Jim. You know you can't interfere and come out of this clean."

Nettleman shifted the chaw in his mouth, turned his head aside, and shot a long stream of spit onto the dust. At least it was on his side of the gate.

"Yeah, I know that. And you'll notice I'm not armed, or anything. Unlike the people in the houses, I might add. The Senator asked me to come up as a mediator. I'm going to be as neutral as I can. First thing is, I want to see the warrants. In fact, we've got a lawyer here, at least he used to be, who wants to look 'em over. That's got to be step one, they say. By the way, is this all the help you brought?"

Ayala looked at Annette—good man, she thought—and she shook her head.

"Mr. Nettleman, you are impeding our lawful performance of our duties, I'm sure you know that. Because of your status, we can be flexible. But please don't jeopardize your future by aiding and abetting."

"Lady, I don't really know who you are or why you're here. But I do know Tom here, been playing cards with him for years. So if I'm talking to anyone, it's him. Got it?" To Annette's amazement, her sense of calm only deepened,.

"Now, Jim, she's my boss in this operation. It's her show. No point in antagonizing her."

"Lieutenant Ayala, I want to settle this as peacefully as possible. I'll defer to Mr. Nettleman's wishes. Feel free to consult with me as needed. Here are copies of the warrants for him. Let's give them an hour to look them over." She rummaged in her briefcase, handed the copies to Ayala, and returned her steady gaze to the man behind the gate. This fellow, she thought, is on very thin ice if he wants a future in law enforcement. But maybe he can be helpful in this situation. She watched Nettleman walk back up to the main house.

An hour later, she used the radio patch to call the house. After four rings, the telephone was answered by a woman with a heavy Spanish accent.

"This is Annette Trieri, Colorado Bureau of Investigation. Who am I speaking with, please?"

"I am Consuela. I work here, I cook." Consuela, Annette could tell, was quite nervous.

"Consuela, I'm sure you can tell that things are a little strange just now. But I don't think that you have anything to worry about. I need to speak with Senator Schoenfield. Is he there, please?"

"He said that he is not going to talk with anyone." Annette heard a voice in the background, and Consuela resumed. "Oh, he is not talking with anyone yet. I guess maybe later."

"I see. Consuela, I need to know something else. Are there three people there, two men and a woman, one of them is Tim Langer, Michael Oswald's nephew, and are they all right?"

"Si, they are fine. In the basement." Annette heard a roar of outrage in the background.

"Oh, I cannot talk any more." The phone went dead.

Annette looked at Ayala. "Well, it sounds like our hostages are doing OK. At least we know that much. Let's deploy, and then we can go to work on that chain on the gate. It looks sturdy."

There was backing and filling of the cars to create a semi-circle around the gate, and everyone put on radio headsets. Annette and the officers positioned themselves

Excess Homicide
A Four Corners Mystery

behind the cars, and one officer, probably the most junior, Annette thought, crept forward with large bolt-cutters.

When he got halfway to the gate, a hefty chunk of wood was blasted loose from the right post on the gateway almost simultaneously with a booming report of a large-caliber rifle. The junior officer duck-walked, apparently without really touching the ground, back to a position behind the cars. If the situation had been different, it would have been quite amusing.

"Well, that sets a tone, doesn't it?" Annette was wondering just what she should do next.

"Lieutenant, that was quite some weapon. Kind of sounded to me like one of those antique Sharps buffalo rifles. .50 caliber maybe. Probably from the Senator's collection." One of the older officers seemed to know his firearms.

"I bet you're right, Larry. And that means it was a warning shot. If there's someone with a Sharps in the gate house there, they're ready for a fight. Damn." Ayala looked worried.

Annette switched on her radio and said into the headset, "Trieri. I need two snipers at the gate, quietly."

"Already here, ma'am," came the quiet reply. "One on either side in the trees. If you can see us, we screwed up. I was watching the gate house and saw the shooter. George, it's the upper left window. See how it's open just a crack?"

"Got it," came a second voice. Neither had screwed up, for Annette had no idea where they were.

"Look, up the road." Ayala was pointing toward the main house. Jim Nettleman was walking toward them, hands aloft.

"I'm coming out, OK? I'll climb the gate." He still had his hands up when he reached the gate. Over he came, and then he scurried around to the back of the cars with the others.

"I heard the shot. Oswald's in the gate house, with an closed-circuit phone link to the Senator. They've been discussing the warrants. Oswald saw your guy, and the Senator ordered him to hit the gatepost as a warning to you. He said to Oswald that the next one should be for real, and to aim for the head. Oswald's a crack shot." He was breathing hard, not from exertion, Annette thought, but from nerves.

He looked at her. "Listen, ma'am, like I said, I was just being a mediator. As a favor to the Senator. But if they're shooting, I'm done with that. Also, he, I mean the Senator, he's been drinking a lot, and I'm a little worried about his judgment. Hope it's OK with you if I just sit this out." He stared at the ground, rather like a four-year old caught with a mess in his pants. Annette was thinking that he had undergone a remarkable attitude adjustment.

She switched on her radio again. "Snipers, we're going to try the gate again. If you see that rifle poke out that window, or anywhere, lay down steady fire at it." She took a pair of small binoculars out of her briefcase and trained them on the window.

"OK, let's see if we can get that gate open. You'll be covered."

As the officer duck-walked, zig-zagging, back toward the gate, Annette peered at the window, periodically scanning the others. When he was about half way to the gate, she noticed movement behind the upper-right window, and it opened a crack. She switched her radio.

Excess Homicide
A Four Corners Mystery

"Upper-right window opening. Protect the officer. Fire at will." She couldn't quite tell what was happening behind the window, but she knew that the snipers' telescopic sights had better optics than her binoculars.

A shot rang out, from the woods to her right.

"Shooter down, head shot," came a voice in her ear.

"You sure you got him?" Annette was looking at the junior officer lying flat in the dust of the road, trying to burrow beneath the gravel.

"Absolutely, ma'am. We're using hollow points. I saw his head explode."

Nineteen

It took about five minutes for Ayala's car radio to crackle, "Telephone call patch for Trieri." She switched her radio to the other channel.

"Trieri, CBI"

"I seem to recall meeting you briefly, maybe back in May or June, Ms. Trieri. In Denver." The voice, slightly slurred, was smooth and pleasant.

"Yes, Senator, you did. Just before I joined the CBI."

"And, let's see, you were with the police department in Durango before that?"

"Correct. Senator, surely you realize that your situation is hopeless and is not going to improve. We came here to serve the warrants that you have seen, and we're doing things legally and properly. You're not. Shooting at us will not make this any easier."

"Speaking of shooting, that last shot wasn't the Sharps that Mike's using. What was it? And where's Mike? He's not answering the phone."

Annette's mind raced. No point in telling him things that could make him mad.

"Well, Senator, he fired a warning shot at us, and we fired one back at him. At least he's got some sense. He came out with his hands up. He's lying on the ground in

Excess Homicide
A Four Corners Mystery

front of the gate house, waiting for us to come get him. We will, as soon as we get the gate open."

She heard a slow chuckling noise. "Well, I'd sure hate for Mike to lie around on the ground too long and get all mussed up. He's really fussy about his clothes. You go ahead and open the gate and get him. But if I see anyone come closer than the gate house, you're going to have a dead hostage. I think I'll start with our industrialist here. I'd hate to disappoint Mike by killing his nephew, and I have some ideas for the chickie."

"Senator, I'm sure you know that our first priority is to ensure the safety of the hostages. So we won't be doing anything to endanger them. But we also need a plan to resolve this. Do you have any suggestions?" She realized that if this were to continue, they would need to call in an experienced negotiator.

"Well, I reckon I'm just fine here. Got food, water, booze, and women. That should last me for as long as I need." His recurring references to the women began to bother Annette.

"Senator, if you'll excuse me a minute, I'll tell my people to go and get Mr. Oswald. You said you didn't want him lying on the ground too long." You didn't say anything about him lying in it, though, she thought.

She switched the radio channel and it occurred to her that Schoenfield could have a police-band scanner. She hoped he hadn't heard the news about Oswald.

"Trieri. Move to gate house, but no farther. Hostages well so far. Radio silence. Out." She motioned to Ayala and turned her radio off.

"Lieutenant, let's wait until dark to remove the body. I don't want Schoenfield to know that Oswald is dead, OK?

Thanks. Oh. And see how quickly we can get a real negotiator up here. I'm not really well trained for this."

She switched back to the channel with the telephone patch.

"Senator? Thanks. My people will go no farther than the gate house."

"That's a good idea, because I've got another Sharps, an even better one, up here with me. Longer range, with a tripod. Much longer range than anything you folks have. And, of course, I've got the three hostages. Plus others on my staff, who really have no role except as additional hostages."

"Senator, are you interested in negotiation, or what?"

"Well, I suppose that depends on the definition of 'what.' But I'll talk, if you'd like."

"Thank you. Now, the longer this goes on, the more attention it will draw. And even if you have some agenda that needs attention, that kind of attention isn't what you need. For one thing, the FBI is going to want to get involved. If they put pressure on the Governor, I'll lose control of things and it will be downhill from there. One thing that could help me retain control, and to do things the way you'd like them done, is for me to establish that you and I have a credible negotiation going. Understand?"

"Sure. And you're probably right. It's far more pleasant talking with you that it would be with some federal stormtrooper. Why don't you come on up here for a drink with me?"

"I'm afraid not, but I'm glad you're comfortable talking with me. So, something that would help establish the credibility of our negotiation would be a gesture on your part."

Excess Homicide
A Four Corners Mystery

"A gesture? Like what, not shooting that cop I've got in my sights just now?"

"Well, any shots by either side will prove to anyone who's interested that we have no negotiation and then the feds will take over, probably. So not shooting is fundamental. But a gesture of trust would be an additional step. The best thing you could do would be to let some of the hostages go. Send them walking down the road, just like Jim Nettleman did."

"I'll think about it. Got to keep my cook, though. Man gets hungry during a negotiation. But which of the others would you suggest?"

"Ms. McFarland is the least involved in all this. She was just along for lunch with Tim. Completely removed from the whole thing. Why don't you send her out?"

"Well now, I just don't know. Letting a pair of tits like that get away is just something I'm not sure I want to do. Like I said, let me think about it." Focus, Trieri, she thought. Don't let him get to you.

"Senator? Please reassure me that they are safe and unhurt. That's also fundamental to our negotiation."

"Oh, they're fine. Consuela was right. They're in the basement. There's an apartment down there, with a bathroom and everything. They're locked in, of course, but Consuela's feeding them and they're fine. Hell, I don't even have the key—I gave it to Consuela. Look, I'm getting bored with this. I'll call you back later this afternoon. Got some thinking to do. Don't you folks try anything now. This Sharps has quite a range, and I've practiced with it. Got an elk in the head, aiming for the head, at 500 yards once. Nearly a third of a mile. And you folks are only about half that far. So don't try anything foolish. And don't call me, I'll call you."

IT WAS A LONG AFTERNOON. They set up a base of operations in the gate house, and Oswald's body was zipped into a body bag. Annette called Hal on the radio patch, just to let him know she was fine. Word came that an experienced negotiator was on the way. Food and drink arrived. Annette had messages sent, by runners and hand signals, to the SWAT officers in the woods to ease their way in toward the house on all sides except the front, but to remain concealed.

And they waited.

Annette had brought a laptop computer with the most revealing of Schoenfield's files on it, so she spent time re-reading them. She also noticed that Lieutenant Ayala was keeping very busy, busier than he needed to be. Time for a chat, she thought.

"Excuse me, Lieutenant. Can we talk? And I'd like to be informal, so please call me Annette."

"Uh, OK, that's fine. Call me Tom by all means. What's on your mind?"

"Well, you don't know me very well, but people who do think of me as a straightforward person. It's all just out there. So here's some of it now. It seems to me that you're uncomfortable about something. Of course, I don't know you at all, either. But it seems like you're fidgeting. Are you OK?"

"Uh, well, Annette, this is your operation, and that's fine with me. You know the background and so on. But, well, it seems like you ordered that guy shot awfully quickly. I mean, with hostages and all, we usually go very,

Excess Homicide
A Four Corners Mystery

very carefully. At least that's what we're trained for. And he wasn't shooting, he was just opening a window, right?"

"Oh, he was going to shoot, I have no doubt. I saw the rifle barrel come out the window. And I had to assume that your guy Larry was right about the rifle's being a Sharps. And Schoenfield confirmed it after the fact. But given that, and given the history of these guys, I wasn't going to take any chances. Also, I'd heard that the hostages are up at the main house, and I figured that some action here wouldn't necessarily endanger them. It was a little risky, for sure. And I think that you're right, in general. I moved quickly, more quickly than you learn in training, that's for sure. What do you bet that the negotiator will be upset, when he gets here?"

"Well, it turned out all right, so far at least. But you sure surprised me, there."

"You may not know these guys the way I do. Remember that lawyer, Bill Campbell, the guy that got murdered back in June down by Norwood?"

"Sure do. Still open."

"These people were behind that. They probably weren't the shooters, but they were the masterminds. And Schoenfield planned the assassination attempt up in Boulder earlier this month. And they're behind that fire down in Cortez that killed those two guys a little more than a week back. Have you heard about what CBI's calling the 'environmentalist portfolio'?"

"I did hear something, but no details. Bunch of people have been killed here in Colorado, some down in New Mexico. No leads."

"These same people are behind all of them. A dozen murders. And they have plans for lots more. Kind of a militia movement thing. And, here, read this." She had opened one of Schoenfield's files that she remembered. It would be especially interesting to someone named "Ayala," she thought.

He began reading from the screen of her laptop, and she decided to take a little walk. Evening was approaching, and at home she'd be eating dinner. What do you suppose Hal would fix tonight? she thought.

More to the point, where is that negotiator? And even more to the point, why hasn't Schoenfield called? It's been almost four hours. What's going on up there?

He said don't call me, but I think I'd better, she thought. She returned to the gate house.

As she was figuring out how to use the closed-circuit phone system, so she wouldn't have to go through the radio patch again, Tom Ayala walked into the room, a look of serenity on his face.

"Thanks for showing me that, Annette. And thanks for handling this the way you are. If you ever need me, especially if there's anything like a board of review hearing about this, just call me. OK?"

"I will, although I hope it doesn't come to that. But, look, you live here, right in the Senator's home town."

"But I had no idea. Now I do. What can I say? He had a secret agenda that none of us knew about. If we had, he wouldn't be dog-catcher, let alone a senator. Anyway, where do things stand? Any word on the negotiator?"

"Haven't heard a thing. So I think I'll call up there, if I can figure this out. It says 'house phone' on it, so let's just try old reliable, zero."

It rang twice and then was answered. Annette recognized Consuela's voice.

"Consuela? This is Annette Trieri, calling from the gate house. Are you OK?"

"Si, I'm fine. And your friends downstairs are fine, too."

"Can I speak with the Senator?"

"No, I'm afraid not."

"He won't speak with me?"

"Oh, I don't know. Probably. But not now."

"Maybe later?"

"I don't know. Maybe. If he comes back."

"Comes back? Where did he go?"

"I don't know. He went through the—how do you say?—tunnel."

"When?"

"Oh, about an hour ago, I guess."

"Can we come up to the house?"

"I don't think he would like that."

"But is there any danger if we do?"

"No, I don't think so."

"Thank you, Consuela. I'll be seeing you shortly." She looked at Ayala in exasperation.

"Schoenfield slipped out through a tunnel or something about an hour ago." She switched her radio on. "This is Trieri. Move in, move in. There should be no resistance. There isn't really any rush, I guess. And be nice. Schoenfield has escaped."

She and Ayala started up the road toward the main house at a brisk walk, and the others followed. Around her, she saw shadowy figures emerging from the landscape, the SWAT. She had no idea that they were so close.

They entered through a side door, into what turned out to be the kitchen, a large, elaborate kitchen at that. A short, round woman was singing to herself and peeling potatoes. She looked up when Annette and her retinue crowded through the door.

"Yes? Oh, you must be Señora Trieri. I am Consuela. Have you had supper?"

Annette looked at Tom Ayala, puzzled. "This is unworldly. Do you speak Spanish?"

A rapid-fire conversation in Spanish ensued, and Annette had the remainder of the officers spread out through the house, carefully. At last they were going to be able to execute their search warrant. Apparently, the arrest warrant would have to wait.

Finally the Spanish waned, and Ayala turned toward Annette.

"All she knows is that the three hostages, she calls them your friends, are downstairs and the Senator's gone. The other cook and the housekeeper, who's the boss, are off today, it turns out."

"Where's downstairs?" More Spanish led to Consuela's pointing at a door at the back of the kitchen. Annette led Ayala through and down a flight of narrow, steep stairs. More of a cellar than a basement, Annette thought. At the bottom, there was a locked door, with a key in the lock. Annette unlocked it and opened the door slowly, carefully.

There was a light on in the room, and the first thing she saw was carpet, Berber carpet in an off-white with darker tan flecks. As she continued to push the door open, she began to see furniture, a couch against the wall, a lamp, and finally the legs of a dining room chair. Then there was someone's back, someone with no shoes on, hunched over a table. As she opened the door farther, two other chairs, with other people hunched over the table, became visible. And she began hearing a strange conversation.

"So we take the high-voltage capacitors and their power supply from the TV tube and rig them to the reading lamps, right? Like this circuit here." Annette recognized Tim Langer's voice. So, she thought, that must be his back. So that means the one on my right is probably Shure and the other one is Jamie McFarland.

"Right." It was Shure's voice this time. "It'll be tough to get solid connections without tools, but at least you've got your fingernail clippers, so we can strip the insulation from the wires. And I bet there are some wire nuts inside the lamps or the TV or somewhere that we can borrow. Anyway, the connections only have to last for a couple of milliseconds, long enough to energize and blow out the light bulbs in the lamps. The flash and pop, and the glass shrapnel, should be enough."

"Do you guys really think that will be enough of a distraction for you to jump Schoenfield?" To Annette, Jamie sounded highly skeptical.

"All we can do is try, Jamie. We can't rig the door, because we don't want to hurt Consuela. So we've got to see who comes through it before we can do anything. And this will blind him and disorient him long enough for us to jump him. C'mon, there's three of us. I'll conk him on the head with the lamp base, and then we're outta here." Shure, Annette could tell, was looking forward to the conking part.

She cleared her throat, in a way that she hoped would be authoritative. "So, I hate to break this up, but does anyone want to be rescued?"

The three prisoners practically hit the ceiling coming out of their chairs before they recognized Annette. Wow,

Annette thought. Talk about kids with their hands in the cookie jar. Shure was, predictably, the first to recover.

"Annette! Whew—I sure am glad it's you and not Senator Shithead. Although I would have liked to try out our little plan on him. Did you hear?"

"Senator Who?"

"Ah, well, we made up a new name for him. But did you hear the plan?" Shure was looking pleased with himself.

"Just enough to know it's a good thing I got here when I did."

"So have you got him?"

"No, he seems to have vanished. We still have some searching to do. But we can get you three out of here and home. That's the first thing I've been worried about. Get your shoes on and come on upstairs." She left the door open, and she and Tom Ayala returned up to the kitchen.

BY THE TIME the former prisoners made it upstairs, Annette and Tom Ayala had related their find to the others, and a series of jokes was in progress, none very flattering to Senator Jarvis Schoenfield. The "conking" part, and his new name, received extra attention. Annette finally decided it was time to get back to business.

"OK, look, this is all healthy. Really. We had the shoot-out earlier and then we waited and tension built. And now we can all breathe a big sigh of relief. We actually needed something like this. But we still have a bad guy to catch. And he's got more than an hour's head start and he knows the territory. Anybody have any suggestions?" Annette wanted get things back on track soonest.

Excess Homicide
A Four Corners Mystery

"Well, we're really not set up for a search in these mountains. Let's have our guys here search the house and the buildings, and maybe Consuela can tell us where the tunnel is. The SWAT guys outside have some wilderness experience, so maybe they can help with strategy. But I don't think we ought to run off into the woods chasing this guy tonight." Tom Ayala was still grinning, but he was serious now, too.

"I agree. Gentlemen, the search of the house is on. Go for it. Consuela, would you be so kind as to make a big pot of coffee? Oh, and do you know where this tunnel is?"

"Si. Under the basement stairs. I do not know where it goes, just outside somewhere, I think."

"Well, Tom, are you game for a little expedition? Maybe we should get a couple of the SWAT guys in here." She switched on her radio. "Trieri. We are going to check out this tunnel, Tom Ayala and I. Please send in two SWAT members. Out. Oh. No, not out. Can someone in communications please call whoever is sending the negotiator? We won't be needing him. Out. Oh, wait, one more thing. If anybody has a set of those night vision goggles, they'd be useful in this tunnel, I bet. Out, for real."

It took only about 30 seconds for two of the camouflage-covered SWAT members to arrive, one carrying a bulky set of goggles. Conseula began to look very nervous, so Annette figured they should just go look at the tunnel without any more delays. They followed her down the stairs.

With the door to the suite left open by its former occupants, there was enough light on the base of the stairs that Annette could see a small passage to the side of the staircase and a door underneath it.

"Want to draw straws, or what?" She was being flip, but she also really didn't want to go first.

"Excuse me, ma'am. The smaller of the two SWAT guys eased past her toward the hidden door, goggles on his face. He motioned Annette and the others aside and, protecting himself as much as he could, he jerked the door open.

The darkness of the empty tunnel stared at them, and then it seemed to exhale with a cool, earthy breath. The SWAT officer took the goggles off, and then he reached into a cargo pocket and came up with a flashlight, which he pointed down the tunnel and turned on. It showed more tunnel, a passageway about five feet tall and three wide. It seemed maintained, because the roots that hung from the ceiling were trimmed. There were post and beam supports about every five feet, and they receded past the reach of the light. It appeared that the floor began to climb on a gentle slope after about fifty feet.

The SWAT guy reached into another pocket and produced a compass.

"Ma'am, please have someone upstairs sight along a heading of 098 degrees. If there are no turns, and if that slope down there is steady, this thing should surface a couple hundred yards out. Is there a building out about there, or something?" Annette heard the other SWAT guy taking the stairs two at a time. I really need to get their names, she thought.

He was back in a surprisingly short time, hollering into the tunnel, "Looks like the hay barn, Al."

"Thanks, Rafe," came the response. Well, she thought, that takes care of that.

Excess Homicide
A Four Corners Mystery

"Ma'am, Tom, with all due respect, you folks aren't really dressed for this. It's not only dirty in there, we really don't know what we're going to find. He may be holed up. Excuse me." And Rafe eased his way into the tunnel after Al.

"He's right, Tom. Let's go have a look at that hay barn." She switched her radio on as they started up the stairs. "Trieri. SWAT please converge on the hay barn east of the main house. We think it's where the tunnel surfaces. Out."

"Hay barn, eh?" Alaya was thinking out loud as they walked toward the barn. "Annette, did you grow up on a farm, or ever visit one much?"

"We used to visit my uncle in downstate Illinois in the summer, for Labor Day. Big family reunion. He raised corn and soy beans, some hogs."

"I grew up on a ranch, cattle and a hay operation. Sometimes, we used to make tunnels in the hay loft, using bales like bricks, you know? All sorts of passage ways, little rooms. We used to play hide-and-seek."

"Yeah, we did that, too. I think that's where I got hay fever, from breathing all that dust." Just thinking about it made her sneeze.

"Bless you. So, what do you suppose we'll find out here, in this barn?"

"Are you thinking that the tunnel surfaces in some kind of cave in the hay?"

"No idea. It just occurred to me, about my childhood and hay lofts."

"Trouble is, it's getting dark."

"Yep. If we have a real search, it's for tomorrow. But maybe we'll find something here that will help tomorrow."

When they reached the barn, there was a cluster of camouflage-clad people standing around, talking with one another. They came to a sort of casual order in Annette's presence. She supposed that her handling of the Oswald situation was getting around. Ayala took charge.

"Guys, what Annette said over the radio is about all we know, until we hear from Al and Rafe. They should be under us somewhere, I guess."

"Not quite, Tom, we're here." It was Al, walking around the corner of the barn. "Come look at what we found. The group followed him.

On the east side of the barn, a car-sized sliding door had been rolled back, revealing a little room made out of hay bales. In its center was an open trap door. The room, about the size of a small garden shed, was empty.

"Look at this." Al was pointing at tracks in the dust, from the knobby tires of an all-terrain vehicle, leading down the hill toward the forest.

BACK IN TOWN, Annette showered and washed her hair before calling home.

"He must have waited us out and rolled the ATV down the hill after the SWAT guys had closed in past the barn. They searched it, of course, but not well enough to find this hide-away. The sliding door was locked, from the inside, when they tried it earlier."

"So the Senator gave you the slip. But Jamie and Tim are OK and on their way home?"

"And Chuck Shure, too. They should be there by now. Tomorrow, they're supposed to see you and tell you all about it. Please try not to laugh too hard. They need the Stern Dean look on this one."

Excess Homicide
A Four Corners Mystery

"Stern Dean look?"

"You know, when someone needs an authority figure to clamp down on them. Discipline. That sort of thing."

"They need discipline?"

"Oh, not really, but it would be better if you acted like it. They were concocting a hair-brained escape scheme, not something we like hostages to do. They're supposed to sit quietly and await their fate. At least that's what the book says."

"What are you talking about?"

"You'll see. And nothing, really. I'm just tired. The yo-yo day I described has me exhausted and babbling. I'll call you tomorrow."

"You be careful out there."

"I will. Superman isn't around to save me."

"Right. But those SWAT guys can, right?"

"You bet. Good night, sweetie. I miss you."

"Me, too. The house is too empty. Hurry home, OK?"

She felt lucky to have found room at a bed and breakfast down in Norwood. Tom Ayala was across town at a motel with some of his officers, and most of the SWAT officers were still at Raven's Roost, having taken over the bunk house as well as the gate house. Someone had pointed out that one tunnel with hidden entrances could mean more, so they had all-night guards posted.

The next morning, a Saturday, dawned gray and gloomy. It appeared that the southwest monsoon might pay the Four Corners a visit, just in time to wash away whatever tracks Schoenfield had left. Annette and the entire team gathered at the gate house for a morning briefing and strategy session.

As they were assembling, Jim Nettleman, forgotten in yesterday's action with Oswald, walked in. Yesterday, he had borrowed a ranch pickup he found by the gate house and driven home at the first opportunity.

"Here's the keys, Tom, Ms. Trieri. Uh, my car's up by the main house. I'd get it but it doesn't look like you got much further with this thing than yesterday."

"You can go on up there. We got the house searched, but Schoenfield got away through a tunnel to the hay barn. We found some ATV tracks leading down the hill over to the southeast there." Tom Ayala was pointing in the general direction of Lone Cone Peak. "Got any idea of where he might have gone, Jim?"

"Well, now, I reckon that the more I work with you folks as a civilian, the more temporary that civilian status is likely to be, hmm?" Nettleman looked Annette in the eye for the first time.

"I'm just in charge of this operation, Mr. Nettleman, not your future. But the more you help us, the more I can help you. And I'm perfectly willing to overlook our bad start yesterday, to begin all over with you. You didn't do anything that had any real effect on yesterday's events. It didn't all turn out the way we would have liked, but I don't know how we would have got anywhere at all without your presence at the start. And you climbed that gate at exactly the right time." She smiled, trying to be as disarming as possible. He actually smiled back, a sort of half smile that twisted his moustache around, and nodded.

"Well, thanks for that. Now, as to the Senator... Say, I guess I'll have to learn to stop calling him that, won't I?"

Excess Homicide
A Four Corners Mystery

"Oh, I imagine that his new friends at the state pen will continue to call him that, and have a lot of fun in the process." Ayala was grinning.

"You're probably right about that. Anyway, if he headed off toward Lone Cone, he's probably making for his hunting cabin. He usually goes in there on horseback, but in the past he's had people take supplies in with four-wheelers, and groups sometimes go in using off-road pickups. It's about three, three-and-a-half miles southeast, on a saddle between a couple of little draws, near a spring. Hidden away pretty well, but not too hard to find because there's an old logging road. It's part of a network of old roads in there. Got a map?"

They unrolled a USFS quadrangle and Nettleman pointed out the location and approaches. Annette noticed the dashed-dotted line first.

"Well, isn't this ironic. Mr. Nettleman, you're off the hook anyway. If he's gone to this cabin, he's out of your jurisdiction. This is Dolores County, isn't it?"

"Just barely, yeah. I've been down there several times on hunting trips with the Sen... with Schoenfield. Uh, y'see, ma'am, he's a community leader here and being invited to hunt with him, or to come to his parties, or anything like that is a real honor, or has been in the past. So I've been there. And I always figured that because it was in the next county, I could take off my badge and kick back, if you know what I mean."

"What's the cover like?"

"Ponderosa forest, mixed with aspen and some spruce. Lots of rocks. We grow rocks good in these parts, as they say."

"You know, Annette, it won't do to have civilians along on this operation, and Jim's a civilian. Maybe he would benefit from reading some of the stuff you showed me yesterday." Ayala wanted to give his friend the perspective he'd seen. "Wait 'til you see this, Jim. Some of Schoenfield's thoughts written down. Surprised the hell out of me, I'll tell you."

"Good idea, Tom. I'll leave you with my laptop computer, Mr. Nettleman, and you can get educated about Senator Jarvis Schoenfield's political philosophies, his private ones. Meantime, we'll see if the ranch vehicles sitting around here can negotiate these old logging roads."

IT WAS BUMPY, and several times even the high clearance of the pickup Annette was in scraped something, but they worked their way down the roads. There were three pickup trucks, with the beds full of the SWAT officers, wedged in and hanging on. Tom Ayala, driving the lead truck, seemed to have a global positioning system in his head, for he made turns onto connecting roads at seemingly random intervals, all the while managing to maintain more or less the same heading.

Eventually, he stopped the truck in a clearing, and the other two pickups pulled up beside.

"I think we're close enough that we need to do the rest on foot. Let's see that map, Annette."

"If we're not lost, you're in the wrong line of work. You should be a navigator."

Ayala looked embarrassed. "Well, to tell the truth, I've been here, once. I couldn't have put it on the map like Jim did, but I did remember the trick to getting here. There are marks on trees where you turn."

Excess Homicide
A Four Corners Mystery

She handed him the rolled up quadrangle, thinking that it had been a wise idea to wear sensible outdoor shoes today. He opened the door and stepped down, amid the SWAT members, who were stretching and rubbing spots that had gone to sleep. He unrolled the map on the hood of the pickup next to his, and everyone gathered around.

"I think we're about here," he was pointing to a spot on a dashed line to the west of where the cabin had been marked. "It's about a half mile away from the cabin here. By road, it's half again that much, probably, because you can see how there are these sort of switchbacks. If we fan out, we should be able to cover any additional escape attempts, at least on the road and uphill toward us."

"You think he's still got that Sharps?" George, one of the snipers, was well aware of the potential of that weapon.

"We didn't find one in the main house, so we have to assume he does. Also, there was an arms cabinet left open, and there appeared to be handguns missing. Can't say what they are, although the only ammo left was large-bore. So I think we've got a heavily armed crazy person on our hands."

"What's the drill?" Everyone, even Ayala, looked at Annette. She tried to think fast.

"We'd like to take him in, of course. But he may not let us. So, first and foremost, protect yourselves and each other. I'm hoping we can get close enough to the cabin to hail him, give him a chance to surrender. We certainly can't just go in blasting."

She paused to gather her thoughts, and before she could continue, Ayala held up a hand. "Listen. Is that a horse?"

The familiar sound of a horse at full gallop caused the SWAT officers to melt into the landscape, and Annette and

Ayala, along with the uniformed officers, took up positions on the opposite side of their pickup. Presently, the horse appeared, running flat out down the road, carrying Jim Nettleman. He pulled the horse up short at the trucks and swung easily down.

"Tom, ma'am. I know you don't want me here, but I need to say something to both of you. I mean, I had no idea. Schoenfield helped get me elected and re-elected, and I owe him for that. That's probably why the Governor suspended me during this operation. But, honest, I had no idea. Tom, after reading that garbage, I have to tell you I'm ashamed. Ashamed to be associated with the man, and, well, just ashamed. And Ms. Trieri, well, I had the wrong idea about you altogether. I guess I figured there was some kind of political vendetta at work, but I can see how wrong I was. If there's anything I can do, just say the word." He was breathing hard from the ride and this speech, so he stopped to recover.

"Well, tell you what. You can show us where we are on the map and give us more details about the cabin and the layout. And, hell, I guess you could help by guiding us down there. I thought to cut off the next big curve by bushwhacking through the woods. Does that make sense?" Ayala, who knew Nettleman well, was convinced, and Annette decided to follow his lead.

So they gathered around the map, and the SWAT members re-emerged from their concealment.

Twenty minutes later, they were in position. Annette could see the front of the cabin from her position amid a cluster of large granite boulders. The boulders were high enough above the cabin to provide a clear view, and they were large and numerous enough to provide cover for her, Ayala, Nettleman, and two uniformed officers.

In front of the cabin was an eighteen-inch ponderosa pine, standing like a sentinel with long, jagged stubs of two broken-off limbs about street-sign height pointing both right and left along the logging road. She knew that, to her left, downhill slightly from the cabin, the road was blocked by one of the pickup trucks. It had been moved into position quietly by letting it roll with its engine off for the last two hundred yards to the road's low spot.

She could just make out the remnants of a long-unused road heading straight away from her on the left side of the cabin. It wasn't likely to be Schoenfield's choice for a quick exit, as it was blocked by deadfalls. To the right, the logging road swept upward and away from them around a curve. There was a group of SWAT officers at about the apex of the curve, where they had cover. Because that direction led away from the ranch buildings, everyone thought it would be Schoenfield's first choice for flight. But even this would be difficult, as the old road, while serviceable, was eroded badly. Near the stately ponderosa in front of the cabin, there were several deep ruts completely across the road, and she could see erosion channels running down the hill as well.

On the porch of the cabin sat an ATV, and the view through binoculars suggested its tires were candidates to have made the tracks leading away from the hay barn.

Annette was not looking forward to what had to happen next. Megaphones were not her favorite method of communication. For one thing, she thought they were just flat obnoxious. For another, she didn't like the way her voice sounded through one. But there was really no alternative, and she was in charge. She took it from the officer who had carried it down from their truck, and turned it on.

"Senator Jarvis Schoenfield! You are surrounded by officers of the Colorado State Patrol and the Colorado Bureau of Investigation! We have lawful warrants for your arrest on felony charges. We order you to surrender to us. Exit the cabin through the front door, keep your hands on top of your head, and lie face down on the porch. Do it now!" She paused to take a breath. Why, she thought, couldn't her voice sound like, say, Melissa Etheridge, instead of like Britney Spears with a bad sinus infection?

"Senator, we know you are armed. You should know that I lied to you about Michael Oswald. He's dead. The shot you heard was not a warning shot, it was a kill. He pointed that rifle our way, and we used deadly force. We're prepared to do the same with you. And despite the power of your rifle and your skill, you are outnumbered and outgunned. So please don't do anything foolish. Surrender peacefully and you will be treated well. So come out with your hands on top of your head. Now!"

And, after a tense minute of waiting, he did.

The front door of the cabin opened part way, and Annette could see a cowboy boot kick it fully open. Then Schoenfield was standing in the doorway, hands on top of his head as ordered. He began walking out onto the porch, slowly, looking around, up and down the road, at the boulders up the hill toward Annette and company. He walked to the ATV, and then he began the process of lying down. He lifted his hands off his head, fingers splayed, and extended them in front of him while beginning to bow from the waist.

Excess Homicide
A Four Corners Mystery

Annette realized that she had been holding her breath, and she exhaled in relief. So did everyone else.

But when Schoenfield's hands were about waist high, he moved. Instead of lying down, he leapt sideways, onto the ATV. He grabbed the handlebars, pushed a button, and it roared to life. It lurched off the porch, and then it turned left up the road, in the direction everyone had expected Schoenfield to flee. Annette switched on her radio.

"Trieri. Subject bolting, on an ATV up the road toward the SWAT. No weapons seen, and as long as he's got hold of the handlebars, he won't have any. Hold fire. Guys, get out your ropes."

But they must have shown their hands too soon. When he was up the road 100 yards or so, Schoenfield twisted the handlebars and spun the ATV completely around, and then he accelerated back down the hill toward the cabin, standing on the foot pegs and leaning forward on the handlebars to absorb the rough road. As he approached the first of the ruts across the road by the cabin, he squatted and then suddenly jerked the handlebars upward, gunning the engine. The ATV hopped across the rut.

But the second rut got him when the ATV's front wheels landed squarely in it. Because they were turned slightly to the left, the handlebars were wrenched from his grasp. And because the suspension had compressed on landing, the ATV bounced, and Schoenfield was thrown clear while the ATV did a somersault.

It is said that victims of accidents such as this always see things happening in slow motion. Certainly, Schoenfield had time to scream while flying through the air. But he didn't have time to twist away from the ponderosa. It caught him head-on, and his body looked like a rag doll as it smacked squarely into the trunk. His arms and legs wound up wrapped completely around it in the sort of embrace small boys use to shinny up trees.

But he didn't fall. This puzzled Annette and her team, until Jim Nettleman pointed out that the sentinel's right-pointing branch was nowhere to be seen.

Except, suggested Tom Ayala, for the bump under the back of Schoenfield's jacket.

"That," someone said, "has gotta hurt."

It took only a couple of minutes for Schoenfield's arms and legs to go slack, and for his head to sag back.

But he still didn't fall.

SUNDAY MORNING was much better for Annette than Saturday had been. For Hal, too, but most certainly for her. She'd managed to get home late Saturday night, and sleeping in her own bed, curled up with her favorite Dean, was an antidote to the previous 48 hours.

Breakfast, a quiche Lorraine, on the deck in the late July morning sun, was the finishing touch to her recovery. It also helped that she could tell the story to someone who really listened rather than merely to a computer file. She'd have to do that later, for her official report, but for now talking helped.

"So you're telling me that Jarvis Schoenfield, who was so set against the environmental community that he plotted to kill them off, with considerable success for a time there, actually died hugging a tree? Talk about irony. What's going to happen to his empire?" Hal was working on his second piece of quiche.

"Well, of course it's too soon to tell, really. But it was interesting. When we got back to Norwood yesterday

Excess Homicide
A Four Corners Mystery

afternoon, there was this committee wanting to talk with me, most of the directors of the foundation that now owns the X-S Ranch. They had already voted, unanimously, to change their name to something besides Resources For Humanity. It seems that Jim Nettleman is an enterprising sort of guy. After he read Schoenfield's stuff on my computer, he figured out how to use the ranch phone to e-mail a bunch of it to the directors of this foundation. So they were falling all over themselves to point out how the X-S had no real connection to any of Schoenfield's other activities and on and on. I guess that the foundation will now figure out what to do with itself, presumably something constructive."

"And what about those two hit men? The ones that the FBI thinks tried to kill the President?"

"We've got 'em dead to rights. The material we found in Schoenfield's house, found with valid warrants, means they're going to be tried and convicted for several murders and for attempting to assassinate the President. And the same goes for several other unsavory individuals as well. The guys who burned the law offices in Cortez, for example. And a bunch of people who were in line for other operations like that. The whole Resources For Humanity thing is simply over with. Especially since its so-called spiritual leader, Michael Oswald, is dead. Say, that reminds me. He was Tim Langer's uncle. And Tim and Jamie were supposed to come and see you yesterday. When I told them to, I forgot it would be Saturday. Did they?"

"Indeed they did. Along with Charles Shure, industrialist nonpareil and all-around pretty good guy. And not a bad schemer, from what they told me."

"So they told you?"

"Yeah, all about how they were fed up and were trying to concoct an escape plan when you showed up. Shure took responsibility. He also offered Tim a job, which Tim said he knew about from Shure's computer security guy, and almost offered Jamie a job, too. But I changed the subject before he could, because I want to keep her at the U. And now the real question here is your experience with the CBI. You were doing this as a try-out, last I heard." He arched his eyebrows and looked the question right at her.

"Well, I think I'm hooked. Hmm. It feels like anything I say will imply bad things about the Durango PD. And I really like those guys, all of them. And the connection to the people in town, serving the citizens and all that, is really rewarding. But I guess I'm ready for a change, new challenges."

"Well, this first case, I mean all the cases in that portfolio and the other stuff, up to and including a Presidential assassination attempt, that's indeed a change. But how can the CBI, or anyone, top that?"

"I don't think that's necessarily what I'm looking for, I mean big, high-visibility cases. But variety is good." She paused to chew, and to think. "Even though I was working with the counties in the region when I was with the PD, the CBI offers more, on a broader scale. And the connection to the feds is tighter. The FBI takes a lot of flack, but they never get much credit for all their good work. And that's interesting to be involved in. But one thing worries me a little. CBI is a state government operation, and they like to move people around. What happens if they want me somewhere else?"

"Well, as long as it's west of I-25, I don't think there's anything to be concerned about. Say the word and we'll move there."

"West of I-25?"

"You know, in the mountains. I mean, I'd hope that they would offer you some choice. You're going to get a lot of points for solving this case. Er, rather, clearing it. Surely they won't insist on sending you to, oh, some place like Julesburg."

"I'd hope so too, the choice, I mean. And, hey, I do my best work in the mountains. But what about your job?"

"Alice is going to retire before too long, and I'm ready for a sabbatical. I'm about burned out on this Dean stuff. Like I said, say the word."

* * * * * * *

H. P. Hanson

Excess Homicide
A Four Corners Mystery

AFTERWORD

The X-S Ranch, of course, is purely my invention, although the political views of its patriarch are not. Also invented are UNELECO and all of the various organizations that play roles in this story except the National Center for Atmospheric Research. NCAR is real and, besides providing the nation with an outstanding capability to tackle difficult problems in the atmosphere, the oceans, and the climate system, it has a history of celebrity, including starring roles in movies such as Woody Allen's *Sleeper*. If Hal and Annette lived in Boulder, I'd probably have to write a book called *Murder at the Mesa Lab*. As things are, NCAR's small role here is, like my use of other public institutions, meant as a tribute.

Also, due to the presence of Frémont State University, Durango is once again portrayed in terms somewhat less flattering than that delightful community really deserves. Big research universities, even fictional ones, can do that to small towns.

I'm thankful for the help of several people who improved the story and its telling and who persuaded me to avoid several pitfalls of self-indulgence: Craig Tigerman, Julia McKee, Andrea Maestas, and Claire Hanson. My own common sense gets fogged in by my prose sometimes, and they do a great job of seeing through the haze.

HP Hanson, Santa Fe
February, 2003

H. P. Hanson

ABOUT THE AUTHOR

After earning a Ph.D. in Atmospheric Science at the University of Miami, Howard Hanson spent over 20 years in environmental research and administration at the University of Colorado at Boulder and, more recently, at the Los Alamos National Laboratory. A Certified Consulting Meteorologist, he is also president of Southwest Environmental Research and Education (SERE) and serves on editorial boards of several technical journals. This background, combined with his interest in and love for the southwest's spectacular and fragile landscapes, provides a context for the Four Corners Mysteries.

He lives with his wife Claire in Santa Fe.